Catherine Dunne

set in stone

MACMILLAN

First published 2009 by Macmillan
an imprint of Pan Macmillan Ltd
Pan Macmillan, 20 New Wharf Road, London N1 9RR
Basingstoke and Oxford
Associated companies throughout the world
www.panmacmillan.com

ISBN 978-0-230-74230-7

1 3 5 7 9 8 6 4 2

A CIP catalogue record for this book is available from
the British Library.

Typeset by Set Systems Ltd, Saffron Walden, Essex
Printed in the UK by CPI Mackays, Chatham ME5 8TD

Visit **www.panmacmillan.com** to read more about all our books
and to buy them. You will also find features, author interviews and
news of any author events, and you can sign up for e-newsletters
so that you're always first to hear about our new releases.

To

Celia de Fréine, Ivy Bannister,
Lia Mills, Mary Rose Callaghan and Helen Hansen:
my friends in this writing life.

Heartfelt thanks for precision, patience
and Prosecco . . .

Prologue

ON THE EDGE of shadow, something moves.

A figure advances. It pauses, briefly, and stoops to pick up the bits of debris that litter its path. Last night's heavy rain and high winds have scattered the grass with gnarled snatches of branches; roots; upended plastic flowerpots. One gloved hand brushes these obstacles aside, pushing them beneath the straggly bushes, where they lodge, trapped. At least the wind is starting to drop.

The figure remains bent, keeping low to the ground. Its progress is soundless. One heavy, laced boot presses into the mud, then the other. Although it is still dark, the cover afforded by the trees and hedges is poor, winter-thin. The figure crouches, pulling back the dark hood that keeps falling forward, like a monk's cowl. A man's face is revealed, cheeks ruddied by the cold, eyes smarting. The eyes are watchful, bright even in the darkness. He lifts the small silver camcorder to his eyes, one hand adjusting the strap around his neck to a more comfortable position. A wood pigeon startles, rustling in the branches. The man shoos it away.

Just then, light floods one of the gardens below. The watcher adjusts his gaze at once, moving the camera several degrees to the right. A woman steps out onto the deck. She pulls the belt of her dressing-gown tighter and folds her arms, hugging her elbows for warmth. She looks around, absorbed in what she sees: gravel, the bleakness of stone, the bareness of winter. Nevertheless, she looks pleased with herself.

The watcher shifts a little. The effort of crouching has put a strain on his knees and thighs. Pins and needles will not be far behind.

But the woman doesn't stay long. She appears to look up in his direction once, when the outside light goes off. He lowers the camcorder quickly, just in case. He doesn't want to risk a careless glint giving him away. But he feels sure he has not been spotted – it is much too dark. The woman takes a last look around the garden and goes back inside, locking the doors behind her.

'Same routine as before,' the watcher murmurs to himself. He checks the time, the small numerals on his wrist showing greenly in the darkness. 'Well, give or take five minutes.' He trains the camera on the house to the left. Just checking. But there is no movement; still nothing. Not everyone is an early riser, he supposes.

From his standpoint above the gardens, the house on the right looks even more inviting than before. The curtains have been left open and the freezing air makes the interior look alive: somehow warmer, denser. There is now a view to be enjoyed. An ordinary scene of tables, chairs, the familiar clutter of a kitchen, the pleasure of watching a woman's movements, knowing that she is unaware of his presence, that she suspects nothing. It is a particular pleasure, this one. One he has almost forgotten. He lingers for a while, feeling a stab of envy. The sharpness of it takes him aback. He has not expected to feel that; envy above all things.

Time to go. No point in spoiling the ship.

The man stands up to his full height now and backs away from the top of the stone wall. He needs to be careful here: he has already snagged a sleeve on the barbed wire and those shards of glass are dangerous. The night they'd met in the pub, Wide Boy had mentioned every detail about the house and garden, other than this. Maybe he doesn't know. He will, though, and soon enough. But it's worth the risk: this vantage-point gives the watcher a perfect view of the two houses beneath. A view that will be all the better come spring, too, with a leafy covering of new growth. Nature can sometimes be generous. And, as he understands it, this will be a waiting game. Slow work is still paid work, and he is in no hurry to get a result. Not any more.

A few gardens away, a dog barks. Somewhere in the distance, a car starts, engine gunning into life. A local boy racer, probably. More sound than fury.

Satisfied now, the man moves away, down the muddy walkway that has emerged, straight and narrow, from underneath his daily footsteps. Once he reaches level ground, he bends down and undoes the laces of his boots. He wraps both boots in plastic and pushes them well down into the belly of the rucksack that he carries, slung loosely over one shoulder. He changes into city shoes and unwinds himself from the strap of the camcorder, placing it carefully on top of the boots.

His shoes are looking a bit worn, he notices. Could do with a lick of polish, too. Amy used to do that for him, back in the day. He straightens up again. Not a whole lot to report to Wide Boy when he sees him this evening, but still. He's earned his money, done what he was asked to do. That's the important thing. One final delivery and then the day's work is done and dusted.

The thin branches quiver behind his departing back as the watcher makes his way down the slope, hat pulled low across his forehead. He hunches forward and shoves his hands into his anorak pockets. He wonders, just for a moment, if these sheltered people have any idea of what's coming next. Of how fragile, how precarious all their comforts are. It's nothing to do with him, of course. He's just doing the job he's being paid to do . . .

When he reaches the street, things are still quiet. The early morning commute is not in full swing, not yet. To the east, the sky is just becoming light: a greasy, yellowish pall that lingers over the still-sleepy city.

1

MONDAY MORNING; three minutes to six. Lynda woke.

Her eyes were drawn at once to two pinpoints of light blinking redly on the clock's digital display. She reached over, groped for the switch and pushed it to the 'off' position, before the alarm had a chance to ring. She lay still for a moment, waiting for her eyes to become used to the dark. Something had startled her out of sleep, but she couldn't figure out what it was.

She half-turned now and checked on Robert. Had he woken her? Sometimes he called out in his sleep. Sometimes one arm would flail towards her in the dark. Lynda was disturbed by this restlessness, although Robert never seemed to remember it. He was still unconscious now, as far as she could tell, his mouth slightly open, slack, his breathing barely audible.

Lynda slid the duvet away from her and eased herself towards the edge of the bed, careful not to wake her husband. She searched along the floor with her toes but, as usual, she couldn't find her slippers. When she found them at last – surely not where she'd left them during the night – she wriggled her way into the fleecy lining. Then she lifted her dressing-gown from its hook and closed the bedroom door quietly behind her.

She liked this time of morning. The house was quiet, more or less. Over the years, she had grown used to its elderly groanings and sighings, the murmurs of wood and water.

Robert's childhood home: a place so familiar to him that he no longer heard its night-time mutterings, but Lynda did. They often kept her company when she couldn't sleep. And that's how she thought of them: as companions, friendly voices during the hours of darkness.

She crossed the landing now to Ciarán's room and slowly turned the handle of his door. It wasn't locked. She nodded to herself. Good. That meant he'd got home at some stage last night. Safely. No matter what, that was something to be grateful for. She paused on her way past Katie's door. It was wide open. The room had an emptiness that somehow filled it, as though it was holding its breath. Lynda still hadn't got used to her daughter's absence. At twenty-one, Katie was a passionate student of Irish and History at University College Galway. She often declared that wild horses wouldn't drag her back to live in Dublin.

Downstairs, Lynda followed her usual routine. She drew back the curtains, cleared the newspapers from the coffee table, picked up the stray mugs and glasses that littered the counters. She even took a moment to empty Ciarán's careless ashtray, before Robert saw it. It was easier to do it herself, Lynda had decided a long time ago. Much easier than nagging her son.

Katie used to help her with these chores, once upon a time. She was an even earlier riser than her mother, another addict of the slow, uncluttered hours. Lynda wished she could make it home more often. Even the occasional weekend would do: Galway wasn't a million miles away. But We Mustn't Grumble, Robert kept telling her, tongue in cheek. He liked to claim that he and Lynda had, by the standards of the day, raised two trouble-free young adults. Not many parents could say that.

Not even me, Lynda has thought on many occasions. *Not so sure I'd say it with such conviction.* But she had never voiced this. She believed that she and Robert saw these things differently, that sometimes even the best-chosen words were not enough to close the gaps between them.

Now Lynda opened the doors to the garden and stepped outside on to the wooden decking. The sensor light snapped on instantly. The grey-green boards were slippery underfoot; they felt treacherous. The thought came to her suddenly. It surprised her, the force of it. It was freezing out there, the January air biting and bitter. She pulled her thick dressing-gown more tightly around her, her hands gripping her elbows. But she could still feel the cold. The wind stung her cheeks, continued to bite at her feet and ankles.

No matter what the weather was like, Lynda always took this time to gaze at her garden, her creation. Just below the deck, there was a wide, undulating sea of grey, raked gravel. A few crumpled, brown-papery leaves fluttered across the calm surface; there was a stray crisp packet, too. Its shiny foil eye winked at her. And the lid of a Styrofoam cup, rolling cart-wheels around the garden. A striped straw was still attached, poking its way through the opaque surface.

Despite the high walls and hedges and railings, all of this rubbish still managed to make its way into Lynda's garden with a tenacity that baffled her. For a moment, she imagined the wilful determination of inanimate objects, the gleeful sense of malice behind these invasions of her space. She laughed at herself. She'd clear them all up later, once the day was aired.

A stone tortoise, oblivious to these foreign bodies, seemed to swim towards her across the garden, its lumbering head pushing through the gravel waves. Lynda loved the sense of stilled energy all around it, admired its blunted purpose. This, according to the oriental legend, was her rock of good fortune, her isle of immortality. Surrounding the tortoise, the evergreens threw their shadows. Soon, in spring, their growth would become luxuriant. She liked the predictability of her Japanese garden, the way that no matter how much the seasons changed, her island still stayed very much the same.

The sensor light clicked off, having grown used to her presence. Shivering now, she turned to go back inside. As she did so, she thought she saw something move, high above the garden. Just last year Robert, with Ken from next door, had had to string barbed wire across the top of the old stone wall. A rash of burglaries along the street had made everyone feel on edge. Ken had embedded rough pieces of glass into a new layer of cement, too, just for good measure.

She glanced to her right now, into Ken and Iris's back garden. She couldn't help it. It was an old habit, and old habits were the ones that took longest to die. As Lynda waited for any sign of life, a wood pigeon cooed and took flight, flapping its way across the garden. She tensed, looking up again, but the trees along the high wall were blank, dark. She felt a surge of relief. Just a bird – nothing to worry about. She made her way carefully across the deck and stepped back inside, locking the double doors behind her.

She had an hour or so to herself, before the house began to stir. She made tea and toast and sat at the long wooden table, rustling her way through the pages of yesterday's *Irish Times*. She settled into the crossword. The central heating clicked and hummed steadily, filling the kitchen with warmth. Down time, she thought. Warm-up time, before the real day began.

This was the time she missed Katie the most. She missed the clatter of their early morning conversations. And the phone, too, of course. These days, the phone hardly rang at all, it seemed to Lynda, although she knew that that was nonsense. It still rang for her. And for Robert. It was just an impression, that telephonic silence. But still. The absence of Katie was a resonant one. It made itself felt above all in these early mornings, even though more than a year had passed.

But Robert was right. She shouldn't complain. She was lucky, really. Luckier than so many other people. Particularly these days.

'Ciarán, it's gone half-past. If you don't get up now, you're going to be late again.'

Lynda heard Robert's voice booming across the landing. Automatically, she stood up and filled the coffee-maker. Strong and black: Robert said his heart wouldn't start without it. His heavy footsteps made their way downstairs, abruptly silenced by the carpet as he crossed the hall. Lynda looked up and smiled as her husband opened the kitchen door.

'Morning, love . . .' He kissed her on the cheek. 'Your man above is out for the count. Did you happen to hear what time he got home at last night?'

Lynda shook her head. 'No,' she said, firmly, not wanting this conversation again. 'I heard nothing until six o'clock. No idea what time he came in.'

Robert frowned. 'Has he lectures this morning, do you know?'

'I'm not sure.' Lynda pushed the plunger down into the coffee, wiping the granite countertop as she did so. Some of the grounds always managed to escape.

'Anyway, I've called him twice already.' Robert lifted his keys and mobile phone from the kitchen table and put them into the pockets of his suede jacket. 'I'm not going to call him again. He's big and ugly enough to look after himself at this stage.'

Lynda said nothing. She'd call Ciarán herself, later. Perhaps bring him up tea and toast, once Robert had left. Breakfast in bed helped to ease Ciarán into the day. It made the certainty of his bad temper recede a little. And that made her morning easier, too. The joys of working from home. But at least she had no need to brave the tangle of city traffic; no need to hurry up and wait. 'Toast?' she asked Robert.

He nodded. 'Yeah, thanks.' He accepted the cup of coffee Lynda offered him, but he didn't sit down. Instead, he took his briefcase from its perch at the end of the kitchen table and opened it. He handed Lynda an envelope. 'Can you lodge that for me this morning? It's a draft – I don't want to leave it hanging around.'

Lynda suppressed a rush of irritation. She hadn't planned on leaving her studio this morning, had things to do, drawings to finish. Her time was accounted for, all of it. 'Sure,' she said. 'Business account or personal?'

Robert hesitated. It was a fractional delay, but enough for her to notice. 'Personal,' he decided. 'As soon as you can. I've a site meeting in Blessington at ten and I'm tied up for the rest of the day.' He glanced in her direction, gestured towards the envelope with his coffee cup. 'I know you're busy – I wouldn't ask you if it wasn't urgent. Sure you can get to it?'

She nodded, feeling suddenly guilty. Sometimes, she thought, she underestimated the pressures he was under. Some-times, she forgot to understand. And at least he had acknowl-edged her day. 'No problem,' she said. 'I'll get to the bank just as soon as it opens.'

'Great, thanks. Appreciate it.'

There was the sound of the letter box flapping open, the thud of post hitting the floor. 'Postman's early today,' Robert commented.

'Always is on Mondays,' said Lynda. She was surprised that he had forgotten that. It was one of the more enduring, predictable rhythms of their home. She began to empty the dishwasher. At the same time, she switched on the radio for the eight o'clock news. The headlines astonished her, all over again.

The last few months had been like life lived in another country. Crisis after crisis – job losses, plunging house prices. It was as though the miracle of the nineties had never happened. How come the Celtic Tiger had turned tail so quickly?

She turned around to see if Robert was listening to George Lee's latest economic forecast. The 'busiest man in Ireland', as Robert called him. More banks were toppling, lurching drunkenly towards collapse, bringing directors and shareholders with them. But Robert was no longer in the kitchen. Lynda reached up instead to open the cupboard door.

And then, suddenly, he was beside her again, looming out of nowhere. They collided clumsily and Lynda dropped one of the three mugs she was clutching, still slippery from the dishwasher. She watched as it fell from her hands and shattered on the tiled floor. The white shards dispersed everywhere, sputniks flying. She watched their starry explosion with dismay.

'Jesus, Robert,' she cried. 'Don't creep up on me like that!' The anger in her voice caught her unawares. She glanced uncertainly at him but he didn't respond. They both looked at the litter of china on the kitchen tiles.

Then Robert turned away from her. 'I'll get the brush.'

Lynda stooped and picked up the larger pieces. Homer Simpson's yellow face grinned up at her, lopsidedly. One of Ciarán's favourites. 'Sorry, hon,' she said as Robert returned from the cupboard in the hall, carrying the brush and pan. 'You startled me.' His face was white, tense. Still he didn't reply. 'Robert? Are you okay?'

He handed her the dustpan full of broken china.

Lynda took it and thought: why doesn't he just put it in the bin himself? It's right behind him. She could feel her defensiveness growing. 'I said I was sorry – and you did give me a fright.'

He looked at her, not understanding. 'What? Oh, no, don't worry about it. No need to apologize. It's not that.'

'Then what?' she said. 'What is it? What's wrong?'

He shook his head impatiently. 'Nothing – just a letter from Danny, that's all. More of the usual bullshit. Nothing for you to worry about.'

'From Danny?' Lynda didn't try to hide her alarm. 'That's *always* something to worry about.'

Robert stooped and kissed her. 'We'll talk later. It's nothing to get upset about. Just Danny being Danny, all over again. Same old, same old.' He shrugged. 'Trust me.' He drained his coffee cup and smiled at her, but it was a smile without conviction. 'Now I've really got to run. Call you later, okay?'

Lynda saw the strain around his eyes, the pulled-down corners of his mouth. She noticed the shadowy bit under his chin that he always missed while shaving. Her stomach went into freefall. But she squeezed his hand. 'Yeah. 'Course. I'll be here all afternoon. Has Danny said anything in particular to upset you?'

Robert shook his head. 'No, no, not at all. I just don't relish hearing from him, you know that. All his "poor me" crap. Danny, the eternal victim.' His tone was impatient.

Lynda's questions hovered in the air between them, but she didn't ask them. Instead, she searched Robert's face for the truth and didn't find it. His silences always made her feel edgy. She had never got used to them. 'Let's talk about it when you get home, then, all right? We'll keep saying "no" to whatever it is he's asking, just like we agreed. Don't you worry about him – and I won't either.' She gave him a quick hug and brushed imaginary specks of dust off the shoulders of his suede jacket. She wanted to hold onto him for a few minutes longer.

Robert missed a beat. 'Yeah, well, I'm certainly not babysitting him again, not after the last time.' He seemed about to say something else, but then changed his mind. 'Look, gotta run. See you tonight.'

She blew him a kiss; he waved from the front door.

'Have a good day,' Lynda called. She watched from the porch as he struggled out of his shoes and into his work boots, holding onto the Jeep's open door as he did so. He fired his yellow hard hat into the back, and settled his briefcase beside him. With one arm slung across the back of the passenger seat, he glanced over his shoulder and reversed down the long driveway. All his movements were swift, confident. Lynda had always admired Robert's physicality: it was one of the things that had attracted her to him in the first place, the best part of thirty years ago. He had towered over everyone else she knew in those days. His longish dark hair and grey eyes had been a striking combination, one Lynda had found irresistible. His body did what he asked of it: tennis, football, pouring cement, sawing wood. There was nothing too much for it. She still loved its solidity, tending now towards heaviness. Predictability made flesh.

Lynda watched the receding headlights, saw that the Jeep's paintwork was almost completely covered by a thick layer of greyish mud. She waited on the front step until all traces of Robert's presence vanished and the car had disappeared down the hill towards the traffic lights.

She stepped into the hallway and walked quickly back towards the kitchen. Once inside, she turned to where Robert had dumped the morning post on the counter under the microwave. Just the usual stuff: ESB bill, gas bill, flyers for yet another pizza joint. Impatiently, she pushed them aside and riffled through the remaining envelopes one more time. She must have missed it first time around. But there was nothing. Nothing from Danny.

For a moment, Lynda looked at the strewn counter with

disbelief. Then she moved over to the sink and filled a glass with cold water. She sipped at it, keeping both hands around the heavy tumbler. It helped to anchor her. Anchored by water, she thought. Not very substantial. Still, it was better than nothing.

She went back out into the hallway and glanced at the bottom stair. But there was no envelope here, either. Sometimes, Robert tossed the post there, just outside his office. He'd leave it, reminding himself to deal with it later. She stood, feeling even more puzzled now. She and Robert kept no secrets from each other concerning Danny. That had always been their most solid, their most united, front.

There was a faint breeze making its way through the flap of the letter box that still needed to be fixed. She must remind Robert, again, that there was a new one waiting to be installed. She wished that she could block off the letter box completely, seal it closed for good. Too much news of Danny had reached them that way over the years. That, and his sporadic phone calls, all of them brittle, all of them needy, sucking her and Robert in again before they even realized it. But it was well over three years since they'd heard from him now, long enough for memories of his last visit home to be, if not forgotten, then at least gratefully put aside.

She decided now not to 'go there' as her children would advise. She didn't care to remember. Instead, she tried to shrug off the images that were flashing by, thick and fast now, all their bells and whistles zinging. She walked back into the kitchen and poured a fresh mug of coffee for herself, put tea and toast onto a tray. Then she made her way upstairs to Ciarán's room.

Time he was up, and out of her hair.

Time she got to work. That, at least, was a distraction.

*

Danny is remembering.

It's been happening a lot, these days. Whenever the time approaches to go *back* – he no longer cares to think of it as 'home' – it's as though his own personal cinema knows it. It plays the same vibrant reel over and over again – Technicolor, complete with sound effects – and reminds him of all the things he can never allow himself to forget. Before he knows it, his past becomes the most immediate present he has ever known, somewhere much more real, much more insistent than the here and now.

Danny has begun to walk more quickly, his steps speeding up to keep pace with his thoughts. He is conscious of something stirring, prodding at the inside of his skull, needling him to respond. It's like his recent practice bouts in the ring, where his opponent kept on hitting a vulnerable spot, a small, hot cut just above his right eye. Apart from the pain, and the trickle of warm blood that kept blinding him, what he can remember most is the rage. The other man's jabbing left, the incessant, relentless focus of it, meant that someone was aware of his weakness; someone was taking advantage, exploiting it.

Not for the first time, Danny finds it strange the way that tiny, insignificant things detonate memories. Right now, it's the shadow that falls on the railway sleepers as the weak January sun creeps along the valley. But his day, the day he is remembering, was summer. He knows that because they were all wearing shorts.

He can see his ten-year-old self and Tommy and Mick – both boys known locally as Twinnie McCormack, because nobody could ever tell them apart. In fact, the boys made sure that nobody could ever tell them apart. They got away with more, far more, that way. They made it their business to confuse the ever-watchful mothers standing in gardens, looking out their top windows, keeping an eye on their own brood as well as everyone else's. The Twinnies didn't fool *their* mother, of course, not even for a moment. That would have been impossible. But they fooled pretty much everyone else's.

Danny can see the three of them now, skinny freckled figures, playing by the railway tracks that used to run behind the council houses, seven streets over and a lifetime away from home. His mother didn't like any of them playing there. Her lip would curl a little, saying it was no place for nice children. But Mrs McCormack didn't mind. So Danny learned to go along with Tommy and Mick and just say nothing. He still remembers the excitement of retrieving the pennies, flattened hot and thin by the wheels of the train, the copper hen distorted, elongated, forever caught in mid-squawk. They were inseparable, the twins and him. Until the day of the cat. That was the day Danny realized that the world was not as he believed it to be, that it had a method and a logic of its own that could defeat him, sideline him, pushing him off his own rightful place at the centre of things.

The cat had been a poor show, he remembers that, too. It was scrawny, wild, its orange fur matted and dirty. But catching it had still been a triumph. Danny and Mick had made the trap together. First, they'd dug a hole in the hard summer ground, softening the soil with a bucket of water drawn from the McCormacks' rain barrel, the one that squatted in their back yard. Into the hole the Twinnies placed the fish heads, stinking their way through the *Evening Herald* of the day before, bloody streaks making the print run.

The Twinnies had claimed ownership of this part; Danny had been allowed only to watch. Their fish heads, their *Herald*, their privilege. Never mind. Danny had other, *better* things planned for later. He watched as the black ink stamped the news of yesterday's events onto the Twinnies' sweaty palms and forearms. Watched as the blackness made its way underneath their fingernails and into the creases – bendy ones, just like tiny smiles – around their knuckles.

Mrs McCormack had wrapped up the fish heads the afternoon before, folding the newspaper at the top and bottom to make a snug parcel. Danny had watched at the kitchen table, fascinated at the way the fish eyes stared, cold and glassy, their mouths open, taken by surprise. Into the newspaper nest they went, along with the slimy, stringy guts and the glittering scales from their wavy blue and silver flesh.

Mrs McCormack had filleted the dozen or so mackerel without fuss, joking away with the three boys as they drank glasses of MiWadi and ate fluffy biscuits – white ones only: the boys wouldn't touch the pink – three pairs of elbows resting on the kitchen table. Danny had often seen Mrs McCormack use her swift, precise knife. He admired the way she moved, the whole cut and thrust of her. She'd put the tightly wrapped parcel into the bin when she was finished, washed her hands with Sunlight soap and dried them on the tea towel.

'Off you go, boys,' she'd said, throwing the words back over her shoulder as she looked out the window. 'Off you go outside and play. The sun is still shining.'

Once she'd left the kitchen, the Twinnies lifted the lid off the galvanized bin that stood just outside the back door, trying not to make any noise. Then Tommy leaned in very carefully and pulled out the parcel. All three raced to the embankment together where adventure lay, waiting for them to begin.

Danny and Mick covered the hole with a length of blue sacking, stolen from Mr McCormack's shed. On top of that, they placed leaves and twigs and a handful of dirt. That was Tommy's idea – he had insisted on it. He'd seen it in a book, some story or other about hunters in India trying to snare a lion. Or was it a tiger? Danny could never remember that bit. Tommy had probably got it wrong, anyway. But the twin claimed that it would fool the cat into thinking it was on solid ground. Even Mick had thought that that was stupid. The cat wouldn't have time to think about anything at all, he said. It would fall into their fishy trap and then they'd capture it. But they did it anyway, sprinkling the thin surface of the sacking to camouflage it.

The Twinnies always stuck together, even if they didn't agree with each other. Danny knew it would not be a good idea ever to try to come between them.

It was Tommy's job to make the noose. He was good at making things; his long, sure fingers plaited the strands of twine together. When everything was ready, they hid, the three of them, crouching behind a clump of wild, scratchy bushes that produced millions of fat blackberries in autumn.

They hadn't actually thought about what they would do afterwards, once they'd caught the cat. At least the Twinnies hadn't. But Danny had. The previous night, that was all he had thought about, with a hot, hard pleasure stirring between his legs. He knew exactly what he wanted to do.

'Here it comes,' Tommy's voice was a high, excited whisper. 'Here's the cat.'

The scrawny animal, sure enough, was making its way across the scorched ground, heading straight for the sacking. Its tail was up, flicking from side to side. It was as though the tip had an eye, like a periscope breaking the surface of the sea. It glanced jerkily first right, then left, checking for trouble. The cat's ribs seemed to undulate along its orange coat. They were so prominent, so distinct that Danny could count them. The paws were furtive, taking soft, sneaky steps, as though the cat was already suspicious of what lay ahead.

The three boys kept very still, and Danny remembers holding his breath. Suddenly, there was a flurry of movement: of cat and clay and sacking. Tommy darted out from among the trees, a blood-curdling, whooping sound coming from his normally quiet lips. Mick followed, stumbling forward, his hands already in the hole, pressing down on the sacking, keeping the spitting, writhing cat in one place while Tommy slipped the noose over its head.

It was done, over, almost before they realized it. Tommy pulled sharply on the noose, and the cat dangled at the end of his home-made rope, clawing wildly at the air. The boys were all laughing now, shouting, doing an Indian war dance around the struggling cat, who was showing no signs of quietening.

'It worked!' Mick was jubilant. He punched his fist in the air. 'It worked!'

'Will I let him go now?' Tommy's arm was tiring. He was holding it out from his body, leaning forward, his arse stuck out in the air. The cat was frantic, clawing, hissing, trying to make contact with something, anything at all. No wonder Tommy was keen to keep his distance, keen to let it go now that the thrill of the chase was over. But it was the wrong question to ask. *Danny* knew it was the wrong question to ask. Letting the cat go was not in *his* plans, whatever the Twinnies might feel.

'NO!' he shouted.

The Twinnies stopped and looked over at him. He thought that Tommy looked frightened. The freckles were standing out on his thin face, his cheeks were getting redder by the minute.

'I have an idea.' Danny walked over to the Twinnies, holding out his hand for the cat. They didn't stop him. In fact, he could see relief pass over Tommy's flushed face, like a cloud shadowing the sun. He held out the cat, its hissing silenced now. Tommy's gesture was an abrupt, sinewy one. *Here, you take it, then. I've had enough.*

Danny grabbed the noose with both hands, hoping that he wasn't already too late. The cat was still breathing, just, although its eyes were becoming milky. He didn't have any time to waste.

Turning his back on the Twinnies, he raced down towards the railway tracks. Danny could hear them shouting behind him, but he didn't stop. He was always able to run faster than they were. He could see the train now, snaking its way towards him, although he couldn't hear it yet. His hands started to tremble and he could feel his thing beginning to grow hard again. He stumbled as he reached the tracks, almost losing his balance. The cat was quiet now, its paws jerking weakly at the air from time to time.

Quickly, he bent down. He pushed the animal into position on the rail, its head dangling uselessly to one side. The metal glinted back at him, warm in the sunshine. Using the noose, he tied the cat's head as close to the rail as he could manage, laughing out loud as the rest of its body flailed, its paws making feeble contact with nothing at all. Fresh air – just like when Tommy tried to box and his punches fell back uselessly to his sides.

Then Danny ran, further down the tracks, seeing the Twinnies standing a good way up the embankment. He waved to them to come and watch, but they seemed to be rooted to the spot.

And then he forgot all about them. He stopped and turned to watch the approach of the train, his heart hammering. He had a great view of what came next: the loud, fat slam of the wheels, the blood spurting high up into the air, the rusty blur of colour. Grinning hugely, he waved to the train driver, who hooted back at him, heard the train's shrill, mournful whistle. The man didn't even know what he had done, would never know. The cat's head had been sliced off cleanly, more cleanly than Danny would have thought possible, and rolled to one side, as though it had just turned to go to sleep. The rest of its body was reduced to mush. All that was left was a dark stain on the railway sleepers, a furry shadow of its former life.

When he looked up, the Twinnies were gone. He was disappointed. They should have stayed, should have waited for him. He was filled to the brim, tingling with excitement over what they had just done: the chase, the capture, the execution, all of it. But when he went to knock in for the Twinnies, their mum, tight-lipped, told him they weren't going out to play. They were staying in to have their tea.

That night, Mr and Mrs McCormack came to call. He could hear their voices downstairs, make out his father's answering rumble. Then light, cautious footsteps up the stairs: Robbie, his pansy older brother. At thirteen, he was still weedy, scared of his own shadow.

'You're in trouble,' he said, breathless. 'Daddy's goin' to kill you!'

Danny stuck his two fingers up in the air, and his brother retreated, startled into silence.

It wasn't the worst hiding he'd ever had. Even if it had been, he wasn't going to show it. Part of him felt that it was worth it, anyway, and part of him didn't feel anything at all. He had always known, somewhere deep inside him, that this was not the sort of things mummies and daddies wanted to know about. They'd have preferred it if he hadn't brought it home to their doorstep.

He remembered the way *his* mum had shrieked when their own cat, Titus, had brought back stiff and broken birds, trophies, and placed them gently at her slippered feet. But she didn't want them. She'd shouted at Titus and screamed at Dad to take the bodies away. Because they made her sad.

Danny hadn't known what to make of that.

But he knew that his mum and dad felt they had to fix something he had broken. Or stop him doing it again. Or both.

Whenever he got into trouble, there were usually tears from his mother, hiccups as she dabbed at her eyes with a tiny lace handkerchief. Then an earnest talking to from his father, and sometimes, but not always, a hiding. His father seemed unconvinced by punishment; his heart was never in it. This will hurt me more than it hurts you: that kind of thing. But still, it seemed that he felt duty bound to show his wayward son the error of his ways. That was why Danny had learned to keep things separate, private. He could never trust others to see the world the same way he did.

The Twinnies should have been different. He couldn't understand why they had gone over to the other side, why they had left him as they had, right at the best part. And then *told* on him.

But he didn't care – he didn't need them.

He'd go back to the tracks tomorrow, see if the skull was still there. Once all the fur and stuff fell off, it would be a good souvenir.

He slept that night, and dreamt of flying.

2

'HELLO, MUM?' Ciarán, home from college.

'In here,' Lynda called.

Ciarán stuck his head around the studio door. 'Still wor-kin'?' he said.

What does it look like? Lynda wanted to ask. She felt tired, cranky. Her day had not been a good one. 'Yep. Still at it.'

He edged his way closer to her, negotiating a passageway between the bench, the coffee table strewn with books and the Indian footstool. All the low surfaces in the studio were littered with photographs and sketches. As Ciarán passed, the piles of paper trembled, threatening a landslide.

'Mind that rucksack,' Lynda said, sharply. 'Make sure you don't disturb *anything*. I've just sorted out all that lot.' She waited, expecting the usual response. But there wasn't one. That surprised her. No bristling; no swearing. No throwing his eyes up to heaven.

'Okay, okay,' he said. He looked around him, disbelieving. 'I'll leave it outside, then. Yeah?' He'd brought with him the smell of cold air and stale cigarette smoke.

Lynda nodded, bending over her drawings again. 'Do that,' she agreed. And tonight, she thought, he could smoke for Ireland, for all she cared. At least he hadn't flung his way up to his bedroom and slammed the door. Or complained about all the shortcomings of home. Lynda had learned, lately, to dread the sound of his key in the lock, the stamp of his foot in the hallway.

Robert never saw these outbursts of temper. By the time he came home in the late evenings, the anger was spent. Ciarán would be subdued. Sometimes, he was even apologetic. Robert's eyes would glaze over whenever Lynda tried to explain how it had been, how it still was, in his absence. Eventually, it had become easier to stop trying.

She heard the thud as Ciarán dumped his rucksack in the hall, and was reminded of the post hitting the floor that morning. Reminded all over again of Danny. She sighed. Then she heard Ciarán mutter something. She looked up sharply. She hated his *sotto voce* complaints: he always made sure they were barely audible. Most of the time she didn't challenge him. Today, though, she was in no mood for it.

'Ciarán. Did you say something to me?'

There was no reply. She went to call out to him again and was made suddenly curious by a scuffling sound from behind the door he had just closed. She pushed her chair back from the bench and stood up. The door opened abruptly and Ciarán was framed there, looking, she thought, as he used to look as a small child. *Defiant.* That was the word. It leaped its way across the distance between them, crossing the bridges of all those years. She had a sudden memory of a childhood photograph: Ciarán in red Wellington boots, holding a single daffodil. Squinting up at the camera, refusing to smile. He elbowed his way back into the room now, dragging someone behind him.

'I'd like you to meet a friend of mine,' he said.

At first, Lynda thought her son's reluctant follower was a girl. She saw fair hair, expensive clothes, a tanned face. The figure was tall – almost as tall as Ciarán – but there was no evidence of breasts beneath the tight white T-shirt. A fellow, then, Lynda thought, taken aback. She made to move towards him at last – the least she could do was be polite. But Ciarán began to speak and forestalled her.

'This is Jonathan, but we all call him Jon.' He gestured awkwardly at the young man just behind him. 'I invited him to have dinner with us tonight.' His eyes challenged her.

'And you're very welcome,' Lynda said. Ciarán never brought anyone home. She'd always known who Katie's friends were, but Ciarán's life was a mystery to her. Now, it seemed that he had taken somebody captive. He gripped Jon's shoulder tightly. The other boy – Jon – stood up straighter and detached himself. He looked as though he was standing his ground. He held out his hand, beating Lynda to it.

'Mrs Graham,' he said. 'I'm very pleased to meet you. I told this ... this reprobate to behave himself and give you more notice, but you know how impossible he is.'

Lynda was disarmed at once. Reprobate. That was Robert's word. 'I do indeed,' she agreed. 'I know just what he's like. It's very nice to meet you, Jon. Please, make yourself at home.'

His smile was dazzling; so were his pale green eyes and dark lashes.

'Are you an artist, Mrs Graham?' he asked her at last, his eye caught by the drawings that littered her bench.

'Oh, well,' she said. She never knew how to answer that. 'I paint and I make jewellery: silver stuff, mostly. And I design Japanese gardens as well.'

'Wow,' Jon said. He was clearly impressed.

'And please, don't call me "Mrs Graham",' Lynda added. 'It makes me feel old. My name is Lynda.'

He smiled. 'Okay, then. Thanks, Lynda. Does that mean that you design Zen gardens, the dry landscape kind of stuff? And the meditation spaces?'

Lynda was startled. That was an odd sort of knowledge for a young man to have.

'Take a look out the window and see,' interrupted Ciarán. 'She's done one out here, in the back garden. I already told you. We can pull up the blinds, if you like.'

But Jon ignored him. It was as though he hadn't heard. He kept his gaze fixed on Lynda, his pale eyes searching hers.

'Well, yes,' she said. 'That *is* what I do. That, among other things.' Jon's interest intrigued her – she wasn't used to it. She glanced over at Ciarán, conscious of him standing by the footstool. His way was barred as Jon moved swiftly towards her bench.

'May I look at the drawings?' he asked. She could hear the excitement in his voice.

'Of course.' Lynda moved back to her chair and pulled out the garden sketches she had just started working on. Jon took one of the A1 sheets she offered him. He peered closely at it. As he did so, Lynda noticed that his hand was trembling. When he looked up at her again, the green eyes were almost translucent.

'These are beautiful,' he said. 'I've always been interested in design.'

'Yeah, yeah, yeah,' Ciarán interjected. But his tone was benign. 'Never mind all this artsy-fartsy stuff, I'm starvin'. What's for dinner?'

'I haven't decided.' Lynda was annoyed at his interruption. 'If you're so hungry,' she said, 'why don't *you* start to cook dinner? What would you like to make?'

He looked at her sideways. 'Takeaway?'

'You pulled that stunt the last time,' she said. 'How about some real food, for a change?'

'Nah. I think it's vastly overrated,' he said. He dragged one hand back and forth through his hair. As a small child, he'd do this whenever he felt frustrated, whenever he was expected to do something he didn't want to do.

'Let's have a stir-fry,' she said. 'You can make a start and I'll join you both in a few minutes, once I put these drawings away.'

He nodded. 'All right then. Sound.' He made a show of strangling Jon, placing both hands around his friend's slender throat. 'Come, slave!' he said. 'Your task awaits! Your master commands!'

Jon followed Ciarán as he led the way towards the kitchen.

'Don't you make Jon do all the work,' Lynda called after them. 'I know your style.'

Jon turned and smiled at her. For an instant, his eyes seemed knowing. He glanced towards Ciarán, and then back again at her. Lynda was startled, unsure how to respond. Almost at once, the tanned, handsome face was smooth again, neutral.

Her gaze followed her son as both boys left the room together. Ciarán was good-looking too, but in a different way from Jon. He had Robert's dark hair, strong features and his easy, lanky height. He had an air of self-possession that could be convincing. But as he walked away, she saw the innocence of his back, his longish hair, his loping strides. There was a vulnerability that lurked just beneath the surface of Ciarán's skin. Even Robert acknowledged it.

On the other hand, this new friend seemed very grown-up. Lynda wondered where all that confidence had come from. She glanced at her watch and made a pencilled reminder to herself of the time, on the right-hand corner of the latest of her drawings. That way, she'd know which version to start with in the morning.

'We entertaining royalty, or what?' Robert asked, as he came into the kitchen. 'Do I need to dress for dinner?' He was shrugging out of his jacket and looking around him with exaggerated amazement. Lynda had set the table with her best china and glassware.

She put her finger to her lips. 'Shhh – not so loud! Ciarán's brought a friend.'

Robert grinned at her. It was a grin that said: *See? Told you so. Told you it was only a matter of time. You fret too much.*

Lynda ignored it. 'It's the first time he's had *anybody* here since – I can't remember. We should celebrate, be welcoming.'

Robert nodded. 'Sure. Why not? Male or female?'

'Male. His name is Jon.'

'Okay. Right. Let me just go and get out of all this muddy stuff first.'

Just then, both Ciarán and Jon burst into the kitchen, laughing, trailing a cloud of energy with them. They stopped short when they saw Robert, Jon looking unsure, even wary. He glanced from Robert to Lynda, and back again, almost as if he were appealing for help. He *is* shy after all, Lynda thought, amused.

'Jon – come and meet Robert. Robert, this is Jon, Ciarán's friend from college.' At that moment, Robert's mobile rang. He held his hand up and fished his phone out of his pocket. 'Just a minute,' Lynda heard him say. 'Give me a second.' He pointed towards the door, apologetically. She could still hear his voice, even after he'd closed the kitchen door behind him.

'That's my dad,' Ciarán said, with ironic cheerfulness. 'Making his second million. He gave up on the first, though. The going was too tough.'

But Jon didn't laugh.

'That's enough, Ciarán,' Lynda said. She felt uncomfortable. 'Your dad works very hard.'

'Pity about the credit crunch, though, isn't it?' Ciarán put down two cans of beer on the counter in front of him. 'They say things are goin' to get even worse. Particularly for builders. Sorry, I mean *developers*.' Ciarán made imaginary inverted commas around the word, waggling his two index fingers in the air. He tugged at the ring pull on one of the cans until it made a hissing sound. He pushed the second beer towards Jon. 'Help yourself,' he said.

But Jon didn't move. Nor did he acknowledge Ciarán's offhand invitation.

Lynda felt a surge of anger. And where do you think all of *your* comforts come from, you little shit, she wanted to shout. *Your* allowance, *your* clothes, *your* mobile phone? Even the beer in your hand. But she calmed herself. She was aware that Jon was looking at her. The air around him was puzzled, thick with questions. Lynda glanced at her son's face. The shadow of a sneer still lingered. Jon's presence made her see Ciarán as though from a distance, as a stranger might. And she didn't like what she saw.

Finally, Jon spoke. 'Anything I can do to help?' he asked. His tone was casual. He pushed the can of beer very slightly back in Ciarán's direction, then he turned to face Lynda.

'Yes,' she said. She was glad that the silence was broken. 'Thanks. Chop these peppers for me, if you don't mind. I'll go and put on the rice.' Lynda walked past Ciarán on her way to the larder.

Her anger simmered. She'd deal with him later.

Robert joined them just as they were finishing their meal.

'Sorry, guys,' he said. 'Never a dull moment.' He put his plate in the microwave. Then he turned to Jon, smiling. 'Well, Jon, very nice to have you here.' He held out his hand. 'Don't get up. Please excuse that rude interruption earlier – but we live in interesting times.'

'You don't need to apologize, Mr Graham,' said Jon, shaking Robert's hand. His face flushed slightly. 'It's very nice to be here.'

'So, how do you two know each other?' Robert took his meal from the microwave and sat down at the table.

Lynda was glad that she hadn't risked asking the question earlier. She knew how much Ciarán hated what he saw as prying. But Robert's curiosity was normal. It was a natural, friendly thing to say.

'Are you doing the same subjects?' Robert looked from one to the other.

At first, neither answered, then they both spoke together.

'Yeah, but . . .'

'No, because . . .'

Then they each laughed at the collision.

'So, which is it?' Lynda smiled at them. 'Yes or no? Same course or not?'

'Well, kind of both, really.' Jon paused. 'I'm doing History, same as Ciarán, but . . .' There was silence. Lynda could feel Ciarán's eyes on her. It wasn't a glare, not yet, but it was close to becoming one.

'I should be a year ahead, but my parents had some . . . problems . . . lately, so I'm repeating a couple of courses with Ciarán's year and . . . well, working part-time.' Jon's face had sagged. 'It's going okay, though.' He began to speak quickly, rushing ahead, filling the gaps. 'I'll just get it over with right now and tell you that I do part-time modelling as well – sometimes for department stores, sometimes for hairdressers. People often have a problem with that. They think that "pretty face" means "empty head".' His voice was unsteady.

Robert looked up, but said nothing. Lynda reached over and touched Jon on the shoulder. 'You don't need to explain, not about anything. We didn't mean to give you the third degree. Your private life is just that.' She could feel Ciarán's eyes boring into her. 'Please, accept my apology.' She stopped, aware of Jon's struggle to compose himself. 'And I don't think that modelling is empty-headed, either,' she added.

He looked at her, and she saw that the luminous green eyes were almost opaque.

'It's fine, really,' Jon said at last. 'And I know that my family situation is anything but unique.' He gave a short laugh. 'At least, not these days.' He seemed about to say something else and then stopped.

'My mother, the Grand Inquisitor,' said Ciarán, after a pause.

Lynda flashed him a look. 'I *have* apologized,' she said.

'That's enough, Ciarán,' Robert's interjection was quiet.

'Well, maybe if you were a bit less of a Silent One, your folks wouldn't need to ask,' Jon's voice was sudden, full of mischief. He took all of them by surprise, Lynda in particular. She looked over at him, not knowing what to say.

He glanced back at her and laughed. 'This,' and he jerked his thumb at Ciarán, 'is one of the most secretive people I've ever met. I call him Silent One, or Reprobate.' And he let one of his hands hover back and forth in mid air, as though considering. 'You know, whichever fits him best at the time.'

Ciarán looked over at Jon. He pretended to pick up his knife. 'Don't y'all even think of gangin' up against me, y'hear?' But he was laughing.

It felt as though the room had just exhaled. Time to move before the tension had the chance to gather again. Lynda stood up and gestured towards the empty plates. 'Hand me those, love, will you?'

Robert began to pile up bowls and dishes.

'That was really good, Mrs Gr . . . um, Lynda,' said Jon. 'Thanks for looking after me.'

'Not at all,' Lynda said. 'You're more than welcome.'

'Yeah, Mum, thanks.' Lynda could hear a note of apology in Ciarán's voice. She smiled at him, wanting to show him how easily he could still be forgiven. 'You're welcome, too. Better than a takeaway, then?'

He yawned. 'Dunno about that, though.'

Jon nudged him. 'Move,' he said.

Ciarán looked at him in surprise. 'What? Why?'

'Duh – dishes time. C'mon, get up.' Jon was already on his feet, clearing the rest of the cutlery and glasses.

Robert pushed his chair back from the table. 'Well, seeing as you guys have everything under control, I'm going to go and do a bit of work. I've some invoices to catch up on.' He turned to Lynda. 'I'll be in my office if you want me.'

'Okay,' she said. 'See you later.'

Ciarán began to load the glasses into the dishwasher. At the same time, Jon was filling the sink with hot water.

'What're you doin'?' Ciarán demanded. 'That's what a dishwasher is for.'

'Not for those glasses, it's not,' Jon said. 'Give them here.'

Lynda walked to the other end of the room, smiling to herself at Ciarán's complaints. She saw Jon plunge his arms into the hot, sudsy water, while Ciarán went in search of a tea towel. There was reluctance written all over his face. He rummaged in the drawer for a minute and then flung a clean cloth over one shoulder. He bent down and fiddled about with the CD player. Suddenly, the sound of Neil Diamond and 'I Am I . . . Said' filled the kitchen.

'Ciarán! Not so loud!' Lynda called. He turned and grinned at her. He waved and lowered the volume fractionally. Then, both boys began to sing along.

'C'mon Jon, give it loads!' cried Ciarán.

Lynda watched, delighted. Ciarán played an air guitar while

Jon threw his head back and sang. His voice was good. He could carry a tune. She watched his dramatic, rock-star movements while he kept standing at the sink, up to his elbows in water. When the song finished, he bowed to his audience. Lynda clapped, laughing, and Ciarán sashayed back down the kitchen to change the CD.

'Well done, both of you,' she said. 'My, to be in the presence of such undiscovered talent!'

She bent down to put the table mats in the drawer. She was still smiling. It had been a long time since she'd seen Ciarán happy. As she closed the drawer, something, some movement caught her attention and she stopped halfway. She glanced in Jon's direction. He was still at the sink, but he had grown very quiet. He was staring out the window, his entire body arched forwards. Everything about him seemed to be on high alert. She approached him, concerned.

'Jon? Are you all right?'

He turned, his face blank. His eyes seemed shuttered, as though he wasn't seeing her. He opened his mouth to reply, but no words formed. The absence of expression lasted only for an instant, was gone so quickly that Lynda wondered whether she had imagined it.

'Yeah, fine.' He nodded towards the kitchen window. 'I just thought I saw something move at the end of your neighbour's garden – just in front of that high wall.'

'Really?' Lynda was alarmed. Ken and Iris often worked late. And even though so many things had changed over the years, she still kept an eye on the house for them. Had done so ever since they'd moved in. She'd take in deliveries, gather post off the porch floor, look after lights and curtains when they weren't there. She peered into the garden now, but was unable to see anything, only her own and Jon's reflection in the steamy kitchen window.

33

Then he pointed, his forearm gloved in bubbles. 'Look – it's just a cat.'

Lynda followed the direction of his arm, and froze. There, in the crook of his elbow, was a patch of blue and purple and yellow skin. It was livid, ugly, some of the veins prominent. She flinched. She couldn't help herself. She had a vivid flash of imagination: a grainy, black and white photograph of Jon sitting in the half-light somewhere, his arm strapped, forcing veins to the surface as he injected. She stopped, horrified at herself.

What on earth was wrong with her?

Jon caught her looking at him. At first his expression was puzzled. Perhaps he had spoken to her and she hadn't heard? With an effort, she pulled herself back. And he was laughing.

'Lynda? Are you okay? I had blood tests three days ago – and I bruise very easily.' He rubbed his hand over the inflamed skin. 'I've suffered from anaemia, ever since I was a kid. What did you think – that I was some sort of a junkie?'

Ciarán was back beside them, now, frowning.

Lynda was acutely aware of his presence. She shook her head. 'Of course not,' she said. Her tone had just the right amount of dismissal. 'Don't be daft. I was just concerned at the size of the bruise, that's all. It looks very painful. Would you like some Arnica?'

'No, thanks,' Jon said. 'Don't worry. It looks loads worse than it is. It was hurting on Friday, but it's fine again now.' He continued rinsing the glasses and placing them, very carefully, on the drainer. He had turned his back to her. Lynda felt as though she had just been dismissed.

'Are you sure?' She could hear herself talking, just for the sake of it.

'Nah, it's fine,' he said. 'Thanks anyway.'

'Stop fussing, Mum.' Ciarán was right at her shoulder. She could feel his breath against her cheek.

'Well, let me know if you change your mind, Jon,' she said. 'Now I'll leave the two of you to finish up here. I'm going to see if Robert needs any help.'

She left the kitchen. As she closed the door behind her, there was a gust of raucous laughter. It sounded like a joke shared at someone else's expense. Don't be silly, she told herself. It's just two young guys having a laugh.

But instead of going into Robert's office, Lynda changed her mind and went upstairs. A bath, she thought. Something to clear away the day.

On the way, she stepped into Katie's room. She liked spending time here, looking around at all the remnants of her daughter's childhood. It was as though the years had stayed still . . . Dolls, teddies, posters, even books that had survived baby-hood. Katie had always been the orderly one, the careful one. This was a space that was very different from the chaos of Ciarán's bedroom. A space he had always guarded jealously. Even now, he locked his door each day before he left the house. Lynda left clean sheets and pillowcases outside his room every ten days or so. He'd change the bed and deliver the linen to the basket in the utility room. She now accepted the arrange-ment without comment.

It hadn't always been like that, of course.

'What are you doin'?' he'd shouted at her, one afternoon the previous summer, when he'd returned home to find Lynda standing on a chair at his window. The suddenness of his arrival had made her jump. She'd almost lost her balance.

'Jesus Christ, Ciarán, don't do that! I'm taking down your curtains to wash them. I could have fallen and broken my neck.'

'I'll do it,' he'd said. His voice was cold, remote. 'Get down and I'll do it.' Lynda had obeyed. She'd said nothing, but his reaction had made her suspicious. Frightened and suspicious. What was he hiding here? What did he not want her to see?

35

When she'd spoken to Robert about it later, he'd groaned. 'Lynda, he's eighteen. What do you expect?'

She hadn't understood. 'What do you mean?'

Robert had closed the kitchen door. 'He's probably got porn stashed away there. Maybe even a bit of dope. Are you going to jeopardize an entire relationship by discovering whatever it is that he might be trying to hide?'

'What relationship?' she had countered, stung. 'That's exactly the point, Robert – what relationship is there to jeopardize? He's become a stranger. An angry, bitter stranger.' And she'd burst into tears.

Robert had sat down beside her at the table and taken both her hands in his. 'Sweetheart, he's not a boy any more. He's finished school, he's on his way to university, probably has a girlfriend we don't know about. His life is full of secrets right now. It has to be. That's how he gets to be independent.'

She'd opened her mouth to speak, but Robert had held up one hand. 'You took him by surprise. Yeah, sure he was angry. Probably felt you had invaded his privacy.'

'But—'

To her surprise, Robert had kissed her, silencing her. 'Katie is not the template, Lynda,' he'd said. 'Lads are different. You and Katie will probably talk dresses and lipstick until you're ninety. Boys don't do that. Remember the first time I brought you home here, to my parents?'

Lynda had nodded.

'Remember the way Emma asked could she be your bridesmaid? And how my mother talked about stuff between her and my dad that would've made his hair stand on end, had he known about it?'

Lynda had nodded again, smiling now.

'You females are just more open. Give Ciarán time. But remember, he's different. He may not want to share everything

with you. In fact,' and here he'd grinned, 'I hope he doesn't.
I'd have serious worries about him if he did. Telling everything
to his ma!'

But there was still something about Ciarán's withdrawal
that made Lynda suspicious. And his recent rages, never far
below the surface. What if these rages were coke-fuelled, or
ecstasy-induced? The stuff seemed to be everywhere these days,
part of a lifestyle and culture that she didn't even pretend to
understand. And the talk shows had been full recently of young
people addicted to something called 'skunk'. She'd listened to
the stories of parents at their wits' end; to tales of teenagers'
personalities changing overnight; to stories of verbal and physical abuse. So many families on the brink. Lynda had needed to
know, needed to find out for herself what Ciarán was so
desperate to hide.

Shortly after the incident of the curtains, she'd called a
locksmith to the house. 'My son has lost the key, and we don't
have another.' She'd made light of it as she showed the man to
Ciarán's door. He'd muttered something about all teenagers
being careless, all teenagers being the same. Hungry, useless
creatures. Within moments he had handed her a duplicate from
his box of tricks. Lynda was surprised at how easy it had been.

'These keys are standard internal ones,' he told her. 'If you'd
known the serial number, you could have bought it at any
supermarket hardware. Or from a builder. No big deal.'

But she hadn't known it – and it *is* a big deal, she'd
thought. It's a big deal to me, breaking into my own son's
room. She'd thanked him and paid him and he'd left. She'd
run back up the stairs after she'd locked the front door securely
behind him. Just in case.

Once inside, she'd begun her search – although she hadn't
known what she was looking for. She had decided not to care
about porn, or the odd bit of dope, or any of the other things

that Robert had said Ciarán might be hiding. What she was really looking for was the source of his anger. Perhaps I shouldn't be looking here, she'd thought, suddenly, in the middle of her careful turning over of the mattress, her methodical leafing through books. Maybe that's to be found elsewhere. Maybe with me. Or with Robert. Or with Robert and me: parents from hell. She'd cried then, and left the room as she'd found it, locking the door behind her.

Locking the stable door, she'd thought, even as she left.

She'd never told Robert about that. It had seemed such a grubby thing to do. But a grubbiness born of desperation. She'd discovered nothing, except that perhaps she didn't like herself very much for doing it.

Katie's room, on the other hand, was open, trusting. A bit like Katie herself. Lynda stood up now and smoothed the bed where she'd been sitting. She looked at the gaily coloured bedspread, embroidered by Katie herself, with all the fierce concentration of an eleven-year-old. Lynda remembered the day she'd finished it. Her small face had glowed with pride.

And then the other memory that came with it. That same evening, nine-year-old Ciarán had burst into the living room, his face flushed, his eyes bright.

'Mum! Mum!' he'd shouted. 'Uncle Danny's on the phone! He's sending me a Scalextric for my birthday next week!'

By the time Lynda reached the phone, Danny had hung up. There had been tears and tantrums as Robert had told his son, sharply, that he could forget about that promise: his Uncle Danny was not a man to be trusted. That's just how things were.

And Katie's face, crestfallen. Her thunder stolen by Ciarán. By Danny. She'd been sitting on the floor, her finished bedspread laid out in front of her, waiting patiently for her parents' praise. Instead, Lynda had rushed from the room and Robert and Ciarán had become locked in an angry argument that was going nowhere. Lynda had tried to make it up to her afterwards, but Katie had refused to be consoled.

Memory, sharp as salt. Katie, folding up her bedspread, stealing from the room.

And Danny, as usual, tainting all before him.

'Well?' asked Lynda, when Robert joined her later. She sat on the bed, putting her rings away safely. 'What did you think of Jon?'

'Very charming,' said Robert. He sat down on the opposite side of the bed, his back to her. There was a pause. 'But he's a bit effeminate, isn't he?' Another pause. Lynda could guess what was coming next. 'Do you think he might be gay?' He turned to look at her.

'Would it really matter?' Lynda countered. 'Would it matter to us if Ciarán was gay?' She spoke quietly, with just enough emphasis on the 'us'.

Robert slid into bed and pulled the duvet up to his chin. He looked uncomfortable. 'Life's tough enough. Without that, as well.' He hesitated. 'Besides, I'm pretty sure Ciarán isn't. And I'm not saying anything about the other lad, either, except that I didn't know whether he was a boy or a girl when I was introduced. Did *you*?' Now his tone was challenging.

'It did take me a moment,' Lynda admitted as she slipped in beside him. 'But then I forgot about it once he started to talk. What I saw was someone who made Ciarán look happy again.' There was no response. She moved closer to Robert as he put one arm around her shoulders. 'For what it's worth,' she went on, 'I think they're just friends, good friends. They're easy together. There was a lot of clowning about in the kitchen after you left.' There was still no answer. Lynda could feel her irritation growing. This was not the time to mention her reaction to Jon's bruised arm. Robert believed her imagination to be overactive enough as it was. She tried again. 'And Jon's an intelligent lad. Didn't you think so?'

Robert reached over to turn off his bedside light. 'Hard to judge, from the little I saw. But he looks intelligent enough. And you seem to be impressed.' He sounded amused.

'I don't think Ciarán has fitted in at all at UCD,' Lynda said, after a moment. 'He started off well enough, but he seems to have gone back into his shell. Jon is the only person I've seen him relate to in a very long time. If that's impressed, then yeah, I'm impressed.'

Robert didn't answer at once. Lynda could feel him thinking about it.

'Mmm. Well, this lad's no shrinking violet, anyway.'

'Didn't you like him?' Lynda was curious.

'Yeah, I liked him well enough. There's something familiar about him, though – something I can't put my finger on. I feel as if I've seen his face before.'

'Well, you probably have. He seems to do a lot of modelling. Reading between the lines, I'd say that his parents have split up and I get the feeling that he more or less supports himself.'

'Does he indeed.' Robert sounded interested. 'I didn't catch that. I was probably a bit preoccupied over dinner. But that speaks volumes.'

That was Robert's seal of approval: that Jon was someone who didn't cadge off others. It was a bone of contention between himself and Ciarán. But Ciarán had dug his heels in. No minimum-wage job for him in shitty conditions; no way.

'Well,' Robert said now, rolling over to kiss Lynda goodnight. 'You never know. He might even be a good influence on our reprobate.' He yawned. 'I'm done in. Sleep well.'

Lynda smiled. Seemed like the entire evening had been full of echoes. 'Goodnight, love.'

Lynda remembered Jon's excitement as he'd looked at her drawings. His body language as he'd helped with the meal. She'd make sure he felt welcome. He'd be good for Ciarán.

Just as she drifted off, she remembered the letter from Danny. She'd forgotten to ask Robert for details about why he had been so upset this morning. The arrival of Jon had put all thoughts of Danny to one side so she had more than one reason to be grateful for his arrival.

Danny would just have to wait.

And maybe she wouldn't have to deal with him at all. Robert had said it was nothing – just more of the same old, same old. Perhaps she should leave it to him.

Yes, she thought, fitting herself around the curve of Robert's back. She'd leave the worrying to him.

The watcher has begun to wonder about the predictability of ordinary people's routines. If they know they're being observed, do they behave differently? Do the unremarkable comings and goings of a household become more significant, more loaded, in the knowledge that someone else is looking on? He finds these to be interesting questions; and he has plenty of time to think about them just now. He's considered them in the past too, during what he likes to think of as his official working life.

Back then, you had two distinct groups under surveillance. Each of them guilty. The guiltier they were, the more ordinary they tried to be. Their patterns of behaviour were *studiedly* ordinary: too mundane, too unchanging. There was never the surprise caller to the front door, the unexpected domestic crisis, the bin forgotten on collection day. All was precisely as it should be – which really meant that all was as it *shouldn't* be.

All was surface, like tinted glass – built to obscure whatever might lie beneath.

And then there was the other lot. Brazen, tough, streetwise. Dropping their trousers or giving the finger to whoever might be watching. Come and get me, they sneered. This is *our* world. Enter at your peril.

Scumbags, the lot of them. Although, in many ways, the watcher understood where they were coming from. What you saw was what you got. They swaggered, radiating that particular kind of power that always comes with danger. They were invincible, the Tony Sopranos of Dublin's suburbs. It had a certain dark attraction, their view of life. He'd watch them show, over and over, that they saw no need to hide the business they did. Because in their world, the rules were different. The only wrong was getting caught.

Lately, though, he's been wondering about all of that. About crime, and what it really means. He no longer feels able to explain what it *is* any more, or maybe, what it has become. Somehow, the definition keeps getting murkier, keeps slipping away from him. It seems to him that things were a lot simpler, back in the day. You knew who your enemy was, then: there wasn't so much blurring of the boundaries.

Like in the Westerns. White hats for the good guys, black for the bad. He liked knowing where he stood: who to root for, who to hate. Now, though, he can't see much difference between the 'criminal classes' and their refuse sacks stuffed full of cash, and the collar-and-tie brigades that rip off a whole country. It's all about scale, really. A difference of degree, as his old boss used to say, not of kind. The watcher likes that. It helps to make some sense of what he's feeling these days. Bankers/burglars. Consultants/conmen. No difference. Except that they used to catch some of the burglars back then; punish them. Most of the time, anyhow.

The watcher reaches the front of the house now and begins to move more quickly. He's left his rucksack and his postman's bag hidden around the back, in his usual spot behind the high wall of the garden. He's covered them in leaves and branches and stuff. It's easier to move fast and keep low without them. This will only take a few minutes and the porch light won't come on, Wide Boy has assured him of that. Even if it does, he'll be gone, sharpish, the deed done.

He steps carefully across the gravel driveway of number nineteen and kneels at the back of the Jeep. It's been parked just right for him: back wheels facing towards the road. Sometimes, you get lucky. He unscrews the dust caps and puts them into his pocket. Then he inserts the tip of his screwdriver into the valve, pressing it downwards, and waits for the satisfying whoosh of air. Disabled, not damaged, Wide Boy has said. At least not this time. He treated it as a bit of a joke, which – in the scale of the things that he seems to have planned – the watcher supposes it is.

He pulls the envelope out of his anorak pocket and tapes it carefully to the inside of the Jeep's wheel arch. It's inside a Ziploc bag, sealed with insulating tape: Wide Boy had been very precise. It is to be hidden, he insisted, but immediately obvious to anyone checking the tyres. The watcher presses down on the sticky tape with his thumb, making sure that decent contact has been made. He is aware that in this cold, it may not stick for long. But there is not a whole lot he can do about that. Now he moves across the driveway towards the navy-blue BMW convertible, still keeping low. Nice. Front tyres for this baby. Easy peasy. Right, time to go time. He makes his way quickly down the driveway. A final glance over his shoulder shows him the house is still in darkness. He turns right and slows his pace: purposeful, rather than hurried.

The watcher wonders what these people are like. Wide Boy has told him a bit, but then he would gild the lily, wouldn't he. He wouldn't come right out and say whatever it was they were hiding, though, what sins they were guilty of. As Wide Boy told it, these were crimes the law could never punish them for; serious stuff that they had got away with in the past. The watcher understands that frustration, but he doesn't do detail and the less he knows the better. He's convinced that everyone is guilty of something. In his experience, even decent folk have something indecent to hide.

He makes his way back down the street, making sure to keep close to the walls and gardens, away from the street lights. A couple of houses have the curtains open, even at this hour. Shift workers, maybe. He sees the blue flicker of television screens. And shakes his head. He doesn't like TV; doesn't believe in it. Particularly what they call Reality TV. Amy, on the other hand, loves it.

She watches nothing else when Tina visits, the pair of them glued to the screen. She and her sister are peas in a pod, in that regard. Their addiction irritates him. But then, Amy has always believed in what she sees. She has always trusted the evidence of her own eyes. Tina, on the other hand, is that bit more worldly-wise. But not as far as celebrity is concerned. Each of the sisters, one for the sake of the other, is besotted by what they see on screen. Once it's on TV, then it has to be true, has to be real, has to be believed. Gospel. Hooked, lined and sinkered, the pair of them.

The watcher's experience of life has made him different. Given what he has seen of human nature, he knows that all those programmes are one big set-up, designed to sucker in the people who'd sell their grannies for ten minutes of fame. And of course, that's what the advertisers cash in on, too, leaving people – like Amy, like Tina – with their mouths open, waiting for part two. Thirsting after shiny happy people; bowled over by the glossy photographs in *OK!* and *Hello!*.

The sitting room at home is always littered with magazines like that. And they aren't cheap. Not that the money worries him, not as such. His Amy spends very little on herself. He often wishes she cared about her appearance a bit more, took care of herself better. But instead, she dives into those bloody magazines and rarely comes up for air.

Once, in the past week or so, he's even caught her tying her hair up in the same way as Amy Winehouse. Now that worries him. He has seen, often enough in the past, the way cops identified with the people they were supposed to catch. How they grew to admire the villains, in a strange kind of way, for what they did, what they managed to get away with. Even though it was supposed go against the grain of everything they believed in themselves. Projection, isn't that what it was called?

A car approaches from behind. The watcher can hear the hum of the engine in the distance; he sees the beams of the headlights illuminating the slick roadway to his left. He adjusts his hat and hunches forward suddenly, as though lighting a cigarette. The car passes. The watcher memorizes the number plate, slows his pace until the car has made a right turn and disappeared down the hill.

He's trying to remember now the psychologist from a long-ago training day. That idea of projection, identification, admiration – whatever it was – has stuck with him, down through the years. It astonishes him that you could long so much to be someone else that you kind of become them. You muddy the waters that separate you; submerge yourself in the other. You start to see everything that they do, everything that they are as a reflection of some unlived part of your self. He wants to understand it, that frame of mind. Maybe, if he can understand it better, he'll understand Amy better.

If only there was somebody he could ask. But there isn't, not any more. One way or the other, he misses the camaraderie of the job. This, now, is solitary work, with no change of shift, no chance to share a bit of banter with the lads coming to relieve him. Nothing to ease his aching knees, either – and no one to watch his back. This job may be well paid, but apart from the money, it's unrewarding; nothing for him to take pride in. He can never hold out hope of making an exciting discovery – the secret past, the skeleton in the cupboard, the juicy, hidden misdemeanour.

He pauses for a moment now, keeping well under the shelter of the trees. He waits for a few minutes, but there is no sign of anything untoward. Still keeping to the shadows, he makes his way up the steep slope towards the garden wall which is becoming all too familiar to him. Sitting still for so long makes him feel restless.

All this surveillance is insignificant to anyone other than Wide Boy, of course. He's loving it. Can't wait to hear the latest. Can't wait for the watcher to transfer the video files so that he can view them on a laptop. The watcher hands over the memory stick every evening, having edited out the dull stuff. He wonders what happens when Wide Boy gets them home. Although he doesn't seem to be a sex pervert in any obvious kind of way, this boy. He might be something even creepier. Anyhow, one way or the other, this is the sort of stuff that will never lead to an arrest, or a shipment intercepted, or even a little bit of dirt on a misbehaving politician.

The watcher crouches into the small hollow he has made for himself behind the stone wall. He scratches the back of his neck where his woollen scarf has begun to get prickly. Amy knitted it for him, one Christmas, a few years ago. It was a short-lived craze of hers, one that followed the flower arranging, the cake decorating, even origami, for Christ's sake. He's never liked the scarf, but not to wear it would provoke tears or vision-and-no-sound for days on end and he can't cope with that, not any more. He glances at his watch. Five-twenty. Time for a coffee.

He settles himself more firmly into his fleece. For the past two weeks, he has avoided bringing anything with him on these early mornings that might leave a trace. Cigarettes, hot drinks, food. But this morning it's just below freezing and his knees will seize up if he doesn't have some sort of heat. He has wrapped a fine woollen blanket around him, too, pulling it from the depths of his rucksack. Amy has given him a Thermos of coffee and he pours himself a cup. She doesn't ask where he's going, or who he's working for. In the past, he used to think it was because she had learned to be discreet. A cop's wife has to be. Later on, he realized it was because she didn't care.

That had hurt, he won't deny it. He has often wondered why she married him so quickly in the first place; who she was rebounding from. He was free; no baggage. He'd not had a serious relationship since his early twenties when Nadine had left him for somebody else. One of his colleagues, as it happens; one of the graduate boys. He had a lot more drive, she'd said, more ambition. Turns out she was right.

Amy had definitely been with someone before him. He'd caught her on a few occasions in the early years, her and Tina, in a huddle together over something. Amy'd emerge, red-eyed, trying to smile. But the watcher took the decision not to ask. He was afraid that asking might shatter whatever there was between them. He was aware that it was already fragile. The fact that she seemed to want to stay with him was enough; he could live quite happily with that.

He'd been no great catch, after all. Big, ungainly – that was his mother's word – and dull. He knows that's how other people saw him. How Amy saw him. On the other hand, he offered her stability, reliability. She didn't seem to mind that he was fifteen years older than she was. He liked looking after her, felt grown-up and responsible in a way he never had before. He'd set up a joint bank account for the two of them, just as soon as they were married. Whatever he had was hers, too. That's what his own father had done. It seemed natural for him to do the same. And at first, things like that seemed to keep her happy. That, the occasional holiday, flowers on a Friday. The slow ordinariness of it all.

He finishes his coffee and replaces the Thermos in his rucksack. Now he shuffles a bit of dirt over where he's emptied the dregs. Experience makes such attention to detail almost as instinctive as breathing. But it's so bloody-well-freezin' up here that he doubts if anybody will ever chance upon his hideout. No reason for anybody to come pokin' around.

He keeps a close watch on the house on the right. The routine there has been like clockwork. Plenty of time yet; everything is still in darkness. Things begin to happen around six o'clock every morning. Curtains are drawn, lights flare outwards and upwards, and the woman comes out onto the deck, hail, rain or shine. Takes the same few minutes every day to look around, then disappears back inside again.

For the life of him, the watcher has no idea what keeps on bringing her – Lynda her name is, with a 'y', not an 'i' – outside. A few rocks strewn here and there, a bit of a pond, some low trees and shrubs. Not what *he* thinks of as a garden at all, not really. No proper flowers, no colour – although there wouldn't be in winter, would there. But she seems to like what she sees. Sometimes, she picks up the junk that blows in from the street, stuff that has snaked its way through the bars of the gate that guards the side entrance. Up from the gutter, around the corner, making its way in without permission. A bit like him, really. The thought makes him want to laugh. The garden fills with the sort of skinny bits and pieces of rubbish that the wind catches and dumps whenever it stops to take a breath.

On those mornings, he can see annoyance written all over her movements as she takes careful steps off the deck and onto the gravel. She picks up the papers and sticks as though they have no right to be there. That amused him, the first time he saw it. The rich are all alike, in his opinion. They think they don't have to – shouldn't have to – put up with the same shit in their lives as other people do.

Hang on – the downstairs light has just been switched on. He checks his watch. That's almost half an hour earlier than normal. Suddenly, the curtains are drawn back, but nobody appears on the deck. The watcher lifts the camcorder. He can see two figures moving about the kitchen. One of them, Mrs Lynda, looks agitated. Her movements are jerky – not her normal serene self. And she's dressed, too, which is unusual: in some sort of a puffy jacket. Shit – maybe they've already discovered his morning's work. Jesus, it was a close-run thing, if that's the case. Can't have been more than ten minutes since he left the front driveway.

Right, that's it. Time to go. Too dangerous to be hanging around here this morning. The watcher shifts a bit first, getting his feet planted solidly underneath him. Then he hauls himself up to standing. At least today's letter has already been delivered and he doesn't need to do his usual sneaking around to the front door. That is the only bit that makes him nervous. He feels exposed at the front of the house, particularly in this cold, clear weather. There is nowhere to hide should anybody suddenly open a door or a window.

Of course, he has his cover: a postman's sack full of charity flyers, begging for clothes and bric-a-brac in aid of the third world. He grunts. Third world, me arse. Most of the boys collectin' this stuff put the proceeds straight into their own pockets. But people in nice houses fall for it over and over again. Helps to ease their consciences, probably. Besides, it gets rid of their junk, and no questions asked.

He reaches the level ground, changes his shoes, dusts himself off.

Wide Boy has paid him two grand as a deposit, another three due when the job is done. Maybe he'll buy himself a boat when it's all over. One of those little ones he'd seen on Lough Conn when he went fly-fishin' with Jimmy, five maybe six years back. They still kept in touch, the two of them. Jimmy had hated the tranquillity. All that silence made him nervous. But he'd loved it. Funny, for an inner-city man like himself. Or maybe not so funny. Maybe that's why . . .

He checks his watch, shoves the rucksack into his Postman Pat bag and settles the lot comfortably on his shoulder. Then he heads for home. He'll have a cooked breakfast in The Pantry in Talbot Street, first. Then, his morning paper, a bit of a snooze on the sofa and a couple of games of pool before he meets Wide Boy tonight.

He suspects that they are going to have quite a few things to talk about.

3

FIVE O'CLOCK. Lynda was waking earlier than ever these days. It had begun to exasperate her, the way this thin sleep had suddenly begun to unravel any time after three. Her eyes were hot and sandy when she woke. She felt restless, alert in ways she couldn't explain.

She eased herself out to the edge of the bed now and searched the floor for her slippers. Might as well get up. Anything was better than just lying there. The last few mornings had taught her that. She made her way downstairs, shivering a little in the cold. The weather had been bitter for what felt like weeks now. She had hardly left the house.

When she reached the bottom stair, she suddenly remembered. It was Tuesday. Bin day. It had been sleeting last night when she'd thought about it, and besides, she'd been feeling lazy. She'd decided to leave that job until this morning. She opened the cupboard in the hallway and switched the heating on. She kicked off her slippers and shoved her feet into the pair of old Wellingtons that she kept there for gardening. Then she pulled on Robert's parka, and wriggled her fingers into the woollen gloves that she found balled up in one of the pockets. She walked through the dimly lit kitchen to the back door, unlocked it and stepped outside.

The cold took her breath away. The side entrance was icy and underfoot was glazed with danger. Lynda took small steps, keeping one hand on the wall of the house. Then she pulled the wheelie-bin behind her as she made her way towards the front garden.

She pulled the side gate open, its hinges whining. The metal was freezing; she could feel its steely cold, even through the gloves. She began to manoeuvre the bulky green bin between her car and the Jeep, wondering why it was suddenly so difficult to see where she was going this morning. Then she realized. The outside light hadn't come on.

Puzzled, she walked over to the porch and stood underneath the sensor, waving her arms. But nothing happened. Bulb must be gone. She'd get Robert to pick one up on his way home. As she turned, something about her car struck Lynda as strange. It looked collapsed, somehow, as though the body had suddenly lost its shape.

Then she saw the cause. The left-hand front tyre was flat. 'Oh, bloody hell,' she said aloud. Time her car breakdown people earned their money: there was no way she was dealing with *that*. Not in this weather. She'd put in a call as soon as she got back inside the house. Lynda was just about to reach for the bin when she looked down again and saw that her right-hand tyre was flat, too. Alarmed now, she walked around the convertible. Rear tyres looked fine. And the front tyres of the Jeep looked fine, but there was something odd about the back.

As she walked around the Jeep, she saw that both of the back tyres were flat, the boot sagging. She looked at it in disbelief. It took several seconds to process what her eyes were seeing. From *surely not*, to *what on earth?* to *this must be deliberate*. It had to be. This couldn't all be coincidence, could it? But why would anyone want to do a thing like that?

Quickly, Lynda left the bin outside the gate and went back

into the house. She'd have to call Robert. He had an early meeting in Wicklow this morning . . .

'Little bastards,' said Robert. He looked dishevelled, angry in the sudden light.

Lynda looked up. 'The sensor,' she said. 'It's working again.'

'What do you mean, "again"?' Robert sounded impatient.

'When I came out here earlier with the bin, the light wasn't working. But it is now.'

Robert glanced at the fitting above the porch. 'Some kind of intermittent fault, maybe,' he said. 'I'll take a look at it later.' He shook his head. 'Meanwhile, I'll have to call the roadside assist number. There's no way we can handle four flat tyres. Although Christ knows how long they'll take to get here in this weather.' He sighed. 'I'd like to wring their necks.'

'Whose?' asked Lynda, slowly.

Robert gestured towards the cars. 'Whatever little fuckers did this,' he said, glaring at her. 'Whose do you think?'

But Lynda didn't want to say what she was thinking. That no vandals were likely to have been abroad in sub-zero temperatures last night, letting the air out of hapless neighbours' tyres. That no other car on the street seemed to have been touched. That for some reason, *they* had been targeted. Robert would call her paranoid; he'd blame her overactive imagination. And in fairness, he might be right.

Or maybe this was part of a new culture of envy, something they would just have to get used to for the future. Perhaps that's why it had happened to them, and not to any of their neighbours. In an already upmarket street, theirs was easily the biggest house, extended, gardens landscaped, with two fancy cars in the driveway. Maybe someone saw them as just too rich and too lucky.

Lynda shivered. Nothing like this had ever visited them before, in all the years they had lived here. She felt violated. And to her, the attack began to feel like a personal one, rather than the random nastiness that Robert seemed to think it was.

'Come on,' he said, taking her arm. 'Let's go back inside. No point in standing around here. It's freezing.'

'Coffee?' Lynda offered, getting out the mugs.

Robert nodded. 'Yeah. They'll be here in about forty minutes to fix the tyres. Or so they say. I'll just make a few calls, warn James I'm going to be late.'

'Sure. Fire ahead.'

As he left the kitchen, mobile already at his ear, Ciarán and Jon came in.

'What's all the commotion?' asked Ciarán, yawning. 'You woke us up.'

Lynda looked at him. 'Well, it couldn't be helped. We had two flat tyres each this morning. It's a bit of an inconvenience, to say the least.'

Ciarán frowned. 'How did that happen?'

'I don't know. When I left the bin out this morning, I noticed it. I called your dad and we've arranged for someone to come and fix them.'

'Are they punctures?' asked Jon.

'I don't know,' said Lynda. 'I presume so.'

'But you haven't been driving. Not for ages,' said Ciarán, reaching for the Corn Flakes. 'You said you were getting stir-crazy.'

Lynda smiled. 'Well, it's a mystery. Your dad thinks it might have been some local kids. Their idea of a joke.'

'Some joke.' Ciarán rummaged in the fridge now for milk.

Jon stood by the kitchen table, looking over at her. 'Pretty horrible thing to do, in this weather,' he said. 'Someone with a strange sense of humour. Why would anyone *do* that?'

'Jon, sit down, please,' said Lynda, suddenly realizing that he was standing while Ciarán had looked after himself. 'What would you like for breakfast? We don't usually have such a chaotic start to the morning.'

'I'm fine, thanks. Whatever Ciarán is having.' Jon pulled out a chair.

'Ciarán, get out a bowl for Jon, please. And some cutlery.' She glanced at the clock. 'You two are up early,' she said. It was a long time since she had seen Ciarán up at half-past six.

'The field trip to Newgrange, remember?' said Ciarán, his mouth full of cereal. She was about to tell him not to speak while eating, and then stopped herself. Not in front of Jon, who was looking groomed and polished even at this hour. Beside him, Ciarán looked, well, a bit lumpy. Like an unmade bed.

She was growing used to Jon's presence. Since that first evening Ciarán had brought him home, they were spending more and more time together and when Jon was there, Ciarán was less angry. Yesterday evening, when Lynda had emerged from her studio around seven, she'd found both of them in the kitchen. They'd emptied the dishwasher and Jon was folding clothes from the tumble-dryer.

'Well,' she'd said. 'Thank you. That's most thoughtful.' She'd caught Ciarán glancing in Jon's direction. As though he was saying *you got that one right*. She wondered what her son was leading up to. Ciarán had always been transparent as a child.

'Do you want to get a beer for yourself and Jon?' she'd said to Ciarán, pulling salmon out of the fridge. 'There's some in the utility room. Help yourself. And bring out a bottle of white for us as well, will you?'

He'd nodded, and headed towards the farthest end of the kitchen. She'd heard him stamping about in the utility room, heard the chink of bottles as he pulled open the fridge door.

'Ciarán has been very kind to me, you know,' Jon had said quietly. 'Especially in the last few months when things were really bad at home. He's probably the only one I can talk to. He speaks very highly of you and I just thought you'd like to know that.'

Lynda had looked at him. Ciarán? Kind? That had surprised her. 'Thank you,' she'd said. 'It's good to know that.'

Ciarán had reappeared, carrying cans and a bottle of wine. 'Want me to pull the cork on this one?' He'd held up a Chablis.

She'd nodded. 'Please. Here's the corkscrew. And get your-selves some glasses from the cupboard in the dining room.'

'I know, I know,' he'd grumbled. But his tone had been good-natured. 'No tinnies at the table.' This time, though, there was no muttering under the breath, no 'Jesus Christ' as he marched off to do as she asked. Jon had smiled at her, watching Ciarán's departing back.

'Is there anything else I can do?' he'd asked.

'Really? You don't have to.' And Lynda had smiled. 'A bit of chopping and we're done.'

'Yeah, no, really,' he'd said, earnestly. 'Honestly, I don't mind.' He'd paused. 'To tell you the truth, I kinda like being in a home kitchen again. My mother doesn't cook any more. In fact, she's hardly ever there. Not since my dad moved out.'

Lynda had felt a wave of compassion for him. He'd looked forlorn as he'd spoken, almost fragile. 'How about setting the table, then?' she'd said. 'The dishes and plates and things are in the cupboard over there.'

He'd nodded. 'Sure.'

'You want a glass of wine, Mum?' Ciarán was standing in front of her, glass in one hand, bottle of Chablis in the other.

She'd noticed that he had brought her favourite crystal. She'd smiled at him. 'Yes, please, why not?'

He'd poured for her, then said suddenly, 'We've a really early field trip tomorrow morning, Mum. Part of our history project. We're goin' to Newgrange. It'd be much easier for us both to go to UCD from here.' He'd looked over at Jon. 'The bus is leaving at eight. No point in Jon going all the way home to Shankill and all the way back again in the morning.'

Jon had made as if to protest, politely.

Lynda had waved it away. So that's what the domestic bliss had been all about. 'Of course, that's no problem. Jon, you can stay in Katie's room. I'll change the bed after dinner.'

'If you're sure it's no trouble.' There it was again, that flash of vulnerability.

'No trouble at all.' She'd smiled at him. 'It's a pleasure to have you.'

But this morning, the discovery of the flat tyres had made her forget all about their field trip. 'Sorry,' she said, 'I'm losing my memory as well, thanks to all this commotion. What time do you reckon you'll be back tonight?'

Ciarán looked at Jon and then shrugged. 'Dunno. I'll text you if I'm coming back for dinner. There might be something going on afterwards.'

'Right,' Lynda said. 'I'm going for a shower. Jon, you're very welcome to come back here for dinner tonight. Both of you – just let me know.'

'Oh, no it's fine – really, I—' Jon's voice trailed away.

'Ah, shuddup,' said Ciarán. 'Thanks, Mum. Text you later.'

'Have a good day,' called Lynda over her shoulder, as she left the kitchen. She hoped that Jon wasn't embarrassed by their hospitality. If he was, he and Ciarán would just have to sort it out between them.

Just as Lynda reached the end of the hallway, she saw a light flashing outside. She could make out nothing else through the frosted glass, so she stepped into the television room and pulled back the curtains. She saw two men standing in the driveway, talking to Robert. Behind them, the lights of the tow-truck flashed orange.

This morning's discovery was making her uneasy in a way she couldn't explain. Robert's anger had been a straightforward, less complicated response – and she hoped that he was right. As far as he could tell, the tyres had not been damaged. He'd insisted that letting the air out was a mindless piece of vandalism. But harmless, really. Lynda wished that she could feel so certain.

One of the repairmen bent down, his head level with the wheel arches of the Jeep. She watched as he inserted the jack and began to lever the car upwards. Suddenly, he stopped and lifted something white from the top of the wheel. He handed it to Robert, and then turned back to his work.

Lynda moved closer to the window, her heart pounding. She knew by Robert's reaction that something was wrong. He walked away from the car, and stood close to the gateway. His whole body stiffened as he looked at whatever it was in his hands – he had his back to her, but Lynda knew by his movements that he had just opened the package the man had handed him. Then his shoulders slumped forward and he ran one hand across the back of his neck, as though trying to dislodge something that gripped him there.

He turned around suddenly and Lynda ducked away from the window. She left the room and ran, taking the stairs two at a time. She reached the upstairs window in time to see Robert fold whatever it was he had in his hand and stuff it into the back pocket of his trousers.

She started to tremble.

A letter from Danny. It *had* to be. Another one, to follow the one that had arrived a week ago. The one Robert had never shown her.

Lynda sat heavily on the bedroom chair. She knew what this was. There was no point in pretending she didn't. Maybe Danny wasn't under her roof this time, but it made no difference. His reach was long.

This was the start of another campaign. Clever, focussed, relentless. She knew the drill by now; had learned that lesson three years ago. She couldn't wait: she'd have to confront Robert, now, today. Not just about this, but about the last letter, too. And by the expression on his face, he would not want to share whatever it was he had just read and hidden away in his back pocket.

Lynda felt a strange sense of calm surround her. It was here, at last. This was what she had been waiting for, for three whole years.

Without even knowing it.

Danny takes a calculated risk and walks past his old house.

A Thursday night; a blanket of midweek quietness all around him. Chancy, nevertheless. He is aware of that. But it's very late when he goes walkabout and the streets are dark. It's a good neighbourhood, a safe neighbourhood, where people look after their own.

Danny has taken good care to disguise himself, to shield his face from any random, prying eyes. He's enjoyed it, the dressing-up: it brings him right back to the games he used to play with Emma. He's always liked being someone else. Superman. Spiderman. Secret agent. Tonight, though, it's the good old-fashioned spy-movie disguise that appeals to him. The Humphrey Bogart Look. It's a classic: the turned-up collar, the belted trench coat, the tilted fedora. Perfect for retreating into yourself, like a tortoise into its shell.

Except that that isn't what he's really wearing, of course; that would make him stand out even more, had anyone been looking. Instead, he's put on a dark beanie, pulled low over the forehead. And he keeps his head down, his nose assailed by the slightly sour smell of his old donkey-jacket. Head down and shoulders hunched. That takes a good three or four inches off his height. He has proven that, on more than one occasion.

All of the house lights are off, everywhere. As he passes number nineteen, he glances at the front garden. Gravel where the old path used to be. There is no longer any grass – or 'lawn' as his mother used to call it. Instead, he can see the dark outline of shrubs, something low-lying and creeping, off to one side. And two cars in the driveway, of course. That makes him smile. It must have been a happy little interruption to the household, the discovery of four flat tyres. He was pleased with that bit of inspiration. The perfect kick-off. The Jeep sits squarely now, all black and arrogant. Behind it, and closer to the house, there's the sleek and sexy BMW.

He's never been much into cars, himself. They've always been Robbie's territory. Danny's more of a motorbike man. Ah: the Harley Davidson he'd once owned, briefly; and the second-hand Kawasaki, all those years ago. Nothing like a motorbike. The freedom. The open road. He nods to himself. Those days will come again.

This time, ever since he's come back, he has been trying to get a handle on the years after Emma was no longer around. He thinks of them as the grown-up years, when Lord Robert had himself nicely installed, thank you very much, along with that wife of his, Lynda. Lynda with a 'y', who was probably plain old Linda with an 'i' until she met Robert and got the taste for tennis clubs and a little social climbing.

But the way things turned out afterwards is not Danny's fault, has never been his fault. The forces of destiny conspired against him, that's all. Things went wrong from time to time, and all that wrongness meant that he was left with fewer and fewer choices. Life's like that: once the doors start to close, particularly after the first time, they close against you with startling speed. And then, one final slam and it's all over. You're trapped, in whatever kind of life you've ended up with, right then, right there. The noose is around your neck, you dangle from the string of chance, spitting and clawing in vain. Change is no longer possible.

For years, bad luck seemed to seek him out. It followed him around. Great waves of it, breaking along the shoreline of his life. Sometimes, others got pulled in underneath the surface along with him; sometimes they drowned in the undertow.

A bit like Amy. He met her after things had fallen apart, after he had been cut adrift. But they didn't last, the two of them. Even after it was over, though, he thought about her from time to time. He'd heard that she married, a year or so after he'd left for England. A fella called Phelan. He wonders what she looks like now. Is she a stout, matronly, forty-something, following the pattern of her sister and her mother? The mother only glimpsed from afar, it is true: Danny had never had any intention of meeting her. The sister, Tina, had been quite enough on her own.

Amy was so very pretty, with those big brown eyes, that gorgeous, innocent mane of blonde hair. He had loved the slenderness of her, too, the way his hands could almost meet around her waist. And he *had* loved her, no matter what they said. In his own way, sure: but that was love, too, of a kind. Amy knew it. And trusted it.

So breathless, she was, the first night they'd spent together.

He could see that she was overcome, that she'd never felt about anyone the way she felt about him.

'Hello, gorgeous,' he says. Walks right up to her in the club, pushes aside the others hovering nearby. The girls on either side of her look stunned. They are far better-looking, in a low-necked, self-assured kind of way. But it is Amy he wants. Petite, just like Emma. He has eyes only for her. He makes sure to let the other girls know it, too. He catches the whiff of resentment, as they each peel themselves off their barstools, stubbing out their cigarettes, saying: 'See ya later, Amy.' 'Yeah, Amy, see ya.'

He's seen it all before, with young women like these. Heard it, too – that sour edge of mockery, the insolent disbelief. 'Why her?' 'Why not me?' Especially the really good-looking ones. Danny'd been quite a catch in those days, too, at least at first acquaintance – and he still has the photographs to prove it. Six foot four, dark hair, pale eyes, rugby-player's build. He could have picked up anyone he wanted – but it is Amy he wants on that night. All five-foot nothing of her, Madonna-eyed, shy.

'Hello,' she says, the word ending in a gulp. She glances down at her glass and then puts it behind her on the bar. He notices that her hands are shaking a little. He smiles. It's a good feeling that, sweeping someone off their feet. And he is ready for a girl to find him special. It has been a while since anybody has come even close to finding him special.

'So,' he is saying. 'You're Amy and I'm Danny. That's all the necessary introductions over with.'

Her eyes widen in surprise. She hasn't copped the other girls' use of her name as they leave. She's only had eyes and ears for him. That gives him more confidence.

'Well, okay, let's do surnames as well and get it over with. I'm Danny Graham,' he says, and he takes her right hand and shakes it, gravely.

'Amy Munroe,' she says.

'Like Marilyn?'

She smiles at that. 'Yeah, but with a "u", not an "o".'

That figures. She is about as different from Marilyn as he could want. All that blowsy, frowsy stuff is not to his taste, not at all. 'Would you like us to go somewhere quieter?' he says then, still holding onto her hand. 'Can't hear my ears in this place.'

'Quieter?' she says. 'That would be some trick. It's two o'clock in the morning. And it's Christmas. Everywhere's jammers.'

But she goes with him, willingly. Out in the street, he lifts her, literally sweeps her off her feet and she shrieks with delight. He places her back gently on the footpath and kisses her, both arms wound tightly around her.

'Ah, Amy, Amy,' he says, 'where have you been all my life?' It is a cliché, of course it is, but he figures he'll get away with it with her.

'Waiting,' she says. 'Amy and Danny, Danny and Amy.' She cocks her head to one side, looks at him demurely. 'We sound good together.'

She is a little tipsy, he thinks, or else more forward than he'd believed. 'Yeah,' he says softly. 'I think we'll be very good together.' Her skin, he notices, lights up from within. This is what happiness looks like, he remembers thinking.

She goes home with him to his flat and stays until morning. He is reluctant to let her go, the memory of her shy passion lingering. She promises him she'll be back. She's never stayed out a whole night before, she says. She needs to go home to spin her mother and father a yarn, but she will come back to him. Promise, promise, promise.

And she keeps her promise. 'I'm here!' she calls, as he throws open the door of the flat to welcome her. He's not surprised, not really, but nevertheless he's glad that her mother and father haven't been able to stop her.

'I told them nothing,' she says. 'I'm really good at keeping secrets. Besides,' and she looks suddenly coy, 'you're Dan*ielle* now. We work together. In the accounts department of Arnotts.' She smiles the slow smile that he comes to know well, at least at first. 'I'm keeping you company, while your family are away on holidays.'

'And afterwards?' he asks. He's curious. He never makes plans, himself. He's surprised to have found someone else so like him.

She shrugs. 'We'll tell them when we have to. And by then,' she kisses him, 'it'll be too late for them to do anything about it.'

We'll tell. We.

Danny doesn't like the word. '*We*' has always been used against him, to shut him out, to let him know that he is not welcome as part of the charmed circle of family. He says nothing, though. He doesn't want to spoil the moment. And Amy is very cute when she smiles.

In only a matter of weeks, Amy moves in with him, leaves everything behind for him. Danny still feels good about that: it makes a difference, that someone would love you that much. Not to ask, not to question. He tells her about his life, his family, even weeping when it comes to the bit about Emma. Amy fills in the gaps in his story for him, fills them with indignation on his behalf. She glows with righteous sympathy, with loyalty. He lets her.

She is right, of course: she helps him to believe in his story, the one that he hasn't been able to tell until now. It feels like a kind of liberation, leaving blame behind. At last, someone seems to understand what he has intended, not just what he has done.

Amy's sister doesn't like him one bit and does not trouble to hide the fact. At first, the strength of Tina's hostility amuses Danny. Then it angers him. He knows that he needs to pull Amy away from her, before she, too, becomes infected. He wants her to himself. At least until he is ready to let her go: not the other way round.

Amy's love for Danny reminds him of those bits from the Bible that Mr Lennon used to read out loud to them, back in first year of secondary school. Religious Knowledge, said the printed timetable on the cover of his school journal, but there was precious little knowledge. Not that he can remember. Lennon only read them the dirty bits. His big voice would boom around them, sometimes making the windows hum and shiver. He read while the back benches sniggered.

'And so Adam and Eve cleaved unto one another,' he'd intone. 'Genesis, Chapter Two, verse 24. "Therefore a man leaves his father and his mother and cleaves to his wife, and they become one flesh. And the man and his wife were both naked, and were not ashamed."'

Then Paddy McGrath would ask, all innocent, what 'cleave' meant. Lennon would frown and bark '"One flesh", boy,' and hurry on to the next bit of the lesson. Paddy McGrath would make spit balls and fire them at Tom Joyce's head, just at the part where the hair was all rubbed off, from some horrible disease that seemed to run in his family. Horrible and smelly.

But like Eve, cleave to him she did, the lovely Amy.

'I love you,' she used to whisper to him, her voice the voice of a child in the dark. 'I love you so much. Don't ever leave me.'

She can't have known back then that that was the wrong thing to say to him – is *always* the wrong thing to say to him, if anybody still cares to know. A man needs freedom, great gulping breaths of it. A man mustn't drown or be pinned down, or stopped in his tracks by others who can't keep up. 'You're a man in a hurry,' one of his bosses had once said to him, and scowled. Jealousy, Danny had put it down to. It had been time for him to move on. Danny knew that he could earn far more on the road as a salesman than he ever would stuck behind the counter of a bar.

The flat grows too small for them, for him and Amy. It happens quickly, almost at once. Much more quickly than Danny would have imagined, had he been able to anticipate it. But you can't foresee these things, living in the moment. It is not what he has intended; it is simply what has happened. And the present becomes the past, something he cannot change.

His restlessness grows and keeps on growing until it fills all the spaces around them. Until, finally, there is no longer any room for him there. The flat becomes full of Amy, full of what *has been*, that winter, not what still is. A winter, followed by a spring of discontent, and no 'glorious summer' to follow. Danny has always liked that play, likes the ruthlessness of the king, although his teacher was horrified at his admiration. At his lack of moral centre, she called it. The king's lack, that is, not his. Although, sometimes Danny has cause to wonder about that. About whether Miss Madden really had seen something in him for the future, something of significance that her other pupils did not have, could never have.

There is some fighting, of course, between him and Amy. Perhaps more than he cares to remember now. It gets easier, the not remembering. It just leaves a bit of a hole, but one that can be filled by other things. Imagining. Storytelling. Old photographs. Miss Madden always said that he had a strong narrative sense. Anyway, it isn't his fault, the fighting, the crying, any of it. The money just keeps on getting tighter, the spaces between the fights shorter.

When Amy cries now, she loses that luminous look that has drawn Danny to her in the first place. She begins to look thin, rather than slender. And she is always tired, not up for fun any more. Her shy passion has turned to clinging. Danny feels, again, that he cannot breathe.

In the end, he knows it is better to leave, better for both of them. Certainly better for Amy. After all, she can always go home, make like it has never happened. She has a home to go to. And a sister, who will no doubt take her in, forgive her, as long as Amy accepts the extent of her foolishness. Betraying Danny will be the cost of her finding her way home. Whereas he – well, best not to go there. Betrayal and home are always words in the same sentence, as far as Danny is concerned. A year and a half in a shitty flat on the northside is just about as much as he can take. London calls and Danny is more than ready to answer.

He arrives at their flat on what he has decided will be his next-to-last evening. He's earlier than usual, but he has things to do. He'll need the next two nights to get all his ducks in a row. But when he steps into the narrow hallway, he is surprised at the emptiness. There is no TV blaring, no sound of pots rattling in the tiny kitchen. And it's cold. Amy hates the cold. He walks into the sitting room and snaps on the light. He can feel the pulse beat beginning again, just above his right eye. The flat is clean; the kind of clean that is bare and silent. He makes his way to the bedroom, curious now. The bed is stripped, blankets folded neatly.

Then he hears it, the key in the door. Despite himself, he is relieved. And then, his neck prickles with irritation. What has Amy been playing at? He's the one leaving her, not the other way around.

But it's Tina who stands in the hallway, a rucksack in her

hands. She is visibly startled to see him, but she recovers quickly. He'll give her that. They look at each other for a moment and neither speaks. He decides to wait her out.

'I'm here for the rest of Amy's stuff,' she says. But there is a rasp of uncertainty in her tone. She clutches the rucksack more firmly, like a comfort blanket.

Still he doesn't reply. She pushes past him and makes her way towards the bathroom. He knows she wants him to ask, can see it written all over her departing back. He doesn't want to give her that power, but finally, he can't help himself.

'This is my place,' he says. 'Where do you think you're going?'

'I told you.' Now she's her usual sharp self. 'I've come to get the rest of my sister's things.'

'Leave them,' he says. He lights a cigarette, looking at her through the haze of bluish smoke. 'If she wants anything else, tell her to come and get it herself.'

Tina leaves the bathroom, comes back and stands in front of him. '*You* don't tell *me* what to do,' she says. And then: 'You don't get it, do you? She's left you, walked out on you. She's had enough of your bullying.' Now her eyes are blazing.

He feels a curious respect for her. She should fear him, but she doesn't. Her feet are planted firmly beneath her. She looks up, meeting him eye to eye.

'So, you got your way, did you?' he says, drawing insolently on the cigarette, blowing the smoke into her face. 'You finally got her to leave?'

Tina slings the empty rucksack over one shoulder. 'My way?' she says. 'It's nothing to do with me. Sure, I didn't like you from the first time I met you, but nothing would have made me happier than to see my sister with someone she loved. Someone who'd take care of her.' She shoves both hands into her jacket pockets.

He can see that she's getting ready to leave. A small victory, keeping her from taking the rest of Amy from him, but nonetheless a victory.

'You drove her out. You've broken her heart, left her no choice. It's *you* who've got your way. You were never serious about her in the first place.' Tina's gaze is level. 'Why else would you have nothing to do with her family?'

He knows she's right, recognizes what she says. Her words find some echo inside himself. 'Are you finished?' he asks, his voice cold.

'Yeah,' she says, 'yeah, I'm finished here. And so is Amy. I figure she can live without her make-up. Keep it, with my compliments.' And she's out the door. She's quick. He almost hasn't noticed her edging her way back towards it. And now she's gone, the door slammed hard behind her.

He's restless for the rest of the night. He wanders around the empty flat, not so much remembering as storing up memories, to be called on later.

There's nobody to be trusted. Nobody. First Pansy Robert and his Lady Lynda, kicking him out of his own home. And now Amy, leaving before he had his chance. He scribbles her name and address on a piece of paper, leaves it on the stained and scratched coffee table. He notices she has been careful to remove all traces of herself.

Well, let the landlord chase her for the rent. See how she likes that. The time has come to shake the dust of this place off his feet. He'll take the ferry to Holyhead tomorrow. No passport, no ID. He'll disappear. He never wants to see any of them again.

But that was then and this is now.

Danny finishes his walk around the block. It's good, seeing

all the old haunts again. But strange, too, to see just how much the old neighbourhood has changed, how much more . . . upmarket it has become. Many of the large back gardens now sprout mews houses where kids once kicked footballs. Corners and green spaces are occupied by small blocks of apartments – 'gated communities' – copper-clad, exclusive, painfully fashionable in Danny's view. Every available inch of space has been used – but *tastefully*, of course. Infill development, isn't that what it's called? The sort of thing that makes rich men out of guys like Robert. He's done well for himself. Might be feeling a bit of a squeeze these days, but that's all to the good. What goes round, comes round. And Danny reckons it's his turn, now. This time, success is assured. He's worked hard at putting all the bits of the jigsaw together.

He's glad he's come back again. It's time to reclaim something of what was stolen from him. He's entitled to it. Life lately has involved a fair bit of ducking and diving. London and Liverpool are big places, but nonetheless they have felt smaller, more uncomfortable in the last couple of years. Things that he had thought long buried have started catching up with him again. Some relationship things, but mostly money things. It seems that the arm of the law is long when it comes to debt. Or creative borrowing, which is how he likes to think of it.

It is, of course, a very gratifying irony that Lord Robert and Lady Lynda have unwittingly paid for this little venture. Danny had managed that thirty grand from three years ago very cunningly, using it only to further the Grand Plan. If his brother was so careless as to leave money like that lying around, well then . . . he'd got what he deserved.

Six months back, Danny had been wondering if it would ever be possible to put any kind of a plan together again. After the last time, three years ago, he thought he'd blown it for good. And then, the astonishing coincidences that sometimes happen in the way that they do. They converge in a wholly satisfying way, knitting themselves together seamlessly. All of them producing opportunities that couldn't be ignored, *shouldn't* be ignored.

First, the letter, then the meeting: a strangely easy one, given the difficult circumstances. And then all that flowed from that. Coming back to Dublin, just when he needed to leave stuff behind. Followed by the carefully arranged, but yet apparently random conversation with a man in a pub. Effortless, all of it; timely. He was able to feel the justice of it, the balancing of the scales, the rightness of grievances redressed.

Things are moving along nicely now, and that is all that matters.

4

'MUM, IS IT OKAY again for tonight?'

Lynda looked up, startled. Ciarán was standing in front of her. 'Okay for what?' she said.

Ciarán threw his rucksack onto the kitchen floor and pulled a chair towards him. He sat noisily at the breakfast table. Lynda looked at him, her mind a blank. She wondered what was happening this evening that she had forgotten about already. Ever since the flat tyres on Tuesday, she knew that she had become jumpy, forgetful. And she also knew that Robert had been avoiding her.

'I mean Jon. Can he stay with us again?'

Lynda didn't hesitate. 'Sure. Katie's room is already set up. Of course he can stay.' Anything, she thought, anything to keep you happy. One less thing to worry about.

'Great. Thanks, Mum.' He stood up and lifted his rucksack from where he had just dropped it.

'Aren't you having breakfast?' Lynda was surprised.

'Nah,' he said. 'Meetin' Jon.' He turned to leave and then stopped. 'Can I ask you somethin'?' His question was sudden.

His tone made Lynda look up quickly from the newspaper she had just pulled towards her again. 'Yep. Fire ahead.'

'It's just that . . .' he dragged his hand through his hair with that old, familiar gesture. 'Jon's having a really hard time right now.'

Lynda nodded sympathetically. She remembered how Jon had described Ciarán as kind, a word that had surprised her. He was being kind now, it seemed. His expression was boyish, almost bashful, but his tone was gruff. As though he was trying to conceal the fact of his kindness.

'I was just wondering if, like, he might be able to stay here for a bit, just until he gets his head sorted out? He needs to have a bit of space, away from home, like, for a while.'

Lynda felt the need to be cautious: she didn't want to offend anyone. 'How would his parents feel about that?' she asked. 'I wouldn't want us to cause any more upset for Jon – and they might not like it.'

'His parents don't care,' Ciarán said, already growing impatient. 'That's the whole point. His dad has moved out and his mum's never there.'

'Is he an only child?'

Ciarán looked at her. 'I don't know, do I? All I know is he hates going home to an empty house. Seems daft when there's room here, and we're friends.'

Lynda nodded. 'It's not that I think it's a bad idea – I'd just like to make sure his parents are okay with it. They may be very wrapped up in their own problems, Ciarán, but I doubt that they don't care. It might just feel that way to Jon.'

'Well, it's the same thing to him in the end, then, isn't it? When he goes home, he's on his own.' Ciarán eyed the clock and hoisted his rucksack onto one shoulder. 'It'd be nice to be able to help him,' he added.

'I've no objection, if he clears it with his parents first. And you'll have to talk to Katie about it. It's her room, and I don't know how she'd feel about a stranger moving in.'

'He's not a stranger, he's my friend,' said Ciarán. He was defensive now, almost aggressive.

Lynda sighed. 'I meant a stranger to Katie. Look, if you

want to do this, then you need to take responsibility. Talk to Jon, by all means, but not before I've had a chance to speak to your dad.'

'Will you talk to him this morning? Please?'

'Yes, all right, I'll talk to him this morning.' If I can get him, she added to herself.

'And text me afterwards? Straight away?' He was edging towards the door.

'Yes, yes, all right. But you've got to promise not to say anything to Jon until I get back to you. And even if it's a "yes" from your dad, you still have to negotiate with Katie, do you hear? I'm not doing that for you.'

Ciarán was walking quickly down the hallway, glancing back at her over his shoulder. 'I'm not asking you to do anything – just talk to Dad. I'll do nothing till I get your text.' And he was gone, front door slamming shut behind him.

'Why not?' said Robert, later that morning. 'I've no objection. It'll probably mean more work for you, though. One young lad not picking up after himself is bad enough. You sure you want two?' The mobile signal was patchy. Robert's voice kept coming and going – but that reservation was loud and clear.

'That's a point,' admitted Lynda. 'But I think Jon's actually more house-trained than Ciarán. Some of it might rub off.'

Robert snorted. 'That might be stretching things. But at least it'd be company for Ciarán, and he's been much better for that, lately. I've no problem, Lynda – I'll leave it up to you. Look, I have to run – I'll talk to you in the morning. It'll be late when I get home; don't wait up.'

'Robert – we have to talk.'

She could hear the evasion in his reply. 'About what? I'm really up to my ears here, Lynda. Can't it wait?'

'It's about the other morning. The flat tyres.' It sounded more blunt than she'd intended.

Robert sighed. 'Look, there was no real harm done. The tyres were just deflated. They could have been slashed. I don't want to make a song and dance out of it.'

'Don't you think that that's odd, in itself?' she demanded. 'Why would anyone go to that much trouble *not* to do any damage? It doesn't make any sense.' She waited. *Please*, she thought. *Tell me about whatever it was in the package.*

'Kids are kids, Lynda, and I really don't have time to talk about this now.' He was impatient, his voice wavering down the line at her. 'Stop letting your imagination run away with you.'

'Fine,' she said, angrily. 'You can stick your head in the sand if you want. *I* know what's going on.'

The call ended abruptly. Lynda sighed. She'd give him the benefit of the doubt – bad signal as opposed to cutting her off. She'd just have to wait until he got home. She had started to compose a text to Ciarán when her mobile rang again.

'Mum? It's me. Did you talk to dad?'

'Yes. I've just got off the phone—'

'Mum, I don't have much credit left – what did he say?'

Lynda felt a prickle of irritation. No please, no thank you. 'He said that he has no objection – as long as there is no extra work involved for me.' She could hear his voice, excited, relaying this to Jon.

'That's brilliant! I'll talk to you tonight! Is it okay if—' His credit ran out.

Lynda shook her head. There was no point in ringing back. This would need to be done face to face, later. For a moment, she had a surge of apprehension. She hoped she wasn't getting herself into something she might regret.

She glanced at the clock and pushed her chair back. She'd almost forgotten it was Friday. Time to get a move on. Her students would be waiting. Another long morning's teaching, when she'd much rather be painting.

'Mrs Graham – Lynda, I mean. I really want to thank you for this.'

'Yeah, Mum, me too.'

Lynda looked at the two young faces in front of her. Jon seemed to have a light shining under his skin; Ciarán couldn't stop grinning.

'Sit down, both of you,' she said.

They sat at the kitchen table. Lynda filled the kettle and sat beside them. Jon was expectant. What an open expression he has, Lynda thought. Far less guarded than Ciarán.

'We all want this to work.'

The two boys nodded, looking at each other. 'Particularly me,' said Jon. 'And I'm *very* grateful. I need to know what your house rules are.'

'First of all, we'll have a trial period of a month. If things aren't working out, we'll reconsider. One way or the other, Jon, I'm taking it on trust that your parents don't object to your moving in here.'

He leaned towards her. 'To be honest, I haven't seen either of them in three weeks. I spoke to my mother today and she was fine with it.' He paused.

Lynda could almost see him search for the right words.

'She was relieved, I think,' he said, finally. 'Now she doesn't need to bother about me. That came across loud and clear in the five minutes she had to spare.'

Lynda said nothing. His expression spoke volumes.

'I wrote my father off a long time ago,' he added. 'Besides, I'll be twenty-one soon. I make my own decisions.'

Lynda could hear the distinct burr of bitterness just below

the surface of his words. She stood up to make tea. 'I'm not arguing with you; I'm just stating my position. It's your business to clear this with your family, not mine.' She turned to Ciarán. 'Just as you've got to square it with Katie. I told you that this morning. That's not my responsibility, either.'

For the first time, Lynda regretted the lack of a proper spare room. Five years ago, when they'd extended the house to build her studio, she'd insisted on one of the bedrooms being renovated as a luxury bathroom.

'Jacuzzi an' all, I suppose?' Robert had been mocking, but indulgent.

'Why not?' she'd agreed. 'Might as well take advantage of you being in the business.' She'd then redesigned the original bathroom as walk-in wardrobes. If Katie objected to her room being used by Jon, then she supposed that Robert's office downstairs might do, although it wasn't ideal. Besides, there were bad memories of the last time that that sofa bed had been occupied. Danny had seen to that.

'I texted Katie this morning,' Ciarán said quickly, looking over at Jon. 'We're both going to talk to her tonight, at nine. She's working until eight, she said.'

Lynda nodded. 'Okay, then.'

'Rule Number Two?' asked Jon. He was smiling at her.

'No smoking in the house,' she said promptly, 'and no butts left lying around in my garden if you smoke outside. Take an ashtray.'

They both nodded. 'Deal,' said Ciarán. 'What's Number Three?'

'You pick up after yourselves,' said Lynda. 'I don't see that as my job and, even if I did, I don't have the time to do it.'

'I'll cook a few times a week,' said Jon, at once. 'I love cooking. Ciarán and I will work it out between us. We can draw up a roster.'

Ciarán looked as though he was about to protest and then changed his mind.

'That's it, then,' said Lynda. 'Those are the rules.'

Jon looked puzzled. 'Is that everything?' he asked.

'Yes. Why?'

'Well – what about rent? I've been handing my mother fifty euro a week, ever since I decided to go to college,' Jon said.

Lynda felt embarrassed. She hadn't even thought about money. But maybe he should be asked to contribute; maybe it would hurt his dignity to have a home for free.

'Perhaps you'd like to think about it?' said Jon. He lifted his head. 'I've always paid my own way. It's kind of a principle with me. Obviously,' he said, looking around him, 'I can't . . . I mean . . .'

'Fifty is more than enough,' Lynda said, quickly. She poured tea for the three of them. She could feel Ciarán's eyes on her. She wouldn't even begin to explain.

'That's very generous.' Jon's voice was quiet. 'I know that that is a token payment. Thank you.'

'No need,' said Lynda. She paused. 'And we'll review everything in a month.' She glanced at her watch. 'I need to leave shortly. There's lasagne in the oven. Just leave enough for Robert, in case he wants something when he gets home.' She turned to Jon. 'What about your stuff? Do you need a lift to bring your things here?'

Jon pointed to his rucksack. 'They're here.'

Linda made no comment. She hoped her surprise didn't show. Even a bulging rucksack couldn't contain clothes, books, college materials, all the bits and pieces of daily existence.

'I've things in my locker at UCD,' he said. 'And I can always nip home to pick up more stuff, if I need it.' He smiled. 'I travel light.'

'Well, if you're sure, then,' Lynda said. 'I'll be off. I'll see you both later.'

'Where are you going, Mum?'

'Art exhibition,' she said. She picked up her handbag. 'I probably won't be late. But if I am,' she added, slipping on her jacket, 'I'll see you both in the morning for breakfast.'

'Make that lunch,' said Ciarán, grinning at her. 'It's Saturday.'

'Have a nice time,' said Jon.

'Yeah. Enjoy yourself.'

'Don't forget to ring Katie,' she called, as she made her way down the hallway. 'Or your ass is grass.'

'Promise!' Ciarán called.

'Thanks again.' Jon's voice.

He sounded amused, she thought. 'See you both later.'

And she was gone.

When Lynda got home, just before midnight, the house was quiet. There was no sign of Ciarán, or of Jon and Robert's Jeep wasn't in the driveway. She'd made her decision on the journey home and now Robert's absence confirmed it. It was time to act. She couldn't wait any longer.

She hadn't been able to concentrate on anything since Tuesday. Somehow, routine had felt hollow, insubstantial. And Robert's evasions were making her jumpy. She'd rather *know* whatever it was that Danny might be threatening. Imagining made things so much worse.

She moved around downstairs, tidying up, switching off lights. She decided to take a last look around the garden before she went to bed, aware that she was delaying what she now knew to be inevitable. But she unlocked the double doors anyway and stepped onto the deck. Light spilled everywhere.

Outside, nothing was amiss. Her garden always made Lynda feel more tranquil. She picked up some stray leaves and the inevitable burger wrappings. The stone tortoise was solid and still, its presence a comforting one. It was a stillness she loved, a calm that radiated energy.

She missed Robert. The thought came suddenly, formed out of all the past days' misgivings. She could feel the distances opening up between them again, just like before. It frightened her: the possibility that they might have to go through all of that again. Living like uneasy strangers; passing like ships in the night.

She glanced over to her right. Ken and Iris's lights had just been switched off. Out of nowhere, memories began to crowd around Lynda, memories she thought she'd dealt with a long time ago. Someone switching off their lights shouldn't have such an impact. But that's the way it was, from time to time. Sometimes a glance, a half-remembered conversation, even the way sunlight fell on her garden: each was enough to remind her of the times she and Ken had spent together. After it was finished between them, she had tried hard over the years – they both had – to keep the neighbourly patina from cracking.

It hadn't been easy. Lynda still found it strange: to move freely around another woman's home, picking up her post, drawing her curtains. Seeing all the careless intimacies of another couple's life. After what had happened between herself and Ken, it felt like an unwelcome intrusion on her part; another breach of trust. But she and Ken had both agreed that it would look odd, even suspicious, to stop the easy traffic between their two houses, and so she'd continued as normal.

But he hadn't. Ken had suddenly acquired an office space away from home, once he and Lynda had parted. She'd felt bereft, had grieved the loss of him, and in some ways still did. She'd missed the companionship, the tenderness of Ken's friendship above everything. She and Robert had been living as strangers back then, their lives shadowed by the ghostly presence of Danny. Lynda shook off the memory. Things were different now. And there was no harm done. No one hurt except herself and Ken.

Sometimes, Lynda wondered how much Katie had known. She'd always been an acute observer, even as a child. Especially as a teenager. Well, there was nothing to be done about it now. Lynda stepped inside the kitchen again and made sure the doors were securely closed behind her. Then she turned off the lights and made her way upstairs.

Once inside the walk-in wardrobes, Lynda locked the door behind her. Robert's jackets were hanging there in orderly rows along the top rail, with several pairs of trousers on the bottom. It felt wrong, this subterfuge. She seemed to be making a habit of it. Searching behind closed doors. But right now, she needed to know whatever Robert knew. Danny was looming large between the two of them, all over again. Hovering, dangerous.

Lynda's mouth was dry now, her palms sticky as she fumbled at the pockets of her husband's jackets. For a moment, she felt a bubble of hysteria gather. What an irony this might be. What if she were to find evidence of a mistress, nights in a fancy hotel, unexplained credit card transactions? She shook her head at herself. That only happened in fiction. This was real life. Get on with it.

She remembered the brown suede jacket that Robert had been wearing on the morning of the broken mug. She'd try that first. She pushed her way through the rail now until she came to it and searched all the pockets. She pulled out a neatly folded wad of paper. Receipts for stationery, business cards, web design consultations. Lynda frowned. Surely he wasn't thinking of expanding the business? People were going under every day. She replaced the papers in the inside pocket. Nothing to help her there.

She began to feel almost glad: perhaps there was nothing to be found, after all. If Robert had destroyed Danny's letters, then she couldn't do anything about it. She'd have to leave it to him. And in many ways, that would be a relief.

And then she spotted it. At the bottom of the wardrobe, slipped in between shoes that Robert hadn't worn in some time. It looked as though it had fallen. An accident: it was not hidden enough to have been deliberately concealed. A folded white envelope.

There was a charge of elation, sudden electricity at her fingertips, as she stooped to pick up the letter. She smoothed out the envelope and then, fingers shaking, pulled it gently apart. But there was nothing inside. Something like a sob escaped her, a sob of disappointment and frustration.

She turned the envelope over, looking for *something*: a return address, a clue as to where it had come from, anything. As she read the familiar, sloping handwriting, she began to understand. Robert's name was there, plain and legible. But there was no address. She stared at the name, Robert J. Graham. Comprehension crept towards her at first, then suffocated her.

There was no stamp. So he was here. Danny was *here*.

Danny, standing at her front door, slipping his bombshell through her letterbox while she, innocent, uncaring, made coffee and emptied a dishwasher. Danny, at their cars, creating havoc. Laughing at them again. She could still see Robert's face, remembered his clumsiness as he and she had collided that day, shattering china all over their kitchen floor. And then the other morning, his hunched shoulders. The look of desperation on his face.

'Jesus Christ,' she whispered. 'God Almighty. It's happening again. I knew it.'

Just at that moment, there was a knock on the door.

She jumped, suddenly filled with terror.

'Lynda?' Robert's voice. 'You in there?'

'Yeah – with you now.' Lynda's hands were trembling; she could feel her heartbeat speeding. Quickly, she replaced the envelope where she'd found it and closed the wardrobe doors. She tried to breathe deeply before stepping out onto the landing.

Robert was standing at the top of the stairs. He looked puzzled. 'Didn't know where you were,' he said. 'Are you okay? You look a bit pale.'

'I'm fine.'

'I'm going to have a drink. Join me?'

'Yes,' she said. 'That'd be nice.' She followed him downstairs and into the kitchen. He poured a brandy for both of them.

'You look tired, yourself,' she said, as soon as they were both sitting down. 'You were talking in your sleep again last night.'

'Was I?' he said. 'I've no memory of that. I thought I'd slept well. Didn't wake until nearly eight.' He raised his glass to her. 'Cheers,' he said.

'Cheers.' Lynda sipped at the brandy. But her hand felt unsteady and she placed the glass carefully on the table in front of her. It was now or never. 'I know you don't want to talk about it, Robert, but I can't wait any longer.'

He uncrossed his legs and placed both feet on the floor. 'Lynda,' he began.

'No, Robert. Listen to me.'

He sipped his drink, not looking at her. His smile had

vanished. Instead, he glanced at his watch. Then he reached into his pocket and pulled out his mobile, checking the screen for messages.

Lynda watched him. These were techniques she knew of old: distractions, busy things to postpone whatever it was that he didn't want to tell her.

She began carefully. 'I know that Danny has been in touch with you again. You wouldn't show me the first letter. And another one came on Tuesday, the day of the flat tyres.' She kept her gaze level.

Robert looked over at her. 'Okay, right,' he said, lifting his hands in resignation. 'So now you know. But I told you before – it's just the usual bullshit.'

'What does *that* mean?' she said.

'You know what it means.' Robert looked down at his glass. 'It's poor Danny. Look what I took from him. Nobody understands how hard his life is. If only I'd helped him, things would be different.' He shrugged and drained his glass. 'It never changes.'

'He's here again, isn't he?'

Robert poured more brandy. 'I don't know. And that's the truth. I don't know if he's delivering the letters himself, or if somebody else is doing it for him. He knows not to come near me. Not after the last time.' His tone was flat, blunted with an edge of anger.

'And you think he'll obey? You think he'll stay away because you told him to?' Lynda was incredulous.

Robert sighed. 'Look, he's not here, under our roof this time. Last time, he was in our *home*. He took us unawares. The tyres were an irritation, I agree. But no real harm was done. Just let it go, will you?'

'*Unawares?* Is that what you call it? Robert, why are you

84

denying what's happening?' Lynda hated the shrillness she could hear in her own questions.

'I'm not denying anything,' he said, exasperated. 'Look, I just don't want us getting things out of proportion.'

What proportion would that be, she wondered. She tried to calm herself. This conversation was about to run away with her. 'Is he in debt again?' She kept her voice quiet. 'Why don't you just show me the letters?'

Robert looked at her, his face closed. 'I can't show them to you because I tore them up, okay? I don't want any reminders. And I didn't think you would, either.'

Lynda didn't believe that he had torn up anything. Robert was far too meticulous a man for that. He'd have kept them safely somewhere, held onto them in case he might need to produce them at some future date.

She could feel the air around them becoming charged again. She was angry; he was defensive. If she fought him now, she'd never get an answer.

Suddenly, the front door slammed. There were voices, loud in the hallway. Robert stood and opened the kitchen door. Ciarán and Jon stood there, laughing at something.

'Keep it down, you two,' snapped Robert. 'It's late.'

'Sorry,' said Jon, looking from one to the other. 'We didn't realize.'

Ciarán looked unsteady. He went to speak and then seemed to change his mind.

'Go to bed, Ciarán,' said Robert, bluntly. 'Sleep it off.'

Lynda saw her son glance at Jon, who tugged at his sleeve. 'Goodnight, then,' Jon said. 'We're sorry for disturbing you. Come on, Ciarán.'

'Night,' mumbled Ciarán. They made their way towards the stairs.

Lynda frowned. How come he looked so unsteady, while Jon seemed to be in such perfect control? She could see Robert looking at her.

'Don't go there, Lynda,' he said. He raised his hand, warding her off. 'He's just had a few beers. Stop mollycoddling him. I'm going to bed.'

'Robert,' she said, feeling suddenly helpless. 'Please. Let's not be like this. We're pulling against each other again. I hate it when we're like this.'

Robert put the brandy glasses on the draining board. 'We're both tired,' he said quietly. 'It's been a tough couple of days. Let's just go to bed. I'm sorry for being short with you.' He squeezed her hand. 'Let's go out for lunch tomorrow and talk when we're not so upset. Okay?'

She nodded. 'Okay,' she said. She wasn't giving in, not this time. 'That's a promise, then?' she said.

He nodded. 'Yeah. And try not to worry,' he said.

She looked at him.

'I mean it. You worry too much. About Ciarán. About Danny. About everything. It's not as bad as you think it is.'

Lynda woke just before six. She'd slept better. Nothing had pulled her to the surface before she was ready. She glanced over at Robert. He seemed deeply asleep. She left the room quietly, making sure not to disturb him. She could hear voices as she approached the kitchen. She stopped, surprised. Ciarán: at this hour?

She opened the door and saw both of them, Ciarán and Jon, at the breakfast table. She looked from one to the other. 'It's Saturday,' she said. 'I thought you weren't going to get up until lunchtime.'

Jon laughed. 'Good morning. I hope we didn't wake you?'

'No, not at all. This is my usual time. I'm just amazed to see the two of you, that's all.'

Ciarán jabbed his spoon in Jon's direction. 'His fault. We're goin' to see a match. Some mates of his are playin'. We've left you a note.'

'But it's only six o'clock!'

'It's in Galway. We're taking the ten past seven train,' said Jon. 'Here – it's all in the note.' He handed her a piece of paper.

She waved it away. 'It's fine, it's fine – there's no problem. As long as I know.' She looked at Ciarán. 'I don't think you've been to a match in years, have you?'

He grinned. 'You can put it down to his good influence,' and he pointed to Jon.

Lynda decided to say nothing about the previous night.

'And we're stayin' over in Galway. We might even see Katie.'

'Did you talk to her about her room?' Lynda asked.

'Yeah,' he nodded, looking over at Jon. 'She said it was grand with her, didn't she? She just asked that we take away her teddies and dolls and all the girly stuff. We promised we'd keep them safe.'

'Really?' said Lynda. She was surprised. 'Is that all? Didn't she ask anything else?'

'She was very generous,' Jon said, quickly. 'We had a long chat. She said she's off to France soon for a residency, or something?'

'Yes,' said Lynda. 'She won a scholarship to a college in Toulouse. A kind of exchange, for part of this term. Robert and I hope to fly out and see her.'

Jon smiled. 'Well, I'm very glad to be taking her place here. And I'll be very careful of the rest of her things.'

'I'm sure you will.' But Lynda wasn't satisfied. She decided to call Katie herself, once the boys had left. She waited until she thought her daughter would be up and dialled her number.

'I can't talk for long, Mum. I'm giving a grind at ten o'clock. Is everything okay?'

'Sure. Everything's fine.' Lynda paused. She knew that Katie had to get away to whoever she was tutoring – it was a great way for her to make some extra money. But she needed to know whether the two boys had been telling the truth. 'I gather you spoke to Ciarán last night, and to Jon, his friend.'

'Yeah,' said Katie. 'Jon sounds cool.'

Lynda smiled with relief. 'Yes, yes he is. He and Ciarán get on really well. They're thick as thieves. So you don't mind him moving in, then?'

'Of course not,' said Katie. 'Why would I mind? And even if I did,' and here she laughed, 'I'm off to Toulouse! I'm *sooooo* excited. You and dad still going to fly over for a weekend?'

'Absolutely,' said Lynda. 'We're really—' There was noise in the background. Shouting, laughter.

'Mum, I have to go. I'll talk to you later.'

'Do you need anything? I mean before you go to—'

'I'm fine, I'm fine.' Katie was impatient now. 'Gotta go. Love you.'

'Love you, too.' But Katie had already hung up. Okay, Lynda thought. Ciarán's happy. You're happy. Jon is happy. I suppose I should be happy.

She was, as Robert liked to remind her, apparently worrying over nothing.

Now, before Robert got up, Lynda went out into the garden just for a couple of minutes. Last night's heavy frost had made the deck dangerous. The sun wasn't high enough yet to have made a difference, but the garden was beautiful: a stark, still-white photograph. The tortoise glistened; the gravel seemed even brighter than usual.

And she and Robert had a whole day together, on their own. She allowed herself to feel optimistic. They'd come through so much in the past. She'd have to believe they could come through this, no matter *what* Danny was threatening.

Without even glancing at next door, Lynda stepped back inside into the warmth of the kitchen and closed the doors firmly behind her.

At precisely five-thirty a.m. on Monday the ninth of February – according to instructions – the watcher tips six refuse-sacks full of rubbish over the garden wall.

He'd been concealing them, one by one over the past few days, behind a clump of spindly bushes. If anybody'd found them, they'd regard them as abandoned bin-bags. And no harm done. As it was, at five o'clock this morning, they were exactly as he'd left them, each of them filled to bursting point with Styrofoam containers from Burger King, food tins, used tea bags, vegetable peelings. Volume was all-important, according to Wide Boy. There was to be no ambiguity, as he called it, no chance of this being seen as a random lot of litter dispersed by the gales. This Event, he declared, would be the putting down of his marker.

The watcher looks at the garden below. He has cast his net wide, as it were, and a respectable amount of the gravel has been covered. The rubbish is smelly stuff, too. It has that peculiar, pungent smell that rotting vegetation has. Even from here, it catches him at the back of the throat. He folds the black bags carefully and puts them into a separate, clean sack, which he pushes well down inside his rucksack. He'll dispose of them all when he gets home.

Wide Boy has been very specific about his instructions. It still feels strange, not having a real name to call him. But he refuses to give one, saying it is in everyone's interest not to get too pally. That's actually what he said: too pally. Pally, me arse, thinks the watcher. The thing is, he'd always been used to showing his employer a bit of respect. That's the only reason he wanted a name in the first place. But he's not getting one and so the watcher has kept on thinking of him as 'Wide Boy'. It sounds good: just the right undertone of contempt. And he'll find out his real name, soon enough. Someone, somewhere is bound to let it slip. And the watcher will catch it as it falls. That's what good training does: keeps you alert to detail, makes you anticipate and add to your store of knowledge, bit by little bit.

Wide Boy reminds the watcher of a type, one he had come to know very well during the course of his more official working life. Smooth, big, probably good-looking once upon a time. Blue-eyed, dark-haired, still with an eye for the ladies. One who knows how the world works, who deals in cash and never pays full price for anything. Oh yes, the watcher has known plenty of pricks like that during his long career. Jumped-up, two-bit little gobshites who believe the world owes them a living.

But money is money and the bills still need to be paid. And at least Amy has stopped giving him grief about hanging around at home. You're under my feet, she used to say. Go and find something to do. It made her cross, having him there. She had her routine, liked the house to herself. Without meaning to, he kept getting in her way, tripping over himself in his eagerness to help, to be useful. But she didn't want help; didn't need useful. His retirement, earlier than he had expected, a lot earlier than he would have liked, had left him feeling rudderless. He hated having nowhere to go.

Shame, that they never had any kids, Amy and himself.

She'd have been a good mother. She always had a way with her. Tina's three boys flocked to her, filings to a magnet. Children would have occupied her, kept her a lot happier than spending all that time celebrity-watching. He's never really understood why babies didn't happen for them. His brothers all had kids, large broods of them. And Tina had her three, bang bang bang. So it's nothing that runs in either family, like. But anytime he tried to talk about it in the early years, Amy would just turn away from him. Her face would shut down. He'd get the silent treatment for days afterwards. It was eventually easier to let things slide. Easier than making her sad.

He jerks himself back to focusing on the job. Wouldn't do to miss anything. But the garden below is still quiet; no lights yet, flaring upwards and outwards. He zips his jacket right up to his chin, and burrows further into the blanket. As soon as six o'clock comes, he'll get the camcorder going. Wide Boy's appetite for the recordings is insatiable. Name or no name, he's probably right. It's safer to keep the anonymity going. You can't be too careful with freelance jobs like this. That way, there will be nothing to tie the two of them together if . . .

The watcher has never got around to finishing that thought. If what? he asks himself. He's been told not to worry, that this isn't really serious stuff, no big league crime or anything like that. Like *he* has needed to be reassured about that? But WB has taken the trouble to reassure him at almost every meeting. This isn't about drugs, or protection rackets or extortion – nothing that will bring them face to face with Dublin's criminal underworld, nothing like that.

Wide Boy laughs when he says that: 'Dublin's criminal underworld'. The most he'd known as a lad growing up, he says, is petty thievery, the occasional bits and pieces falling off the back of a lorry. The watcher says nothing to this. It is always best not to reveal too much about yourself. Best to remain in the shadows, on guard. Nevertheless, he can't help but feel a surge of impatience when Wide Boy talks in that ignorant kind of way. He, the watcher, knows more *about* Dublin criminals – and more *of* them – than he can shake a stick at. WB isn't even at the races, as far as that's concerned.

Wide Boy keeps going on about the people in this house paying for their past crimes; about them showing him a bit of respect. The watcher wonders, though, how flat tyres and a few bags of harmless rubbish are proper payback for past crimes. And where does respect come into it? Keeping tabs on the enemy is one thing – but it's all supposed to *lead* somewhere. But he keeps his powder dry. He's felt from the start that this man is someone who needs to be humoured a bit; sometimes he's even wondered if WB is all there.

The watcher recalls how Wide Boy has mapped out in great detail what he needs done, sitting in the back bar of O'Neill's on Pearse Street, his ever-present notebook on the table in front of him. No text messages, he has warned, no calls, no emails. Ever. Memorize instructions and just do the job.

Or this tape will self-destruct in ten seconds, jokes the watcher. But WB looks back at him blankly and continues with his list.

Jaysis. Not even a glimmer.

But – hang on, here we go. It's time for the watcher to get ready. Lights, camera, action.

The woman, whose name he's known for some time to be Lynda, emerges onto the deck as usual. It has started to rain, that kind of fine misty rain that soaks everything, it seems, even more completely than a downpour. Visibility is poorish, but he is still able to see how her two hands fling up to her throat and her body jerks from side to side as she tries to take in whatever it is she believes she is seeing. The garden is a right old mess and the watcher now feels a kind of guilty pride in his work.

She screams 'Robert, Robert!' and a man, presumably the husband, comes charging out onto the deck, loses his balance on the wet surface and falls heavily onto his back, both legs flying out from under him. As the watcher watches, he thinks that this is an even better result than Wide Boy has asked for. There are raised voices then, and he distinctly hears the man called Robert cry out 'For Christ's sake, Lynda – someone has dumped their rubbish, that's all. I thought you'd been attacked!'

But she is sobbing, weeping as though she *has* been attacked. She has helped her husband to his feet, and is clutching at his arms.

'Look at it, Robert! Look at it! Are you still trying to tell me this is some sort of *mistake*? Are you crazy?'

He shakes her off, anger moulded into every movement. The watcher feels a new glow of respect for the man who is paying him. He should enjoy this one. He's getting every detail now, rain or no rain. Wide Boy and his bags of rubbish have pushed Mrs Lynda's buttons, all right. She is trembling, he can see it from where he's crouching, can see the look of fear on her face. He is careful to keep the camcorder low, to make sure that no flash of silver gives him away.

'Can't you see?' she is crying, shouting after her husband's retreating back. She lifts her fists, shakes them impotently in the air. 'Can't you see that it's him again? It's Danny! His name is written all over this!'

Then he can hear no more. The husband comes back outside at once and puts his arms around his weeping wife. The watcher can see his attempts at comfort. He can also see that she is having none of it. She wrenches herself away from him and stumbles back through the doorway into their comfortable, warm, middle-class home.

Danny, eh? That's a useful little bit of info. And the resemblance between the two men is unmistakable. Danny is heavier than this guy Robert, sure, and his jaw is more square. But the build is the same; even the way they hold themselves is the same. That makes Danny Mr Daniel Graham, brother to Mr Robert Graham. That might just come in handy. Might even get Jimmy to run a computer check, just in case. See what the files throw up. You have to cover your arse in this line of work.

Satisfied now, the watcher stands up, very slowly. He places the camcorder into his rucksack and secures all the straps. The Cantek has become as familiar to him as his own eyes, over the last few weeks. He likes the way he has really come to grips with the technology. And he's proud of his ownership: single channel digital video recorder. Hard to say, easy to operate. The highest definition, all the bells and whistles. Jimmy and some of the lads at work recommended it for the last job and they were right. It was worth every cent of the four hundred and fifty bucks it cost. Nothing like the Internet. Buy what you like, no questions asked. He's able to capture every movement, every gesture; he's particularly proud of the close-ups.

Lights next door have just gone on – they must have heard the commotion. The watcher backs away from the wall and begins to make his way down the slope. A most successful morning. Wide Boy will be pleased. And so is he. Now he has a bit of information that Wide Boy doesn't know he has.

Knowledge is power.

And Danny is pleased, very pleased. He spends the entire evening being pleased. But he is also cautious. They mustn't lose the run of themselves, he says. Each Event must be followed by a long period of inactivity. Simple observation will suffice in the interim. Then, when things have settled back into predictability, it will be time to strike again. When the guard is down, that's when the attack is most effective. Vulnerability is the greatest weapon of all. The more vulnerable your enemy, the less power you need to use.

On and on and on he goes; doesn't even come up for air. Gets more excited with every thought, dragging on a cigarette as he paces up and down in front of the pub. As though he's just discovered the greatest battle strategy of all time. Like Patton, lusting after glory. Teaching an old dog, the watcher thinks, but says nothing, as usual. It is manners to wait until invited so to do.

You just keep chipping away at things, Wide Boy is saying, over and over, his face glowing, and fear will do the rest.

5

LYNDA LEFT the curtains closed across the patio doors. She couldn't bear to see her garden this morning, not after what had assaulted her yesterday. She didn't want to look at what she might be forced to see.

She put on the coffee as soon as she heard Robert's step on the landing. The images of the previous day haunted her. They kept returning, a jerky, hand-held camera, the pictures too bright, the colours gaudy. They hurt her eyes, even if she closed them. Last night, when she eventually slept, her dreams had been full of Danny.

Robert came into the kitchen now. 'You okay?' he asked.

She laughed shakily. 'I don't know. I haven't looked out there yet.'

He went over to the doors and pulled the curtains across. Lynda sat at the table and kept her forehead in her hands. She wanted not to hear what he was going to say. If she kept her head down, maybe it would all just slide away, disappearing into the winter dawn. She heard Robert unlock the doors and step outside onto the deck. Then she heard the click and knew that the sensor light had just switched on. She held her breath.

She didn't want to fight him again. Their recent rows had left her exhausted and trembling. She couldn't remember the last time she had been so angry at Robert.

'You just refuse to see it!' she'd screamed yesterday. 'You knew Danny was here and you kept on denying it! You wouldn't even let me see the letters!'

'I didn't deny anything!' Robert had blazed back. 'I've no evidence that those letters were delivered by Danny! You're obsessed by him!'

'And you wonder why?' she'd spat back. 'He lies to us, steals from us, cheats us – we've even had to pay his debts. You just *refuse* to see how dangerous he is. Don't you understand? He'll stop at nothing to get revenge.'

Robert had stared at her. '*Revenge?*' he'd said. 'Revenge for what? Danny's the only one responsible for what he did. No one else.'

Lynda's anger had seeped away. 'You don't get it, do you?' She'd looked at her husband's baffled face. He doesn't understand, she'd thought. He really doesn't understand. 'Danny wants revenge for *this*,' and she'd spread her hands out. 'He doesn't just want money; he's not looking just to be taken care of.' She'd stopped, lowered her voice. 'He doesn't see the world the way we do. In his fucked-up head, we *owe* him.'

'Maybe if I just pay him off—'

Lynda had shaken her head. 'Even if we could, it'd never be enough. You said it yourself: Danny the eternal victim. And a victim feels *entitled*.' She'd paused, memories crowding. 'That's what he said after he stole from us, three years ago. After he ripped off your credit cards. "I'm entitled," he said. "I needed it," he said. And your *rationality* will not change that.'

Then she'd started to tremble. The room swam. Robert was beside her in an instant. 'Sit down, Lynda,' he'd said. 'I'll get you a glass of water.' When he came back, she'd started to weep, silently. Tears of rage and frustration.

'Don't let him destroy us, Robert, please. I have such a bad feeling about this.' Lynda had rummaged for a tissue in the pocket of her dressing-gown. She'd been frightened at how isolated she felt. Robert did not see what was happening all around them: at least, not in the way she did. Last Saturday, over lunch, he had tried again to reassure her.

'Even if it is Danny,' he'd said, 'he's sabre-rattling. The letters, the cars – he's doing it because that's all he *can* do. He can't *get* any closer.'

But Lynda didn't believe that. She'd leaned towards Robert, aware of all the other people around them. The restaurant tables were much too close together. 'I feel vulnerable in a way I never have before. Last time, I could *see* what Danny was doing. We were able to fight him. But now, he's both every-where and nowhere.'

Robert had reached across the table and taken her hand. 'You're looking down the wrong end of the telescope,' he'd said. 'And it's not like you.' He'd paused.

Lynda had looked at him. She'd wondered if she could guess what was coming next.

'You're very stressed,' he'd said, trying to be gentle. 'I'm just wondering if there are . . . other things going on. Physical things.'

'Like what?' She had felt rage igniting. She'd pulled her hand away from his.

He'd shrugged. At least he'd had the grace to look uncomfortable. 'Well,' he'd begun, 'you've been complaining of hot flushes and forgetting things and I'm just worried that—'

'I'm mad and menopausal,' she'd said flatly.

'I didn't say that.'

'You don't need to. Don't insult me, Robert. Whatever you do, don't insult my intelligence. Your brother is the dangerous, paranoid, delusional monster. Not me.' And she'd stood up from the table. 'If I stay, I'll say things that I'll regret. I'm going home.'

'Lynda, please, wait – all I'm saying is that you may be getting things out of proportion.' He'd started to rummage in his wallet for a credit card. Robert hated scenes.

Lynda had had every intention of causing one. Nothing else made him listen. 'Stop right there,' she'd said, raising her voice. 'And think for a moment about three years ago. And the time before that, when he forged your name as guarantor. And before that again, when your father was still alive – paying Danny's debts so as not to damage the family name.'

'Keep your voice down!' He'd glared at her.

'No,' she'd refused. 'I've been quiet for far too long. And you've been blind; you just won't accept that Danny *can* do it, will do it – all over again.' And she'd left the restaurant, letting the door swing closed behind her.

Ever since, they'd had an uneasy alliance. When he arrived home, he'd apologized for upsetting her; she'd apologized for walking out on him. But really, nothing around Danny had been resolved.

And then, less than forty-eight hours later, her garden had been defiled. There was no other word for it. Danny was getting close, much too close.

The attack on her garden had felt like a physical assault. How had Danny got to know her so well? How had he figured out the kind of ambush that would leave her feeling defeated, helpless? She'd wept for what seemed like hours when she and Robert had come in from the garden. Everything that she'd believed to be secure and solid had been violated. But she couldn't explain that to Robert.

'Sshhh,' he'd said and held her close. 'We'll clean it all up. We'll get everything back to the way it was, I promise.'

That was yesterday. She'd wondered if he'd ever be able to keep that promise.

And now, this morning, she waited edgily until he came in from the garden. All her senses were primed for disaster.

'It's fine. Everything's fine.' Robert pulled out a chair and sat at the table beside her. 'Look, I know how upset you are. But this *could* just be some lazy bastard who can't be bothered going to the dump. I'll take a walk around the back later, see if I can find anything.' His voice lacked conviction. But he was trying hard, she'd give him that.

She didn't answer. 'I want to make sure the back gate is secure,' she said. 'I want more locks. And maybe even put in an extra light. The outside light always wakes me when it clicks on. I don't know why it didn't last night.'

'Lynda . . .' Robert said.

She knew by his tone that he was going to try again.

He looked at her. 'There's the laneway to the left of us, remember?' His tone was gentle. 'Anybody could have chucked that stuff all over the garden. I don't want you obsessing over something that just might not be true.'

She went to speak and Robert held up his hand. She'd been about to say: *Over the garden is one thing. Such methodical distribution of filth is altogether something different.* But he wouldn't be stopped. She decided it was easier not to interrupt.

'And I'm sorry that you're upset about the letters. But there was nothing new in them. They were just . . . Danny as he always was. Poor me, and all that crap. It still makes me mad as hell.'

Lynda shook her head. 'The difference is he's *here*. We know that now. And he's always created chaos when he's here.'

Robert sighed. 'This could well be one of Danny's mind games. Giving somebody else letters to deliver on his behalf – you know how he can manipulate people. The point is he's not under our *roof* this time. He can't steal from us again, or fool us again.'

Lynda didn't reply. She couldn't. Robert hadn't the imagination to see how Danny might steal from them again, fool them again. While not coming anywhere near them.

'We fell for the sob story three years ago. I admit that. We believed in his illness shit. And his remorse.' Robert stood up angrily. He began to search in the dresser drawer for one of his occasional cigarettes.

Lynda waited until he'd found them. 'We can't blame ourselves for that,' she said, quietly. 'He looked ill enough, down-and-out enough. It's hard to abandon someone who needs that kind of care.'

Just then, the kitchen door opened. Jon hovered, uncertainly, at the threshold. 'I just wanted to see if everything was all right. This morning.'

Robert gestured towards the garden. He sighed. 'Everything out there is fine. I'm not so sure about in here.'

'I'm sorry,' said Jon. 'I'm intruding. I just wanted to see if any help was needed.' He turned to go.

'Come in, come in,' said Robert. 'You're not intruding.' He ground his cigarette butt into the ashtray. 'You're part of the family. I think we're beginning to feel a bit under siege. But it's important not to get things out of proportion.' He paused. 'By the way, thanks for yesterday. You and Ciarán certainly got stuck in. You did a great clean-up job, both of you.'

'Thank you,' said Jon. He waited, as if getting ready to say something.

'What is it, Jon?' Lynda had been watching him.

'Oh, nothing really,' he said. 'It's just . . .'

'Go on,' said Robert.

'Well, it seems to me that the dumping of all that stuff yesterday was deliberate. I mean, there were dozens and dozens of Styrofoam containers, and huge amounts of vegetable stuff. It really stank. It didn't look like anybody's *normal* household rubbish. It was kinda half domestic, half industrial, if you know what I mean.'

Lynda glanced at Robert. He looked away from her. He shoved his hands into his trouser pockets, agitated.

'So, I was wondering,' Jon went on.

They both looked at him.

'Is there anybody who has a grudge against you? Some neighbour, maybe? Nobody could have dragged sackfuls of that stuff very far. It has to be someone local.'

Robert nodded, considering. 'You may well be right,' he said. 'But let's hope we don't have to test the theory again. At least there's no harm done this time. We all got a bit dirty, a bit smelly, but that's the end of it.'

Lynda sipped at her coffee. She wouldn't look at Robert.

'Right,' he said, abruptly. 'I've got to run. I've a meeting in half an hour and the traffic is going to be the pits. I'll see you later.' He came over to where Lynda sat at the table and squeezed her shoulder. 'I'll try and get home early, okay?'

She nodded. 'Yeah.'

'Take care,' and he kissed the top of her head. 'Look after her for me, Jon,' he said, as he hurried from the kitchen. 'Make her a nice breakfast.'

'Of course I will,' said Jon, and smiled at her. 'Don't worry,' he called after Robert. 'I'll take good care of her.' He turned back to Lynda. 'How do you like your eggs?'

After Lynda had finished breakfast, Ciarán shuffled into the kitchen in his pyjamas. 'What's up?'

'Not a thing,' said Lynda. 'All quiet this morning. Jon has just made me breakfast.'

Ciarán snorted. Then he grinned and jerked his head in his friend's direction. 'I wouldn't trust him if I were you. He's just butterin' you up for his birthday present.'

'Well, I dunno how,' Jon interjected quickly. 'As you're the only one who knows about it.'

Lynda looked at Jon. 'Happy birthday, Jon,' she said. 'I didn't realize.'

'Thanks,' said Jon, grinning. 'I can't believe I'm twenty-one.'

Lynda smiled. But she felt a stab of dismay. Who would celebrate his birthday with him? Jon had already admitted to her that he didn't call his parents: didn't want to call them. And certainly nobody had come looking for him. It worried Lynda, this silence between himself and home.

'What if something happens?' she'd said to Robert. 'What if he has an accident, or something, and we need to contact them? We have no address, no phone number, nothing. It's not right.'

'Leave it,' Robert had advised. 'He's probably still feeling raw. Maybe a bit of time and distance will help to heal the breach. He'll get back in touch with them when he's ready.'

Lynda looked over at Jon now. He was smiling. He seemed happy. The banter between himself and Ciarán was constant. 'You guys in College today?' she asked.

Jon nodded. 'Yeah. We'll be leaving in about half an hour.' He turned to Ciarán. 'Smoke before we go?' He stood up from the table and took the ashtray off the counter beside him.

'Yeah,' said Ciarán. 'Just a sec.' He left his cereal bowl on the draining-board and made to follow Jon out to the garden.

'Ciarán,' said Lynda.

He looked at her. 'What?'

She tried not to let her exasperation show. '*Into* the dishwasher. If you can carry your bowl as far as the sink, then you can bend down and place it *inside* the dishwasher.'

He was about to protest, then Lynda caught the look that passed between Jon and him, and he thought the better of it. Sighing, Ciarán opened the dishwasher door and placed the bowl on the rack inside. He made as much noise as he could.

'Thank you,' said Lynda, when he had finished.

'No problem,' he grunted, and followed Jon through the patio doors. Lynda got up from the table and looked out, hoping that, one of these days, her garden might show signs of spring. The light today was good: clear and bright, with an unusual amount of blue sky. Ciarán and Jon stepped off the deck and onto the gravel, Ciarán scuffing the pebbles with the toe of his slippers. Lynda watched the two of them as they stood, deep in conversation, wisps of smoke trailing above their heads. One dark head; one fair. Each of them at the beginning of their lives. She was struck by how different they were from one another.

On impulse, she walked quickly into her studio and took her digital camera off the top shelf. She moved back through the kitchen, and nudged the patio door open, just a crack. She took a photograph of their heads and shoulders, each young man leaning towards the other, intent on conversation. She was satisfied with the result: it was a good portrait, their profiles natural and unposed. She'd give each of them a copy just as soon as she got around to printing them.

Meanwhile, she'd better go and do some shopping. It seemed they had a birthday to celebrate tonight.

Lynda waited until she heard the key in the lock. Then she set the musical candles going. Ciarán burst into the kitchen first, as he usually did, and stopped short. His mouth fell open.

Lynda heard Jon stumble into him at the doorway and mutter 'Jesus, Ciarán, whattya at?' Then he looked around him, too, and became suddenly very still.

'Happy birthday, Jon,' called Lynda, 'and many happy returns.' The candles sang their tinny tune, the plastic '21s' glittered all over the tablecloth, the garish birthday banners fluttered in the draught from the open door.

Jon's eyes darkened. His face filled with emotion. For an awful moment, Lynda felt embarrassed. Had she done the wrong thing? Then his expression softened and his face relaxed into the smile she knew so well.

'Lynda,' he said. 'This is really great of you. I never . . .' and his voice trailed off. He came over and gave her a wordless hug. She understood. His gratitude came mixed with resentment. This was something his own parents should be doing for him and she felt almost angry on his behalf.

'C'mon, mate,' said Ciarán. He was oblivious to the moment. And for once, Lynda was grateful. 'Blow 'em out!'

Laughing, Jon did as he was told. Lynda gestured towards the table. 'Everything's ready,' she said. 'Just help yourselves.'

'Aren't you joining us?' Jon looked dismayed.

'I have a lot of work to do,' Lynda said. 'I've had an online order for a dozen matching rings and bracelets, *and* an invitation to exhibit my paintings in Belfast and there's something I must finish tonight.' She couldn't stop smiling.

'Wow!' said Jon. His eyes widened. 'Congratulations! That's a really big deal, isn't it? Which ones? Which paintings do they want?'

'They want a selection of the silk ones, the Japanese scrolls I've been working on. And some of the gouaches, as well. And yes, it *is* a big deal and I'm pleased.' Lynda smiled at him. 'Now go and enjoy your birthday.'

'Way to go, Mum!' said Ciarán. 'And thanks for this.'

'You're welcome.' As she left the kitchen, Lynda reflected that this was not the first time that Jon had shown an interest in her work. It was flattering, she supposed. And it took some of the sting out of the fact that Ciarán didn't seem to care much, one way or the other, what she did for a living or what her successes and failures were.

Later, Jon came into her studio to thank her again. Ciarán was watching television. 'Am I disturbing you?' he asked. It was always his first question.

'No, not at all,' Lynda said. 'I'm finishing off a garden design. It's due tomorrow. No pressure, you understand.'

He laughed. He leaned over her shoulder, his face close to hers. She became intensely conscious of his presence. His aftershave, the rhythm of his breathing.

'What's this?' he asked, pointing to a detail in the drawing.

Lynda took the opportunity to move away from him, just a fraction. Immediately, he drew back.

'Sorry,' he said. 'Didn't mean to get in your space. It's just that I find this Japanese stuff really fascinating.'

From down the hall, Ciarán's guffaws at the TV could be heard. Jon smiled at her, shrugging a little, as if to say, *young people these days.*

Lynda felt her annoyance flare. Sometimes, just some-times, his overt maturity grated on her. Jon was insistent now, pointing at her drawing again. 'This here,' he said, 'what is it?'

'It's a ceremonial bell,' she said, more abruptly than she had intended. 'They're associated with hunting and harvesting in Japan. The client wanted something that—'

'It's a *dotaku*, isn't it?' he interrupted, impatient.

Lynda was shocked. 'Yes,' she said slowly. 'It's a bell-shaped bronze called a *dotaku*. It's a design I came across in the museum. Jon, how on earth did you know that?'

He cocked his head to one side. 'About 200 AD?' he asked. He seemed not to have heard her. He focussed on the drawing, following the flow of its elements with his index finger.

'Yayoi period,' she said. 'The bell dates from about 200 BC to 250 AD.' She stopped. Somehow, this knowledge of his unnerved her. 'How did you know that?'

He looked at her. The dark lashes were spiky, she noticed. His eyebrows were fine, like a woman's. He straightened and smoothed the sheet of paper in front of him, his fingers long and tapering. 'I told you I found the Japanese stuff fascinating.'

Lynda was at a loss. She watched as his hands moved across the sheet of paper. His fingernails were clean, shaped. In the studio light, they looked almost polished.

'Can you explain the design on the bell?' Jon demanded. 'Is this drawing here a copy of the original or is it an interpretation of your own?'

'Well, yes, it's my own,' she said. She felt flustered, and annoyed at herself for feeling flustered. What was wrong with her? 'But the designs are all based on the original. The Japanese engraved horizontal bands to decorate ceremonial pieces like this, with blocked patterns.' She pulled out a larger-scale drawing that she had done some weeks back. 'Like this one here, can you see?' she pointed to an example. 'They often used to use criss-cross designs like these, as well as scenes from rural life. All very delicate, very intricate. I've stuck to patterns here, though, rather than figurative scenes. I prefer their simplicity.'

Jon nodded. 'Good choice,' he said. 'Figurative scenes of huntin', shootin' 'n' fishin' just wouldn't cut it these days, would they?' And he smiled up at her, his eyes shining.

'Well, yes,' she said. 'I mean no, they wouldn't. That's what I feel, too.'

He nodded. 'Are these the scrolls?' He pointed to the silk hangings around the studio, each of them suspended from the ceiling on fine steel wire.

'Yes,' she said. 'I'm ready to do the final touches, all the tiny brushstrokes. They've taken me months and I'm almost sad to be finished. I've grown very fond of them.' And she smiled at him, wanting to make up for any earlier stiffness on her part.

'I can see why,' he said, looking up intently. 'They are stunning. So much work.'

Just then, there was a bellow from the TV room. 'Jon – c'mere and see this!'

He glanced at Lynda. But this time, there was no complicity, no knowingness in his expression. Perhaps she had imagined it earlier. 'Gotta go,' he said softly.

She watched him leave the studio. There was something odd about him tonight; something she couldn't put her finger on. Then she heard the gusts of laughter from down the hall and shook her head at herself.

Worrying again. Over nothing.

Danny is fascinated by the surface of things.

Glass. Water. The sheen of light on a lake. It's what still draws him to photographs: what drew him in the first place. Even as a child, he loved the shine on his dad's black-and-white family photos; the shine that glides over the stories they told. And even more, the stories they didn't tell.

As Danny grows older, these untold stories become more and more important. They keep on rising to the surface, breaking through the glossy coating that has kept them captive for all those years. A while back, no more than a year or so, Danny spent long evenings poring over the shoebox of photographs he had taken – stolen, really – from his mother's airing cupboard. It had happened on the last occasion he'd set foot in his family home. Over a quarter of a century ago.

He goes back, by appointment. He remembers how grudgingly Robert lets him in. 'Ten minutes,' his brother says. 'That's all you have. Don't make me come and get you.' He waits at the bottom of the stairs until Danny opens the door to his own bedroom.

Danny has decided to make plenty of noise, opening and closing wardrobe doors, dragging a chair to stand on, slamming boxes onto the floor. After a few minutes, he stamps his way across the landing to the bathroom. On the way back to the bedroom, a quick glance over the banisters shows that Robert has retreated from the hallway.

Quickly, Danny partly opens the door of the airing cupboard. He knows just when to stop to avoid it creaking. He used to hide his dope in there, years back. Emma had caught him, once.

'What are you doing?' Her eyes had been wide.

'Ssshh,' Danny had said, his fingers to his lips, warning her. 'It's some of my special cigarettes. I don't want Robbie to find them. He'll smoke them on me like he did before.' He liked having Emma on his side. And she didn't know which of his stories were made up and which weren't.

'Can I try one?' Her nine-year-old face had been full of mischief.

She'd always made him laugh. 'Maybe, one day. But you have to keep the secret, okay?'

She'd nodded. 'Okay. But promise I can try one?'

He'd grinned. 'I promise. But you'll have to be a bit older. Mum would kill me.'

'I won't tell, you know that!' Emma had been indignant. 'I *never* tell. I'm good at secrets.'

'I know you are,' he'd said. 'That's why I'm giving you this one.'

And in the process of hiding his dope, he discovered the box of photographs. And the other one – a smaller, sturdier box, hidden right at the back, under the bath sheets.

After things fall apart, those pictures haunt Danny, particularly the ones with Emma. He wants them. He can't explain why he wants them so much. Partly, he knows it's because they'd be precious to the others, and he isn't letting them get their hands on them. Why is he the only one to get punished? Partly, too, he feels that if the pictures are his, if he has control of them, then he might be able to change the ending.

He lifts the box very carefully now off the top shelf. He freezes for a moment, thinking he hears Robert's step in the hallway. Nothing. He breathes again. He knows that this box is a fragile thing, donkeys' years old. The cardboard will need to be folded in on itself, flattened, in order to contain the photos safely.

He flips the lid of the second box now, and pulls out the contents, three small packets. He replaces the empty box under the bath sheets, pushing them well back towards the wall of the cupboard. The envelopes he stuffs into the waistband of his underpants. He's worn his baggiest jumper for the purposes of concealment. Then, soundlessly, he moves back into his bedroom and continues his rummaging and his packing.

He comes downstairs, just a bit over his allotted ten minutes. He has his rucksack on his back, filled to bursting-point. He hefts a black plastic bag over his left shoulder, shoving the rucksack to one side so that he can balance both across his broad back. The sack is filled with clothes and shoes and personal bits and pieces, the flattened box of photographs safely at the bottom. He knows Robert will not look. He is much too much of a gentleman for that.

As soon as he hears Danny's foot on the stairs, Robert appears in the hallway. They look at each other. Robert's face is grey, he notices, with a pronounced five o'clock shadow.

Danny spreads his hands, a gesture of innocence, of resignation. 'Want to search me?' he asks softly.

Robert's face flushes. Danny sees his fists clench, the way they used to when Robert lost a fight back when they were kids. Or when Danny had succeeded in goading him to lose his temper. Pansy, he used to call him, and watched his brother's rage ignite.

'Just go, Danny,' he says, tiredly. 'Go now.'

Danny, there and then, decides to try one more time, just for the hell of it. He settles his feet more firmly, stepping a bit wider, squaring up to his brother. 'I'd like to see Mum before I go.'

'Out of the question,' Robert holds up one hand, a cartoon Mr Plod. 'I've already told you.'

Danny settles his rucksack more comfortably across his shoulders. 'Who gives *you* the right?' he says. But Robert does not respond. Danny waits, but this seems to be some sort of new tactic on his brother's part. The Silent Treatment. Danny tries again. 'So,' he says, 'I'm being cast out into the exterior darkness. Just like that.'

Robert looks at him. Shock registers, yellowly, across his features. Danny is interested to see that. He'd never known before now that shock had a colour.

'I don't believe you,' Robert says. He shakes his head in that maddening, superior way he has. 'I really can't believe you. Have you still got no idea what you've done?' He stares at Danny. Then something seems to occur to him, and he changes tack. He becomes all brisk, almost businesslike. 'Nobody's casting you anywhere,' he says. 'You've done this all by yourself. As usual. And you've torn this family apart.'

His tone is flat, dismissive, without emphasis. He might almost have said 'You forgot to close the door again.' Danny wonders why Robert does that: he speaks of important things as though they are of no significance at all, as though *Danny* is of no significance at all. He feels as though Robert has just waved him away, as though he is a fly that keeps circling, pestering others.

Danny has his reply ready. He has been waiting for this opportunity to deliver it. He opens his mouth to speak but his brother's response surprises him. He has to admit that.

Robert shakes his head and smiles a slow smile. 'No more talking, Danny. No more listening to you convincing me that one and one makes five. I'm not falling for poor vulnerable Danny, Danny who always means well. Not any more. Now leave.' He opens the front door. 'Go,' he says. 'And don't come back.'

Danny feels caught off-guard. That has never happened before.

Robert is looking past Danny, as though there is already something compelling over his shoulder, something that Danny keeps getting in the way of. His new future, perhaps. One without Emma and now, one without him.

Danny can feel the pulsebeat beginning to gather in his ears. 'You're all sorted, then,' he says softly. 'Got the whole lot of it to yourself now, haven't you? And a new girlfriend, an' all.' He gestures towards the house and garden, a sweep of his arm encompassing all that he sees, and more. 'Maybe I did you a favour.'

Perhaps it's turning his head that does it; perhaps it's because his vision is already clouding over with rage, pinpoints of black and white dancing madly. Whatever it is, he doesn't see it coming. Robert's fist catches him just under the right eye, and pain explodes in great scarlet sunbursts, no matter what way he looks. He staggers, trying to right himself, to find his balance somewhere between the pull of the black plastic bag, the rucksack, gravity. He falls, sprawled on the driveway, arms and legs every which way. He can feel his hands already smarting, bits of the tarmac lodged in the soft flesh just below the thumb. Instinctively, he tries to protect the packets that are threatening to unleash themselves from the waistband of his underpants.

He looks up. Robert is standing over him. His face is contorted. Not with rage, Danny is surprised to see, but with something else. Something that has rage within it, but more besides. Tears roll freely down his brother's face, a face that is now flushed with high spots of colour on each cheek.

'Don't you ever darken this door again,' he says, 'or I swear to Christ I'll kill you. I mean it.'

Danny has scrambled to his feet by then. 'Fuck you,' he says evenly, and walks away. He makes it to the bus stop in less than five minutes. A good, steady pace. When the bus comes, he swings himself aboard and dumps his stuff in the luggage section. He begins to feel in his pockets, to see if his John Player Blue and his lighter are still there. He hopes he hasn't left them behind him, scattered in the flowerbed, or something.

As he shifts on the seat, a girl opposite turns to look at him. He catches her eye and she looks away, quickly, a pink flush beginning just along the fine line of her jaw. Danny smiles to himself. The three packets are still there, still safely hidden – and a girl has just half-smiled at him. A gorgeous, sexy girl. They are the only two on the bus – at least downstairs. He moves towards her, pulling his wallet out of the back pocket of his jeans. He bends his head to the level of her ear. She doesn't even turn round, although he knows she knows he's there. Her heightened colour tells him that.

'I get off after two more stops. That's where I live. I'd love to buy you a drink.' He watches as her shoulders stiffen. Now for the best part. He allows his voice to falter, just a little. 'I mean no disrespect. I think you're beautiful. I won't disturb you again.' He makes to move back towards his seat, but hesitates, just before he goes. He allows his voice to drop even further. 'If you'll join me, I'd consider it an honour. My name is Danny Graham.'

For the next couple of hundred yards, he watches her. He can see the indecision written all over her bent head, her shoulders. He knows she's dying to look back at him, but she won't let herself. He's in with a chance, here. He can feel it.

He'd kill for a smoke, though. Must have dropped the cigarettes when Robert hit him. He pats the three envelopes for reassurance, their bulky presence making him happy all over again. Five hundred quid in each, part of Mum's secret stash. She was always hiding money, always. Rainy days loomed large in her philosophy.

Well, it's pouring now, as far as he's concerned. And these will see him home and dry. Not a bad day's work, all in all. He pats his cheek where Robert has hit him – a punch that carried surprising weight for Pansy. It feels as though it will grow into a right shiner.

Fuck him, fuck them all. He doesn't need them.

The bus pulls into his stop. The girl makes no move. She keeps her head bent, her hair falling like a dark curtain over her cheek. Danny hoists his stuff onto his shoulders and eases himself off the platform onto the waiting kerb. His leg still hurts since the accident. His foot is badly swollen where they said some small bones were chipped. Not that anybody gives a shit about that. And his face hurts, too. He is reminded of just how much as the pain seems to jolt up from the pavement and lodge somewhere around his eye. For a moment, pain is all he can think about. As the bus pulls away, something tugs at his sleeve.

He turns, already having forgotten her. She is smiling up at him.

'Hi,' she says. 'I'm Julie, and I've never done anything like this before.' Her smile is tentative, but her eyes are like a blue flame. He knows desire when he sees it.

He takes both her hands in his. 'Julie,' he says, savouring her name, 'I'm so glad you decided to join me.' He gestures across the green. 'I live just over there. Let me dump my stuff in the house and we'll go and have a drink.' He pauses, as if it has only just occurred to him. 'But, please, why don't you wait for me in Reilly's, in the lounge.' He points to the pub on the corner. A dump. Even from this distance. 'There's no need for you to come to the house.' And he shifts the rucksack, making sure to stumble a little under the weight of the black sack.

'Please,' she says. 'Let me help you with some of that. It'll only take a minute. Besides, I don't like sitting in pubs on my own.' And she smiles at him.

'Well, if you're sure?'

She nods.

'Okay, then. Let's go.' He leads the way across the green. The flat is reasonably clean, the bed made, and there is at least one bottle of plonk in the cupboard in the kitchenette.

They climb the stairs to his place, pain lighting up his face with every step he takes. She looks younger in the bright light of the flat, but he doesn't care. They drop the bags on the floor in the tiny living room and she comes to him easily enough.

*

He calls a taxi for her afterwards, at her insistence. She won't stay the night. Seems edgy, anxious to be gone. That's fine by him.

When Julie leaves, Danny upends the plastic sack onto the bed. He holds onto the two bottom corners and shakes the stuff out, most of it landing where he aims it, some of it slithering across the floor. He rummages for cigarettes in the bedside table, lights one and sits cross-legged on the rug. He pulls the box of photographs towards him and scatters the contents all around him. He pushes them back and forth, waiting for the ones he wants to come to the surface. He watched someone read Tarot cards once. He likes to think that this reading of photographs is kind of the same thing. It's just another way of seeing the future in the past.

Now Danny's eyes alight on one particular photograph, one that has made its way to the top of the black-and-white landslide on the floor. He sees the old rambling house, his family home, bathed in the sunshine of early childhood summers. Were all those summers sunny ones? That's how they seem now, although he is sure some sort of meteorology anorak would tell him different.

The tartan blanket is on the front grass – what his mother grandly likes to call the lawn – in the same way that she says 'lounge' for other people's 'sitting room' and 'lavatory' instead of 'toilet'. He sees the three of them, Robbie, Danny and little Emma, having a picnic. Emma likes to pour, the pink teapot full of MiWadi orange, a teddy bear emblazoned on its pot-bellied surface. Other, smaller teddies decorate the tiny plastic teacups and plates that occupy all of Emma's attention. A drink of orange and a plate of biscuits: all the delights of a summer afternoon. Sometimes, ice cream – but that tends to come in fat wafers, the ice cream melting, sometimes running in a thin white river down your arm.

His mother emerges from the front door, smiling, a damp cloth in her hands to wipe their hands and faces. Danny's most of all: he always manages to drop everything on his clothes – ice cream, orange drink, biscuit crumbs – and that always makes her crease her forehead crossly, two little lines springing up in the space between her eyebrows . . .

But wait – there's something wrong with this image. When Danny looks at the familiar photo again, he is not there. For a moment, he feels confused. He knows that he *was* there, but in the photograph, he is missing. And yet he can remember the day clearly. Robbie and Emma are on the blanket and there are three doll-sized cups, three plates, a scattering of biscuits, all captured, frozen by the glossy weight of photographic paper. He realizes he must have been standing on the edge of this scene, a scene recorded by his father, like all of the others, proud of his new Leica. Danny is outside the frame, on the edge of the happy family action.

He starts to rummage again now, looking for other stories, other days. He comes across Robbie's First Holy Communion, his Confirmation, his first two-wheeler. The firstborn, the favoured one, the one-who-could-do-no-wrong son. And there are others, too. Robbie's first day at secondary school. Robbie in the first eleven. Robbie in the local *choir*, for Christ's sake. And, by extension, these photographs tell Danny's story, too, by the act of omission. Oh, sure, the school photographs are all there. The ones that got taken by other people. But he's missing from too many of the family ones, as though he'd been cut adrift long ago. All the important ones are of somebody else.

Sins of omission . . . he remembers Mr Lennon at school, his voice booming as he warmed to his theme. The not doing of something can be equally as sinful as the doing. Even worse, *thinking* about doing something bad – even if you don't end up doing it – is as bad, as sinful as if you already have.

Then why not go ahead and do it anyway, and enjoy yourself, sniggers Blue O'Dwyer, hiding his mouth behind his hand. But he isn't quick enough. Old Lennon catches him, makes him repeat what he thinks he has heard. Blue doesn't have the wit to deceive. There is no way Loony Lennon can have heard what he's said, not at that distance. All he's seen is the tilted head, the hand to the mouth: all he has is the conviction that words have been spoken. Blue ends up getting three of the best for that. Never could keep his mouth shut.

Other photographs reveal the same thing. Omission after omission. Emma is there, over and over again, dressed in pretty dresses with ribbons in her hair. As a fairy in the Christmas play. Like a miniature bride on her Communion day. God, he remembers the way she loved those white lace gloves, and the little bag that hung around her wrist, all satin and beading. His brother and sister are like bookends, he thinks. The pair of them: the oldest and the youngest. It's the one in the middle that's missing. Much too often. And his story, too, is missing. Like him, it lurks on the outside. It's one that has never been properly told, never properly seen. A story that once took place, and is still taking place, beyond the image. On the margin; on the edge.

Funny the way these were the words they had kept using to describe him. The hospital just outside London, the one he'd managed to get away from before anyone noticed he was gone. Danny remembers their questions, some of them solemn. All of them to do with boundaries, and borders and being outside. His 'frame of reference', one psychologist offered, and the phrase delighted Danny. He liked the way everything came together: he'd wanted to talk about the photographs, and the man with the pointy head wanted to talk about frames, frameworks. It had a nice kind of symmetry to it.

Danny knows that someday very soon now, he will restore himself to the centre of things. It's been twenty-something years, but he will get back to the core of his own life. It has taken planning and willpower and money. A *lot* of money. And it will need more planning, and persistence, and, curiously, courage. No more fuck-ups, like the one three years ago.

It is time to gather up the pieces for the last time and remake the jigsaw, to line the photographs edge to edge, so that the real picture emerges.

6

IT COULDN'T BE. It simply could not be. Lynda rummaged in the drawer again, opening jewellery boxes, closing them, tossing them onto the top of the bedside table. She had to be losing her mind. She checked again. It was the same blue box, velvet, heart-shaped. The one she always used. But it was empty. The neat, vertical cut into which she slipped her diamond ring at night before going to bed, was empty.

She couldn't stop looking at it. She turned it over, shook it and let it fall onto the duvet. It stared back at her, yielding nothing. She sat on the side of the bed, feeling her legs heavy, about to give way. 'Think, Lynda, think,' she said aloud. She lifted the small box off the bed now and held it in both hands, pressing down on the tiny silk pillow inside. Maybe the ring had slipped underneath, somehow, and lay there, silent. Hiding from her. She pressed down again, using both thumbs. Nothing.

She reached over and pulled the drawer of the bedside table from its moorings. Then she tipped the entire contents onto the duvet and began to search through them, opening and closing boxes she hadn't used in years. Bits of old necklaces fell out, single earrings, a few tarnished brooches that had belonged to her mother. She ran her fingers through whatever she found. At the same time, she tried to think back over the past few days.

Today was Friday. Yesterday was Thursday. She hadn't worn the ring since Wednesday. She'd removed it and her wedding band and placed them both carefully into their separate boxes on Wednesday night. That much she was sure of. Rings off, hand cream on. The usual routine; nothing out of the ordinary. She could see herself, sitting on her side of the bed, just as she was now. She'd taken longer than usual that night, waiting for Robert to come home.

And yesterday, she'd been taking cuttings and potting plants all morning in preparation for her horticulture students today. So she hadn't put her rings on because she hated the texture of gardening gloves. Part of the pleasure of it all was plunging her hands deep into compost, firming the plants into their new containers, the delicate roots clean and snug. She loved the optimism of all the gardening rituals of spring. She even loved the grit under her fingernails.

Slowly, she replaced all the jewellery boxes into the drawer now, fitting it back onto its runners again. At least her head was clear. She was able to piece together the last few days with surprising accuracy. It was three weeks now since the rubbish had been dumped in her garden; three weeks since she had begun to understand that Danny was back in their lives again. Lynda had used the time to get ready.

Without saying anything to Robert, she had become alert and vigilant. She had decided to behave as though someone was watching her. Her movements, even inside her own home, were more guarded. She varied her daily activities as much as possible. Sometimes, she'd go through all the routines of locking up and putting on the alarm. She'd leave the house, then, full of purposeful efficiency. Once inside the car, she'd drive quickly around the block and come straight home again.

She wanted to catch Danny in the act – whatever that act might be. She wanted to be the one wielding the element of surprise, this time. Right now, she didn't fear him physically. Perhaps she should, but each day that he didn't appear made her feel stronger. She was ready for him, finally; would be almost happy to meet him. Draw him out of the shadows and into the light.

Everything that was happening to her was part of yet another spiral. Lynda understood that now. This was how Danny operated, how he'd always operated, it seemed to her. But it would take something dramatic to make Robert believe that the threat from his brother was as real now as it had always been. Every time she'd tried to talk to him, to get him to see what she saw, he became impatient. 'Leave it, Lynda,' he'd say, his face creasing in annoyance. 'You're getting things out of proportion again. This isn't like before. We're on top of it.'

The flat tyres, the rubbish in the garden – these things were nothing to worry about, as far as Robert was concerned. *We're on top of things. This is not like before. He can't touch us this time.* Robert's mantra: denying the menace of Danny. Despite what had happened in the past. Or perhaps because of it: the memories of the last time were still painful ones. But Lynda was convinced. This gradual escalation of destruction had Danny's prints all over it.

First something small, just as it had been three years before. There had been the innocent smashing of a vase on the day he'd arrived. One of Robert's favourites, it had belonged to their mother.

Danny had been all apologies. 'Jesus, Robert, I'm sorry. It's the illness. It affects my balance, sometimes. All the medication . . .' And he'd shrugged, his face grey, ghostly. Then it began in earnest. Lynda could see it clearly now, of course, but she couldn't have back then. Within a couple of days, Danny needed money. His requests had been apologetic. 'Wouldn't ask if it wasn't crucial,' he'd say with his small, sad smile.

'Haven't been able to work much, recently. You know. The tiredness . . .' He'd let his voice trail away.

Robert had been visibly horrified at Danny's appearance. His brother had simply turned up on their doorstep, less than a week before. No letter; no call; no warning. Just the element of surprise. He'd looked haunted; gaunt and unkempt. Lung cancer, he'd told them. And, coughing harshly, said he'd prefer to take his chances in Dublin rather than Liverpool. At least he had family here, 'even if you'll never forgive me for Emma'.

It had been an emotional evening, the evening of his return. Lynda remembered how she had left him and Robert, talking late into the night. The following morning, Robert had taken her aside, quietly. 'It's serious, Lynda, no doubt about it. It looks like he has about six months. I know what he did, and I don't excuse it. I can never forgive him for that. But he *is* my brother, and there's no one else but us. Can you bear it, us having him here for however long it takes?'

Lynda didn't even need to think. 'Of course,' she said. 'It won't be easy – particularly for you. But if you can let go of the past, then so can I.' She'd been shocked, too, at how ill and grey Danny had looked. Like a homeless man, rootless and wandering.

'Not let it go, as such,' Robert had said, after a moment. 'But I think I can let it lie, for now.'

Lynda had almost welcomed the opportunity to take Danny in. It might, in its own strange way, allow her to atone for her affair with Ken. Robert had never known about it, she was almost sure of that. He may have suspected, but he'd let that lie, too. They both had. This return of Danny's would help her make her own amends for a betrayal that her husband might never even have known he'd suffered.

Robert had smiled at her then, grateful. 'Thanks, Lynda. I know my father would never have let him across the threshold again, no matter what. But this was my mother's house, too. I'd like to do it for her sake.'

Lynda watched as all the familiar griefs made his face sag. Are we ever going to be finished with this, she remembered thinking at the time.

'I think Mum would have wanted him looked after,' Robert had said to Lynda. 'No, I'm sure of it. He can have the sofa bed in my office downstairs. There's plenty of room. He has hospital appointments almost every day. I'll deliver him, if you can collect him, even a couple of mornings a week.' And he'd held her; they'd held each other close for a long time. Lynda felt that, at last, the same river had just been crossed by both of them.

'I'll do whatever I can, Robert, you know that. We'll look after him together.'

Robert held onto her; his grip on her hand now was almost painful. 'What should we tell Ciarán and Katie?' he asked, after a moment.

'The truth,' she'd replied promptly. 'We'll tell them that their uncle is seriously ill and we're going to look after him. They're old enough to help.'

She remembered saying that now. *The truth.* If only she'd known. But that time had been a dress rehearsal for today. She'd never let Danny fool her again. She'd be waiting.

Back then, it had taken just three weeks for her to find out that Danny's illness was a lie. Quite by chance, Lynda had discovered traces of make-up on the clothes she'd taken from Danny's room to wash. He'd kept protesting that no, he didn't want to be any trouble, he didn't want her picking up after him, he was perfectly capable of using a washing-machine himself.

But one morning, after Danny had already left for the hospital with Robert, Lynda had gone into the office to leave him clean sheets and towels. She'd spotted a pile of crumpled clothes at the end of the sofa bed. On impulse, she picked them up. She'd have them washed and dried and back again before Danny even knew they were gone.

She went straight to the utility room and began to sort the laundry before putting it into the machine. Something around the collars of Danny's shirts began to stain her fingers, making them look grey and powdery. At first, she didn't know what it was. She was puzzled. There was something vaguely familiar about it . . . She rubbed her fingers together. She knew she'd seen this shadowy stuff before.

Finally it hit her. A long-ago memory, from her days in the college drama society. This was make-up; theatrical make-up. Thick, putty-coloured.

The implication stunned her. It couldn't be, surely. Danny was so thin and ill-looking. The pallor was only part of it. But anger had already begun to surface. Jesus – if this was another one of his tricks . . .

She replaced the shirts on the floor of the office where she'd found them and said nothing to anyone. But that evening, she'd watched Danny closely. He was thin, yes, but the gauntness was an illusion. The hollows on his face were expertly done; the pallor was a masterstroke; so were the dark shadows under his eyes. But she needed to be sure of what she was seeing before she said anything to Robert. In case she couldn't trust the evidence of her own eyes.

After dinner, Lynda announced that she'd take a lift with Robert and Danny on the following morning. 'I've a pile of stuff to do in town,' she said. 'I might as well go in with you two. I'll get the Dart home when I'm finished. Maybe Danny will be ready by then and we can come home together?'

She saw the way he looked at her. The quick glance, the quicker calculation. Lynda was struck by how powerful her sudden new knowledge was. It allowed her to interpret what she saw before her in a radically different light. She was surprised at how it energized her, made her feel fiercely protective towards her two children. Although Danny was no threat to them, surely. But, suddenly, she didn't want either Katie or Ciarán in their uncle's presence. He tainted all around him.

'Sure,' Danny'd said. 'I'd like that. Thing is, I can never guarantee what time I'll be finished at.' He shrugged then, a little helplessly.

Nice touch, thought Lynda.

'Sometimes,' he added, 'these clinics go on for ages. I'd hate to think of you hanging around.'

'Mum,' said Katie, interrupting. Lynda didn't correct her. 'Can you pick me up the German text-book I need? O'Connor's are sold out.'

'Sure,' said Lynda. 'No problem. Just write down the name for me.' Right now, she thought, I'd buy you anything you wanted. 'Ciarán?' she said. 'Do you need anything for school while I'm in town?'

He shook his head, his mouth full of roast potato. Wish you wouldn't do that, she thought. But I'm saying nothing, not in front of Danny. This family's ranks are now closed. She turned to Danny. 'You still have Ciarán's old mobile?'

He nodded. 'Yeah.'

She was satisfied to see he was looking uncomfortable now. 'Then there's no problem,' she smiled. 'We'll keep in touch by text. I can wait for you. I'm in no hurry tomorrow.'

Early the next morning, Danny looked greyer than ever. He was agitated, twitchy. He insisted he needed to leave at once. He'd forgotten that today was the day he had to be fasting, to have his bloods done.

'Come on,' said Robert to Lynda. He was anxious. 'We'd better skip breakfast. We can always pick up something later.'

Lynda turned to Katie. 'You're last out. Make sure you lock up and put on the alarm.'

Katie looked up to heaven. 'Yes, Mum.'

'Ciarán, your gym stuff is in the hall. Don't forget it. If they send you home, I'll bring you back. I mean it. You're not missing school again.'

Ciarán nodded. 'Yeah. I know. You already told me.'

'Have a good day, both of you,' she said. Then she followed Danny and Robert out to the Jeep.

When Robert pulled up at the hospital entrance, he and Lynda waited until Danny had gone inside. Just as Robert was about to pull out into the traffic again, Lynda said, as though she'd just thought of it: 'I might as well get out here, too. Save you stopping again. You go on ahead.'

'But it's miles from the centre,' he protested. 'Let me take you to Dame Street, at least.'

But she shook her head. 'No. It's ages since I've been up this neck of the woods. And it's a lovely day. I'll walk. Talk to you later.' She leaned over and kissed him. 'Take care,' she said. His expression made her feel guilty, all over again. She knew he believed Danny, that he wanted to forgive him. Despite all that had happened, she knew that he felt in part responsible for what had become of Danny's life.

The prodigal son. Shouldn't he always have a welcome home, always have the fatted calf? And what about the one who stayed at home, Lynda often wondered. The faithful, patient one. Danny had had too many homecomings, of one sort or another. Too many fatted calves over the years.

Leaving others nothing but the bones.

*

Lynda was surprised at how easy she found it to lie to all of the consultants' secretaries. About her brother, ill and confused and mixing up his appointment dates. Would it be possible to check when his next one was? Date of birth? Of course. All correspondence to this address.

There was no Daniel Graham listed anywhere. Two hours after she'd arrived, Lynda left the hospital. Outside the gates, she hailed a taxi and went straight home. On the way, she called Robert.

At first, he didn't believe her. Then he seemed to freeze. 'Jesus, Lynda,' he said. 'I gave him five hundred euro this morning to keep him going. Felt sorry for him.'

Lynda was puzzled. 'But that's not the end of the world,' she said.

'No,' said Robert, slowly. 'But I took it from my stash in the office. Danny was in the shower, so I just nipped into the room while he was gone.'

'Go on,' said Lynda.

'He walked in on me just as I was putting it back into the safe. I turned around and suddenly he was there. I got paid for the job in cash yesterday. I was going to lodge it today, but—'

'But he distracted you,' Lynda finished for him. 'This morning. He distracted both of us.' She could see Danny's face even now, pale, avid. The lips twitching from time to time.

'Thing is,' said Robert. 'I don't think I locked the safe after me. He was in such a state all I wanted to do was get on the road. Christ.'

Lynda drew a deep breath. 'No wonder he was in such a hurry. I think you'd better come home. If he's there, I don't want to confront him on my own.'

'You're not to,' said Robert, sharply. 'Wait for me in Cronin's coffee shop. I'll be there within the hour.'

By the time they'd got home, the damage was done. The safe was empty. Danny had disappeared.

'How much?' asked Lynda.

Robert looked distracted.

'How much, Robert?' she persisted.

He looked ashamed. 'Thirty grand. And that's not all. After you called, I checked my wallet. My credit cards are missing.'

'Call the police,' Lynda said, at once.

Robert looked at her. She could see all the familiar hesitations, all the family loyalties, all the old humiliations.

'I mean it,' she said. 'It's probably already too late, but this is too much, just too much.' She paused, afraid her anger was about to get the better of her. 'There is nobody left to protect, Robert. We have let Danny away with so much over the years. Way too much. Like the time he stole from your mother. I'll never forget that.'

Lynda stopped. She'd promised herself never to bring that up again. She had seen the pain it caused, all those years ago. 'And my little Emma only dead,' Mrs Graham had whispered to her. She'd clutched convulsively at the lace handkerchief she held, twining it around her fingers again and again. 'How could he? Oh dear God, how could Danny do that?' Her lip had trembled. 'He stole it. Stole the money I need to bury my daughter. My baby.'

Even now, Robert flinched at the memory.

'Do it, Robert,' Lynda said, her voice quiet. 'Do it or I will.'

But Danny had fled by then, of course he had. Vanished. But he'd left plenty of traces behind him. Soiled clothing; unhappy memories. She had looked around her, surveying once more the devastation caused by Danny.

*

Lynda felt ambushed by memories of that morning now as she continued to search for her ring. It was the same mix of disbelief and panic. How could this be happening all over again?

She'd have to stop for now. It was time to go to work. But when she came home, she'd have to pull apart every corner of this house, starting with the probable and ending with the impossible. She had no idea how Danny's hand could be part of this. All she knew was, every instinct she had was screaming his name.

Somehow, he had got under her roof. His presence kept making itself felt.

Like a low growl, crawling under her skin.

When Lynda came home from work, she began her search immediately. First, in the bedroom, a methodical search that included turning out pockets, looking in shoes, rummaging through folded clothes.

She was about to go downstairs when she heard the front door opening. Please God, let it not be Robert. Not just yet. Ciarán and Jon fell into the hallway, laughing.

'Did you ever see anything like her?' Jon was saying. 'Talk about a slapper!'

They both stopped short when they saw Lynda, standing at the top of the stairs. Jon's expression immediately became serious. He glanced at Ciarán, who was staring at his mother. 'Lynda? Are you okay?'

'You're very white, Mum,' said Ciarán. 'Has something happened?'

'I need your help,' Lynda tried to keep her voice firm. 'Both of you. I have mislaid my engagement ring. I have no idea where I left it.'

'We'll help you find it,' said Jon at once.

'When did you have it last, Mum?'

'Wednesday night,' said Lynda. 'I know I had it on when I was writing up notes for class. I know because I remember saying to myself that I had to leave it off on both Thursday and Friday, or it would get damaged.' She stopped. 'I remember distinctly putting it into my ring box before I got into bed. But it's disappeared.'

'Where have you looked?' asked Jon.

'I've torn my bedroom apart. It's definitely not there.'

'Okay,' Jon's voice was brisk. 'We'll start downstairs. What does it look like?'

'It's a solitaire – a single diamond.' She paused. Robert had had it reset for their twenty-fifth wedding anniversary. She was afraid to speak. Too many memories, too much emotion.

'Let's do the studio first, Ciarán,' Jon was saying. 'We'll divide it between us, come on.'

Both boys disappeared. Lynda went into the downstairs bathroom, running her hands over all the surfaces, getting down on her hands and knees. Then the kitchen. But she found nothing, apart from some dust balls and safety pins. The boys found nothing in the studio, either.

Just then, she heard Robert's key in the lock. She could feel her heart plummet.

'What is it?' he said, as soon as he saw her. 'What's up?'

When she told him, he looked relieved. His relief angered her. 'Aren't you even concerned?' She could feel herself glaring at him. 'My ring is missing!'

'Yeah,' he said. 'Of course I'm concerned. But at least this is something we're responsible for ourselves. Not something out of our control.' He glanced over at her. Danny. He meant Danny. She made no reply.

They searched for over three hours. Lynda was close to

accepting that the ring was gone; close, even, to doubting herself, her memory and her certainty. Then there was a sudden whoop from outside, in the hallway. Ciarán came bouncing in. 'We've got it!' he said. 'We've found it!'

Jon followed, proudly holding out the ring. 'Here it is,' he said. His voice was jubilant, eyes shining with delight.

Lynda took it from him. Her hands had gone suddenly cold. 'Where did you find it?' she asked.

'In the downstairs bathroom,' Ciarán said. 'Behind the – the whatever you call that thing that holds up the basin, yeah?'

'The pedestal,' said Lynda automatically.

'Yeah,' said Jon, nodding his head. 'Behind the pedestal. We were just about to give up, and there it was!'

'Thank you,' said Lynda. She was aware that Robert was looking at her strangely. 'Such a relief,' she said, and smiled at the two boys. They looked at her, then at Robert. She could feel their puzzlement. Nobody spoke.

'I think I'm going to have to lie down for a while,' she said at last. 'I'm really sorry, but I feel kind of overcome, to be honest.'

Jon nodded. 'Yeah, you don't look well. You must have been really worried.'

'Frantic,' she said, trying to smile. 'I've been frantic about it, all day. Thank you both.' And she left the room.

She could hear voices, low murmurs as she climbed the stairs. After a few minutes, Robert came into the bedroom. 'Close the door,' she said.

He obeyed. His eyes were troubled. 'Are you okay? All's well that ends well, eh?' But his question was a tentative one.

Lynda tried to breathe deeply. 'I'm not so sure,' she said. 'Robert, I know you're not going to believe this, but I know I put that ring in its box on Wednesday night. I am absolutely certain of it.'

Robert said nothing. He didn't need to: she could see what he was thinking. Could write the script for what came next.

'Lynda,' he said slowly, and sat on the bed. 'You've been under a lot of strain in the past few weeks. We've already talked about this. Frankly, you've been forgetting things lately. You said so yourself.'

'This is different, Robert, I—'

But he held up his hand, that gesture she knew so well.

'And there's nothing wrong with forgetting,' he went on, as though she hadn't spoken. He took her hand. 'We all do it. What is more natural than leaving your ring on the side of a basin when you wash your hands?' He spread his palms, a gesture of resignation, of forgiveness. 'Maybe you knocked it onto the floor and then forgot that you'd been wearing it. It happens.' He patted her hand now.

She could feel her irritation growing. But he didn't notice.

'There's nothing strange about this, Lynda,' he said. 'Please don't make something out of it.'

She looked at him, her gaze steady. 'This is something to do with Danny,' she said.

'Ah, Jesus,' said Robert. 'Not again.' He let go of her hand abruptly and stood up. He was angry now. He began to pace around the bedroom. 'Tell me how, for Christ's sake? How on earth could this have *anything* to do with Danny?'

'I don't know,' she said, truthfully. 'But I know that it has. And I'll tell you something else.'

He looked at her.

'Remember last week when I told you that the sinks downstairs were blocked? When I'd to stop using the one in my studio? Well, when I tried to wash my brushes in the downstairs bathroom, the water kept backing up there, too.'

He nodded, wary.

'I called your plumber guy, last Thursday, the number

you gave me. Naturally, he hasn't come, but that's not the point.'

'And what is?' asked Robert. He sounded tired.

'I haven't gone near that bathroom since. I've used the en-suite, and made sure the boys used the main bathroom upstairs. I didn't want us to make things worse.' She paused then, afraid of the storm that she could see gathering across Robert's face. 'And I wore that ring all week, up until Wednesday night. How do you account for that?'

'What are you saying, Lynda?' his voice had an edge to it.

It sounded ludicrous, even to her own ears. 'Someone took that ring out of the box, here in the bedroom, and put it downstairs. That's what I am saying.'

Robert looked at her, his eyes glazed with disbelief. 'Ah, you can't be serious,' he said. He stopped pacing; couldn't take his eyes off her. He dragged his hair back from his forehead with both hands. The gesture was loud in its fury. 'Why the *fuck* would anybody do that? And how *could* anybody do that? It just doesn't make sense.'

'I know. But I am serious.' She was calm now. For her, the mystery had been solved. Somehow, Danny had come in from the garden. In from the cold. Somehow, he had got inside.

Robert just looked at her. His face looked unhealthy all of a sudden, almost yellow. 'I'm going downstairs,' he said, finally. 'You are definitely losing the plot. And I'm going *now*. I can't take any more of this.'

Lynda watched him leave. The door closed, none too gently, behind him.

She had a sudden, vibrant memory of Ken. He'd said exactly the same thing to her, five years ago. When he'd told her it was over, that Iris suspected another woman. 'Not you,' he'd said. 'Her friend. She'd suspect anyone but you.' He'd paused. 'I'm not risking my marriage for this, Lynda. I'm sorry you and Robert are falling apart. But it's over. *We're* over.' He'd stood up. 'I'm going now,' he'd said. 'I can't take any more of this.'

And he'd left the restaurant where they'd met that night, one that was miles away from home. Discreet, expensive. Where they wouldn't run into anyone they knew. She'd watched him leave; watched him so that she could gather memories. She knew that she'd always known this time would come. But hating it, nevertheless.

Ken had saved her: that was the simple truth of it. Seven years ago, when Robert's parents had died within six months of each other, it was as though Robert went missing from his own life. He still came and went, ran his business, spoke to his clients, but it was as though *he* wasn't there. His home was something he left each morning, returned to each night. That was all: he spoke to no one. Not to his children. Not to her. His grief had frightened Lynda. She couldn't reach him.

And then the threats from Danny began: the challenge to the will, the accusations of undue influence over elderly parents, *his* rights and entitlement to a share in the family home. 'Well, perhaps he has a point,' Robert had replied when Lynda showed him the solicitor's latest letter. She'd looked at him in disbelief. 'What are you saying?' She could hear the hysteria in her voice.

'Let him have it. I don't care any more. I'm tired of looking after everybody.' Then he'd shrugged his way into his jacket and left the room. Stunned, Lynda had followed him down the hallway.

'Robert – we have to deal with this. We need to talk.' She'd forced herself to speak quietly.

'You deal with it,' he'd said, not looking at her. 'I've had enough of it. All of it.' He'd opened the front door.

'Enough of me?' she'd asked then. 'Enough of your children?'

He'd paused at that. 'I don't know. I just don't feel that anything matters any more. What's the point?' And he'd left, closing the front door behind him.

Lynda had walked back into the kitchen and sat down, hunching over the table. Almost immediately, the doorbell had rung. Robert. He'd come back. She'd felt almost dizzy with relief, had leapt up from the table and raced down the hallway, flinging open the front door.

Ken had stood on the step. 'Lynda,' he'd smiled. 'Hope I'm not disturbing you, but—' He hadn't got any further. Lynda had sobbed, her legs had given way and she'd slid to the floor. Ken had caught her, helped her back into the kitchen, made her tea.

And that was how it had begun. With concern, tenderness, friendship. She'd known all along that it was wrong; they both had. But she'd craved the intimacy Ken offered her. He'd made her feel less lonely. It was as simple as that. When they'd parted, she knew it was because the time had come for a decision that neither of them was prepared to make.

Katie had found her when it ended, crying at the kitchen table. She'd been about sixteen at the time, sharp-eyed, hostile. Lynda had brushed her away. But from time to time afterwards, she felt that Katie had burrowed deep into the truth of things. She watched her whenever Ken or Iris were around. Followed her, when Lynda went to pick up the post next door, or to open curtains. They'd never spoken of it. Not of it, nor of Katie's sudden, fierce protectiveness towards her father.

And now, Lynda's recent fights with Robert reminded her too painfully of that time, all over again. She couldn't let them drift apart as they had before. They'd managed to struggle back from whatever place they'd been, five years ago. Part of her had always wanted to believe that Robert hadn't known about Ken – or if he had, that he'd chosen not to say. They'd built something good together afterwards, something that had with-stood even Danny. She couldn't risk losing him again, not now.

She had to follow him, do whatever it took.

Now this, even the watcher has to admit, is bizarre.

It's been more than four weeks since the incident with the rubbish. He is in his usual position, ready to proceed with the next 'Event', as Wide Boy calls it. Except that he's been calling it the next 'Exterior Event' and has looked very pleased with himself as he does. So pleased that the watcher hasn't asked. He wouldn't give him the satisfaction.

And so he's here again. Still. Freezin' his arse off in the cold. And likely to be for the foreseeable future. This looks like runnin' even longer than he thought. As long as my knees last, the watcher grumbles to himself.

He has come to think of this as a war of attrition. Every day, he chips away a little more at the composure of the house that lies below and it might be his imagination, but the house has begun to look untidy of late. The curtains aren't properly closed, sometimes, and outside in the garden, several bits of paper litter the gravel. He's been leaving little things around the place, too, these mornings. And sometimes, they're not being picked up as quickly as normal. A pity, that. He's chosen things that have plenty of ambiguity about them.

Whatever you like, Wide Boy said. Maybe a few old photo-graphs, newspaper clippings, the odd bottle or two. Something that raises questions.

And so, for the past few mornings, the watcher has scattered a couple of dozen black-and-white photographs around the gravel. There's nobody special in them. He's bought them in one of the junk shops along the quays. Then some food wrappers. And beer bottles, bits and pieces of old crockery, placed strategically around the place. Stuff that can't make its way there on its own. Puzzle-making stuff.

Have they been carried there by the high winds? Or has some malign hand delivered them to Mrs Lynda's stone tortoise? Your starter for ten.

He remembers now that a few days after the incident with the rubbish, the patio door was opened tentatively. It was the first time Mrs Lynda had stepped out onto the deck since things had been cleaned up. The watcher had recorded that, too, as per instructions. Two young men, presumably the sons, had got stuck in with rakes and brushes and dustpans. Wide Boy had seemed pleased about that.

But when she had re-emerged, the watcher had been able, even from here, to see the uncertainty on her face, in her movements. Mr Robert followed and took her hand. He seemed to be showing her that all was safe, that there was nothing to be concerned about. He'd looked around him, all his movements exaggerated ones. See? His hand gestures kept on saying. Didn't I tell you? There's nothing to worry about.

But Mrs Lynda held herself stiffly away from him, as though she knew something he didn't. As though she knew better.

Then Mr Robert had put his arms around her. His kiss had been a reassuring one. Her answering smile was thin.

You have no idea, the watcher thought, as he trained the camcorder onto Mr Robert's face. You really have no idea.

Now, the watcher pulls the blanket off his legs and folds it neatly. He pushes it well down into his rucksack. Inactivity is all very fine, but early March is a bloody cold time for this much hangin' around. It's time to get ready. He screws the little plastic cup back onto the Thermos, puts it into the rucksack on top of the blanket and struggles to his feet.

Wide Boy is right now planning a future Event, before this one is even finished. But he hasn't as yet shared the detail of his latest plans with the watcher. Talk about being full of it, last night. The watcher wonders what these people ever did to WB to make him hate them this much. He wonders what's coming next. It worries him a bit. He judges that WB is a man well capable of going overboard.

But for now, the watcher has more than enough on his plate. Four o'clock in the morning and he is about to do one of the strangest bits of sabotage he has ever done in his life.

He has reached Mrs Lynda's back garden, having made his way down the slope, around the corner and through the side gate, which he's opened very slowly to stop the metal singing. It is unlocked, as he expected. He is dressed from head to toe in black and his eyes are barely visible under the balaclava. He is moving around stealthily, not really enjoying the feeling that someone might mistake him for an IRA man. Still, probably not too many trigger-happy neighbours in this neck of the woods.

It's now four-fifteen. And the list of instructions is even more specific. A drawing really, rather than a list. Full of arrows pointing this way and that, the precise position of things noted and underlined. The watcher feels a bit wary about this. It's one thing taking up position on someone's back wall, where escape is not just possible, but assured. Quite another thing being on someone else's property. And we all know how sensitive people are about their property, especially these days.

The watcher permits himself a grin. He's never allowed himself to be sucked into all that Property Ladder bullshit. His place is small, central, the lion's share of the mortgage paid off years back. When Amy wanted to extend, put in a new kitchen, change the bedroom he half-gave in, but would borrow only a fraction of what she wanted him to. Just as well, as it turned out, when the job let him go. To this day, he doesn't know who ratted on him. More than likely a member of his own team, but he doesn't go there any more. Inappropriate, the brass said he was. Told him to dig the dirt and then told him what he found was inappropriate.

Well, in fairness, they said his *methods* were inappropriate, not his information. This is a distinction he is now prepared to accept after ten years. Now that it doesn't matter any more. He spent a long time being bitter. Until he found ways to get his own back. Jobs like this, for example.

In the early days, they'd handed him the stuff that the official channels couldn't be seen doing. Didn't want to get their hands dirty, Jimmy had told him. Then 'transparency' became a buzz word and the work kind of dried up. But he didn't care. By then, he had a few small properties under his belt, rented out on the quiet. Nothing greedy, like, just little places that flew below the radar. Cash, of course. The immigrants lined his pockets for years.

Now that they're going, things are tighter, yeah, but not as bad as they might be had he lost the run of himself. The properties will come right in the end. He just has to hang in there, be ready when the good times roll around again. Thank Christ he never bought shares in banks and construction companies. Even cash in the mattress would have been safer than that.

He focuses on the house now, makes sure not to get too close, not to make any *inappropriate* noise. It's a quiet neighbourhood. One of those places you couldn't buy yourself into, even if you wanted to. You'd have to be born there. The best of addresses; the most desirable of locations; the most magnificent of views. From the top of the hill where Mrs Lynda's stately pile is located, he can see the glorious sweep of Dublin Bay. It always makes his throat catch. The surge of the water, blue or grey, makes him feel small somehow. But grateful, too. It's the sort of beauty that humbles you, Amy had once said to him. And it's free. These days, it gives the watcher even greater satisfaction to see these fancy folks getting all bent out of shape about falling values, negative equity, the wobbling stock exchange.

But in a garden that belongs to one of those Fancy People, the watcher feels entitled to be a bit on edge. Wide Boy has told him not to worry – the sensor light will be disabled. I've seen to that, he says. You won't be disturbed.

The early morning is dark and wet. No moon; no stars showing. Just a solid fall of misty rain, the sort that soaks you without seeming to. And the outside light has stayed off, just as Wide Boy has promised.

The watcher places the camcorder to one side, where it can see the action. That way, his hands are free to rummage in his rucksack for the necessary tools. He glances at the windows of the house next door. Another check, just to be sure. All quiet, no twitching curtains. This is burglar time, the time when householders' sleep has become profound and unsuspecting. He is not really expecting any interruptions, but still, it pays to be careful.

Though he is not stealing anything. When he'd asked Wide Boy straight out, like, what this was all about if not nicking stuff, WB had just smiled. The watcher has been very careful never to let slip that he knows WB's name. Now *that* would be inappropriate. 'There are many types of theft,' Wide Boy had said, flicking his cigarette butt away from him, out into the street. 'And I have been a victim of most of them. This is merely settling the score.'

They were standing outside the pub, apparently for a smoke,

but really because Wide Boy had wanted to keep this conversation private, and there had been too many ears at the bar. Settling the score, indeed. In the watcher's book, scores had to be settled with force and finality, that's all there was to it. None of this sneaking around back lanes and tinkering at the edges. WB seemed to be aware of the unspoken dissent, because he started to talk at once, stubbing out the new cigarette he had just lit.

'Just do as I ask. You don't need to take anything away with you, nothing needs to be stolen. Follow the diagram I've given you, that's all. Is it clear enough for you?'

The watcher knew by his tone that there would be no more discussion.

'Sure, boss,' he'd said, easily. Who was he to argue? If things did go pear-shaped, all he'd have to do is leg it out the gate, which he'd make sure to leave propped open. It was just a bit of digging and shifting. Rearranging, like. No real damage.

The watcher gets to work. He begins to concentrate on the smaller stone, first, the one that looks a bit like an animal's head, kind of pointy at the front. He pushes the crowbar into the ground, and feels some resistance. Plastic sheeting; he had expected as much. Amy uses it. Keeps the weeds from jumping up everywhere, in between the gravel. She'd insisted on having it, even though their garden is about the size of a pocket-handkerchief. He pushes harder now, feeling something give. And then he's underneath the covering, deep into the soil. Not too hard a job, considering. The ground is soft enough after two months of almost constant rain and snow. One of the things he remembers from school – about the only thing, if you ask him, useless bunch of tossers they were – is the law of the lever. Arkymeedays, someone like that. He remembers his teacher saying that you could lift the whole world using a lever, if you could only find somewhere to stand. They'd all laughed at that, but he's never forgotten it. It's surprising how useful a small piece of information like that can be.

He begins to work the crowbar back and forth, back and forth. When it's about two thirds submerged in the sea of stones, he presses down on it sharply with his booted foot. The headstone – headstone! – he thinks, like robbing someone's grave, begins to shift. He works the lever for a few more minutes, pushing from side to side, then up and down, until he thinks it might be worth trying now. He bends down and, hooking both hands as far underneath the stone as he can, he aims for a rolling movement, one that will release the stone from its captivity. It begins to yield. Grunting, he heaves it towards him, and it's done, free. Now all he has to do is roll it – or lift it – towards the pond. He decides on lifting. It's less noisy. He's sweating now, the wool of the balaclava prickling against his nose, his breath hot and sour. He lifts it away, pushing it high onto his forehead.

Keeping a weather eye on the windows of both houses, the watcher, little by little, hefts the stone towards the pond. There is a lip of smaller stones and plants around the edge, but they are easily pushed to one side. Gently, so as not to make too much of a splash, he lowers the head into the water, disturbing some green shiny leaves that litter the surface. Lily pads, maybe. They bow to this new arrival, and some are sucked underneath the surface with it. Then what the hell. A bit of showmanship is called for here. He just can't resist it. He turns his face towards the camcorder, grins and gives the thumbs up.

The larger stone is more problematic. Now that the head is gone, the watcher has the uneasy feeling that he is dealing with a real dismembered body. For a moment, its shape in the darkness reminds him of a giant tortoise. He flinches from touching it. A bird swoops suddenly, making him lose concentration. He staggers a bit, cursing. Bloody wood pigeons. But the interruption has done the trick. He gets a grip, focuses again on the task in hand. At least this one doesn't need to be shifted so far, just realigned and prettied up a little.

When he's done, the body stone now lies at right angles to its former position, the gravel all around it disturbed, pushed up into small, angry waves. The watcher removes the can of spray paint from his pocket, taking care to stand well back so that his clothes don't get spattered. Anything at all, Wide Boy had said. 'Artistic licence'. And he'd laughed.

The watcher has already decided on a swastika and a peace sign – that should be enough to confuse anyone. He glances at his watch. Five-fifteen. Time he got a move on. He sprays his signs, crudely, and sticks the can back in his pocket. One more thing, and then he's gotta leg it.

Carefully, almost gently, he tugs at the shrubs that have been planted all around the periphery of the pond. They yield eventually, some with soft sucking sounds, others like sinews tearing. He tries his best not to damage them. Then, he places them in a line across the decking, their roots facing the patio doors. Quickly now, it's almost time. He looks around, grabbing the camcorder for one, good final sweep of the garden. It looks bare, defeated. He is surprised at how lacking in personality it now seems. He's never thought it had much before, but there you go. It must have done.

He packs away his crowbar, brushes the muck from his jacket and boots. On the edge of the gravel, he changes into a pair of shoes. He shoves the boots into a plastic bag, then into the rucksack. That way, no muddy footprints will be left behind. Just enough time to secure the gate, walk around the block, and position himself at the top of the garden wall again. He hopes that Mrs L will come out, according to routine, in about twenty minutes. The last non-Eventful few weeks, he thinks, should have done the trick. False sense of security. Or sense of false security?

He's never sure which.

Once he has hunkered down in his usual spot, the watcher sets up the Cantek. By now, he has all the distances judged just right and the final quality is always superb. He's ready just in time. The lights go on downstairs, filtered dimly through the heavy curtains. Then the drapes are pulled back and the double doors open outwards.

Miraculously, the sensor light switches on again. The watcher grins. Your man has got that right. Perfect timing!

The woman pauses.

The watcher aims the camcorder, compensating for the sensor light.

She steps outside.

Showtime.

7

LYNDA PAUSED just outside the patio doors, blinking. The light seemed brighter than usual. She waited for her eyes to become accustomed to the sudden glare. She looked around her, searching out the comforting contours of her tortoise, her shrubs, the undulating outline of the pond.

But her eyes refused to focus on what she saw before her. For a moment, she didn't know where she was. She wondered had she stumbled into another garden somewhere; a parallel dimension, perhaps, like *Alice in Wonderland*. Shapes had shifted, shadows had grown where there had been none before, nothing was what it seemed. Her garden was suddenly unfamiliar, yet familiar at the same time. Snapshots began to register, quick snatches of colour, of light and shade. She could feel herself begin to process what lay beyond her feet. Then her hands began to tremble and cold perspiration started to gather across her upper lip.

'No,' she heard someone cry. 'No, no, no!' and realized that the voice was hers, that she was weeping, gasping, unable to draw breath. 'Robert!' she screamed. 'Robert! Robert!' Her stomach shifted and her throat filled with nausea. Unable to move, she vomited where she stood, retching until tears came. Dimly, she was aware of the patio doors opening behind her.

'Lynda,' a voice at her ear said, alarmed. Two strong arms were placed around her shoulders. 'Lynda, what's the matter?'

She clung to the hands that held her, afraid that the sensation inside her head was going to make her faint. Points of light and darkness danced in front of her eyes; she could feel hot nausea gather again, wave after wave of it.

'Come inside,' the voice urged. 'I'll make you tea.'

Lynda turned to look. Jon was gazing at her, his face troubled. His hands were kind. But she wanted her husband. 'I need Robert,' she said. To her own ears, her voice sounded like a mumble. But he understood her.

'Yeah, of course,' Jon said. 'Come back inside and sit down. I'll get him for you.'

And then, suddenly, he seemed to see what she saw. His hands gripped her shoulders even more tightly. 'Jesus Christ,' he whispered. 'What the fuck has happened here?'

Then Lynda knew it was real. She started to weep again, could feel the tears sliding down into the collar of her dressing-gown. 'It's Danny, I know it's Danny,' she gasped. 'It's more of his revenge. I know it.'

'Come inside,' Jon urged. 'Please. We'll talk inside.'

She allowed herself to be led back through the double doors. She turned once more to where her stone tortoise used to be. Her eyes searched for the bits of its body, her grief intense. 'I know what's happening,' she said. 'Oh, God, I know what's happening.' She took the tissue Jon handed her, sat on the chair he pulled out for her.

'I'll go and wake Robert,' he said.

'I can't believe he's still asleep,' said Lynda. She could hear the anger in her voice.

'You actually made very little noise,' said Jon.

She looked up at him, puzzled. 'What do you mean?'

'I went to the bathroom,' he said, quickly. 'I thought I heard something and came downstairs to take a look. You were on the deck, but the doors were closed.'

She nodded.

'I knew by the way you were bent over that something was wrong. But I didn't hear you until I opened the door.'

'I suppose so,' she said, distracted. Every time she glanced out at the garden, the tears started all over again. Jon walked over and pulled the curtains closed.

'I'll help you fix it, I promise,' he said. The green eyes were alight with sympathy.

'Thank you,' she said, sobbing again. She watched as he left the kitchen, heard his light step as he ran up the stairs to call Robert.

But she knew that this could not be fixed. Whatever Danny destroyed could not be fixed.

That was something she had learned a long time ago.

'I don't understand it,' Robert was saying.

He was standing with her in the kitchen, watching as Jon and Ciarán gathered up the shrubs and placed them into black plastic sacks. In the early morning light, the garden looked like a moonscape: pockmarked, mysterious, eerie. All the life had left it. 'I don't understand how the light didn't go on. It always wakes you, doesn't it?'

Lynda nodded. 'Always.' She felt a physical pull, as acute as pain, as she watched the boys toss her plants and shrubs into refuse sacks.

'But you could always plant them again,' Jon had said. 'Look . . .' He pointed at the roots eagerly. 'They're not damaged, are they? Ciarán and I can help – you just tell us what to do.'

But Lynda had shaken her head. 'No,' she said. 'They make me sick even to look at them. *Danny* has touched them. I don't want them – don't want anything he has touched in my life.'

Jon had looked at her then, his gaze half-curious, half-bashful. 'I don't mean to pry, but who is Danny?'

'My brother,' Robert had said, sharply, walking up the two steps to the deck, wiping his hands on his jeans. He'd attempted to re-position the tortoise, had persuaded Lynda to direct him. She'd done so, reluctantly. But she knew that it would never be the same again. Robert had been insistent, and she'd been too weary to argue. Her tortoise was damaged beyond repair. Even if she could clean the paint off its back. And she'd been adamant about the plants and shrubs. 'In the bin,' she'd repeated. 'Straight away. No discussion.'

Robert had handed the roll of black refuse sacks to the two boys. 'Off you go,' he said. 'Come on, Lynda. Let's go back inside and leave the lads to it. You don't need to be standing out here in the cold, looking at this.'

Now, he made her coffee, insisted she have a shot of brandy to go with it. 'Sit down. You're like a ghost,' he said. 'Take it. It'll help settle your stomach.'

'The deck,' she said, remembering. 'I was sick . . .'

'It's okay,' Robert said. 'Jon and Ciarán hosed it down. I saw them do it.'

Lynda poured the glass of brandy into the steaming coffee. Without lifting her head, she said, 'What are we going to do, Robert?'

He glanced at her, his face already beginning to close. He poured himself more coffee. The spoon chinked against the china as he stirred.

'Don't shut me out,' she said. 'And don't make me beg. This is Danny's handiwork. You *must* see that.' She kept looking at him. Her eyes demanded that he respond. *Please don't pretend this isn't happening*, she thought. *The only way out of this is together. Please don't fight me any longer.*

He sighed. 'I know. I know it is. You're right.'

Lynda felt relief wash over her. At last. 'Can we call the Guards? We have to do something.'

'And tell them what?' asked Robert. She watched as frustration clouded his face. 'That someone has dumped rubbish and moved stones around? That a ring went missing and suddenly reappeared on a bathroom floor? That nothing has ever been stolen? Or that a few plants have been damaged?' His voice kept getting louder. Each question seemed to anger him more.

She went to speak and he held up his hand. 'I know what you're going to say, but I'm talking from the police perspective, Lynda. And from their point of view, nothing has been destroyed. Things could be planted again – but you don't want to. How do you think that sounds? It doesn't even qualify as vandalism.'

'It's intimidation and deliberate damage to our property,' Lynda cried, feeling anger surge all over again. 'Doesn't that count?'

He looked at her, his expression weary. 'Sweetheart, this is a city where thugs are shooting each other over drugs. Bus drivers get their fingers broken at night by drunks. Business premises get set on fire: where would your priorities be?'

She felt the sobs catch in her throat. 'I can't live like this, Robert. I just can't. I wake up terrified every morning wondering: What next? What today? First the cars, then the rubbish, then the ring. Now my tortoise.' She stopped. She hadn't told Robert about the other daily reminders of Danny's existence; she had known that he wouldn't want to hear her. But she had his attention now. 'And bits of stuff all over the garden every morning, like calling cards. I haven't even told you about them, because you wouldn't want to listen.'

He looked at her, alarmed.

She nodded. 'Yes, every single morning. Things like old photos, bottles, broken cups and saucers. Deliberate stuff – things that can't just get there on their own.' She saw his face. 'Some mornings, I can't even bear to pick them up. And no, I'm not being paranoid. It's like Danny's taunting us. Telling us how close he's getting. What's to keep him from getting into the house again?' This was too important to let go. 'And you've never showed me his letters, never even told me what was in them.'

'Because it's the usual stuff – you've heard it all before.' But he looked away from her.

'No,' she insisted. 'Because this time, the letters weren't posted. This time, they were delivered by hand. That makes it different: it means he *is* here again.' Lynda made an effort to lower her voice. 'It's not just the garden he's destroying, can't you see that? It's *us*.'

Robert reached for her hand, held it between both of his. 'I suppose I didn't take him seriously enough.'

'We have to take him seriously. He's left us no option. Tell me what he said, Robert. All of it. You can't protect me. I can't protect you. The only thing we have is trust. Tell me what he said.'

Robert nodded. His face was white, his lips bloodless. 'He said he was coming back to finish what he'd started. Three years ago.'

Lynda felt something creep along her spine. She glanced over at the double door that led to the deck. Once Ciarán and Jon were safely inside, she'd make sure to lock it again. 'Have you still got the letters?' she asked quietly. 'I need to see them for myself.'

Robert left the kitchen without a word. When he returned, he had three envelopes in his hand. He pushed them across the table to Lynda. 'Here,' he said. 'You're right. *I* can't protect you. I can't even protect my own family!' His voice was bitter. 'They're the latest three to arrive.'

Lynda looked up, sharply. 'This is not your fault,' she said. 'Danny is destructive and manipulative. We couldn't have prevented what happened last time. But maybe we can stop it from happening again.' She pulled the first letter out of its envelope. The pages of handwriting were familiar, too familiar. She scanned them quickly.

The double doors were opened and Jon and Ciarán came back into the kitchen. They stopped to take off their trainers which were caked with mud. Instinctively, Lynda put her hand over the pages of Danny's letter.

'Anything else we can do, Mum?' asked Ciarán.

She shook her head. 'No, thanks. Not for now.'

'May I ask something?' Jon's question was sudden. He addressed himself to Robert.

'Sure,' said Robert.

'This Danny person. Your brother. Can't you tell the police?' He sounded angry.

Ciarán was nodding. 'Yeah, Dad, why not?'

'It's complicated,' said Robert. 'I don't rule it out. But it's complicated.' He was going to say more and stopped.

'I understand that family is precious, but if someone did this to me, to my home . . .' Jon stopped, his voice full of emotion. 'I don't have brothers or sisters. You guys feel like my family. I just can't bear to see this . . . this havoc. You're good people.'

'Thank you, Jon,' Lynda tried to smile at him. 'And thank you for your support, and your help.'

'Keep us in the loop, won't you?' asked Ciarán. 'I mean about what you're goin' to do. He can't be allowed to get away with this.'

'We will,' said Robert. 'Now, Lynda and I have some things to discuss. Thanks for the clean up. You did a really good job.'

'Yeah,' said Ciarán. 'No worries. We're outta here. Back around seven. Okay, Mum?'

She nodded. 'That's fine.'

They left the kitchen and closed the door quietly behind them. Lynda got up from the table and locked the patio doors. When she sat down again, she leaned towards Robert and spoke softly. 'I know it's a strange thing to say,' she whispered. 'But what Danny is doing may well backfire on him. Ciarán is actually behaving like a grown-up. That's some comfort.'

'Don't be too optimistic,' said Robert with a faint smile. He stood up to put on the kettle again. 'Read the letters. Then tell me how you feel.'

'More coffee?' asked Robert. He'd sat, silent, while Lynda read and re-read the letters.

'Please,' she said. 'I know you tore up the first couple, but can you remember anything, anything at all about any specific threats?'

'It's more than two months ago,' said Robert. 'To be honest, I scanned them, rather than read them. They gave me the creeps and I just wanted to get rid of them as fast as possible.'

Lynda held out her cup and Robert filled it. 'There's something he's not saying,' she said. 'Something he's expecting us to guess. Like here: '*But things change. Nothing stays the same. Life rewards you sometimes, when you least expect it. You lose something – or somebody – and something else takes its place. There's a kind of law of compensation. Too much has been taken away from me. Too much stolen. It's time to balance the scales.*'

Robert frowned. 'I have no idea what he means. It's the ramblings of a lunatic.'

'But he keeps coming back to it, again and again. It's in all of these letters. This harping on about "compensation".' She shuddered. 'I can feel the menace. It's laced into every word.' She pushed the pages away from her.

'So does reading them help?' asked Robert quietly.

'Yes,' she said at once. 'At least I can be sure that I'm not losing my mind.' She stopped and looked at him. 'And *you* can be sure that I'm not losing my mind. Which might be even more important.' She tapped the closely written sheets. 'This is a deliberate campaign to make us suffer. And you're right. They'd make your flesh crawl.'

'I'll put them away safely,' said Robert. His voice was grim. 'We may need them in the future as evidence.'

'Oh, God,' said Lynda. 'As if we didn't have enough to contend with.'

Robert looked as though he was about to tell her something but his mobile rang and he jumped. He left the kitchen, and headed for his office. What now? wondered Lynda. When he came back his face was unreadable.

'What were you going to say to me?' she asked.

He looked at her, his eyes blank.

'Before your mobile rang,' she prompted. 'You were going to tell me something.'

He shook his head. 'Can't remember. It'll come back to me.'

Lynda knew he was lying. 'Robert,' she warned. 'Don't keep anything from me. We're in this together. Any chink in the armour and Danny will slide right in there. Don't shut me out.'

'And you've never shut me out?' he snapped. 'Not once, in all the years we've been together?'

There was a long silence in the kitchen. Lynda could hear the ticking of the clock on her studio wall, through the half-open door. So, she thought. We've come to it at last. 'That's a long time ago, Robert,' she said cautiously. How much did he know? How much did he suspect? 'And we were in a very different place. I thought we'd put it behind us.'

'So did I,' said Robert. 'So did I. I don't know why it's tormenting me now.' He shook his head, angrily.

Lynda swallowed. 'I won't insult your intelligence by telling you it meant nothing. But the truth is, you and I mean a lot more – so much more . . .'

Robert rubbed his unshaven cheeks. 'Look, I'm sorry for bringing it up now. A case of straw and camel's back, and all that.' He looked at her, his face ashen. 'It'll keep until I come back.'

'Why?' asked Lynda, suddenly terrified. 'Where are you going?'

'James and I are in one hell of a lot of trouble.'

Lynda stared at him. She'd never known him to be so blunt before.

'Business is bad, credit is worse. We have to try and pull something together, and fast.' He shrugged. 'I didn't tell you because I hoped it would get better. We both did. Now we need to work out some sort of a salvage plan.'

Lynda pulled out one of the kitchen chairs and sat down. She couldn't think of what else to do. 'Will the business survive?' she asked.

He picked his keys up off the kitchen table. 'I don't know yet. I hope so. I'm prepared to do anything, even if it's on my own – attic conversions, painting and decorating, extensions. All the stuff people do in a recession instead of moving house.'

She nodded. That made sense.

'We're meeting in Wicklow,' he said. 'That was James on the phone. He's managed to get a hold of our accountant and a tax expert. So,' and he struggled into his jacket, 'we're going to hole up there until we've sorted things out,' he said. 'Sorry it's so sudden, but the money men have only just confirmed that they'll be there on Friday morning and James and I need to hammer out a proposal first.'

She nodded. 'Are you okay?'

'I'll text you later and let you know.' He came over to her. 'I'll do my damnedest to see us through this.' He squeezed her shoulder. 'I've already done a lot of research, Lynda. I can repackage myself, and what I offer. I've a website ready to get up and running and I'll work as hard as I need to.'

'I know you will.' Solid, dependable Robert. Predictability made flesh. 'And so will I. We'll pull together, just like before.' She reached up, put her hand on his.

He nodded. 'Talk to you when I can.'

'Okay. Sooner rather than later.'

As he left the kitchen, Lynda called out. 'Robert?'

He turned. 'Yeah?'

'Take care. We've done it before. We'll do it again. Survive.'

He smiled the ghost of a smile and closed the door softly behind him.

Lynda felt stunned. She sat at the table, watching what she thought of as her life begin to fall away from her. After a moment, she stood, shakily, and made her way out into the hall. She reached the window just in time to see the tail lights of the Jeep disappear down the road towards the roundabout.

She sat on the bottom stair, just outside Robert's office. Gradually, her mind was becoming sharper, more focussed, the fog of shock beginning to lift. She was not going down without a fight. *They* were not going down without a fight. She'd find a way.

She *had* to find a way before their life slipped through her fingers and changed into something they no longer recognized.

First Danny. Now this.
What next?

The day is thundery. Sky like a bruise. The leaves of the trees
are livid against pewter, like someone has spattered green paint.
They stand out too much, etched against the stillness.

'Come on, Danny,' Emma is saying. 'It's goin' to be my
birthday soon. *Please?* As part of my present?'

Danny grins at her. 'Part of your present?' he teases. 'How
do you know I'm givin' you any present at all? You're gettin'
far too big for birthdays, anyway.' And he flicks his cigarette
butt into the flowerbed, using his thumb and middle finger to
make it go the distance. It is a gesture his mother hates.
Occasionally, he forgets, and she catches him in the act.

'Don't do that, Danny,' she sighs, 'if you must smoke. It
makes you look like a guttie.'

He laughs then and says he's sorry, keeps forgetting. Then
he promises not to do it again, and that makes her happy. It
works every time. For his mother, a promise made is as good as
the deed done.

They are sitting on the front step, he and Emma. He's
taken the day off, to celebrate his new bike: a second-hand
Kawasaki 1000 GTR in great nick. He's buffed up the leather
and polished the chrome and changed the oil. Danny likes
doing these things himself – it gives him a sense of competence,
of grown-up ownership. She's ready to rock 'n' roll. He needs
the open road, though. Pottering about suburbia is no place for
this baby.

It is July, the heat intense. He can smell the bike's leather
from over here, see the sunlight harsh on chrome. Nineteen
years of age, and he's itching to get going. But Mum has
insisted he stay with Emma till she gets back.

'I'll be no later than three, Danny,' she says, 'and I don't ask you to do much. I can't take Emma with me, she'd be bored silly. And in this heat.' She fans herself, as if to make a point that he might otherwise miss.

'I'm relying on you,' she says, squeezing his hand as she gets into the car. 'Don't let me down.' Looks him right in the eye as she drives off.

Relying on you. 'Unreliable' is his father's word for Danny. He's big into your 'word': if a man gives his 'word', then he should stick to it, come hell or high water. These speeches piss Danny off. Always have. Mum often sticks up for Danny. He has to give her that. He *will* look after his little sister today, though. He will be the reliable one. In fact, Danny's even kind of glad that she's asked him. He feels in a really good mood. One, because he's just collected his new bike and two, because Robert is stuck all day today at his shitty summer job. And Danny is the one who is free. Danny takes great care, always, to make sure that his days off do not coincide with Pansy's.

Emma jumps up off the step, her fists clenched. She opens and closes her small hands, as if she's squeezing her impatience. 'Well, if you won't bring me for a spin, then at least let me sit on the seat.'

He laughs and sweeps her off her feet and onto the pillion in one easy movement. Her eyes are shining. Just two days away from being ten, she has more life to her, more grit and determination than Pansy ever will.

Pixie, Danny calls her. She loves her pet name. Danny can still recall the day when Mum brings her home from hospital. He is nine, Pansy twelve. He can't believe his eyes when he sees her. Is she really that tiny?

'Careful, now,' Mum warns him, as he pulls back the honeycomb pink blanket to see her face. Mum is always telling him to be careful. She doesn't tell Robert nearly as often. He,

Danny, usually ends up getting the blame for whatever it is that goes wrong.

'She's like a little elf,' Pansy blurts out.

Mum laughs, and ruffles Robert's hair. 'That's because she was born a little bit early. She only weighs five pounds. You two monsters were over nine pounds, each of you – almost twice her size!'

He and Robert grin at each other then, a rare moment of shared monstrosity.

'My precious little girl,' Mum croons, while Dad paces proudly up and down in front of the television.

Suddenly, the baby starts to wail. Danny stands transfixed, wondering where all that noise is coming from.

'She's got a right pair of lungs, all the same,' laughs Dad. 'Five pounds or no five pounds. This little lady'll make us all sit up and take notice. Beware, boys: the boss has arrived.'

Right there and then, Danny decides he will call her 'Pixie'. An elf is far too wishy-washy a thing: pixies are bright, darting creatures. They get up to all sorts of adventures. Danny can still remember the stories Mum used to read to them at bedtime when they were small. Elves were the boring ones – a bit like Pansy. Elves only swanned around the forest, mooning over flowers and fairies. At least pixies knew how to get up to mischief.

And Emma – Pixie – more than lives up to her name.

'Come on, Danny,' she is saying now, her small shoulder wheedling against his arm. She has just finished eating an apple and he can smell the green sweetness of it off her breath. 'Just one little spin around the block – I'll hold on really tight. And I won't ever tell Mum.'

He is tempted. What harm can it do? The breeze would be nice: a change from all this humid stickiness, the air around them heavy with the threat of rain. Pixie is now kneeling behind him, her face resting in the space between his shoulder and his ear. 'C'mon, Danny. I won't tell. You know I won't.'

Danny grabs her around the waist, then, and tickles her till she shrieks. He can feel himself weakening already. It can't do any harm, not if he's really careful. And no one ever needs to be told. Pixie is able to keep a secret, as Danny well knows. And she's right. If he doesn't do it now, he'll never get another chance to treat her. It *is* her birthday, after all, day after tomorrow.

'Okay, Pixie,' he says. 'But this has to be our secret, yours and mine. You're not to tell anyone, or I'll end up in a shitload of trouble.'

Emma giggles. She loves it when he uses bad words in front of her.

'Promise,' she squeals. 'No one will ever know.'

She wriggles backwards, her bare legs squeaking on the hot leather, leaving room for Danny to hop on in front of her. He shows her where to rest her feet, carefully placing each sandaled foot on the chrome bar. 'Keep 'em there, now,' he says. 'Otherwise, you'll get oil on your socks, and then Mum will know.' She nods, thrilled by the conspiracy of it all.

Danny kick-starts the engine, taking pleasure in its throaty growl. Then he swings himself on, turns to grin at Pixie, and says, 'You hold on, now. Hold on for dear life.'

He won't go fast. He'll proceed at a leisurely, steady pace. Down the driveway, out onto the road, down the hill towards the sea and back again. A spin of maybe ten minutes. More than enough for Pixie. And it's more than enough time to get back before Mum arrives home.

Pixie shouts with delight as they move off sedately. He can feel her small hands holding on fiercely, just as he's told her. He checks the traffic right and left, and begins the steep descent towards the sea. Pixie is chattering away: he can feel snatches of her words just underneath his shoulder blade, where she has pressed her face. But whatever she is saying is being whipped away by the breeze that keeps getting stronger, the closer they come to the sea.

He slows as they come to the last roundabout, waits for the only car – a clapped-out Mini – to make its careful exit. Pixie is shouting to him. He can hear her excitement as he slows down.

'Go faster, Danny, just for a minute! This is cool!'

Danny has no intention of going any faster. He is being Reliable. A couple of hundred yards more, then back towards home. He turns his head, so that she can hear him. 'You just hold tight, Miss Speed-Freak. Leave the driving up to me. And Happy Birthday!' He puts the bike into gear and begins to move forward, the Mini puttering away in front of him.

He has no chance. The Merc comes at him out of nowhere. It careens onto the roundabout, then off it again, silver-flashing, glinting, blinding in the sunlight. And Danny's thoughts hurtle in the split second that's left: *of course it's going to stop Christ what's happening fuck it's not stopping Jesus.*

He jams on the brakes, but the Merc slams into them, just catching the motorbike's front wheel. All Danny is aware of is impact. A sledgehammer, gut-churning blow to the chest. He feels winded as never before: all the breath seems to leave his body and, instead, he is filled with a desperate instinct to hold on, to keep control, to keep upright. He struggles with every bone, every muscle, every sinew against the reeling force of the impact, transformed into a human wall. The bike skids backwards across the hot road, keeling over like a yacht in full sail.

When he rights himself, a thousand years later, a horrified knot of people has gathered around something crumpled and bloody, lying in the middle of the road. For a moment, Danny is puzzled: 'Did I hit a dog?' and turns to make sure Emma is okay. Then he realizes that she is no longer holding onto him, that her face is no longer pressed against his shirt.

And it's as though somebody switches the sound back on. Suddenly, there is noise, commotion. A woman's voice keeps screaming, over and over again: 'Call an ambulance! Call an ambulance!' He wishes she would stop. She's hurting the inside of his head.

People scatter to their houses. Danny watches as some emerge with blankets, pillows, all the useless accompaniments of tragedy.

Jesus, has he hit someone? Or is it someone from the Merc, catapulted onto the road? Dimly, he can see the Merc, out of the corner of his eye. It has stopped just off the roundabout, right beside where it hit him. He has already seen its doors opening suddenly and two figures darting up the road. A man detaches himself from the group of people nearby, and shouts: 'Oi, you! Stop right there!' He gives chase. Danny is aware of all of it, but aware only in the way you are aware of the background music to a movie. You know it's there, but it serves to highlight the real action, the stuff that's happening on screen.

And what is happening now is that little mound in the middle of the road. It keeps growing until it fills the entire screen, despite its smallness. A great pool of red seeps outwards. There is something eerily familiar about the small hand that curls towards him from under a pink blanket. The fingers are open, as though they have just now let go of something. Danny limps towards the hand, fear, sickness, terror all fighting for space inside his chest and he realizes that the howl that he hears somewhere outside of himself is him. He finally sees that the crumpled form that lies unmoving, just in front of him now, is his little sister.

People are holding him back, their mouths opening and closing in what he presumes are words. She is lying there, little

Pixie, with her head rolled to one side. Just like the cat on the railway track, he remembers. Broken. A sob escapes him. His head fills with noise, the scene swims before him. He vomits his guts up, while someone holds onto him, making some sort of reassuring sounds.

Then the ambulance arrives and soon after there's the hospital. The grave face of the doctor. The nurses. All of them. And when his mother arrives, flinging back doors, she fights all round her like a madwoman. A lioness in search of her cub.

He's in a cubicle, curtains drawn almost all the way around the bed. But he can still see her. And he knows her voice, would recognize it anywhere. The curtain is wrenched aside and she stands there, just looking at him. A nurse hurries over.

'Please,' she says, 'you can't be in here. You need to wait outside. We need to attend to this man's injuries.'

He wishes his mother *would* go. He can see by her eyes that she doesn't believe it, any of it. Somewhere, she clings to hope, that this is a mistake, this is someone else's daughter – anybody else's daughter except hers.

'It's okay,' Danny says. 'This is my mother.'

The nurse looks from one to the other. 'All right, then. But let me bring you somewhere more private,' she says. 'And you'll have to come back to have that leg attended to.'

Danny nods. He slides off the bed and manages to walk, a kind of half-drag, half-hop motion. But his mother doesn't even ask him how he is, or how badly his leg is injured.

The starched nurse shows them to the poky relatives' room. Danny hates her professional sympathy. He hates all of them. All that white, unfelt empathy.

'Danny,' his mother says as the nurse closes the door. Her eyes are begging him. 'Is it true?' He knows by looking at her that she will sacrifice any child – maybe even her own sons – to make sure that this is not, that this cannot be, her baby.

There is nothing he can say. Then she sags and weeps, she and Danny together.

'How could you?' Her voice is hoarse, pleading now, as though she really wants an explanation, a route towards forgiveness. But Danny knows that really, she is looking for someone to blame.

Some of the numbness is beginning to wear off. His leg is starting to hurt like hell. He wants, desperately, to remake the story, to change the ending. But he's not able to. 'It isn't my fault,' he says, weeping, unable to stop the tears. 'I promise I did nothing wrong. I was going really slowly, really carefully, and then this guy in a Merc just shot off the roundabout and – '

'Danny,' she says, pulling back from him, her voice barely above a whisper, 'I left her in your care. I told you I was relying on you. It was only for a couple of hours. What were you *thinking*? You didn't even have a *helmet* for her.'

He can see that she is struggling to understand something. That her daughter is never coming back. 'She kept begging me for a spin, she wouldn't leave it alone. She kept going on and on about it being her birthday.' Danny wipes his eyes with the back of his hand. 'And anyway, there would be no helmet small enough for her.'

His mother's eyes widen. He can see the rage coming, has seen it before, although not like this. Never as bad as this. She comes at him, taking him by surprise, pushing him off balance. Her fists are up, and now she's pounding on his chest, shrieking. 'She's a child! A ten-year-old child! What have you done to my baby? What have you done?'

Danny tries to ward her off. But she's strong and his leg and shoulder are hurting him. She still hasn't even asked him how he is. And his knee has started to bleed again.

Suddenly, the door slams open, crashing against the wall

with a splintering of wood. Danny's father rushes in, his eyes wild, his face askew, as though someone has assembled bits of it in the wrong order. Danny is aware of two bulky, blue presences behind him, grappling with shoulders, arms. But Danny's father is more than a match for them. Their 'Sir! Sir!', their 'Take it easy, now,' has no effect on him. He and Danny share the same build, the same blunt strength.

He flings all of that strength at Danny now, his tears rasping. 'You're not my son!' he sobs. He lifts one arm, but that is a mistake. It gives the two security men something to hold on to. Both of them grab at the raised fist and force it back down to his side. Then he crumbles, as if he, too, has been winded by the impact. All of the fight has gone out of him.

'Mary, Mary,' he wails. 'Our baby, our baby.'

Danny's mother goes to him then, and takes him in her arms. 'I'll never forgive you for this,' she says to Danny, over her husband's shoulder.

He waits, not knowing what else to do. His parents hold each other, oblivious to his presence. After a moment or two, the security men nod to each other and withdraw. They close the door gently behind them.

Then Danny's father wipes his eyes, his sobbing stilled for now. He looks at Danny. His gaze is steady although Danny can see he's having trouble controlling his chin. It keeps trembling off in the wrong direction, creasing, pulling both sides of his father's mouth downwards.

'Tell me why you did it. Just that. Nothing else. Tell me why you did it.'

'It wasn't my fault . . . I didn't mean . . .' Danny begins.

His father slams his fist on the low wooden table, making the artificial flower arrangement leap in the air and then roll, sadly, onto its side. Even the air feels shocked.

'I said, tell me why you did it.' The tone is even, but Danny can feel all the rage that lurks underneath that surface.

'She kept begging me for a spin,' he says. His tone is flat, now. He senses defeat. 'I didn't know how to say no.'

'You didn't know how to say no,' his father repeats, nodding. Danny has seen him do stuff like this before. It's as though he's considering the wisdom of the statement. Then he locks eyes with his son's. 'But you've known how to say "no" to us often enough, haven't you? About important things, necessary things. And you couldn't keep a little child safe for an afternoon, because you couldn't say "no"?'

He pauses, and the silence is fearful. Then:

'I could never trust you. I knew that, years back. You've never known what it is to give your word and keep it, Danny.' He stops, pretending to think things through, pretending that this speech is not one he prepared ages ago. It's as though he has been waiting for the opportunity to make it. There's no stopping him.

'And then when things go wrong, you just blame somebody else. Usually Robert, sometimes me, sometimes your mother. But never you, never Danny. Danny always means well, Danny's intentions are good – if I've heard it once, I've heard it a million times.'

Danny tries to speak, but his father raises his hand. He's always doing that, not letting Danny speak.

'Your mother was a fool to trust you. But she'll suffer for that now. We all will. For the rest of our lives . . .' His mother begins to weep again, convulsing.

His father looks at him and Danny can see pure hatred in those eyes. 'You've broken this family. Is that what you wanted? Is it?'

At that moment, someone knocks on the door, softly. The three of them turn as yet another nurse opens the door. She looks at Danny's parents. Danny can see Robert's face, white and frightened, just above her left shoulder. 'Mr and Mrs Graham?' she says. 'Would you like to come with me? You can see your daughter now.'

For a second, Danny's heart leaps. Is she alive?

Robert comes into the room now and pushes his way past Danny without even a word. He walks right into his parents' arms and the three of them hold onto each other, sobbing. Danny can see by the way his parents begin to droop as they leave the room that there is no hope. This is the last time they will ever see Emma.

Danny's father stops as he passes. He turns and looks at his son. His hands are menacing. 'Don't even *think* of coming with us. You're not worthy to see her. Not welcome. We'll never forgive you for this. I mean it. Never.'

The three of them leave the room. Robert won't even look in Danny's direction. The nurse takes their mother's arm, Robert puts his around his father's shoulders.

Danny knows now that there is no chance. Once his father says '*We* will never forgive you,' Danny knows that it's over. Not 'I', but 'we'. In that one small word, Danny understands how everything is to be. His mother has been exonerated. Emma has been exonerated. Robert is the perfect son. The fault for everything, once again, is all Danny's. He is to be the scapegoat, forever pushed beyond the 'we'. His intentions no longer matter: only the outcome, over which he's had no control. A pair of joy riders on a bright July afternoon. Who would have thought it?

He tries not to see the blank, blanketed mound in the middle of the road. It keeps flashing back and forth in front of his eyes. Poor little Pixie. And he has a stab of sorrow. They won't even let him see his little sister one last time. He feels aggrieved. It's not fair. He makes up in his head all the things he'll say to his father for treating him like this. He hobbles back out to the ward. He can't keep bleeding all over the place. The nurse from earlier sees him and hurries over.

'In here,' she says, flicking back the curtain of the cubicle. He eases himself onto the edge of the bed, but it seems to swim away from him. Next thing he knows, his head is being forced down towards his knees. Gradually, the cubicle rights itself, his blood stops roaring in his ears.

'Better?' she asks.

He nods. She's young. Pretty. He wonders if . . . But no. Another time, maybe. Not now. She does a good job of stitching up his leg. The bandages feel secure, give him a bit of support. When she's finished, he doesn't know where to go, what to do with himself. The nurse tells him to take care and then goes off about her business. He feels dismissed. So he goes back to the Relatives' Room, opening the door cautiously. His father's coat is still there, his mother's hasty cardigan. They'll have to come back for them. When they do, his father looks surprised to see him sitting there. His mother seems older somehow, her face raw. She leans against his father, who leans against Robert. He seems to be propping both of them up. And still, not one of the three of them even asks about his leg.

'I want you to leave the house,' his father is saying. 'Go this evening, now, otherwise I won't be responsible for what I'll do to you.' And he turns away, gathering his weeping wife in his arms.

Without actually remembering how he gets there, Danny arrives at the house and lets himself in. He packs his holdall from the gym with a few clothes, a toothbrush, his aftershave. He'll have to come back for the rest of his stuff. They'll have to let him do that.

They say he's had a miraculous escape. One leg very badly bruised, but nothing broken, just some small bones chipped.

Painful enough, but nothing that needs plaster. Some ligaments are damaged. His shoulder is painful. But it's nothing that won't heal in time.

He lets himself out the front door, slamming it behind him. Leaving all of them behind. Fuck them. He doesn't need them, any of them. His barman's apprenticeship is nearly over, he can work anywhere he chooses. And the tips are great. Danny's found out how easy it is to be charming to people he doesn't know. All it takes is a little effort, and faces light up. Women, in particular. They laugh easily at his jokes, appraise him with their keen eyes.

Nothing that won't heal in time? he thinks.

He'll see about that.

8

IT WAS FIVE DAYS before Robert came home. Five endless days that saw Lynda become increasingly anxious.

'No, things aren't good, Lynda, I'm not going to lie to you,' he'd said when he phoned her the evening following his departure. 'The business stuff is complicated and frustrating and there are no easy answers.'

Lynda knew of old that there was no point in asking Robert for detail. As far as he was concerned, a phone was for the imparting of information: quickly, succinctly and impatiently.

'I've a few prospects around South Wicklow that I'm going to follow up once we're finished here. I'll let you know when I'm on my way home.'

When she heard his key in the lock at lunchtime, Lynda felt her heart begin to speed up, her breath begin to catch at the back of her throat. He came straight into her studio, looking as though he hadn't slept since he left. She ran to him, putting her arms around him. 'I'm so glad you're back,' she said. 'You look exhausted.'

He kissed her distractedly. 'I am,' he said. 'It's bad, but I'll tell you all the details tonight. Right now, I have to shower and go straight back into town.' He gave her a quick hug. 'I've booked a table for us in *The Merman* tonight. For eight o'clock. Will you bring the Jeep? I've back-to-back meetings today and I haven't the time to scramble for parking spaces.'

'Of course,' she said. 'Do you want a lift now?'

'No, thanks. I've a taxi booked. I'll see you at eight.'

Now they faced each other across the candlelit table.

'So,' said Lynda. 'What's the news? How did the meeting with the money-men go?'

'Badly.' Robert's tone was blunt. 'The last few months have been crazy,' he said. He paused while the waiter refilled his glass. 'It's been crazy for everybody in the business.' He shook his head. 'But I really believed that we could trade our way out of it. When it all started two years ago, we weren't over-extended – at least, not to the extent that some of the guys were.' He sipped at his wine.

Lynda had to curb her impatience.

'At first, I thought it was just us – you know, a bit more competition around than there used to be. And then there was a bit of a slowdown in the market when nobody knew what was going on with Stamp Duty. That sort of thing. We've seen the ups and down before, over the years. We're all old enough to remember the eighties.' He stopped, trying to smile at her. 'Things come and go. But there's always been a market for the sort of high-end builds that we do. That's always been our niche.' He poured himself more wine, his eyes distracted. It was as if he was talking to himself.

But I'm listening, Lynda thought. And what I'm hearing is frightening me.

'Generally, market blips in the past didn't affect us. We pulled through the first dip fine, a year ago, and we might have pulled through this one, too – until the global meltdown happened. Banks that were pushing funds at us eighteen months ago won't look at us now. I can't even get an appoint-ment. Everyone is suddenly very busy and very nervous – even the guys I've dealt with for over twenty years, who know I'm solid. Nothing's working. I had my last stab at it today.' He drummed his fingers on the table. 'And so – we have to let most of the crew go.'

Lynda looked at him. It was probably the longest speech she had ever heard him make about his business. In fact, about anything. She tried to understand what he was telling her. Had he just gone bust? Was he just about to? 'How many?' she asked, after a pause. 'How many have you to let go?'

He didn't answer at once. Lynda counted the beats. It must be really bad.

'At least fourteen,' he said at last. She could feel him wince.

Lynda could feel the shock registering. She was glad that she wasn't standing up. 'Have you . . . have they been let go already?'

'Yes,' he said abruptly. 'James told them. Two days ago.'

Lynda swallowed. She looked over at her husband, careful to keep her expression neutral.

'So. That means just you and James left, then.'

Robert shifted in his seat a little. 'Well, that's the thing,' he said. 'I think that James is going to bail out.' He signalled to the waiter. 'Whiskey,' he said. 'A double.'

Lynda knew at once that James's bail out was already a certainty. Robert didn't deal in speculations – he dealt in facts. 'What's he going to do?'

'He's trying to sell me his half.' Robert spread his hands, both palms facing upwards. The classic gesture of resignation. Lynda wished that he had a little more fight in him. Why did James get to have things all his own way?

'I can't raise the cash to buy him out, not in the current climate.' Robert reached over, put a hand on her arm. 'No one else can raise the cash either, by the way, so I'm not in danger of being taken over, or forced out, or anything like that. Half of the business is still mine. It just means I'll be left holding the baby – running what's left of the show, essentially.'

'Tell me, how does James get to walk away?'

Robert shrugged. 'He has been very canny over the years – he's got a lot salted away. All James wants to do now is ride off into the sunset of retirement.'

His voice was suddenly shadowed by bitterness. He stopped and patted his pockets for the occasional cigarettes he carried with him. He didn't find them and clicked his tongue in irritation.

'And what have *we* got?' Lynda asked. She surprised even herself, asking the question. Robert had always looked after their future. He'd reassured her time and again that their savings were safe. 'Blue Chip', he'd call them. 'Safe as houses.'

Now he looked at her. 'That's part of the problem,' he said. 'I don't know how to tell you this. I've been trying to fight fires for the past few weeks, but . . .'

'Anything to do with Anglo-Irish Bank?' she asked at once. The newspapers had been full of it, radio and television commentators convulsed by it. A spectacular collapse, with suspect dealings and plummeting share prices.

'Yeah,' he said. 'It's a complete disaster. Even more so than the other banks. It's unbelievable.' He shook his head.

'There's been nothing else on the news since you left. What have we lost?' Lynda was amazed at how matter-of-fact she sounded. Robert's long pause made her know the worst before he said it.

'Everything. Or everything that wasn't already invested in Cement Roadstone Holdings.'

'The construction industry,' she said, flatly.

He nodded. 'These days, the share value is pretty much

worthless.' His voice sounded small. 'It's gone, Lynda, all of it. I just didn't know how to tell you. Particularly with all this other stuff that's going on with Danny.'

Lynda leaned across the table. 'The only way we're going to get through this is if you keep talking to me, Robert, let me know what's going on. This is my life, too – *all* our lives. You and I have kept things from each other before, and it's only done damage. To both of us.' She kept her voice low. She was conscious that their silence seemed to have spread throughout the restaurant.

'I need to know what's happening,' she went on. 'Day by day, all the detail. Not just the general stuff. Don't shut me out.' Lynda bit her lip. 'And I won't shut you out. Ever again. We need to plan.'

Robert took both her hands in his. 'I know,' he said. 'It's been rough, and it's going to get rougher. I need you, Lynda. I always have. From the first night I met you.' And he tried to smile. 'Right now, I'm terrified.' He sighed and briefly rested his head in his hands. At that moment, Lynda thought how very like Danny he looked. The thought shocked her. She stroked his face, lightly. 'We've got through tough times before,' she said, quietly.

He looked at her. 'Yeah, well, this is different. Back then, it was just us: we were the only ones in trouble – because of Danny. The whole world wasn't. We were able to recover, with both of us working ourselves to a standstill. That's not possible, not this time.' He gave a thin, bitter, smile. 'There's just not enough out there. Of anything. Opportunity. Work. Credit. Particularly credit.'

Then, as though he had read her mind, he said: 'You're not run off your feet either, are you? When did you last get a commission?'

Lynda nodded. 'It *has* been slow – a few enquiries, nothing much. But I'm due to be paid for the last three jobs – I'm owed quite a bit. And then there's the exhibition coming up in Belfast.' I have a little 'running away money', too, she thought. That had been Robert's mother's advice to her, more than twenty-five years ago.

'Always keep a little bit in reserve, dear. You never know the day nor the hour. Be like the Wise Virgins.' And she'd winked. 'I have my own few pounds that David doesn't know about. It's always a comfort for a woman. That little bit of independence.' She'd smiled then, Emma's smile. 'Just in case the men lose the run of themselves.' That was before Emma, of course. After Emma died, the woman had shadowed into herself, as though her light had gone out. Lynda shivered. She didn't even want to think about what the loss of a child must have meant.

Robert reached for his jacket. 'Let's go home,' he said. 'I'd rather be on our own. This place is beginning to feel oppressive. You okay to drive?' He signalled to the waiter.

'Sure,' she said. 'I've just had the one glass.'

When they step outside, the ferocity of the wind takes Lynda's breath away. She feels her dress slap against her thighs. Rain stings her face.

'Jesus, where did *this* come from?' she gasps as Robert puts one firm hand under her elbow and steers her towards the Jeep. She leans into him, suddenly glad of the comfort his solidity offers her. She holds her handbag in front of her face, shielding her eyes.

He opens the driver's door for her and she struggles into the seat. The wind gusts and threatens to wrench the door from his grasp. His jacket flaps madly about his waist, his tie flings itself over one shoulder. 'Quick!' he shouts. 'I'm soaked through!' He slams the door and runs around to the passenger side. Lynda can see him through the windscreen: his figure distorted by the rain, huge drops of it acting as fat magnifying glasses. He keeps his head down, one arm in front of his face as he battles against the onslaught. She wipes her soaking hair with a handkerchief and drags it back off her forehead. She notices her hands are trembling. The sudden turn in the weather has shocked her.

Robert climbs in and exhales deeply. 'Christ,' he says, 'it's savage out there. Force nine at least.'

Lynda turns on the radio to listen to the ten o'clock news and weather forecast. Robert reaches out one hand.

'Leave it,' he says. Then: 'Leave it, please,' aware that his tone has been abrupt. 'I don't want any more bad news this evening. The worst has already happened.'

'Okay,' Lynda says. She waits until he has his seatbelt fastened. 'Home, James?' she asks lightly.

'And don't spare the horses,' he agrees, smiling at her.

She reaches over, touches his cheek. 'I love you, Robert,' she says, quietly.

He takes her hand, kisses it. 'I love you, too,' he says.

Lynda pulled slowly out of the restaurant car park. At this time of night, and in this weather, it was hard to judge distances. She'd never liked night-time driving anyway. Perspectives seemed to shift, familiar landmarks disappeared. Her eyes tired more easily. And there were always those, too, who drove on full headlights, blinding the oncoming motorists. She slowed again as she approached the roundabout. She could feel the Jeep being buffeted by the gale, even its sturdy body rocking a little from side to side. She glanced over at Robert. Sometimes they acknowledged it, sometimes they didn't, that this was the roundabout where Emma had been killed. Twenty-six, almost twenty-seven years ago. More than a quarter of a century. Lynda shivered. The memory of it was still raw, even after all this time.

'Cold?' asked Robert. He turned up the heating. 'It'll get warm in a minute.' Lynda was glad of the noise the fan made. Tonight, it was easier to drive without speaking.

They had only just met, she and Robert. Lynda remembered that night now, only a few short months before Emma's accident.

'I don't usually do this – come to the theatre,' Robert had confided to her all in a rush, on the evening that Charlie had introduced them. 'But I'm very glad I did tonight.' *Richard II*, she remembered. A rousing interpretation by Dramsoc. She had been spellbound, wondering if she'd ever have the courage in the future to take even the smallest of parts. The stage terrified her – all that empty space. She was happier behind the scenes: the scenery that she had painted.

Robert's eyes had widened when Charlie nudged him towards Lynda.

'This is the extraordinarily talented Miss O'Brien,' she'd said. 'Robert, meet Lynda. Designer, wardrobe mistress, scene *stealer*, sometimes lighting expert,' she laughed. 'She does it all.' Then she'd turned to Lynda. 'Lynda, meet Mr Robert Graham. Rugby-player, tennis-player, engineering student. You're from the same neck of the woods. Get acquainted while I'm gone. Coming!' she yelled, responding to a frantic, gesticulated summons. And she dashed off towards the stage door.

'That's Charlie – Charlotte, if you want to be formal – the Dramsoc whirlwind. Director, stage manager, publicity woman – and she talks about me!'

Robert laughed. 'Seems like the two of you have the world pretty much sewn up between you. This is my first time here –

hope that doesn't make me sound like a peasant. Niall insisted I come along. Bums on seats, he said.'

Lynda nodded. 'Thanks, yeah. It's great to have a full house on opening night.'

'Well, Niall said that Charlie would have killed him if he hadn't gone out into the highways and byways. Saying "no" wasn't really an option.' He lowered his voice. When he spoke again, his tone was conspiratorial. 'Tonight was my first time to meet her. Charlie, I mean. I'm glad I made the decision to come. I don't think I'd be able to bear her wrath. She's terrifying!'

He looked at Lynda sideways then, an expression she was to become very used to over the following years. Half shy, half quizzical. As though he was trying to gauge how terrifying *she* might be. He gestured towards the table in the corner. Lynda could see some wilting sandwiches, some sad and sweaty cheddar cheese. The usual opening night fare, bludgeoned out of some local supermarket, or 'borrowed' from parents' cupboards and wine racks.

'The white wine is warm and the red – well, frankly, you wouldn't know whether to drink it or put it on your chips.' He nodded, as though weighing up his choices. 'You finished here, by any chance?'

She knew immediately what he was asking. Lynda had already decided, the moment she laid eyes on him, that if Robert didn't ask her to slip away on their own somewhere tonight, she would have to ask him. She'd liked him instantly: his obvious strength, his open expression and the way he carried himself. As though he was comfortable with his bulk, even proud of it. He didn't slink away into his body, a tortoise withdrawing into its shell. He was upright and at the same time grounded. Steady on his feet. She tucked a strand of curly blonde hair behind one ear. It was always escaping. She was conscious of how well they would look together, she and Robert: her fair hair and slender build a striking contrast to his dark looks. His tallness, too, felt comforting, protective. Steady on, Lynda told herself. You've only just met.

'Yeah,' she said. 'I'm done here for tonight. I won't be missed.' She was surprised at her own directness.

He grinned at her. 'Then let me buy you a glass of something decent.'

'Guinness,' she'd said bravely. 'Actually, I think I'd like a pint of Guinness.'

His eyebrows had shot up. 'Better and better,' he said. 'I know just the place.'

They ducked out the door while Charlie's attention was elsewhere. Lynda knew that she'd be forgiven, eventually. For once, she didn't care how long eventually took. There was an eager boyishness to Robert that appealed to her more and more. She wasn't about to pass up the possibility of a real date. As they hurried outside, Robert had taken her by the hand. They both stopped. Lynda held her breath.

'I like you,' he'd said. For a moment, he looked bashful again. Lynda wanted to laugh. His expression didn't seem to fit with his body. 'Are you about to make fun of me?' he asked suddenly.

She shook her head. 'No, not at all. I'm *smiling*. I like you too.'

It had been that easy, almost as though they were speaking lines that each had already rehearsed. Their own private theatre. It felt intimate, her hand in his. Natural, and exciting at the same time. Lynda tugged at his sleeve, pointing towards the bus stop. 'Quick, there's a number ten about to leave. If we run, we'll just make it!' He hesitated and she stopped. 'What is it?'

'Promise you won't laugh?' he said.

'Promise,' she agreed. She wondered what was coming next.

'I have my own transport,' he said, with a degree of dignity she found comical.

'Oh – why didn't you say!'

'Well – and this is why you promised not to laugh, okay?'

She nodded, waiting.

'I am the proud owner of a . . . Honda, navy-blue, 500 cc scooter. Bit of a sewing machine on wheels, really.'

Now she did want to laugh. She'd seen the careful scooters around college, put-putting through the car parks. The image of Robert, tall and robust, on one of those machines made her want to smile. But even then, she knew better.

'Glamorous,' she said gravely. 'Most impressive.'

He looked at her. His face was stern. 'You promised not to laugh.'

'Who's laughing?' she said. Then, as a deflection: 'I don't feel it would be right for two of us, though, do you?'

'Maybe not,' he agreed. He seemed relieved. 'I just wanted you to know.'

'Before someone else told me?' she risked teasing him, just a little.

'Pretty much,' he confessed. 'Not great for the image, though – but all I could afford. My brother Danny gives me enough grief about it.'

'I think it's fine,' she lied. 'But tonight, let's take the bus, okay?'

His face brightened then, as though confession had eased his conscience. 'Let's go,' he said. 'Race you.' And he let go of her hand.

Stunned, Lynda watched him take off. Then she gathered herself and followed, long coat flying out behind her. She easily overtook him, and jumped onto the platform of the bus, triumphant. The driver gunned the engine, impatiently. 'Just a minute,' she cried. 'Hang on – my boyfriend's coming!'

Robert hurled himself onto the bus, just as it had begun to leave the stop. Gasping, he put his arm around her and steered her to the stairs. 'Boyfriend, eh?' He pushed her up ahead of him. 'That's pretty forward of you.'

'You objecting?' she asked. 'Because if you are . . .'

Then he grinned. 'Go on,' he whispered. 'Walk up the stairs in front of me. I like the view.'

'Is this how you like to embarrass women who have beaten you, fair and square?' Lynda demanded. She turned to look down at him, one hand on her hip. She was exhilarated after the race. She could feel her heart thumping, the blood singing in her veins. My boyfriend, she had said. My boyfriend. She wanted to tease him, to make him admit that she had won, that he had lost.

He shrugged. 'Not much of a race, really. Besides, I let you win. You have to see that.' The bus lurched forwards. Robert grabbed her and held onto her waist. 'Why don't we talk about it when we're sitting down?' he said. 'There'll be much more time for you to see reason.'

They went to Mulligan's after that, Lynda remembered, pushing their way into the bar already crowded with Friday night students. He'd bought the first drink, she the second and by the time the pub closed, she knew all about him. About his rather proper mother, his sound father; his little sister Emma and his younger brother, Danny.

Almost to her surprise, Lynda told him about her family: about how being an only child had made her feel responsible for her elderly mother and father, as though *she* were the parent, they her children. And she told him, too, about her love of art and design, and how *that* had been a bridge too far in her small family. Something practical, her parents had insisted. Something *teachable*. A good career, teaching, they had said. All this arty stuff is much too unpredictable. And so she'd chosen English and French – but most of her time was spent designing and painting scenery for Dramsoc. Listening to Robert, Lynda realized again how fascinated she was by other people's siblings. The way Robert spoke about Danny in particular had intrigued her.

'Is he like you?' she'd asked. His reply had surprised her.

'I hope not,' he said. 'I'm afraid my brother is a shit.' Seeing her face, Robert laughed. 'Don't worry – it's not a taboo or anything. I accept it. I've always accepted it. He's selfish and wild and irresponsible towards everyone – my parents included. I hate seeing how he hurts them. But there's nothing I can do about it.' He finished his pint in one gulp. 'To tell you the truth, I'm ashamed of him. Just keep that in mind when you meet him.'

She'd liked the certainty then that she would meet him, that Robert looked on her as someone who would be part of his life in the future.

'I will,' she said. 'I'll keep it in mind.' She paused and said: 'Can I ask you a question?' She kept her voice low, serious.

He looked at her. His eyes filled with apprehension. 'Sure,' he said quickly. He placed his empty glass on the table in front of him. Then he faced her with a confidence she guessed he didn't feel.

'This Danny,' she said. She trailed her beads through her fingers. Pretended to concentrate on them. 'What if I like him? What if I fancy him and not you?'

He searched her eyes until she couldn't pretend any longer. She started to laugh and watched as his face lit up in a slow, wide smile.

'Then it's off,' he said softly. 'If you even look at him, I won't ask you to marry me.' And he kissed her.

*

She didn't like Danny when they met, three weeks later. Didn't
like his cocky assurance, or the way he looked at her. Half-
amused, as though Robert had pulled off something that he
didn't expect, as though the territory of women and romance
was his and his alone.

'Well,' he'd said, his eyes appraising her, his hand holding
onto hers for too long. She'd tried to tug it away, but that
seemed to please him even more. 'What have we got here?'

Robert had reacted angrily. 'Cut it out, Danny,' he'd said.
'This is Lynda. Maybe you could pretend to be a civilized
human being, just for tonight.'

Danny had dropped Lynda's hand, pretending to be
shocked. 'Me?' he'd said. 'I was only admiring your taste, brud.
Didn't know you had it in you.'

Just then, Robert's mother had approached, smiling. Just as
well, Lynda thought. Another minute and the brothers might
have been squaring up to one another.

'Lynda,' she said, smiling. Her face was a striking mix of
her sons' – Robert's grey eyes, Danny's square jaw and chin.
She shook hands warmly. 'You are very welcome. Come and
have a cup of tea,' and she led Lynda into the front room.
Robert followed, not saying a word. He'd smiled quickly at
Lynda once, his eyes saying: 'You're on your own!'

They had tea in the oddly formal front room. Mrs Graham
still believed in the concept of 'the good room' – one used only
at Christmas and for family state occasions. The chairs were
deep and comfortable, the carpet olive green, the drapes ornate.
Everything was muted, everything matched, but Lynda had the
sense of having been transported to another time. The room
was about solid, old-fashioned good taste, not fashion. If that
was what Mrs Graham had been aiming for, then she had
succeeded. It was also a room that kept the visitor slightly off

balance. Lynda had been aware of the force of a personality at work here – quite what the force was, she couldn't decide.

Robert had warned her about his mother's pretensions. 'But they're harmless, really,' he'd said. 'Little eccentricities. She'd have liked to live a slower, grander life, with a lot more money and a lot more elegance. All it means is loads of doilies and tiny sandwiches whenever anyone comes to visit. Don't let it put you off. Her heart's in the right place.'

'Don't worry. I won't be put off.'

To her own surprise, Lynda had liked the quiet, firelit sense of occasion. Although it was May, the weather was still damp and chill and the fire was a perfect antidote to the grey outside the bay window. She'd settled into the armchair that Mrs Graham indicated and decided to prepare herself for the interrogation that Robert had assured her would be coming. But if the older woman was scrutinizing her, she gave no sign. The conversation was polite, gracious. Danny was nowhere to be seen.

When they had finished, Mrs Graham stood, brushing her tweed skirt briskly. 'Now, I'm sure you two have a much more exciting evening planned and I'm not going to keep you from it. But Emma has been dying to meet you, Lynda, and I know that she won't be able to contain herself for very much longer. Would you mind?'

'Of course not,' Lynda said, surprised. 'I'd be delighted. Robert has told me all about her.'

Mrs Graham looked at her son, fondly. 'Apple of our eye, isn't she, Robert? No point in pretending otherwise.'

'No point at all, Mum,' Robert agreed. 'I've learned to deal with the trauma of rejection. I'll only ever be second best.' He sighed, theatrically.

'Well, we mustn't grumble. We all know who's boss,' Mrs Graham said. 'I'll just go and get her.'

When she'd left the room, closing the door behind her, Robert grinned. 'You've passed the test,' he said. 'With flying colours. Otherwise, Emma wouldn't be called on to give the seal of approval.'

'Don't exaggerate,' Lynda said. 'Besides, a nine-year-old giving a seal of approval? I don't think so.' But she was pleased. Being liked made life easier.

The door flung open and a small, dense whirlwind in shades of pink erupted onto the fireside rug. The white of the sheepskin was startling against the deep pink of her shoes.

'You're Lynda, Mum said. Robert's girlfriend. Are you going to be married? Can I be a bridesmaid, or maybe a flower girl?'

'Emma,' Robert warned. But Emma paid no heed. She turned her huge brown eyes on Lynda.

'Well,' Lynda said. 'It's very early days. Robert and I only met a few weeks ago. Who knows what will happen?'

The girl regarded her steadily, summing her up. 'But if you do,' Emma persisted, 'can I be your bridesmaid?'

Lynda laughed at her earnest expression. Robert groaned and put his head in his hands. Suddenly, Lynda knew that only a direct, honest answer was going to satisfy this child. Energy radiated from her. She glowed. It was easy to see how the household revolved around her.

'I tell you what,' she said. 'And this is a promise. Whenever I get married, and whoever I get married to, I'll make sure that you are my bridesmaid or my flower girl. Is that a good enough answer?'

Emma looked back at her, her head cocked to one side. 'Yeah,' she said, having thought about it. At that moment, Lynda was struck by how like Robert she was. 'That's a good answer. And I think you keep your promises.'

Lynda was taken aback. 'Yeah,' she said. 'I do. I make a point of it.'

'Okay,' Emma said, turning to her brother. 'I hope you're taking her somewhere really special. She deserves it.' And then she flung herself out of the room in more or less the same way she had flung herself into it.

'That's our Emma,' Robert said, ruefully, 'the human cyclone.'

The air in the room seemed curiously flat and dusty after her departure. 'She's a tonic,' Lynda said. 'And I meant what I said, no matter what happens between us.'

Robert reached for her hands and pulled her to standing. 'We'll keep that promise together,' he said, putting his arms around her and kissing the top of her head, hugging her close to him. 'Watch this space.'

And so when she'd got the call on that hot afternoon in July, Lynda had had trouble understanding.

'What are you saying?' she'd asked Robert, her voice catching in her throat. 'What do you mean? There has to be some mistake.'

But there was no mistake. A hit and run. Out of the blue on a sultry July day. Two seventeen-year-old youths, twins, driving their father's car. It was no consolation that they had been caught, arrested on that same afternoon. By the time Lynda reached the house, the desolation was palpable, like smog in the air. She'd rung the doorbell, expecting Emma's light and mischievous steps down the hallway. Instead, Robert had answered, his face raw, his clothes askew, as though he had dressed in a hurry and mismatched buttons and buttonholes, belts and loops. When he saw her, he threw his arms around her and wept so hoarsely she was frightened. She'd tried to soothe him, to offer comfort, anything that would stop the keening that shivered around her soul.

Even then, Lynda knew that the loss of Emma had catapulted her into Robert's life in a way that might not have happened otherwise. She and Robert were suddenly, inextricably, bound to each other. Their courtship was over. In the space of just a month or two, they had become a couple, defined by tragedy. They were no longer separate people, no longer boyfriend and girlfriend. They were something much more sedate, much more grown-up.

Lynda had felt a hot shudder of guilt at the time. She'd been appalled that she could even think that way, in the midst of grief. But part of her had sorrowed after the carefree part of her life, hers and Robert's, that she'd known was over. She had never voiced it, and neither did he. But both of them knew that it had died along with Emma.

'I'm so sorry, so sorry,' was all she could say as she wept into his shoulder and the image of Emma had stayed with her during all the days that followed. Even now, the memory had the power to throw her off balance, to bring her back to the unfashionable living room with the olive green carpet and the brocade drapes. And as for Danny . . .

'What's that?' she said to Robert now as they approached the end of their road. The rain was still torrential and the windscreen wipers were having difficulty keeping up.

'What?' asked Robert, peering ahead. He looked dazed.

At first, Lynda thought that her memories of Emma had just been transformed into some waking dream that played itself out on the road in front of her. A shimmering figure, luminous in the car headlights, suddenly lurched in front of them and Lynda swerved, pulling the Jeep abruptly to the right.

'Jesus Christ!' she heard Robert yell. 'What the fuck was that?'

Lynda braked, her heart hammering. So he had seen it, too. It wasn't a ghost. It wasn't Emma. That much was a relief . . .

What was she thinking? Of course it wasn't Emma, it couldn't be Emma! The figure that had thrown itself into the path of the Jeep was alive, running – and terrified.

Seared onto Lynda's retina was a pale, oval face: hair matted, eyes wild and rounded. Mascara, eye shadow – whatever it was – streaming in two muddy rivulets down her cheeks. But what Lynda remembered most was the mouth. Scarlet lips, in the shape of an O. Like Munch, Lynda thought suddenly. That was what she had seen. She had just seen 'The Scream' made flesh.

'Jesus, Robert, that girl is in trouble.' Lynda sat shocked, trying to put the gear lever into reverse. 'We have to find her. She looked absolutely terrified.'

'Where has she gone? Which way did she go?' Robert was twisting in the passenger seat, looking wildly in every direction. 'We didn't imagine her, did we?' he asked. His face was white. His eyes looked black and deep in the shadows of the car.

Instantly, Lynda knew that the roundabout had sparked off his own memories of Emma. He had fallen asleep and woken suddenly to the sight of a ghostly young woman, fleeing from something that he couldn't see.

'Look at me, Robert!' Lynda cried. 'She was real, flesh and blood real! We have to find her and help her!'

'Reverse into that gateway,' he said, snapping back to himself. 'She can't have got far. She had her shoes in her hand.'

'What?' Lynda looked at him in horror.

'She had her shoes in her hand,' he repeated. 'Someone must be after her, but I can't see anyone. Jesus, this weather is getting worse!'

Lynda slammed the Jeep into reverse and bumped against the kerb of the opposite pavement. Robert opened the passenger door and leaned out. 'You're fine,' he said. 'Miles of room.'

'Quick, which way do you think she went?' Lynda started to sob. She was filled with compassion for the frightened girl. Even then, she knew that the emotion was intensified by her memories of Emma. It was as though they were connected, somehow. She had not been able to save Emma, but maybe there was a chance that she and Robert could save this girl, whoever she was. She was somebody's daughter, somebody's sister. She could be Katie, in another, parallel life. 'Where should we try first?' Lynda tried to calm the storm inside her that she could feel gathering, despite herself.

'Try that way,' Robert pointed down the hill. 'Go down Cedar Walk. But she could have turned off anywhere. We'll never find her in this weather.'

'We've got to try,' Lynda said. She began to drive slowly, back down towards the roundabout. She kept peering ahead, stopping whenever anything glimmered in the distance. Robert slid the passenger window open, to try and clear the rain from the glass. 'I can see nothing,' he called against the gale. 'There isn't even a trace of her.'

'Let's give it another twenty minutes,' said Lynda. 'She can't have got *that* far.'

Robert closed the window, and rubbed his hands together briskly to warm them. 'Maybe she lives nearby and she's gone home,' he said. He sounded suddenly irritable. 'We can't just drive around aimlessly all night.'

'Twenty minutes,' Lynda repeated, evenly. 'Just to satisfy myself that she isn't in a heap on the side of the road somewhere. Then we'll go home. What if it was Katie?' she demanded. 'Wouldn't you want somebody to help Katie? We can't just *leave* her. Jesus, Robert, what if she's been raped, or something?'

They drove around the new estates for twenty minutes. All

the houses that had sprung up around them in recent years, anywhere there had been a gap. Like veins leading to a main artery. Their road, Ashfield Terrace, old-fashioned and sedate, and once sparsely populated, had given birth to Cedar Drive, Cedar Park, Cedar Avenue. Then Sycamore Road, Sycamore Close, The Saplings. The new roads were endless.

But there was no sign of the girl anywhere. She had simply disappeared. And perhaps Robert was right. Perhaps she had fled home from whatever frightened her, and was now safely back inside her own four walls. Reluctantly, Lynda decided it was time to give up. She'd ring the local Garda station when they got home. The girl's expression haunted her: she'd never forget that face.

She drove to the top of the hill.

As she turned into Ashfield Terrace again, Lynda began looking for clues. Clues to what? She had no idea. For all she knew, the young woman might have been involved in an innocent lovers' tiff. Even now, she could be back in her boyfriend's arms, the row forgotten, the drama enjoyed by each of them, transformed into passion.

'It was one shoe,' said Robert, suddenly. 'Just the one shoe.'

Lynda glanced over at him, feeling suddenly cold again. As she approached the driveway, she could see light from their hallway spilling out onto the slick paving.

'What the . . .' began Robert.

At the same time, she could feel the thump, thump, thump of rock music vibrating through the metal doors of the Jeep. Robert looked at her, his face aghast. 'Christ,' he said, 'the front door is open. What is he playing at? That racket is . . .' But he didn't finish. Instead, he leapt out of the car before Lynda had pulled to a halt. Through the open door, she could hear the pounding bass of Ciarán's favourite band, Nine Inch Nails.

She wrenched open the driver's door and slid to the ground,

aware of the slippery surface underneath her feet. And then she saw it. A shoe. Cream, high-heeled, studded with sequins.

'Jesus, no!' she whispered to herself. She bent down and picked it up. At the same time, the house was plunged into silence. The music had stopped abruptly and the calm was sudden, eerie. Lynda felt something prickle across the back of her neck. She made her way through the open hall door, stepping further and further into silence as she went. Where was Robert? Why hadn't he come back, or signalled to her to let her know that everything was all right?

She pushed open the door of the living room. Robert was standing with his back to her and his stance was what she remembered from the days after Emma's death: stiff, poised. Now, he faced Ciarán and Jon, who were both sitting on the floor. Ciarán's legs were stretched out in front of him, his feet casually crossed at the ankles. The smell of dope was overpowering. Robert's bottle of Bushmills lay on its side on the carpet, a faint shadow where it had leaked onto the wool. Ashtrays were scattered here and there, beer bottles, packets of cigarettes, Rizla papers.

Lynda stumbled through the doorway. The power seemed to have left her legs.

'Drunk again, Mum?' Although it sounded more like 'Srunk again.' Ciarán cackled. He tried to draw on the joint in his fingers, but he kept missing his mouth. 'Fuck it,' he said.

Robert approached his son. Both of his fists were clenched. 'What are you doing?' he asked, his voice very quiet. Ciarán looked at him. 'Shit, Dad,' he said. 'We're just havin' a good time, me an' my ol' buddy here.' And he gestured wildly to his left.

Slowly, Lynda looked away from her son to Jon, who was sitting on the floor beside him. His face was blank, white. She didn't know whether he was drunk, or stoned. 'Jon?' she said.

He looked at her, his face impassive. He was nothing like as incapable as Ciarán. He was very quiet, very still. He made no move to speak. For an instant, Lynda thought he looked at her apologetically, shrugging his shoulders ever so slightly. She was about to speak to him again, to challenge him this time, when Ciarán began to laugh. He was pointing at her, his laughter becoming more and more hysterical.

'The lovely Larissa,' he kept intoning. 'The lovely *Laaaaris-saaaa*, all the way from sunny *Latviaaaa*.'

Robert looked at Lynda. She could see he was about to wade in, to lift Ciarán bodily, to bring this to an end. Already he was moving towards his son. Lynda held up her hand, stalling him for a moment. Who was Larissa? Then she realized. Ciarán was pointing to the cream-coloured shoe she still held in one hand.

'Does this belong to Larissa?' she demanded.

Ciarán nodded. He turned to Jon. 'You remember Larissa, dontcha?' He put down the joint and the glass of whiskey, freeing up both his hands. 'The one with the massive . . .' and he made the gesture for breasts, smiling down at his own handiwork as he did so.

'Yes,' Jon replied. 'I remember your friend, Larissa.' He reached over and took the joint off the carpet. It had just begun to smoulder.

Lynda looked at him, shocked. He was very sober. His eyes were clear. As he stood, his coordination was fine. Lynda looked at each of the young men in turn. What sort of circus was this?

Suddenly, Ciarán keeled over and slumped against the green armchair. Almost at once, he began to snore.

Jon stood and put up both his hands, warding off the attack that Lynda could see Robert was about to make. 'Lynda, Robert, hear me out.' His poise astonished her and she found his use of their Christian names offensive. They were not equals here. He was a guest in their home, one who had just abused their hospitality.

'I tried to stop him, truly I did. It started off with a few beers, and I was fine with that.' He paused. 'I wanted to buy some, but he kicked up a huge fuss. Said there were loads here and I could get some for another night.' He shrugged, his lips trembling. 'I think he'd already had a few joints by the time he got home because he was acting all weird. I didn't know what to do.'

'Why didn't you call us, if you were so worried?' Robert's voice was harsh.

Jon looked at Robert. Lynda could see all the things he wouldn't say, couldn't say. He's not a babysitter, she thought, Ciarán isn't Jon's responsibility. His voice was low, calm. 'I wasn't worried, exactly. I thought something had happened, and maybe a few beers would help him get it off his chest, whatever it was.'

'And?' Robert prompted.

'I don't think that I should—' Jon began.

'Forget any misplaced loyalty,' said Robert. 'What's going on with him?' His voice was almost a snarl. Jon stood up straight, met Robert eye to eye.

'We played some music and shared a couple of joints. There's no point in lying to you about that. We did nothing wrong.'

Robert interrupted him. 'I'll be the judge of that. Tell me what you talked about, what was going on with him.'

'He kept going on about wanting to get out of college. He said that you wouldn't understand.'

Robert made a gesture of impatience. Lynda put her hand on his arm. 'Let's hear Jon out,' she said quietly.

'The next thing I knew,' Jon continued, 'this girl Larissa was on the doorstep. Ciarán said he'd met her last weekend at a club – Zeitgeist, I think – and that she was really good fun.'

'Good fun?' asked Robert bluntly. 'What does that mean?'

Jon looked uncomfortable. He glanced in Lynda's direction.

'Go ahead, Jon,' said Robert. His voice was cold, his anger contained for now. 'You won't shock us.'

'Look, it all started out harmless enough. We'd a few drinks, then she arrived. I made myself scarce.'

Lynda interrupted him. 'Why did she run away from this house like a bat out of hell?'

Jon looked surprised. 'Did she? I didn't know. I went upstairs after she arrived and stayed in my room until about half an hour ago. I didn't even know she'd left at that stage.' He pointed towards the hallway. 'I came down because the front door was open and there was a gale blowin' through the house. Doors were slamming everywhere. I've done nothin' wrong,' he said again, his tone suddenly defensive.

'Why, if you were so concerned, did you leave the door flying open?' demanded Robert.

'Because Ciarán insisted I did. Your woman had thrown a strop but he said she'd be back. I could see he was in a bad way and I didn't want to make things worse. Look, I haven't done anything here.'

Robert pointed to the empty whiskey bottle. 'I suppose you haven't had any of that, either? Or the dope?'

'I told you, I smoked a couple of joints, yeah, but Ciarán drank the whiskey. Him and Larissa. I'm not your son's keeper.' Jon was becoming agitated. His cheeks were flushed, his eyes blazing. 'Ciarán was the one who wanted to party. Try stopping him when he gets started! When he really wants to do something. But obviously, you both hold me responsible.' He stood his ground, just as he had on the day Lynda met him first. He looked her in the eye, then Robert. 'I'll pack my stuff and leave, if that's how you feel. I won't be where I'm not wanted or trusted.'

'You have nowhere to go,' Robert said, evenly.

'Thank you, sir, for reminding me of that,' Jon retorted. 'Then I'm no worse off than I was a few months ago. I'll find a hostel. I don't need anybody to tell me I have no home to go to.' And he turned to leave the room.

Lynda felt her anxiety rise like sap. 'Wait. Jon. Wait. Nobody's trying to blame you. But something has happened here tonight and we need to get to the bottom of it. He obviously can't tell us anything right now.' She gestured towards Ciarán. 'We'd appreciate anything you know about how he was feeling, anything at all about what happened here this evening.'

'Lynda . . .' Robert began.

She turned to face him. 'No, Robert, you listen to me now. I've tried to explain to you before about Ciarán's rages. Just because he's been better-behaved in the last couple of months doesn't mean that the problem has gone away. This,' and she gestured towards her son's slumped body beside her, 'is not a total surprise to me. I'm asking Jon – as a gesture of friendship – to tell us anything that might help us help Ciarán. That's all.'

Jon nodded slowly. 'I'll tell you what I know. But I don't think I'll be much help.'

Lynda felt tiredness engulf her. 'Well, either way, you can't leave at this time of night and in that storm. I'll make tea and we'll talk.'

'What about Ciarán?' said Robert. 'We should try to sober him up, shouldn't we? Make sure he's safe to go asleep? We can't leave him in this state.' His anger was abating. Lynda could see it drain away, leaving him as exhausted as she suddenly felt.

'You and Jon get him up on his feet, try to get him walking. I'll make the tea and we'll get him to drink some. Other than that, I don't know what we can do.'

'How much did he have?' Robert turned to Jon. His tone was conciliatory. Lynda was glad. Jon wasn't guilty of anything: Ciarán was the one lying insensible on the ground.

'He and the girl polished off the bottle of whiskey. Before that, he had about three beers and a few joints. I don't know how many. And I don't know what else. I was in my room from just after Larissa arrived.'

'What time was that?'

'Maybe about half-past eight, nine o'clock?'

'What was he thinking?' said Lynda. 'He knew we'd be back.'

'Not thinking at all,' said Robert grimly. 'That's what seems to be the problem. Give me a hand here, Jon.'

Together, they hauled Ciarán to his feet. His body was limp, his face pale and shadowed. Something struck Lynda. She turned to Jon. 'What did you mean when you said you didn't know "what else"?'

Jon looked at her blankly.

'Just now,' Lynda insisted. 'You listed the beer and the whiskey and then said you didn't know "what else". What did you mean by that?'

He looked away from her.

'Jon, whatever it is, we need to know. This is our son, and he's in trouble.' Robert's voice was beginning to crack.

'We won't say where we got the information,' Lynda said. 'Please, Jon. This is more important than you know.' Lynda could see reluctance written all over his face. 'That's a promise.'

'You've been very good to me,' said Jon. His eyes were translucent against the pallor of his face. 'I can't say for sure tonight, but I know that Ciarán takes coke. And ecstasy. On a regular basis.'

Lynda could hear the intensity of the silence that gathered itself around them. Something seemed to have stopped, and remained suspended in the air.

'And just how do you know that?' asked Robert, sharply.

'Because I've seen him buy it.'

'And you don't? You don't indulge, yourself?' Robert was trying to keep Ciarán upright, but he was losing the battle. Even with Jon's help, Ciarán had become a dead weight. His body kept on sliding towards the floor.

'I can't afford to,' Jon said, simply. 'I don't have the cash. And if I did, if I turned up to even one modelling job stoned, or hungover or with a runny nose, that's it. No more work.'

Ciarán began to moan. 'Let him lie down, Robert, and turn him on his side. I think he's going to be sick.' Lynda dashed into the kitchen and grabbed a bowl and a towel. She ran back to the living room and dropped to her knees beside her son's prone form. 'Get me some water, Jon, will you?'

He obeyed instantly. She turned her face to Robert as they both knelt on the floor. 'There's no point in interrogating Jon,' she said, keeping her voice to a whisper. 'Anyway, what *he* does or doesn't do is not the issue. It's Ciarán we need to deal with. So drop it for tonight, okay? We may have to bring Ciarán to Casualty if he doesn't come round very soon.'

Robert nodded. 'Okay. I hear you.'

Jon returned and poured a pint glass of cold water into the bowl at Lynda's knees. She soaked a corner of the towel and began to dab at Ciarán's temples. Then she moistened his lips.

They looked cracked and dry. By now, his head was turning first one way, then the other, his moans intensifying.

Jon went back to the kitchen and reappeared by her side, this time with a tumbler filled with water and ice. 'If we lift his head, I think I can try to get him to drink some of this,' he said.

Robert positioned himself behind Ciarán's head and lifted it, letting it rest back against his knees. Jon eased a plastic straw between his lips. 'C'mon, buddy,' Lynda heard him say. The tenderness in his voice brought a lump to her throat. Just then, Ciarán's eyes opened. The pupils were hugely dilated and Lynda wondered what he was seeing. Suddenly, he lurched to one side, retching. Lynda placed the bowl under his mouth, just in time.

'Thank Christ for that,' muttered Robert, holding his son's head. 'I thought he was in a coma.'

A good twenty minutes later, Ciarán struggled into sitting and wiped his mouth with the back of his hand. He looked bewildered. 'What's going on?' he said. 'What's happening?'

'You tell us,' said Robert. Now that the crisis seemed to be over, Lynda could see the fury gathering across his face. She reached out, put a hand on his arm.

'Not tonight, Robert. It's almost one a.m. It's been a hell of an evening, one way or another. Let's leave it till the morning.'

Robert nodded but said nothing.

'I can't remember what happened,' Ciarán said. His pupils were still huge. 'Am I in trouble?'

'Come on, mate,' said Jon, gently. 'We'll go up the stairs together. Things'll be better in the morning.' He reached out and took firm hold of Ciarán's arm. He draped it around his own shoulders and half-pulled, half-carried him towards the stairs.

Robert began to follow but Jon turned to him. 'It's okay,' he said. 'I've got him. I can manage him from here.'

Lynda watched as both boys made for the door. 'Will you help me remember?' she heard Ciarán whisper, as he shuffled along.

'Sure. Sure I will. Just let's get you upstairs and into bed. Then we can talk.'

Lynda turned to see Robert's face fill with grief. As though he had just lost someone. She put her arms around him. 'It's okay,' she murmured. 'It'll be okay. Thank God he had Jon with him.'

Robert wiped his eyes quickly, with the back of one hand. 'For small mercies, at least,' he said. 'And now, I need a drink. Will you join me?'

'Yes,' said Lynda. 'I'm weary. Weary and empty.'

Robert handed her a tumbler of whiskey. 'Here. There's none left of the good stuff.'

She smiled. 'Don't think I'd notice.'

The following morning, Lynda's head felt light with lack of sleep. Something hot and sandy scratched across the back of her eyes. She had heard Ciarán and Jon murmur long into the night. Jon had made frequent trips downstairs for water and ice. Lynda, unable to sleep, had got up several times, and knocked on Ciarán's door. She felt like an intruder.

Sometimes, Jon answered, his finger to his lips. Over his shoulder, she could see Ciarán, his face to the wall. He was restless, mostly. Even the room felt unquiet. Other times, the door remained closed, resolute. Once, she had eased it open to see Jon lying on the floor beside Ciarán's bed, a sleeping bag thrown over him, a cushion under his head. She'd been about to go in search of a spare duvet, but something told her to leave well enough alone. She'd stepped back onto the landing then, pulling the door silently to.

Ciarán came downstairs at about ten o'clock. His eyes were red, his skin dry and blotchy. 'I'm sorry, Mum,' he said, as he came into the kitchen. Jon followed him. Despite the late night, Jon looked rested and alert. Lynda was struck by how polished he seemed, particularly compared with Ciarán. She put her arms around her son without a word. He began to sob, the way he used to when he was five. He clung to her. Jon waited, a discreet distance away.

'I don't know what's going on,' Ciarán sobbed. His face was distraught. 'I need to try and work out what happened last night. Right, Jon?' He turned to Jon, who was hovering at the doorway. 'I can't remember anything after the joints. I don't even *know* anyone called Larissa. At least, I don't think I do. I don't know what's happening to me.' He looked back at Lynda now, his eyes wide and terrified. 'I just don't know what's happening. I don't even know if I did anything to her. Jon said she ran out of the house, like I'd scared her.'

'Sit down, Ciarán,' said Lynda. When she looked again, Jon had disappeared. She felt grateful to him for his discretion. 'We have a lot to talk about.'

He nodded, his expression eager for forgiveness. There was no rage, this time, no aggression. Now there was only fear.

'Even if last night had never happened,' Lynda said, aware of the need to tread carefully, 'there are things you need to talk to us about.'

'Like what?' his face was bewildered.

'Whatever it is you're taking,' said Lynda bluntly. 'Drugs can make you paranoid.'

'It was only dope,' said Ciarán. He looked away from her. And there it was again, the old evasiveness. Why lie about it now, she thought, wearily.

Just then, Jon came back into the kitchen. 'I'm really sorry to interrupt,' he said, 'but I have to go. I have a photo shoot in an hour.' He paused. 'Maybe Ciarán might like to come with me?'

Ciarán nodded, his face brightening. 'Yeah,' he said. 'Yeah, I would. We can keep on trying to figure out last night. Right, Jon?'

'Sure,' said Jon. He smiled at Ciarán and Lynda felt soothed by his presence. His affection for Ciarán had been obvious throughout it all. Even Robert had been impressed.

'He's a good lad, young Jon,' he'd said as they finally fell into bed. 'He really cares for Ciarán. I'm sorry if I was a bit hard on him earlier.'

Lynda had hesitated. It was nothing she could explain to Robert, nothing she could even articulate to herself, but something about Jon's *ownership* of Ciarán's distress had disturbed her. She approved of their friendship, of course, was grateful for it – but something about the way Jon had taken over made her feel uneasy. It seemed as though there had been a kind of smugness to his being in charge. She shook the thought away. Jon was loyal to Ciarán; they looked out for one another. That was all.

She'd reached over then and kissed Robert. 'Don't worry about being hard on him,' she'd said. 'He'll get over it. Everyone's emotions are running high. We'll gather our forces tomorrow.'

'No matter what happens,' Robert had said, 'I'll be home by seven at the latest tomorrow night. We can't let this slide. We'll have to confront Ciarán. Christ only knows what's waiting in the wings if he did any harm to that girl.'

He'd put his arms around Lynda, kissed the back of her neck. 'I love you.' He'd slept, curled around her, keeping close. She'd held his hand in hers. But his words had haunted Lynda all night. *If he did any harm to that girl.* Even when she'd slept, fitfully, the girl, Larissa's, face was always before her eyes. Ciarán's memory loss terrified her. What if it was caused by something he wanted to deny, something that was too impossible to admit?

Now, this morning, Lynda felt that it would be a relief to spend some hours on her own, without the constant reminder of Jon and Ciarán, Ciarán and Larissa, everywhere she looked. 'That's not a bad idea,' she said now. 'You could both do with a change of scene. But I want you home by seven, at the latest. Robert will be here by then. And we will *all* sit down together and talk this through.' She wanted to make sure Jon knew he was included.

Ciarán shuffled himself into the jacket that Jon handed him. 'Yeah,' he said. 'And maybe I'll have a handle on it all by then.'

Lynda felt a sharp pang of grief. He looked so lost. And he seemed to have got thinner, smaller. It was something she noticed only now, as he zipped up the oversized jacket.

'Either he is a superb liar,' Robert had said to her earlier that morning, before they came downstairs, 'or he was genuinely so out of it that his memory is a blank. I just don't know what to think.'

She sat at the table after Jon and Ciarán had left. They'd refused a lift. Jon said the walk to the Dart would do them both good. She wished Robert was home. Her life felt precarious, more fragile than it ever had before. As she looked around her, she saw a house of cards, ready to topple if there was even one more tremor.

*

By midday, Lynda had had enough of the silences of the empty house. She couldn't work, couldn't concentrate. She needed to call Katie, now that last night had happened. A weekend in Toulouse was impossible, with Ciarán the way he was. They couldn't leave him on his own. And Katie deserved to know the truth. She was old enough not to be fobbed off with excuses. Lynda reached for her mobile and discovered that it was out of charge. She took the house phone and dialled her daughter's number. To her relief, Katie answered at once.

'Mum, what's wrong? You were supposed to call me last night. Why didn't you answer my texts?'

'I'm sorry, love – my battery ran out. We're okay, but I have something to tell you.'

'I'm coming home,' Katie said, once Lynda had finished.

'No, Katie, there's probably no need and anyway . . .' Lynda could hear her voice trail away. Suddenly, Katie at home seemed like a very good idea.

'I don't care what you say. I'm on my way,' Katie's voice was firm. 'Today. There's a flight tomorrow I can make if I organize myself. I'll keep in touch. And put your mobile on charge, Mum.'

Lynda smiled. 'I will,' she said.

After she'd hung up, Lynda felt energized. She cleaned up the living room, searching for anything that might help her understand what had happened the previous night. The cream shoe was there, a poignant reminder. She could see Larissa's face all over again; the open mouth, the ghostly dress, the rain-soaked hair. And one thing was sure. That girl had been fleeing from something that absolutely terrified her.

Suddenly, Lynda decided she couldn't just sit there and do nothing any more. This house no longer felt like home. She needed to get out. And there was supermarket shopping that needed to be done. A distraction, of sorts.

She gathered together clothes for the dry cleaner's: Robert's suit from last night; Ciarán's trousers; her silk dress, probably destroyed by the rain. Before she left, Lynda put the cream high-heeled shoe into her car. She'd search the local shoe shops, see if she could find anything similar. It was a long shot, but she needed to do something. It felt as though there was a web surrounding her, one that needed to be untangled, strand by sticky strand, before it suffocated her.

She locked the front door, checking several times that it was secure. For a moment, she felt as though she was going through the motions. Nothing had kept Danny out of her home. Security was an illusion.

She passed the roundabout, Emma's roundabout. Lynda negotiated the traffic carefully, aware that some part of her was still distracted. She needed to focus. When she arrived at the shopping centre, she was astonished at how normal everything seemed. People went about their business; babies cried; teenagers lit cigarettes, huddled around shop doorways. It was hard not to feel that everyone else must have been shaken up, just as she was. She and her family; her universe. But the rest of the world gave no sign of it. Lynda parked the car and made her way across the pedestrian crossing into the shopping centre.

As she passed the shoe shop, Lynda glanced at the plate glass window. Boots were reduced. Heavy winter footwear was gradually making way for sandals and smart leather heels. Not that we ever have much of a summer, she thought. And there was nothing in the window that resembled the cream shoe that lay, she now realized, behind the passenger seat of her car. She was annoyed with herself for not having put it into her shopping bag.

Lynda decided to bypass the supermarket and go straight to the dry-cleaner's. She wanted to get rid of the bag of clothing she carried. Apart from anything else, it was tainted with bad memories. As she went by she glanced at the checkouts, trying to see how busy they were. Lynda hated queuing. She'd rather sit and wait somewhere else until things calmed down, buy a newspaper and a cup of coffee. Waiting in line was such a waste of . . .

She froze. The girl had her back to Lynda, of course she did, but there was something familiar about that profile, that white-blonde hair. Unaware of any scrutiny, the girl at the checkout continued to scan groceries, pushing them to the end of the belt where a harassed-looking woman with three children was attempting to pack them away. One child was on her hip, howling. One was in a buggy, wrestling with the restraining strap. The third was attempting to help, but had just dropped a carton of eggs on the ground. Lynda could swear that she heard them smash, although she was much too far away. But it seemed that every other noise had stilled: the howling, the rattle of trolleys, the conversations around her.

It was Larissa. She was sure of it. Lynda looked around her, aware of the perspiration already beading across her upper lip. She could not lose this girl, could not even lose sight of her – but she had to go back to the car for the cream shoe. Without it, she might not be able to convince this girl that she had seen her flee, that she understood her terror. That she wanted to help her.

That she needed to save her son.

Lynda dumped the bag of clothes beside a litter bin. She didn't care if they were stolen by the time she got back: she could run a lot faster without them. She hurried out of the mall, breaking into a run as soon as she reached the car park. It had filled up in her absence. People were circling, waiting for spaces. All the shops were offering special deals for the weeks leading to Easter. Suddenly, shoppers had become very cagey with their money. She reached her car and yanked open the passenger door.

'You leavin', Missus?' she heard.

A car hovered just behind her, its hazard lights blinking. Lynda didn't waste time replying. She reached in behind the seat and grabbed the single shoe. She stuffed it into her handbag, locked the car and pressed the alarm fob. The tail lights blinked twice.

'No need to be so rude!' she heard a voice call after her. 'Snooty bitch!' But she didn't care. She raced back to the supermarket, her heart hammering. She was still there. Thank God. The girl was still there. It *was* Larissa, wasn't it? The similarity was too striking to be a coincidence. There was only one way to find out.

Pulling the bag of clothes from its spot beside the litter bin, Lynda walked quickly into the supermarket. The line at Larissa's checkout had lengthened. Lynda took a basket from the pile at the door and made her way to the aisle that led directly to her. She flung items at random from the shelves into the basket. She didn't care what she bought, as long as the line led her to Larissa. Now all she had to do was wait.

As Lynda approached the checkout, she glanced at her watch. Almost lunchtime. Would the girl be due a break, she wondered. If so, that would be a perfect opportunity to buy her a cup of coffee and speak to her away from supermarket prying eyes.

Lynda was last in the queue. She prayed that no one else would join it. She needed to speak to Larissa on her own, to see her reaction. She was prepared for the girl to run, too. She placed the items from her basket carefully onto the belt and smiled at the girl, noting with relief that her name badge was clearly visible on her uniform. There it was, in black and white. Larissa.

'Hello, Larissa,' she said, and pushed the packets of spaghetti and penne along the belt towards her. 'My name is Lynda. You won't remember me, but we've seen each other before.' She glanced over her shoulder. But no one else had joined the queue.

The girl smiled. 'Hello,' she said, her accent obvious even in that one word. The 'h' almost guttural, the vowels foreshortened. 'Here?' she said, scanning the packets. 'We see each other here, yes?'

Lynda shook her head. 'No, Larissa. Not here. Last night. Out on the street. The weather was very bad.'

The girl blinked. 'No,' she said. 'I stay home on last night. Bad storm.' And she continued to concentrate on her work. But her face had paled and her hands weren't as certain as they had been.

'Larissa,' Lynda said gently. 'I want to help you. You are not in any trouble. I just want to talk.'

Larissa looked up, her lip trembling. 'Please,' she said. 'Go away.'

'Have coffee with me now. I promise I will go away then if you want me to. It's lunchtime. Take your break,' Lynda urged. She reached into her handbag and withdrew the tip of the shoe, just enough for Larissa to recognize it as hers. The girl looked as if she was going to be sick. Lynda felt sorry for her. 'It's yours, isn't it?'

Larissa nodded, bit her lip. Even if she had lied, her face would have given her away.

Poor kid, Lynda thought. 'I'll wait for you outside. We'll go to Bernie's coffee shop. I promise, all I want to do is help. Half an hour of your time, that's all I ask.'

Larissa put the 'closed' sign on the checkout and signalled to someone Lynda couldn't see – she was afraid to turn around, in case Larissa disappeared from sight.

'We go now,' Larissa said. She pulled a fleece from a shelf to the left of her chair and led the way to the front entrance. She did not speak again until she and Lynda sat at a table in the coffee shop, facing each other.

'What would you like?' Lynda asked.

'Coffee.'

'Two coffees, please,' Lynda said to the waitress who hovered.

'It's lunchtime,' the waitress said impatiently. 'There's a cover charge.'

'Fine,' said Lynda. 'Bring us two coffees and two sandwiches, please.'

'What sort?' Her tone was cross now.

'Cheese,' said Larissa.

'Two cheese, please.'

The waitress disappeared.

'Who are you?' asked Larissa.

Lynda noticed her nails were bitten. Up close, her skin was rough, pock-marked. She wore no make-up today: no rivulets of mascara ran down her cheeks. She searched Lynda's face, her blue eyes cloudy with anxiety. She had begun twisting a cheap ring around her thumb.

'I was driving the car that you almost ran into last night,' Lynda said. 'I could see how frightened you were and I drove around the streets looking for you, but I couldn't find you. The only thing I did find was this shoe.'

'You are the mother, yes, of the boy?'

'Yes,' said Lynda, her heart sinking. 'I am the mother.'

The waitress returned and placed the cups of coffee on the table. Liquid sloshed out of each of them, pooled in the saucers. Any other time, Lynda thought ... She waited until the sandwiches were put in front of them before attempting to speak again. But Larissa got there first.

'I am not prostitute,' she hissed suddenly, her eyes lighting up with anger.

Lynda didn't have to pretend to be surprised. 'I never thought you were! Not for a moment.' She leaned closer to the girl. 'But that was my home you were in, and something frightened you. *You* are not the one in trouble. My son is. But before I can punish him, I need to know what he did.'

'You do not punish him,' she said, shaking her head.

'*Yes*,' said Lynda, forcefully. 'Yes, I will. My husband and I are agreed. My son has behaved badly. He will not get away with it. That's how it is in our family. You do wrong, you get punished.' From nowhere, the thought came. Well, not *everyone* gets punished. Danny got away with it. But that's not how things would be for Ciarán.

Larissa looked at her, her expression uncertain.

'He said you would not,' she dropped her eyes. 'That you never punish. That he is golden boy.'

Lynda felt sick. 'What did you call him?'

'Not me,' Larissa said. She sipped at her coffee. 'Him. He called himself that. Golden boy. Apple of your eye.'

Apple of our eye. No point in pretending. Robert's mother. Emma. All those years ago. Lynda shook away the memory.

'Listen to me, Larissa. No matter how much we love him, no matter how "golden" he thinks he is, if he . . . if he hurt you, he will pay for that. But he remembers nothing. You have *got* to tell me.'

Larissa stood, pushing her chair back. 'See? Remembers nothing? And you believe him? You believe that?' She leaned down, her face pushed right into Lynda's. '*If* he hurt me? You do not forget rape, I think.'

Lynda drew back, shocked.

'See?' the girl persisted. 'Already you do not like the truth. You do not come to punish – you come to protect.' She leaned over, so quickly that Lynda wasn't fast enough to stop her. She yanked her shoe out of the handbag on Lynda's lap. 'This is mine,' she said and turned to leave.

'Wait!' cried Lynda. She grabbed Larissa's arm. Her elbow caught the coffee cup and it fell to the ground and shattered. Cloudburst of coffee. White shards everywhere, like the morning of the Homer Simpson mug. A lifetime ago. Heads turned, watching them.

'Tell me where it happened.' Lynda's voice was a whisper. Something had begun to stir in her memory. Something that was struggling to come to the surface.

The girl looked puzzled. 'Where it happen?' She pulled her arm free. 'In your house. The house where you see me running.'

'Sit down. Please.' Lynda could hear the entreaty in her own voice. The waitress glared at her, dustpan and brush already in her hands. 'Leave us, please,' Lynda spoke more sharply than she had intended. She pulled a twenty euro note from her purse. 'Here, that should cover it. Now, please, give us some privacy here. We won't be long.'

Surprised, the waitress scooped up the shards of china and quickly ran a cloth over the floor. Then she made herself scarce, tucking the note into the pocket of her uniform.

'I *know* it was my house,' she said, quietly. 'I *know* it happened. I *believe* you, Larissa. I saw how you ran away, how terrified you were.' She leaned closer, blotting out the other faces in the cafe. 'I just need you to tell me *where* in my house.' She stopped, and prayed.

'Upstairs,' Larissa said. Her voice was harsh. 'Upstairs in your son's bedroom. He take me there to smoke a joint.' She paused. 'I want to stay downstairs, but his friend, he was too drunk and too noisy. So, your son take me upstairs.'

Lynda looked at her. One final, desperate hope. 'Just answer me one more question, please.'

Larissa nodded. 'One more. Then I go.'

'What colour was his hair, the boy who took you upstairs?'

Larissa looked at her as though she was stupid. 'What colour?' she repeated.

'Yes,' said Lynda. 'It's very important. Please.'

She shrugged at the obvious. 'Golden boy. Blond hair. Like mine.' She pointed to her head, as though afraid that Lynda might not understand. Lynda could see that she was puzzled. Stupid woman, she could almost hear the girl thinking.

'Thank you,' whispered Lynda. 'Thank you.'

'Why you thank me?' Her expression was bewildered.

'For telling me the truth,' said Lynda. She scribbled her mobile number on a piece of paper. 'Take that. Please, keep in touch. This boy will be punished – and not by me. By the police.'

Larissa's alarm was palpable. She shot out of her chair. 'No!' she cried. 'I tell police it never happen! Go away! Leave me alone!' And she ran out of the cafe, knocking into tables and chairs as she fled. Lynda let her go. She knew where to find her – and right now, she had other, more urgent things to see to.

Lynda drove fast. Up the hill, past the roundabout. For once, she didn't care about speed limits, Guards, getting caught. That girl, Larissa, had been telling the truth, no doubt about it. She pulled into the driveway, tyres squealing against the still wet surface. To her relief, Robert's Jeep was there. Thank God, he was home early. She stumbled out of the car and rummaged in her bag for house keys. She couldn't find them. Her hands seemed to have stopped working, the fingers frozen and clumsy.

In desperation, she upended her handbag onto the front step and spilled everything out, not caring. Then she had difficulty fitting the key into the lock. Too impatient to try again, she pressed the bell and kept her finger there. She could hear the ring echoing throughout downstairs. She swept everything back into her bag, jamming in the purse that refused to fit.

Through the frosted glass she was able to see Robert make his way down the hallway. Robert and not Jon. Not Ciarán. Just Robert. She almost wept with relief. She pushed the door just as it was opening.

'Hey!' said Robert. 'Steady on! You nearly knocked me over!'

'Are you on your own? Have the boys come back?' She was breathless.

Robert looked at her in surprise. 'No. They're not here. I'm way earlier than I should be. Why? What's wrong?'

'The girl. I found her.'

It took him a couple of seconds to get it. Lynda tried to breathe more evenly.

'The girl from last *night*?' he said. His voice was filled with alarm.

'Yes. Her name is Larissa. She works in Superquinn. At the checkouts.' Lynda stopped. 'I spoke to her, found out what happened.'

'Take your time,' Robert said. 'As it happens, we have all night. Ciarán has just phoned to say that himself and Jon wouldn't be home tonight. He said they were going to a party, that we could always talk tomorrow. He was aggressive, Lynda. We had a row and he hung up on me. Now he's not answering his phone.'

Lynda slumped against the kitchen wall. 'Jesus, Robert. Let's sit down. You have to listen to me! Just stay with me while I try and work this out.' She tried to still the hammering of her heart.

'Take it easy,' he said. 'You're shaking.'

She took off her coat and draped it over one of the kitchen chairs, then she sat, leaning her elbows on the table. 'The girl, her name is Larissa. She's eastern European, I think – I didn't ask. Just heard her accent. I showed her the shoe.'

Robert placed a mug of tea in front of her. 'And?'

'She admitted it was hers. Seemed absolutely terrified. I told her she wasn't in trouble, that Ciarán was the one to be punished.' She stopped. Tears threatened.

'Go on,' said Robert, gently.

'She didn't believe me. Said my son was a "golden boy" and I'd protect him, not punish him.'

Robert said nothing for a moment. Then, 'A reasonable fear, in the circumstances.'

'But she wasn't talking about Ciarán.'

Robert looked startled. 'I don't understand.'

'It was *Jon*. Jon who took her upstairs. Jon who raped her. She called Ciarán "the friend downstairs". The one who was so drunk and noisy that Jon brought her upstairs to get her away from him.'

'How do you know?' asked Robert slowly.

'I asked her what colour his hair was. She said blond. Said that he called himself Golden Boy.'

'Jesus Christ!' said Robert. He looked stricken. 'What the fuck is going on here?'

Lynda reached over and took his hand. 'I'll tell you what's going on. It's Danny, Danny is what's going on. I don't know how, but the two of them have to be linked, in some way. Jon and Danny. This . . . this spiral has all started to happen since Jon moved in in January. Three months ago. Think about it.'

Robert looked disbelieving. 'Now, steady on,' he said. 'I can accept that Danny is behind the garden stuff but—'

'Listen to me!' Lynda's voice was urgent. 'I know it sounds bizarre, but I haven't lost my mind. Trust me. Remember the letters?'

Robert nodded. 'Of course.'

'Go get them. Let's go through them again. With a fine-tooth comb. You said they were "off the wall" and I agreed with you when I read them. But we weren't reading them right. Danny was *warning* us. Those letters are full of clues, they have to be.'

He still looked doubtful. 'I'll go and get them,' he said, but she knew by his tone that he was humouring her.

When he left the kitchen, Lynda rummaged in her handbag. She pulled out her mobile phone and scrolled down to Ciarán's name. She pressed the call button and prayed.

Robert reappeared at the kitchen door as Lynda waited for Ciarán to answer. She held up a hand, making sure Robert wouldn't speak, as the phone clicked on to Ciarán's message minder. She kept her voice light.

'Hi, Ciarán, Mum here. Sorry I missed you. Can you give me a call when you pick this up? I've a nice little windfall for you here. Talk soon.' She snapped closed the cover of her phone. She looked up. Robert hadn't moved. He was still standing there, just looking at her.

'What?' she said. Her mind was buzzing, all her senses on high alert. So many things were beginning to make sense.

'The letters,' he said. 'Danny's letters. They're gone.'

They sat, trying to piece together everything that had happened since January. Slowly, like river mist beginning to clear, markers began to stand out. Now Lynda was suspicious about everything.

'Just think about it for a minute,' she said. 'The sensor light not working on the morning of the flat tyres? Jon had stayed over the night before. Remember how I couldn't understand the way the light worked afterwards? He'd switched it *off* to let Danny – or whoever – do what they needed to do in the dark. He *had* to have.

'And it was exactly the same in the back garden each time something happened. I kept trying to figure out why the light didn't wake me – thought I must be going mad.' She stopped, remembering something. 'And – the morning the garden was destroyed, *Jon* was the one to come out onto the deck and find me. He was awake because *he* was the one switching on the lights again.'

She couldn't slow down. Her mind was making connections, finding links between the improbable and the impossible, illuminating everything.

Robert still looked sceptical.

'I know I'm right,' insisted Lynda. She took his hand. 'And my ring. How else could my ring have disappeared and then suddenly turn up again? You and I don't lock our bedroom door, Robert. We never did and we lost the key for the door almost as soon as we moved in. We're trusting people. We *believed* in Jon.' She stopped and drew breath. 'I know that there are pieces of the jigsaw still missing but we'll find them. In the meantime, Jon is bad news. I don't know how Danny is pulling his strings, but he is. I'm going to find out. This family is *not* going to go under.'

Lynda felt filled with a rage she couldn't describe. It was as though she was suddenly made of steel.

And relieved, at the same time. She wasn't over-reacting, or over-sensitive. Or over-forgetful. This was a real and tangible threat, and one that existed under her roof.

'I'm going up to search Jon's room,' Lynda said. 'Maybe there'll be some clue as to where he comes from, who he is.' She stopped, and looked at Robert. 'I don't even know his surname, do you know that?'

Robert frowned. 'Didn't he mention it? I know I asked him.'

'Can you remember?'

Robert shook his head. 'It was something ordinary and Irish, like Murphy. Or maybe Power, or Phelan. Something like that, I think. I probably wasn't paying much attention. I'll come upstairs with you. God alone knows what you might find.'

Upstairs, Robert tried the handle of Jon's room. 'It's locked,' he said. 'We don't have a key, do we?'

'Yes, we do now,' she said. 'Hang on.'

Lynda went into her bedroom and rummaged for the key in the drawer of her bedside table. It was time to tell Robert. No more secrets. He was looking at her, his expression curious.

'I got this from a locksmith,' she said. 'Seeing as how Ciarán always kept his door locked. And it fits all the internal doors.'

Robert looked at her in surprise. 'When?'

'When I searched our son's room, last summer. I was trying to find out why he was so angry.'

'I see.' Robert was taken aback. 'And did you find any-thing?'

'No,' said Lynda. 'Though I did find out that I didn't like myself very much.' She fitted the key into the lock and turned the handle.

All around the room, Katie's dolls and teddies had been replaced, as though they had always been there. Robert opened the wardrobe door. It was empty.

As if in a final, mocking farewell, the bed had been stripped.

The sheets and pillowcases were folded neatly, the duvet doubled over.

It was as though Jon had never been.

Tonight's the night, Wide Boy tells the watcher.

What's more he has insisted that they meet early. Moving things up a gear now, he says. The tyres and the garden rubbish worked out well; the tortoise turned out to be inspired. But now it's time for the real showdown. This is what we've been leading up to, he says, lighting his cigarette behind his cupped hands.

He's a dirty smoker, the watcher thinks. Clouds of smoke hover around him; his clothes are always speckled with ash. He notes, too, that Wide Boy's index and middle finger are almost black with nicotine stains. His hair looks greasy tonight and he smells as if he hasn't washed in a few days.

The watcher recoils slightly as Wide Boy moves closer. Even the cold air outside the pub isn't enough to dampen down the smells of unpleasantness that seem to halo around him. His breath, his clothes, his hands – it's as though something dark clings to him. Amy would say that he stinks, frankly.

And it's yet *another* pub. Wide Boy will not meet in the same place twice. The watcher hopes that this will be the second to last meeting. Tonight, to plan. Then, next time, to review and pick up his money. And then he's outta there. Your man has really started to give him the creeps. A fishing boat on Lough Conn and some fresh air have never seemed more appealing than they do tonight.

Right, Wide Boy says, back inside the pub again. He settles himself at the table, pint of Guinness in front of him. Here's what's next. The watcher doesn't like what he's hearing. Breaking and entering was never his style. Doin' damage to a garden is one thing, but actually stepping inside a *house*? Even when Wide Boy explains that it's only *technically* breaking and entering, he's not convinced. Of course he's not. He knows the law. If he's caught, it doesn't matter that he hasn't stolen anything: he's still technically a burglar. No can do, the watcher tells him. Absolutely not. At the same time, he is aware of a creeping, uncomfortable sensation, as though he is being dragged slowly towards a precipice. First the top of the garden wall was the deal; then the garden itself; and now the inside of the house? He feels as though he is being sucked into something, that control has somehow been stolen from him while he wasn't watching.

Then Wide Boy goes all steely on him. Oh really? he says. Then I'll have to turn over your recordings to the cops; particularly the one that has you giving the thumbs-up to the camera. Remember? The one where you're vandalizing a back garden? He shrugs. It's my civic duty.

The watcher could kick himself for that one bit of stupid vanity. What had he been thinking? He can feel his mouth go dry. There's no danger of you being caught, Wide Boy goes on, taking a good slug of Guinness. You've logged the movements yourself. Mrs L is never at home on a Friday morning. A smile flickers. She teaches gardening, remember? House is empty until lunchtime. All you have to do is make a bit of a mess. Here he smiles broadly. 'Show that the citadel has been stormed. Know what I mean?'

The watcher feels a wave of nausea that stops close to where he swallows. Should he just cut and run? Take the risk that Wide Boy would never want to explain where he got those images from? He's been paid two grand already. But Wide Boy seems to read his mind. He leans closer. 'There's another five hundred in it, on top of the three grand I already owe you. And the job's risk free. Safe as houses.' And he laughs at his own joke.

The watcher is tempted. Take Amy abroad on a holiday as well. They haven't been away to the sun together in donkeys'. And Wide Boy has delivered on all the other stuff he promised: a good hiding place, no unpleasant surprises, even the sensor light disabled. Maybe it would be all right.

And so he agrees. Reluctantly, but nevertheless. Wide Boy nods and closes his eyes briefly. It's an expression that says he never had any doubt.

Today's Tuesday. They agree on this Friday, three days' time. No point in waiting for another week, although WB tries to push him on it. A little more air between the tortoise Event and this one might have been better, he says. Particularly as he has other things in the mix as well, ramping up the volume. The watcher doesn't rise to this bit of bait and he is adamant about pressing ahead. He wants to get it over with.

He leaves the pub before Wide Boy. His head is buzzing. If he could find a way out of this, he would. He doesn't like all this breaking and entering crap.

Doesn't like it at all . . .

9

'I've just had a text!' Robert called. 'It's from Ciarán!' He raced downstairs and into the kitchen, his face alight with relief. 'He's okay. Says he'll be home tonight.'

Lynda locked the patio doors behind her. Everything in the garden had stayed the same. There were no calling cards this morning. There was some comfort in that. 'Ring him, quickly,' she said, 'maybe the phone is still on.'

'I've tried,' said Robert. 'It's off. But at least we know he's safe.'

Lynda looked at him. 'How?' she said. 'How do we know that? He's been gone nearly twenty-four hours. Jon could be using his phone. We don't know *what's* happening.'

Robert dragged one hand through his hair. 'Let's not assume the worst, okay? If he doesn't come home by this evening, then I'll go to the Guards. Nobody would take it seriously if we reported anything now. A teenager, missing for one night? Particularly after what happened,' he added. 'I'd rather not have to go into that. How would we ever prove that it wasn't Ciarán?'

Larissa. 'Jesus,' said Lynda. 'Not even two days ago. I'm going to call Katie again,' she said, suddenly. 'I want her home, here. Safe with us. She'll be back from Toulouse today and Jon knows her address.' She looked at Robert, could feel fear begin to gather. '*Now* I'm being paranoid, and I know it. But I want her where we can see her.'

Robert nodded. 'I agree. Let's take no chances. Call her. I can go and collect her. One of us should stay here, though.'

'Robert, I couldn't stay here on my own,' Lynda said. 'Just the thought of it terrifies me.' She shivered. 'Let me go to Galway – the drive will give me something to do, something practical. Do you mind?'

Robert shook his head. 'Not at all. I'm happy to stay. I'd welcome a visit from that little fucker.' He paused. 'Though somehow, I think we've seen the last of Jon. He's done his damage. But are you sure you're up to the drive? It's a good three hours.'

Lynda nodded. 'Yeah. It'll make me focus.' She called Katie's mobile. It went straight to message minder. 'Katie, it's Mum. When you get back to your flat from the airport, stay put. I'm coming to get you. Your dad and I both want you home. Love you and talk later.'

Lynda snapped her mobile shut and took her handbag off the chair.

'I'll tell her about Jon, face to face. I want to get on the road straight away. But let me know the minute you hear anything from Ciarán. Or from Jon.' She was about to say, 'Or from Danny,' but changed her mind. 'My mobile will be on the whole time.'

Robert kissed her. 'You drive carefully.'

'I will. And you take care: don't assume, by the way, that we've seen the last of Jon – or Danny. I'll be back sometime tonight.'

As Lynda pulled out of the driveway, she was assaulted by the realization that her whole life had been transformed, turned inside out in less than forty-eight hours. Nothing was stable any more. Or safe. Or predictable.

Only one thing was sure.

She would do whatever it took to save her family.

Just as she pulled up outside Katie's flat, Lynda's mobile rang. 'Robert,' she said. 'Any news?'

'He's here,' said Robert. 'Safe.'

Lynda rested her head on the steering wheel. 'Oh, thank God. Thank God for that. Is he okay?'

'In a manner of speaking,' said Robert. 'He's angry, aggressive and, I would say, coked up to the eyeballs. But he's here. Up in his room. I'm keeping my distance. Oh, and he refuses to talk about Jon.'

'Don't let him out of your sight. I mean, don't let him go out, Robert. Keep him there.'

'Don't worry,' Robert's voice was grim. 'He's staying right where he is.'

'How did he look?'

'I've told you.' He sounded puzzled.

'No, I mean, how was he dressed?' Lynda suddenly, urgently, needed to find out.

'Like a Harlem thug, if you must know. Those awful baggy jeans, displaying half his arse. Shoelaces undone. And a back-to-front baseball cap, with some sort of obscene message on it. Can't remember exactly. Why? What does it matter?'

'I'm not sure,' said Lynda. 'When I work it out, I'll let you know. But you've got to make sure he doesn't leave the house.'

'Don't worry,' said Robert again. 'When he calms down, he has a lot of explaining to do. The other night, for starters.'

'No, wait until I get back,' said Lynda. 'I don't want him stamping off in one of his rages. If he does, we'll never get to the truth.'

'We'll be waiting. Have you reached Katie's yet?'

'I've just pulled up outside this minute. We'll be back on the road in half an hour.'

'Okay. Take it easy on the way home. Neither of us has had much sleep.'

'I will. See you later.'

Katie was waiting. Lynda saw the airline tags still attached to the suitcase and felt sorry for her daughter. What a homecoming. As soon as she saw her mother, Katie started to cry. 'What's going on, Mum? I don't understand. What's happened to Ciarán?'

Lynda hugged her. 'It's okay. Your dad's just called. Ciarán's home, safe. There's a whole lot we don't understand, either. Let me tell you what I *do* know.' And Lynda heard herself tell a story that sounded somehow unreal, even to her own ears. It felt insubstantial, full of coincidence and guesswork. But Katie was angry.

'I can't believe you let him have my room,' she said. 'I can't *believe* you did that.'

Lynda was shocked. 'But he spoke to you, and you said it was okay. *I* spoke to you, and you said it was okay.'

Katie's eyes lit up with fury. 'Okay that he moved *in*. Why would I care about that? I was going to be away, anyway. It didn't matter to me.'

'But they told me you were fine with it – they just had to put away the "girly stuff" and keep it safe?'

Katie was indignant. 'That's Ciarán talking. When would I ever call my things "girly stuff"? They told me Jon was staying in Dad's office, where uncle Danny stayed, that time he was ill. Or when we *thought* he was ill.'

Something Katie said triggered a memory. 'They didn't come here, did they? Just before you went away? After a football match?'

'No,' said Katie. 'I've never met Jon. And I only spoke to him on the phone that one time. Why?'

Lynda shook her head. 'All these lies. I can't keep up with all of them. God knows what the two of them got up to *that* night.' Katie was looking at her, puzzled. 'Look, don't mind my ramblings – lots of things have started to fall into place. I'm sorry about your room, Katie, so sorry.' Lynda sat on the lumpy sofa and accepted the cup of coffee Katie handed her. 'This guy Jon is bad news. I wish I'd never set eyes on him.' She sipped, grateful to avoid her daughter's eyes. 'He arrived out of nowhere. We don't even know his last name, for God's sake.'

'What?' said Katie. 'You gave somebody a home and you didn't even know his *name*? What are you *like*?' Her face was incredulous. Lynda could feel embarrassment prickle along the back of her neck. How easy she had been to take in; how easy they both had been. Had Danny taught them nothing?

'*I* know who he is,' Katie was saying. 'He told me, that night on the phone.'

Lynda looked at her. 'Are you serious?' Something like hope began to nudge.

'Yeah,' said Katie, slowly. 'In fact, now that I think of it, he made a point of it. Said he was the sweetest man I'd ever know. We laughed about it.'

'What do you mean?' asked Lynda, puzzled. 'I don't understand.'

'Sweetman,' she said. 'His name is Sweetman. Told me he came from Waterford.'

He wants to be found, Lynda thought suddenly. He wants us to know who he is, where he came from. And the trail, she knew, would lead them straight back to Danny.

Where it all started, over a quarter of a century ago.

Quickly, she called Robert.

'You be careful,' he said. 'I don't like this.'

'I'll keep in touch,' said Lynda. 'I can't not follow this up. Don't you see? This is all part of the game. He wants us to see how clever he's been.' She pulled the map towards her. 'We're going to Waterford, as soon as I have a sandwich and a shower.'

'Jesus, Lynda, it'll take you hours.' Robert sounded alarmed.

'I don't care. Katie and I will share the driving. You just keep Ciarán safe. I have to do this, Robert. I don't have a choice.'

He sighed. 'Keep in touch, then. Constantly. And stay over in Waterford tonight. You hear? You're not to be driving through the night.'

'Of course we'll keep in touch,' said Lynda. 'You take care.' She hung up and turned to Katie. 'Where's your laptop?'

'In my bedroom. Why?'

'Come on. We need to look up the phone directory. As many Sweetmans in Waterford as we can find.'

'There's just the one,' Katie said. 'Here – look.'

Lynda peered over her daughter's shoulder. 'Maybe there are others, ex-directory.'

'Maybe,' agreed Katie. 'But let's try this one first. At least it's a start.'

Lynda rested her index finger on the screen. 'Jack and . . . is that Martina?'

'Yeah,' said Katie. 'Jack and Martina Sweetman, 49 Waterville Avenue. Wait, I'll look it up on Google Earth.'

Lynda watched as the map appeared on the screen. Katie zoomed in and pinpointed the street. 'There it is.'

'Can you print that?' Lynda asked.

'Sure.'

The printer whirred and spat out an A4 page in colour. Lynda folded it and put it into her handbag. 'Let's go. While there's still a bit of light.'

'Don't you want a shower? And a sandwich?' Katie was startled.

Lynda shook her head. 'That was just to keep your dad from fretting. I'll be fine.'

'Okay, if you're sure.' Katie shrugged. 'I'll do the first bit of the drive. I can get us out of Galway faster than you can, anyway.' She walked over to Lynda and hugged her. 'It'll be okay, Mum.'

Lynda kissed her forehead. 'I know it will. I've got you in my corner.'

The street was deserted. One of the lamps flickered, casting strange shadows across the pavement.

'This is it,' said Katie. 'Number 49.'

Lynda turned off the ignition. 'Great navigating,' she said. 'Right. You ready?'

'Yeah,' said Katie. 'But if there is anything that makes me uncomfortable, we're outta there, okay?'

'Absolutely,' agreed Lynda. 'I'm not feeling one bit brave.'

Lynda locked the car and they both made their way up the short garden path. She knocked at the door. Lynda saw that the outside of the house was cared for, the garden neat, if still a bit bedraggled by winter. There were some cautious daffodils just under the living-room window. Curtains were drawn and things looked cosy. That was always a good sign. Katie stood close to her on the step. They waited, but there was no answer. Lynda began to feel the slow seep of disappointment.

'Let's just hang around for a while, Mum,' Katie said. 'They could be anywhere. On the phone – in the bathroom. Let's give it another minute or two.' And she pressed her finger to the bell. They could hear it ringing, shrill and insistent. And then it stuck.

'I'm coming, I'm coming,' said an irritable voice, making its way down the hall. The door was wrenched open and an angry woman stood just inside it. She was dishevelled, her hair in disarray.

'It's stuck,' said Katie at once. 'We're very sorry, but we can't get it to stop.'

'Just a minute,' said the woman, and disappeared down the hallway. She returned with a knife, and prised the bell-push from its housing. The noise stopped at once. 'Thank God for that,' the woman said, with a half-smile. 'Now how can I help you? I'm not buying anything, so if that saves you time—'

'And we're not selling,' said Lynda, quickly. 'We'd just like to talk to you for a few minutes.'

Her face looked wary. 'What about?'

'About a twenty-one-year-old man, who is in a lot of trouble.'

The woman's face clouded over. 'What's that got to do with me?'

Lynda opened her bag. She pulled out the photograph of Jon and Ciarán that neither had known she was taking; the one where they stood together in the garden, talking, smoking. She'd intended to have it framed for each of them as a gift. Now, she handed it to the woman standing before her. There was silence for a moment or two.

'Jesus,' she said. 'You'd better come in.'

They followed her down the hall towards the kitchen.

'Please,' she said. 'Sit down.' She ran her hands through the tangles of her dark hair. 'Excuse my appearance. I was just about to have a bath.'

'I'm sorry for disturbing you. This won't take long. I'm Lynda Graham, and this is my daughter, Katie. We're looking for this boy, yes, but only because we want to understand what's going on.'

The woman held out her hand. 'I'm Martina Sweetman. Everyone calls me Tina.' She seemed about to say more and stopped.

Lynda could see that she was making up her mind about something. She waited, searching the other woman's face for clues. Who was she? She could see no resemblance to Jon at all. What if this had all been for nothing?

'Where did you get that photograph?' she asked, finally.

'I took it,' said Lynda. 'That's my son, Ciarán, with the dark hair. We know the other boy as Jon. They became great friends at UCD. We know nothing else about him, except what he's told us. He said his parents were separated and he needed a place to stay, just for a while, to get his head sorted. We took him in.'

'So – why are you looking for him?'

Lynda hesitated. 'It's a long story.'

The other woman shrugged. 'You're here. You obviously want to tell it. I can listen.'

When Lynda had finished, Tina said: 'I'll put on the kettle. Would you like tea or coffee? Only instant left, I'm afraid.'

'Instant's fine,' said Lynda.

Katie nodded. 'Yeah, grand.'

'Sweetman is my husband's name. Jack Sweetman.' She nodded towards the adjoining room. 'He's in there with my three sons, watching football.' There was a sudden roar from the room next door. Tina grinned. 'See what I mean? Man U. More important than God in this house.' She paused. 'You found us through the telephone directory, I suppose? There aren't too many of us.'

'Yes,' said Lynda.

'And that's how the boy you call Jon found us, too.' Tina looked sad.

Memories, thought Lynda. Tina's expression had become distant, as though she had been taken away somewhere else.

'What *is* his name, then?' asked Katie.

Tina looked at her, her face now unreadable. 'By a very cruel twist of fate, his name is Daniel. Of all the names in the world, they called him Daniel. Daniel Morrissey.'

Lynda didn't understand, although something had begun to tingle at the base of her neck. It felt as though her throat was constricted. 'Go on,' she said. 'Please just tell us.'

'My maiden name is Munroe,' she said. 'I have one sister, whose name is Amy. We are incredibly close, always have been.' Tina sipped at her coffee. 'Sometime in 1988, my sister, who was nineteen at the time, fell hook, line and sinker for this absolute charmer that she met in a club. He was twenty-one at the time.'

Lynda felt sick. She could feel where this was going.

Tina looked at her. 'It's an old, old story,' she said. 'I loathed the guy, first time I clapped eyes on him. But Amy was very naive. She'd always been fragile, and I suppose a bit protected at home because of that.'

Katie reached across and squeezed Lynda's hand. 'Mum, are you okay?'

'I'm fine,' she said. 'Go on, Tina, please.'

'You could write it yourself,' Tina said, looking from her to Katie. 'Amy leaves home, pretending she's going to stay with a girl that she worked with. She and I had the most massive row, but there was no stopping her. She said I was jealous. That I didn't want her to have somebody of her own.' Tina looked down at her hands, hugging the cup of coffee. She shook her head. 'Nothing could be further from the truth. But he was a dangerous man. I could smell it. In six months, it was all over. She got pregnant, he fucked off, end of story.'

'And the child?'

'Sorry,' said Tina. 'I must be accurate. She got pregnant and left him, before he knew about the baby. But he was going anyway. She was so terrified of him and so unhappy that she knew there was no way they could have the baby together. I admired her strength. It really surprised me.' Tina looked at them. 'I need a cigarette. I'm trying to stop, but in the circumstances . . .' She reached into the cupboard behind her. 'Anyway, Amy upped and left and came to me. To us, Jack and me. We'd moved from Dublin, so we were a safe distance from my parents. She didn't want them to know.'

'And the child?' Lynda repeated, hardly trusting herself to speak.

Tina nodded towards the photograph. 'That's him. That's Daniel. I couldn't believe it. That's what his adoptive parents called him. Of all the names.' She shook her head again.

'And the father?' asked Lynda, heart hammering.

Tina looked surprised. 'Oh, I thought that was why you were here. To track him down.'

'In a way,' Lynda admitted. 'I just need you to confirm it.'

'His name is Danny. Danny Graham. He's the father.'

Lynda exhaled. She felt as though she'd been holding her breath for years.

'This guy is my *cousin?*' blurted Katie. 'What is going *on* here?'

Lynda put one hand on Katie's arm, the pressure asking her to hold on, just a little bit longer. She turned to Tina. 'If he didn't know that Amy was pregnant, then how did he know he had a son?'

'He didn't, until his son went looking for him. And his son came here first. Talk about a chip off the old block.'

'I still don't understand,' said Lynda.

'We had Daniel adopted when he was three weeks old. Jack and I used our surname, to put as much distance as possible between Amy and Danny. That was what she wanted. She wasn't even able to hold the baby after he was born. She spent months afterwards being almost catatonic. It was a nightmare.' Tina stood abruptly and filled the kettle again.

'The baby went to an adoptive family in County Meath,' she went on. 'And that's all I know about them. When the time came, they didn't stop him looking for his biological parents, although it must have broken their hearts. And so, he came here first. He thought I was his mother.'

'And did you tell him who was?'

She nodded. 'Eventually. The minute he stood on the step, I knew who he was. The apple doesn't fall far from the tree. He intimidated me, I don't mind telling you.'

'And what about his father? How did he get to Danny?'

'I promised to give him all the information I could about his father. As long as he left his mother alone. He promised he would – not that I'd put much store on that. He insisted on knowing everything.'

Tina ground out her cigarette and almost immediately lit another. 'I appealed to his better nature,' she said, dryly, 'said that his mother was very unwell. I told him Danny's name, date of birth, everything I could, including the fact that he had gone to England. I presumed he was still there. He left, then, and I haven't heard from him since.'

'Well,' said Lynda, 'he found his father. Or they found each other.' She rested her head in her hands, suddenly exhausted.

'I'm sorry for you,' said Tina. 'Truly I am. I know how destructive Danny – the father – was. I can only assume that

Jon, as you call him, is following in his footsteps. I'm not all that happy myself that either of them – both of them, now – know where I live.'

'You've been very good to talk to us,' said Lynda. 'We really appreciate it.'

'Not a problem,' Tina said. 'I'm curious – how did you trace him to me? I mean, how did you know what name to look for? Or did you know all along?'

Lynda smiled sadly. 'Well, as you now know, he left our house under something of a cloud. We had no way of finding him. But he'd told Katie his surname. They spoke on the phone one night, just before he moved in. I think he wanted us to find out who he was. It's like some sort of a cruel game.' Lynda stopped. 'And my son is the pawn.'

'Jesus,' said Tina. She was silent for a moment. 'If he's anything like his father, then I don't envy you.'

Lynda nodded. 'He's done a lot of damage. And he's still doing it. He *and* his father. An unholy alliance.'

'I'm truly sorry,' said Tina. 'The two of them, the two Dannys together. Talk about a force of nature. They were peas in a pod. Couldn't believe my eyes, the day young Danny – Jon – turned up here. It's like my mother used to say. Set in stone.'

'What do you mean?' Katie was curious.

Tina shrugged. 'My mother had this old-fashioned belief that badness was handed down, parent to child. If a mother or father was evil, then the child was likely to be evil as well.'

'Evil,' repeated Lynda. 'It's not the word I would have used.'

'It exists,' said Tina. 'Whatever you call it.'

'So you've *no* chance if one of your parents is bad?' Katie's voice was sceptical.

'I'm not sure that that's what she meant, in fairness,' said Tina. 'It wasn't a blanket that covered everything. But she did believe the bad stuff was handed down; that nature was way more important than nurture.'

Lynda stood and held out her hand to Tina. 'Thank you again, Tina. Here's my mobile number if you ever want to contact me. Feel free. You've been very kind.'

'Not at all,' said Tina. 'To be honest, I feel pretty helpless.'

'We all do,' said Lynda. 'But it's some comfort to know what we're dealing with.'

'Jesus,' said Katie as they drove away. 'My own cousin.'

Lynda nodded. 'Yes. I'm not as surprised as I should be. I always felt Danny was behind this. What an awful thing to do, though. To corrupt your own child like that, make them part of your revenge.' How had Danny done it, she wondered. Had Jon just been an innocent teenager, before his father got his hands on him? Or was there something, after all, in what Tina had said?

Katie chimed in, echoing her train of thought. 'It's a very bleak view of life, what Tina says, though, isn't it?' She looked sideways at her mother. 'You don't believe in that stuff, do you, Mum? That kind of pre-destination?'

Lynda concentrated on the road ahead. 'Katie, I don't know what I believe in any more, to tell you the truth. Apart from my family.'

Neither of them said anything for a moment.

'Are you and Dad okay?' Katie's question was sudden.

'How do you mean?' Lynda knew exactly what she meant, but the question had taken her aback.

'I'm not a child. I wasn't a child when it happened, either.

Jesus, sometimes parents haven't a *clue* what their kids see.' Katie turned and stared out the passenger window. She was angry.

'I made a mistake, Katie,' said Lynda. As she spoke, Lynda knew that it was true. 'Probably the worst mistake of my life. I had an affair and I regret it, bitterly. Even more when I realize how many people I hurt. I thought it was just me.' She slowed down, moved into the inside lane.

'I'm not judging you,' said Katie. She still kept her face turned away from Lynda. 'I just want to make sure that you and Dad are okay now.'

'Yes,' said Lynda. 'Yes, we are.' She risked a sidelong glance at her daughter. 'Everything else is falling apart all around us. But strangely, we are okay, the two of us.'

'Good,' said Katie. 'I'm glad to hear it.' She turned back to look at her mother, her face full of emotion. 'I knew all along, and I was really mad at you. But I understand more now how these things happen. Now that I'm older.'

Lynda stifled a smile. Twenty-one. Such wisdom. She asked a cautious question. 'Did Ciarán know?'

Katie snorted. 'You must be jokin'. Ciarán saw nothing but himself. He was always the same. Self-centred little shit.'

Lynda was surprised at her vehemence. 'Why do you say that?'

'He got away with murder. You *spoiled* him.' Katie's tone was furious now. She glared at Lynda. 'You picked up after him all the time – or had me do it. And I bet you're still doing it. You sheltered him – both you and Dad, although I've no idea why. I used to think it was because he was the baby. Then I believed it was because he was the boy. I got used to being second fiddle.'

Lynda felt as if she'd been slapped. 'Katie – that's just not true!'

'It is! It *is* true! You just won't see it!' her voice cracked.

Lynda indicated and pulled over onto the hard shoulder. She turned off the engine and pressed the hazard light switch. The blinking started at once. She turned to Katie, her eyes searching her daughter's face. 'Is that really what you believe?'

'Yes!' said Katie. 'You took me for granted. You expected good marks and good behaviour from me, always. But Ciarán – you always made excuses for his shitty behaviour and let him away with way more than I was ever allowed.' Tears had started. 'And no matter what I did, I was always second best. Why do you think I couldn't wait to get away from home and go to college in Galway?'

Lynda's head reeled. *Second best.* Danny's cry, all his life. She took Katie's hand. 'I'm devastated to hear you say that,' she said. 'I can't tell you how much we both love you, how proud we are of you. And how much I miss you.'

Katie snatched her hand away, and wiped angrily at her tears. 'Yeah, well, I never felt that. Ciarán always came first. He always took up so much room. I felt like there wasn't enough . . . *space* . . . for me.'

Lynda thought about that. She stroked Katie's hair back from her forehead. 'What you say is partly true. Bad behaviour always takes up more room than good, Katie. But he didn't come first, not in the way you think.' Lynda paused, trying to figure out the best way to say it. 'He occupied a lot of our attention and we knew we could trust you. I'm sorry if that made you feel sidelined.'

Katie blew her nose. 'Even the weekend you were going to spend with me in Toulouse got cancelled because of that little shit, didn't it?' She turned her gaze on Lynda. Her face was full of hurts, old and new.

'No,' said Lynda at once. 'That's not true – not in the way you mean. We had to cancel because of Danny. I didn't want to tell you about all the horrible things he was doing, not while you were away from home. We couldn't leave. It wasn't safe.'

'Yeah, well,' she said. 'I guess now isn't a good time. Ciarán's in trouble again. And he is my brother.' But her anger seemed to have abated.

'We'll talk about it again, Katie, and that's a promise.' Lynda started the engine.

'Well, that's one good thing,' said Katie. She glanced over at Lynda, and half-smiled at her.

'What?'

'You and your promises.'

Lynda waited. She almost held her breath. She could feel shadows of Emma all around her.

'You always keep them. That's one really good thing. You always keep your promises.'

10

IT WAS AN HOUR or so before dawn when Lynda pulled into the driveway. She could see that the downstairs lights were still on. Robert was waiting for them. She leaned across to Katie, who was fast asleep. It seemed such a shame to wake her.

Robert appeared at the front door and stepped out onto the driveway. He peered into the car and smiled at the sight of his sleeping daughter, then he opened the passenger door carefully. Lynda released the seat belt and, without a word, Robert leaned in and lifted his daughter bodily out of the seat. She stirred and opened her eyes. With her face filled with sleep, she looked like a child again.

'Dad,' she murmured, winding her arms around her father's neck.

'Ssshh,' he said, and kissed her forehead. 'Let me carry you up to your bed, princess. We'll talk later.'

Lynda watched as he climbed the stairs. What a perfect thing to do, she thought, particularly tonight. She'd tell him. He needed to know just how right he'd got it.

Dawn crept up on the dirty skyline, just as Lynda came to the end of her story. 'And that really is everything,' she said. 'This woman Tina filled in all the blanks.'

Robert nodded. 'I'm sorry,' he said. 'For not listening, for not taking Danny seriously enough. For all of it.' He shook his head. 'My own nephew, my own *family*. Jesus Christ.'

Lynda held out her hand to him. 'It's not your fault that Danny is your brother,' she said, standing up from the kitchen table. 'Come on. Bed. I'm exhausted. But I'm really beginning to feel that we're coming to the end of the nightmare. And you're sure Ciarán hasn't moved?'

'Positive,' said Robert. 'I even changed the locks on the doors, back and front. He can't get out. Besides, I checked his room, just before you got home.' He grinned at her. 'Good investment, that locksmith. Stroke of genius, I'd say.'

'To be continued,' she said. 'Tomorrow's another instalment.'

He reached for her as soon as they got into bed. She went to him, gladly.

'We'll come through,' he whispered.

She could make out his face above hers, shadowed in the lightening room. 'Yes,' she said softly. 'We will.'

Lynda woke again at seven. She'd slept hardly at all and was happy to make her way downstairs at once. She pulled back the curtains and stepped outside through the patio doors. She'd not had the heart to do anything with the garden after her tortoise had been destroyed and, as the days went by, it got harder even to touch it. She still stepped outside each morning, though, reluctant to let go of the possibility. Maybe one day, when all of this was fixed, she'd settle her stones once again.

She went back inside now and made a note to herself to call the college. Her horticulture students would have to do without her this morning. Friday. God. What a week.

*

When Katie came down to the kitchen at nine, Robert and Lynda were still sitting at the breakfast table. Robert stood up at once and Katie walked into her father's arms.

'Dad,' she said, and hugged him. 'It's good to be home.'

Robert kissed her. 'Great to see you, kid. Welcome back. You look terrific.'

'And thanks for carrying me up to bed last night. Hope I didn't wreck your back.' She looked at him archly.

Robert wagged a finger at her. 'No more ice cream, y'hear? Otherwise you'll have to walk.'

She grinned at him. 'Cheek of you.' She sniffed the air. 'You makin' chilli for tonight?'

Robert nodded. 'Your favourite, isn't it?'

Katie nodded.

'It's hard to keep occupied when the women in your life are swanning all over the countryside,' Robert went on. He buttered more toast and looked up at Katie. 'Want some?'

Katie shook her head. 'Aw, poor Dad,' she said. 'Left at home doin' the cookin' while the girls have adventures.' She pulled a cereal bowl from the dishwasher and rinsed it. 'Smells good, though. Chilli always was your party piece.' She pointed upstairs. 'Ciarán's awake. I heard him in the bathroom.'

Lynda nodded. 'Yeah. We're waiting to talk to him.'

'Do I stay or go?' asked Katie, pulling the Corn Flakes out of the cupboard. She looked at her parents in turn.

'Stay,' said Robert and Lynda together.

Seconds later, Ciarán came into the kitchen. Lynda saw at once what Robert had meant. A Harlem thug, he'd said. She looked at Ciarán, took in the sloppy jeans, the unlaced trainers, the back-to-front baseball cap. And all the old defiance was back. It was there, in the way he slouched, in his lowered gaze, in the fists he had thrust into his pockets.

'Hiya, Ciarán,' said Katie.

'Hiya.' He didn't look at her.

Something about the baseball cap caught Lynda's attention. Ciarán never wore one. It had never been part of his style. Suddenly, something disturbed her; something she caught, out on the edge of her vision. 'Ciarán,' she said. 'Take off the cap, will you?'

He glared in her direction. 'Why?'

'Because your mother asks you to,' barked Robert. 'And if you don't, I will.' He made to stand up from the table.

'Fuck's sake!' muttered Ciarán and snatched the cap off his head, tossing it onto the table.

Lynda gasped. Robert stopped in his tracks. Katie stared at her brother.

'Ciarán,' said Lynda. All the implications had started to sink in. 'What on earth have you done?'

He ran his hand through his cropped, white-blond hair. He shrugged. 'We did it yesterday. For a laugh. It's no big deal.'

'Wait a minute,' said Robert. '*We* did it?'

'Yeah,' said Ciarán. He finally let his gaze drift back towards his father. 'Me and Jon. He dyed his black, I dyed mine blond. I don't know why it's such a big fuckin' deal.' He shifted from one foot to the other. 'It's only hair dye.'

'Oh, Jesus Christ,' said Lynda. 'Ciarán, you have no idea what you've just done!'

'What?' said Ciarán, spreading out his hands in front of him.

'I'll tell you what,' said Robert, angrily. 'Your friend Larissa was raped in this house three days ago. You were out of your mind at the time. And guess what? Guess how she identified her rapist?'

Ciarán had begun to look frightened. He fidgeted, looking from Robert to Lynda to Katie. He didn't answer.

'I'll tell you, then, will I?' said Robert. His fists were clenched. ' "Golden Boy", she called him. The *blond* one in the house. Not the noisy one who sat downstairs, pissed out of his head. The *blond* one attacked her. And you, you idiot, you've just made yourself fit that description.'

Ciarán took his hands out of his pockets. He looked bewildered.

'Let me fill in the blanks for you,' said Robert, leaning into Ciarán's face. '*Jon* is the one who raped her. But bottom line, you're the one who's going to get the blame.'

Ciarán looked disbelieving. 'Has she . . . I mean . . . did she say that . . .' And his voice trailed away.

'Where *is* this guy Jon?' demanded Katie. 'Why isn't he here with you?'

Ciarán shrugged, looked at the ground. 'He said he needed to move on for a while,' said Ciarán. 'He's a free spirit. But he'll keep in touch. He has my mobile.'

Robert snorted. 'Yeah, sure,' he said. 'He'll keep in touch all right. He's gone for good. Vanished without a trace.'

Ciarán sagged and Lynda saw his face fill with emotion.

'Sit down, Ciarán,' she said. 'There are a few things that you need to hear.'

He dragged a chair out from the table and slumped into it. Just then, the doorbell rang.

'I'll go,' said Robert. He looked over at Lynda. Jon, she thought for one wild instant. Had he come back? Robert left the kitchen and closed the door behind him. She heard his footsteps make their solid way towards the front door.

'What do I need to hear?' Ciarán asked her. But his voice was dull.

The kitchen door opened again, before Lynda had the time to reply. Robert stood there, flanked by a man in a suit and a woman in uniform. The man was tall and bulky and he looked as though his suit wasn't comfortable. The woman was smaller, slighter. Then Lynda saw Robert's face. The pallor, the fear in his eyes. He didn't speak.

'Mrs Graham?' It was the woman who spoke. 'I'm Garda Fiona Dolan and this is Detective Paul Galvin. We've just been explaining to your husband that there has been an incident reported regarding your son.'

Lynda's mind sped out in all directions. Had Larissa gone to the police, despite her terror?

'What sort of an incident?' asked Robert now, guarded.

'We have had a complaint regarding a serious assault on a young woman at this address on Tuesday night. We—'

Lynda interrupted. She wanted to say: *We can explain . . .* but Robert glanced at her, warningly.

'May we know who is making the complaint?' Robert asked.

The policewoman shook her head. 'I'm afraid not, not at this stage.'

'But my son has been accused?' Robert's voice was cold.

'Yes, sir, that is correct. We have had a complaint against a Ciarán Graham of this address.' She looked down at her notebook. 'We would like him to help us with our enquiries. Ciarán Graham is your son – am I correct in assuming that?'

'I think we'll follow up this conversation in the presence of our solicitor,' said Robert.

Lynda looked at him. What was he doing? They could clear this up right now, tell them that Ciarán wasn't the one responsible, that Jon was. That Jon had taken over this family, that it was all part of a spiral of revenge. She wanted to shout at them that their boy was innocent – and then, suddenly, she realized how it would look. Parents protecting their son. Shifting the blame to another boy. And Jon, suddenly nowhere to be found.

'I'll contact my solicitor immediately,' Robert said. 'You'll hear from us just as soon as I've spoken to her, and to my son. I believe that's all for now.'

'This is an extremely serious allegation, Mr Graham. We will need to speak to your son as soon as possible.' Detective Galvin looked directly across the table at Ciarán. 'It would be much better if he came to the station of his own accord.'

'I am aware of the gravity of the situation,' said Robert, stiffly. 'We all are. I will be in touch.'

'We will need to hear from you no later than six o'clock this evening,' said Galvin. He handed Robert a card. 'That's my number, or you can get me at the station. I must repeat that this is a serious matter. We have in our possession a detailed statement of the events of the other night.'

'You will hear from me this afternoon.' Robert's tone was firm. He was already ushering the two Guards out of the kitchen.

'Not so fast, Sir,' said Galvin. He stood his ground. 'We also have a warrant.'

'A warrant?' Lynda could barely trust her voice.

The detective turned to face her. 'Yes, ma'am. In cases such as this, we need to gather the evidence for forensics as quickly as possible.' The detective replaced his notebook in his inside pocket. 'Our warrant is to collect the bedclothes from the scene of the alleged crime.' He laid the warrant on the breakfast table, in front of Lynda, and Katie's breath caught.

Lynda glanced across at Ciarán, who had now begun to tremble violently. He had placed his arms on the table. Lynda could see him trying to steady himself.

'Well, if you must, you must,' said Lynda. Robert looked as though he had turned to stone. Where will they go? Lynda wondered. To Ciarán's room, or to Jon's? How far ahead of them all was Danny?

Robert spoke. 'I'll go upstairs with you,' he said. The three of them left.

'Is your door unlocked?' asked Lynda.

Katie looked at her in surprise. 'Of course.'

Lynda's mind was racing. Katie had slept in that bed last night. Jon's bed. His sheets were already in the wash. And nothing would be found on Ciarán's bedclothes, because there was nothing to be found. He was innocent of this. She thanked God he had been incapable on the night in question, otherwise . . .

'I can't remember,' Ciarán was saying, his eyes filled with terror. 'I can't remember anything. I don't know if I hurt her. I just don't know.'

Lynda lifted a warning finger to her lips. 'Sssshhh.'

He rested his head on his arms and started to weep. Harsh, gulping sobs that racked his whole body. Katie stood up and went over to him. She began to stroke his head, his face, his hands. She was stricken, unable to speak.

Lynda looked at both of them, Ciarán's white-blond hair stark against the dark blue of Katie's dressing gown. Jesus, she thought. What a mess. What an unholy mess. It can't get any worse than this.

Robert came back into the kitchen. 'They've gone,' he said. 'I'll ring Jennifer's office first. Get an appointment immediately. In the meantime, Ciarán, you'd better start to remember any detail that you can from Tuesday night. We can't protect you from this. A DNA sample would clear you, but it may well be too late for that. And Jon's gone. Your cousin is long gone.'

Ciarán looked up. Shock had registered across his eyes. 'Cousin?' he said. He looked from Robert to Lynda.

She turned to Katie. 'Put on the kettle, love, will you please? This is going to be a very long morning . . .'

*

When Robert came back, he had his coat on. 'Let's go, Ciarán,' he said. 'We have an appointment with Jennifer in half an hour. She's fitting us in.'

Ciarán stood up. He looked from Robert to Lynda. 'What do I tell her?' He looked small, defeated. No matter what Lynda had said to him while Robert was out of the room, he'd persisted in his loyalty to Jon. 'You don't understand him,' he kept saying. 'What he's been through. He was a brilliant friend to me.'

Katie was aghast. 'You can't believe that, Ciarán. Look at the evidence.'

He'd turned on her then. 'You weren't here. You don't know shit, Little Miss Perfect. He's my friend and he's done nothing wrong. There's some explanation for this, I know there is.'

Katie looked as though she'd been slapped. 'He's no friend of yours,' she said, shortly. 'He's disappeared and left you up to your eyes in it. How about that for friendship, or cousinly concern?'

Lynda had intervened. 'That's enough, both of you! Ciarán, you're going to have to face a few uncomfortable truths this afternoon. Use the time to get your head straight. Not to fight with your sister.'

He'd glared at Katie and seemed about to reply when Robert entered.

'Okay. Ready?' Robert took his car keys off the table. 'You coming with us, Katie?'

She hesitated. Ciarán turned to her. 'You can if you like,' he said. 'It's okay . . . if you want to.' There was a hesitant note of apology in his voice. Lynda felt a pull of grief as she looked at him. He felt fragile. He seemed to have disappeared. His clothes were standing there, making their outlandish statement, whatever that was, but Ciarán had retreated from them, and was curled into himself.

'Come on, Katie,' said Lynda. 'We'll all go. Let's all stay together.'

Katie nodded. She picked up her coat off the hall stand and followed her brother out to the Jeep.

At least the morning is dry. Sky the colour of cold steel, but no rain. That makes things easier for the watcher. Not so many tracks to be covered. This morning's five o'clock observations have shown the house on the left to be empty. Ken and Iris – that's her name – daft flowery-sounding name if ever he heard one, are away. That's good. A lucky break. He keeps thinking Ken and Barbie, has to stop himself. Anyway, they're gone since early yesterday afternoon. So that bit of the coast is clear.

Things seemed a bit unusual in the house early this morning, though. There seemed to be more activity than normal, more people moving about in the kitchen. At first it was just an impression. But when the watcher held the Cantek to his eye, that impression was confirmed. A girl. Wide Boy had said nothing about there being a girl. Two boys, yes, but no girl. The watcher felt agitated. This was not in the plan. Any more deviations from the routine and he'd have to consider aborting the plan.

And so he watched for longer than normal. Mr Robert was still there, at nine o'clock, when he should have been long gone. Mrs Lynda just gave the garden a cursory glance when she came out onto the decking. That was not like her. Not like her at all. And she was still there, sitting at the table, long after she should have left for work. This was not the normal Friday routine. The watcher could make out other forms in the kitchen, too, at one stage, shadowy figures. But they were standing too far back for him to get a proper fix on who they might be.

Bingo! At ten-fifteen, finally, there is movement. He watches closely. Four figures leave the kitchen. Time to go time. Quickly, now, he stuffs his camcorder into the rucksack and hurries down the slope. If he's fast enough, he might just see them drive away. This has to be done, over with, even more quickly than he has planned. This Friday is unusual, and unusual makes him uncomfortable.

The watcher's nervousness increases. He still doesn't like going round to the front of the house, no matter how good the story. He has his trusty postman's bag, full of flyers, begging for help in Somalia, this time, and he is wearing his innocent grey anorak. Funny how people don't rate men in anoraks. Trainspotters, potting-shed merchants, dry old sticks: that's how the world sees them. He allows himself a small smile. Bertie certainly bucked that trend. But only after he got rid of the anorak.

The watcher trudges around the corner, making sure to insert his red and black flyers into every letterbox along the street. Easy does it. Whatever you do, don't break the pattern. He spots the Jeep in the distance, making its way down the hill towards the roundabout. He quickens his step. A woman washing windows doesn't even register his presence. Kids kicking a ball flow round him, like a river around stone. The invisible man.

He reaches number nineteen. He bends just a little and pushes the flyer through to make sure it lands in the hallway, that it doesn't get caught in the flap. He notices that the letter box is broken. He takes a quick look over his shoulder. The street is pretty much empty. Window woman has gone inside. Kids are all looking the other way. The watcher walks around to the side gate, his step surprisingly light. His heart begins to speed up. He's forgotten how much he still misses this bit: the pure adrenaline rush of it. Almost better than sex.

He drops his bag of flyers just below the deck. He reaches in and pulls out his rucksack, slings it over one shoulder. Then he steps up onto the wooden surface. He moves stealthily, fast for one of his size. He takes his wire-cutters out of his inside pocket and gets ready. He breaks the window of the downstairs bathroom, the window closest to Ken and Iris's house. He uses a hammer wrapped in cloth to muffle the crash. At once, the alarm begins to scream. The sound is deafening, piercing his eyes and ears, making his blood sing. He reaches inside and cuts the wire to the sensor. The screaming stops at once. The abruptness of the silence is almost painful.

He waits for a moment, but nobody comes. Typical. Chances are, even if he'd left the alarm sounding off, *still* nobody would have come. But he can't afford to draw attention to himself. He eases open the bathroom window which gives without complaint. And then he is inside.

He tiptoes into the kitchen and wipes his feet with systematic thoroughness on the mat just inside the door. Heels, toes, sides, just as he has always done: like a surgeon washing his hands. And he is here, after all, to perform an operation of sorts.

The kitchen is even nicer than it looks from the top of the garden wall. Things are orderly here, neat. The air is warm, as though the central heating has only just clicked off. A slow cooker on the counter breathes chilli into the air. The watcher feels immediately hungry. He hasn't been able to have breakfast today, not with all this looming. Food slows you down. You need to shed as much as possible, to prepare for flight. That's why fear makes people sweat, piss, shit themselves. You've got to be unburdened. A physiological manifestation, they'd called it, back in the days of training courses. The physical results of a psychological state.

He moves into what Wide Boy has called the studio. Over

by the huge picture window, there is a wooden desk with a kind of sloping surface. He's seen one like it before, in the office of an architect he'd once gone to arrest. Your man had been on the take. Thousands of pounds must have passed across that desk in brown envelopes. The watcher is still amused that most people haven't got a clue about white-collar crime. That arrest was back in the good old days when planning corruption was only beginning to hit the headlines. Thing is, they're just more careful nowadays not to get caught, that's what he figures.

Mrs Lynda's studio desk is littered with drawings. And paintings, too, dozens of them. Small, delicate pieces of work. The sort of stuff Amy would like. Kind of oriental looking. Poppies, freesias, the branch of an orchid, a spray of apple blossom. But all single flowers, no bunches, and nothing in vases. He's tempted to slip a few of these small pictures into his anorak pocket. They'd make a nice gift; get Amy to smile at him again. He sees then that these are maybe like sketches, rehearsals for the real thing. And the real thing looks like painted silk – long, narrow wall-hangings, dozens of them, all around the studio. Nice. They're real eye-catchers.

But he resists the temptation. That's how people trip themselves up. It's greed, just as often as carelessness. He learned that lesson a long time back: it only took the once. He prides himself on never again making the mistakes that'll get him caught. And so he moves away from the desk and heads for the wall furthest from the patio doors.

He pulls a Stanley knife out of his rucksack and gets to work. 'All of them,' Wide Boy has said. 'Leave nothing intact. Nothing.' He does the wall-hangings first, slicing from bottom to top, the blade moving along the silk cleanly, as though through water. When he's finished, they look like some sort of weird ribbon-art. Maybe it'll start some sort of arty craze. He might have done Mrs Lynda a favour.

Then he turns his attention back to the paintings. They're done on some sort of stiff paper, full of small lumps and bumps. As though the paper has been made by hand, not straightened and smoothed into sameness by a machine. They tear easily enough, though. He scatters the bits all over the desk, all over the floor. They look quite pretty, really, like large splotches of confetti.

There are several jars on the flat portion of the desk. Half-filled with murky water, they hold dozens of paintbrushes, all of varying sizes. It's easy to tip them over. He watches as the water rushes across the large sheets of paper, and then slows down, soaking bluely into their surface. He shuffles the pages a bit, making sure the water reaches all of them. They look like the architect's drawings, actually, from what he can remember – except these ones seem to be of gardens, not buildings. He pulls out the digital camera and takes a couple of shots of his handiwork. They look clearer, starker than the reality. The light seems harsh. He has a moment of uncertainty. A slithery feeling of guilt that snakes around the back of his neck. Not his business, this. Just acting on behalf of another. Nevertheless, the feeling lingers. He'd prefer to be out of here.

He checks his watch now and goes back through the kitchen. He drops his rucksack just outside the door. He doesn't need anything from it upstairs. Keeping low, he makes his way down the hall and up the stairs. He moves quickly between each of the bedrooms. 'All of them,' Wide Boy has insisted. 'Don't leave anything untouched.' He does the usual stuff: a bit of slashing here, a bit of a mess there. Mattresses upended, drawers turned over, surfaces swept clean. He takes another few photos as proof of the pudding.

He pauses in what is obviously a girl's room. Teddies, dolls, stuffed toys litter every surface. For some reason, they remind him of Amy and he baulks. He can't damage these. What would be the point? Harmless bits of fur and fabric. He puts the Stanley away. Wide Boy will never know.

He leaves and hurries downstairs again. He picks up his rucksack and enters the room that gives out onto the front garden. He doesn't like this exposure, either – the curtains are open. So he works fast.

He takes the files out of the filing cabinet, strews their contents all over the floor. He takes books off the shelves and leaves some where they fall. Others he kicks under the desk, or stuffs behind the radiators.

Now for the most important bit. He checks his watch again. Twenty-seven more minutes and he's gone. Wide Boy has told him how important this office bit is. He wants the laptop, or the desktop, or whatever is there, to be destroyed. 'I want no possibility of any files being retrieved,' he says. 'You know computers, don't you?'

And the watcher says yes, he knows about computers. He likes the question. It means that Wide Boy knows fuck all, and that makes his job easier. But he plays along for now, boasts about how he can get into Robert's system without even knowing the password, that kind of thing.

Wide Boy's eyes light up at that. 'Really?' he says. 'How do you do that?'

But the watcher says not to worry, he'll look after it. 'We call it a worm,' he says, 'and it burrows into files, corrupting them.' He waits, figuring that Wide Boy will be impressed. The watcher thinks that he might even have a bit of fun with this, at WB's expense.

'A worm,' says Wide Boy. And starts to laugh. 'You mean, like a worm in the garden? I like that. Burrowing away into the darkness. A nice bit of symmetry.' He grinds the cigarette butt under his heel. That annoys the watcher. The pub has supplied an ashtray outside, a big one. Why does he have to litter the place like that? The watcher has a bizarre instinct to arrest this man for littering. In his head, he laughs at himself for that.

'Or,' he goes on, 'I could always format the hard drive. That means that everything is wiped. Clean slate.'

Wide Boy looks at him. 'Which is better?'

The watcher shrugs. 'Depends on what you want. Formatting the hard drive is a once-off. The worm causes trouble that lasts longer. Prolongs the pain. It's up to you.'

'I'm tempted by the worm,' says Wide Boy. The watcher sees him consider it. 'But nah. I'll go for the instant fix – the hard drive thing. More dependable. Takes away the chance of repairing it. Am I right?'

The watcher is tired of this conversation. He already knows what he's going to do, so the discussion is pointless. 'Yeah,' he says, 'you're right. Formatting the hard drive is the way to go.'

Wide Boy nods. 'Do it.' He looks at his watch. 'Gotta go. I have another appointment. We done here?'

'Yeah,' says the watcher. 'We're done here.'

'Okay,' Wide Boy says. 'I need to consult one other person about this hard drive thing. Just to be sure it's what I want. Can you meet me in O'Brien's tomorrow night, just for ten minutes?'

The watcher shrugs, annoyed despite himself. 'Sure. What time?'

'Let's say eight. It won't take long.'

When he leaves, the watcher wonders who the 'one other person' is. He doesn't like this, doesn't like the fact that these games are spreading beyond the boundaries of the two of them. Once you move outside a tight unit, it's all so much harder to control. He'll listen tonight, sure, but this time, he's going to do his own thing.

It's one of those little ironies that the most important thing the force ever did for him was to help him get to grips with technology. Before they let him go, they sent him on courses for all the latest and greatest. Made him employable, at least in their eyes. They didn't want to consign a forty-five-year-old man to uselessness. He supposes they'd expect him to be grateful for that. Anyhow, he's kept up the skills, over the years, although things change so fast these days, he finally feels he's being left behind.

Inside Robert's office now, the only thing that worries him is having to stand still for longer than he likes. He moves to the other side of the desk, away from the window. He decides to start with the laptop. That's where most people keep the up-to-date stuff. He wonders why Robert doesn't have it with him.

Fuck it. Just *do* it.

He pulls on a fresh pair of surgical gloves, stuffing the used ones into the pocket of his anorak. He retrieves the set of Philips screwdrivers from the front pocket of his rucksack. Then he draws the laptop towards him, across the desk, and turns it over. He disconnects the power cable, to give him more ease of movement. Quickly now, he removes the four screws that keep the casing in place. He lifts off the cover and places it to his left on the floor beside him. The hard drive releases easily. He pulls it from its slot and places it on the desk to his left. Then he glances at his watch. He can feel the perspiration across his forehead. Get a move on. Time is running out.

He turns to the desktop now. Lifting the box onto its side, he unscrews the casing and pulls out the drive. This one is a bit more tricky, a bit less accessible. Plastic clips can be a bugger. But he's there. He places this one on the desk to his right. Twenty-two minutes to spare. This is cutting it tighter than he likes.

Right, he thinks. Movin' on. He pulls the two replacement hard drives from the main section of his rucksack and places them on the floor to his right. Wide Boy has supplied him with these, pulling them triumphantly out of a briefcase last night, as they sat, briefly, in a quiet corner of O'Brien's pub, said he thought replacing the hard drives would be even better than formatting the old ones. The watcher has asked no questions. WB has taken great trouble to assure him that the specifications are all correct. Count on it, he says, with that self-satisfied smirk that has begun to grate on the watcher's nerves.

Just in case the drives don't fit though, the watcher has brought a selection of magnets with him. If Wide Boy has got it wrong, he has no intention of ever coming back to this house again. When this morning's over, it's over. If the hard drives don't do the business, the magnets will. More and more, the watcher wants this to be done, finished with. Wide Boy is a creep, and hanging around him is making the watcher feel edgy. It feels as though his strings are being pulled, and he doesn't like it. Back in the day, *he* was the one in control. He doesn't like handing that power over to anybody. Ever.

Working fast now, he inserts one of the drives into the slot of the laptop, the other into the desktop. He can feel his shoulders relax as both drives slide into place without any difficulty. Thank Christ for that. He replaces the casing of each machine now, screwing them both securely into place. Then he puts the small screwdrivers into their case and stows them again in the front pocket of his rucksack.

He reaches for the original hard drives and throws these, too, into the open mouth of the rucksack, securing the flap with its belt and buckle. He remembers drilling a hard drive open years back, out of curiosity. Inside, it looked like a three-dimensional map of some sort of surreal city – highways, bridges, the flat metallic roofs of buildings. It had a strange kind of beauty, he thought at the time.

Thirteen minutes. Go.

He leaves the downstairs office and crosses the studio, being careful to stay away from the window. He walks through the kitchen and pulls the patio doors closed behind him. Mrs L should be more careful about leaving keys in locks . . . Once outside on the deck, he pauses and pulls a woolly hat out of his anorak pocket, shoving it down on his forehead so that it covers his eyebrows. Then he picks up his bag of flyers, making sure to conceal the rucksack that hangs over one shoulder. He hunches forward and walks through the side gate, pulling it to behind him.

Out on the street again, he turns quickly into number twenty and resumes his flyer routine. Another dozen or so houses and that should be enough. It's the recycling collection day, so, after a bit, he'll dump his bag at random into a wheelie bin. Preferably one clustered with a few others on a corner somewhere, so that ownership might not be obvious should any nosey parker be looking.

Then, around the corner, he'll take off his hat and stand up straight. Crossing the next street, he'll shrug himself out of his anorak. Once he reaches the Dart station, he'll put it on again, this time with the green inside, rather than the grey outside, showing. A great boon, the old reversible jacket.

He grins to himself as he imagines Robert's face. Both machines intact. Laptop – miraculously – not stolen. Then, he'll switch on and wait, anxiously, for his system to reboot. Instead, he'll watch over and over again as colourful images continue to gyrate on both screens. A repeating image, one that never changes. No matter what he does, that's all there is to see. He can access nothing else, because there's nothing else to access.

The watcher figures that he'll be home by lunchtime. Then, this evening, he'll head out for a casual pint, meet Wide Boy and finish the business. He's decided to bring Amy out for an Indian tonight. He feels exhilarated. Another job done. Another successful outcome. All that early stuff to do with the garden felt dull, low-level. But today has been exciting, satisfying. It's interesting, how close he feels to the people whose house he's just left. Intimate, almost. As though he knows their most secret secrets.

He reaches the Dart station with five minutes to spare. Just enough time for a cigarette. And the prospect of three and a half grand in cash tonight, into his hand. He feels lucky: a chance encounter with a random stranger and he's five grand better off.

It doesn't come much easier than that.

Danny is pleased. His boy has done well. The outcome is even better than he could have hoped. Now Danny sits in the corner of the pub, getting ready for the final act. He sips at his pint and orders a second one just as the watcher comes through the door.

'Good timing,' he says, indicating the seat across from him. 'Another one for my friend, here,' he calls to the barman. The watcher is always punctual. The barman delivers the pints and Danny pays him for both, waving away the watcher's protests. The watcher is on edge. Danny can taste his anxiety. He knows how much the man wants his money. He can see it in his eyes. The man wants to be paid so that he can go home. Home to his wife, his comfortable little nest. Well, not so fast, Danny thinks. I'm not finished with you yet, boy, not by a long shot.

The watcher nods his head in thanks, lifts his glass in salute. He takes one sip of his Guinness and sits back, expectant.

'Well, Mr Phelan,' says Danny. He watches the watcher, enjoys the way one eyelid flickers in surprise. No names, no pack drill. That has always been their agreement.

'Mr *Thomas* Phelan,' he says. He's enjoying this. Nothing like the element of surprise to keep your enemy off balance. He knows what's coming next. He's always been good at being one step ahead.

'I'm well, thank you, Mr Graham.' The watcher gazes at him. His expression is unreadable. 'Mr Danny Graham.' His voice is low now, with an edge of steel to it.

Danny nods in delight. Just as he thought. 'As a former copper,' he says, swallowing the last of his pint, 'it's the least I would have expected. I understand you were good at your job. Once.'

This time, the man's face is impassive. 'Pay me what you owe me,' he says, 'and I'll be on my way. I've no time for games.'

Danny sighs, sitting back in his chair. 'Now, I just don't think I can do that,' he says. 'You see, there are some loose ends here.'

The watcher leans forward. His gaze is intense. 'I did what you employed me to do,' he says. 'Let's keep to the rules. Pay me.'

Danny shakes his head. His tone is regretful, patient, as though he's dealing with a conscientious, but limited student. 'You don't understand,' he says. 'I can't do that.' He reaches into his pocket. 'By the way,' he says. 'These are copies. The real thing is safe.'

He places a CD on the table in front of him. 'Here's the evidence of your vandalism. Won't be difficult to convince the cops. Inappropriate surveillance, wasn't that it? Wasn't that why they fired you in the first place?' Danny has allowed his voice to grow louder. A couple of men sitting at the bar turn to look in their direction. Then they return to their newspapers.

'And in addition,' Danny lowers his voice again, 'you recorded yourself destroying that poor woman's garden. It's all here,' and he picks up the CD and waves it in the air. 'Pretty poor practice for an ex-cop, isn't it? A man of the law?' He

allows his tone to be incredulous at the questions he is driven
to ask. A nice touch, he feels.

The watcher's eyes fill with hate. Danny is pleased. Now
we're getting somewhere. Then something else settles across the
man's face. Danny is not able to read it, not yet. The watcher
reaches into his pocket and pulls out something slender and
black.

'Digital recorder,' he says. 'I've downloaded our conversations – all of them. They're sound files. Already attached to
emails.' He reaches into his inside pocket and retrieves his
phone. 'This is a BlackBerry,' he says. 'And those emails are
ready to send. I've still got friends in the force.'

'But you'd incriminate yourself,' Danny says softly.

The watcher shakes his head. 'You'd be part of my ex-
colleague's investigation. I've checked. My immunity would be
part of the deal. After all, you're the controller here, the
instigator. We have files on you, going way back. And this
time, your brother and his wife have already reported you to
the Guards. Did you know that?' He knows he's flying a kite
here, but it's what most sensible, middle-class people would do.

Danny sits back, considering this. 'I see,' he says. The man
may be telling the truth, he may not. It hardly matters, not any
more. It makes the final card all the more glorious.

'Let's leave that aside for a moment.' Danny pauses. 'We
have other, more interesting things to discuss. How's your wife?'

The watcher looks at him, startled. The defences are finally
pierced now. 'What did you say?'

'I asked you how's your wife. How's Amy?' Danny signals
to the barman for another round. 'Amy Munroe?' Then he
turns back to the watcher and smiles. 'Well? It's a polite inquiry,
after all we've done together. All we've been through. How is
she?'

The watcher pushes back his chair. 'None of your fuckin' business,' he says.

Danny admires him, just a little. Pride, loyalty to his wife, to his life, prevent him from asking how Danny knows Amy. He waits until the watcher has almost reached the door of the pub.

'And Tina?' he calls. 'And, of course, Amy's son? How are they all?'

The watcher turns slowly. Danny sees that his face is yellow, not white. He is reminded of Robert, standing on the doorstep that day. Telling him never to come back.

'What did you say?'

Danny waits until the watcher makes his way back towards the table.

'What did you say?' he repeats.

Danny notices that his hands are now fists, with white knuckles under translucent skin.

He smiles, makes a face full of sympathy, concern. 'Didn't Amy tell you? She and I were an item for, oh, nearly two years. Of course, it's a long time ago now.' He lowers his voice, draws the watcher in closer. So close he can see the pockmarks on his face, see the red veins in his eyes. 'I fucked her,' he says softly. 'Didn't you know that? We have a lovely son.'

Then his cheek explodes under the force of the other man's fist. He hears glass breaking, shouts, the clamour of chairs falling, running footsteps. He stumbles, but catches the back of the chair and rights himself, just in time. He won't be brought down by anyone.

The barman has leapt over the counter and has the watcher's arm twisted behind his back. The other customers are watching, still as a photograph. Some have their mouths open. Others have glasses halfway to their lips. Danny notices, in that heightened way you notice details in a crisis, that some of the women have moved closer to their men. One has her hand on a mobile phone. All are watching, waiting.

'You're barred!' the barman says, pushing the watcher roughly towards the door. 'Get out before I call the Guards. And you,' he says, pointing to Danny, his forefinger stabbing, 'you sit for ten minutes and then make yourself scarce.' His voice is no-nonsense, full of righteous authority. 'I never want to see either of you here again. Take your argument somewhere else. Not in my pub.'

At the door, the watcher turns. His face is stricken.

Danny sits, gathers up the CD, the digital recorder and the BlackBerry off the table. He feels quite calm. He's guessing that the emails are a bluff. Doesn't matter, anyway. First thing tomorrow morning, he's history. Miles away, before anyone can even begin to come after him. When he looks up again, the door of the pub has closed.

'Have you a rear exit?' Danny walks over to the bar. He touches his face gingerly with the tips of his fingers. The barman glares at him. 'Your man is a psycho,' protests Danny, gesturing towards the door. 'Dunno what got into him.'

The barman looks sceptical. 'What do you want?' he asks, pulling pints for the customers who are averting their gaze from Danny.

'A taxi,' he says. 'As soon as possible.'

The barman nods. 'Where to?' he asks, reaching for the phone on the wall behind him.

Danny smiles. 'No offence, but in the circumstances, I think I'll keep that for the taxi-man.' And he goes back to finish his pint.

'Five minutes,' the barman says curtly. 'Out that way,' and he nods in the direction of the Gents. 'I'll let you out when the taxi's here.'

'Thank you,' says Danny, politely. He sits down and finishes his pint. A job well done, he thinks. A satisfying project overall.

Just one more thing and then he'll be on his way.

11

'THANKS FOR seeing us at such short notice, Jennifer,' Robert said.

'Not a problem. Come in. All of you.'

They sat, clustered around the desk in Jennifer's overheated office.

'Right.' Jennifer adjusted her glasses and addressed herself to Ciarán. 'What age are you, Ciarán?'

'Nineteen.'

'We can conduct this interview, just the two of us, if you'd prefer. Do you object to your parents being present?'

He shook his head. 'No. They can stay. It's fine.' He was agitated, pulling at his fingernails. Lynda winced as he made one of them bleed.

'Your father has given me the broad outline of the other night. It seems that a young woman,' she leafed through pages on her desk, 'called Larissa, is that right?'

Ciarán nodded.

'Larissa seems to have made an allegation of rape against you and you have been asked to appear voluntarily at the Garda station and give your own statement. Do you understand?'

Again, Ciarán nodded.

Jennifer took off her glasses. 'A voluntary statement means that you are not being arrested. You will be there of your own free will. You may leave any time. Is that clear?'

'Yeah,' said Ciarán. 'It's clear.'

'What happens in these cases is that the young woman, Larissa, will be required to go to the Sexual Assault Unit at the Rotunda, and submit to an examination.'

'I don't—' Ciarán began.

'Just a moment,' said Jennifer, quickly. 'Don't say anything until you hear me out.'

Ciarán looked at her. His mouth was slightly open. At that moment, Lynda was filled with fear for him. He was so confused, so vulnerable, that he might admit to anything. She hoped that Jennifer could see that.

'If you admit the rape, you will be cautioned and detained for further questioning. I understand from your father that you deny the allegation, is that correct?'

'I don't remember,' Ciarán whispered. 'I just . . .'

'In that case,' said Jennifer briskly, 'I will be advising you to say nothing. And that means what the word says. When asked, you will reply "I have nothing to say". Is that clear?'

'Yeah, but Jon . . .'

Jennifer leaned towards him. 'I don't need to hear any more, Ciarán. The Guards have already taken away bedding for forensic examination. That may, or may not tell them something.' The phone rang, making Lynda jump. 'Five minutes,' said Jennifer picking up the receiver and speaking briskly into it. She turned back to Ciarán. 'I will meet you outside the station at five-thirty this evening. Do *exactly* what I tell you and we'll be out again in half an hour. If things proceed, then we will have a further, much lengthier conversation. For now, it's enough that you understand to say nothing at all when questioned.'

'May I ask something?' said Lynda.

'Sure. Fire ahead.'

'This girl, Larissa.' Lynda paused. 'If she doesn't proceed

with her allegation, I mean, if she refuses to go to the Rotunda or whatever, what then?'

'Then there will be no case against Ciarán.'

'What if the bedding . . .' Lynda trailed off. What an appalling thing, she thought. Poor Larissa. She had to speak to her again. The girl had been right: nobody was going to be punished for this. Except, she thought, looking at her son's distraught face, except those who are innocent.

'One thing at a time,' said Jennifer. 'Let's get today over with, and then we'll see where we are.' She stood up.

Lynda felt a flash of anger. We're just a job to her, she thought. A case. A file. A fee. She stood and took her handbag off the floor. She left it to Robert to thank the woman. All she wanted was to get out of there.

The minute Lynda put her key in the lock, she knew something was wrong. The alarm wasn't working. The air in the house felt disturbed. The kitchen door was creaking back and forth, as though in a draught.

'What's up?' Robert was directly behind her.

'Somebody's been here. The alarm is off.'

'Jesus!' said Robert. 'Is there no end to this?' He was angry; had been angry ever since they'd left the solicitor's office. The journey home had been a silent one. He pushed Lynda to one side and made his way into the kitchen. 'There's a window broken here,' he called back, 'in the downstairs bathroom.'

But Lynda didn't answer. Automatically, she had stepped into her studio. Where she always went as soon as she came through the door. Her space. Her haven.

'Mum?' Katie was right behind her.

Lynda couldn't speak. The whole studio seemed alive with colour. Paintings fluttered on the walls. Brightly coloured confetti littered the floor. Her desk was a tumble of blues and greens and greys. At first, the whole impact was one of curious, chaotic beauty. Then, as things began to settle, Lynda cried out. 'Oh, my God! My God! Robert! Robert!'

He came crashing in behind them. Katie seemed to have been struck dumb. She clutched her mother's hand and stared around her, her eyes wide and unblinking. Ciarán leaned against the door frame. Robert pushed him, roughly, out of the way.

'Jesus,' he said. And 'Jesus,' again. He held Lynda's other hand and together, they looked at the destruction all around them. Katie pulled herself away and began to pick up the pieces off the floor. 'Mum,' she said, lifting her eyes to Lynda, the full impact sinking in. 'They're your paintings.' Her voice was barely audible.

'Upstairs,' Lynda heard Robert mutter. 'Upstairs.' And he fled.

Lynda turned away and walked into the kitchen. She stood in front of the double doors and looked out at her garden. It was as she had left it, weeks back. Bare, sad. Waiting to be fixed. She walked over to the sink and filled the kettle. Then she sat at the table and waited.

She heard Robert and Ciarán and Katie moving about upstairs. Everything else was curiously quiet.

Later, when they gathered around her, she said: 'Well?'

Robert sat. 'Pretty much everything has been destroyed,' he said. His voice was matter of fact. 'Mattresses slashed, stuff broken, drawers upended. And nothing in my office works. It's been trashed, too.'

'Ciarán?'

'Yeah. My room's in bits,' he said. 'Everything's a mess.'

Katie looked grey. Lynda had never seen her this upset without tears, before. 'They left my dolls and teddies and stuff alone,' she said. 'The rest is pretty badly damaged, though.'

Lynda stood. 'Okay,' she said. 'Call the Guards. In the meantime, let's photograph everything for the insurance. Once the police go, we start the clean up.'

Robert looked at her. 'Now? Today?'

She lifted her chin. 'Why not? Any other way, he wins. *Danny* wins. Do you want that?'

Robert didn't answer. Instead, he said: 'I'd better call someone straight away to fix the bathroom window. And the alarm. It's Friday afternoon.' He pulled the mobile out of his pocket. 'Katie – use the house phone to call the police.' He turned to Ciarán. 'Go and have a shower. Get out of those clothes and put on something decent for your interview this afternoon.'

Ciarán left, without a word.

'I'm going into my studio,' Lynda said. 'And then I'm going out to my garden.'

When Robert and Ciarán got back at six-thirty, Katie and Lynda had the studio cleared. Katie had wept her way through it.

'It's okay, love, please don't be so upset.' Lynda looked at her daughter. 'These are things. They can be replaced. The four of us are safe. That's what matters.' They both looked up as they heard Robert's step in the hall.

'Well?' asked Robert as he came through the door of the studio. 'What did the cops say?'

'Oh, you know,' said Lynda, 'the usual.' She stood up from where she'd been kneeling on the floor and wiped her hands in a towel. Spatters of paint clung to her fingers. 'They took fingerprints and photographs and looked around a good bit.' She shrugged. 'They were very nice, but a bit useless, really. I mean, what can they do? I'm just ticking the boxes for the insurance, that's all. We know who did this.'

Katie stifled a sob. Lynda looked from Ciarán to Robert, feeling suddenly afraid. 'What's your news?'

'Larissa didn't turn up to go to the Rotunda,' Robert said. He sounded almost breathless. 'And without her, there's no case to answer. She gave a false address.' He shrugged. 'Doesn't look like there's much the cops can do about it.' He looked exhausted.

'Is that it, then?' asked Lynda, hardly daring to hope.

Ciarán nodded. His face looked raw again, as though he had been crying. 'It's over,' he said. 'I think it's over.'

'You,' said Lynda quietly, 'are only just beginning, Ciarán. Your new life starts now – and it will be absolutely nothing like the old one, I can promise you that.'

Ciarán looked uncomfortable. 'I know I have to do things better,' he said. 'I want to. And I'm sorry about all of this.'

Lynda nodded. 'We all are. And Jon may well not be finished with us yet. But you – you have a lot to make up for.'

There was a silence. Ciaran shifted from foot to foot.

'I'm staying for the next few weeks, here, at home,' said Katie, suddenly.

'What about college?' asked Robert.

'There's only a couple of weeks of term left,' said Katie. 'We finish at the start of April. I'll talk to my tutor. I need to be here. I want to help sort this . . . this . . . wreckage.'

'We'll talk about that later,' said Lynda.

Katie shook her head. 'My mind's already made up.'

Lynda's mobile rang. She pulled it towards her, flipped open the cover. 'Where?' she said. She could feel the others looking at her. 'Give me ten minutes.' She threw the phone into her handbag.

'What?' asked Robert. He looked fearful. 'What now?'

'Larissa. I gave her my mobile number. Told her to call if she needed anything. Let's go, Robert. I want you with me.'

When they entered the cafe, Larissa looked startled. She stared at Robert, then looked quickly back at Lynda. She's still terrified, Lynda thought, poor kid. She couldn't help thinking that this could be Katie, in another life. The thought made her shiver. The girl's face was white, the eyes dark and vulnerable.

'This is my husband, Robert,' said Lynda. 'Robert, this is Larissa.'

Robert nodded and sat opposite her. 'Hello, Larissa.'

Lynda pulled out a chair and sat beside her. Larissa couldn't take her eyes off Robert. 'I'm glad you called us,' Lynda said. She touched the girl's hand, gently. But Larissa flinched and drew back. Lynda paused for a moment. 'We want to help you, Larissa. I promise you we'll do everything we can to—'

'The other man,' interrupted Larissa. Her voice sounded harsh, on the verge of cracking. She spoke directly to Robert. 'The one he look like you? He give me this yesterday.' She pulled an envelope out of her bag. Her hands were trembling.

Danny, thought Lynda. He's got to her. What has he done to her? Robert leaned forward. 'Another man? A man who looked like me?'

'Yes,' she said. She bit her lip. 'He say he is your husband.' She glanced at Lynda. Her eyes were cautious now, wary. She looked as if she might bolt from her chair at any moment.

'My brother,' said Robert. 'I am sorry to say that that was my brother. He was lying to you.'

Larissa looked at Lynda now, confused. 'I do not understand.'

'He is a bad man,' said Lynda. 'A man who has caused us a

great deal of trouble.' And you, she thought. He's caused you more trouble than any of us.

'Did he do anything to you – hurt you in any way?' asked Robert. 'You can trust us, Larissa. We want to help you.'

Larissa looked from one to the other. Her eyes began to fill. 'He frighten me,' she said. She pushed the envelope towards Lynda. 'I do not want this.'

'What is it?'

'Money,' said Larissa. 'He give me money to tell police about your son.'

Lynda shook her head. 'Not our son, Larissa. The blond boy who attacked you was not our son.'

Larissa looked startled. 'Then—'

'Our son,' said Robert, 'was the drunk and noisy one sitting downstairs.'

'*He* is your son?'

Robert nodded, tiredly. 'Yes. And just to complete the circle, "Golden Boy", the one who hurt you, is the son of the man who gave you that money. They are as bad as the other, father and son, and I am so sorry they've made you suffer.'

Larissa blinked. Then her face sagged and she began to weep. Lynda put one arm around her shoulders. This time, Larissa did not move away.

Robert stood up. 'Let me get you something – water, tea, coffee?'

She nodded, sobbing. 'Water, please.'

'Have you eaten anything recently?' asked Lynda.

The girl shook her head.

'I'm sure I can find you something edible,' Robert said and smiled at her.

'Coffee for all of us as well,' Lynda said. 'I think we could do with it.' She kept her arm around Larissa's shoulders. The girl's trembling had started to ease and she was crying more quietly. 'Take your time,' said Lynda. 'Tell us when you're ready.'

She nodded, wiping her eyes. When Robert returned, she was calmer. 'Thank you,' she said as he placed coffee and water and a sandwich in front of her. 'You are kind. Thank you.' Her eyes filled again. 'I do not know what to do. He say his son must be punished, or he would do this again. I was afraid not to do as he tell me. So I go to the police. I give a statement. Then I run away.'

She began to cry again, hunched forward on the table.

'Larissa,' said Lynda, after a moment, 'rape is a very serious crime. And we know who did it. We don't know where Jon is, but we can describe him. We have a witness who saw him bring you upstairs and we both saw you running away on the night – this boy can be caught and punished.'

Larissa shook her head vehemently. 'No. I see police do not *want* to believe me. I *see* it.' She shrugged. 'All the time. They do not care. They do not believe and they do not care.' She paused. 'No hospital, no doctor, no police.' She looked at Robert, suddenly frightened again. 'Please, I want to finish it. Now.'

Robert leaned towards her. 'Nobody is going to force you to do anything, Larissa. If that is your choice, we will accept that. We'll support you. But you must have help.'

'What help?' She looked guarded.

'A doctor, first,' said Lynda. 'A private one – my doctor. Anything you discuss with her will be confidential. I can take you to see her.'

'And no police?'

'No police,' agreed Lynda. 'If you are sure that's what you want. But perhaps a counsellor?'

'What is this?'

'Someone who can help you not to feel so afraid. Someone who will talk to you, and understand how you're feeling.'

'A psychiatrist?' asked Larissa. She stumbled over the word. 'I know what this is.'

'Not quite,' said Lynda. 'But someone with special knowledge.' She paused. 'Are you sleeping?'

Larissa shook her head.

'Do you feel afraid to be on your own? To go out?'

She nodded, biting her lip again.

'Then let us help you,' said Lynda. 'Please. We feel partly responsible. It was in our *home*. And if our son hadn't been so drunk, this might never have happened. We owe you, Larissa.' Lynda waited, hoping the girl would say 'yes'. She had a vision of Jon and Ciarán on that night, of Larissa, running screaming from her front door. She felt a surge of rage at Danny.

'I will go to your doctor, yes,' Larissa said at last. She pushed the envelope further away from her. 'But I do not want his money. It is . . . dirty money.' Her face filled with emotion. 'I'm sorry to cause trouble.'

'You didn't,' said Lynda at once. 'All the trouble was caused by others. None of this is your fault. You just got caught in the net. Do you understand? We *all* got caught.'

'Like fish, yes?' asked Larissa.

'Like fish,' agreed Lynda. 'But it's over. I don't think he'll try again. He's done his worst, this time.'

'I go now.' Larissa stood and put out her hand.

'Are you sure?' Lynda said. 'We can go to the doctor now, if you like?'

Larissa shook her head. 'Now, I must work. But tomorrow, yes?'

'I will call you tomorrow. Are you free in the morning?'

'Yes,' she said. 'In the morning is good.' She shook hands with Robert. 'You are a good woman,' she said suddenly to Lynda. 'I trust you, when I see you last time.'

Lynda smiled at her. 'Call me any time,' she said. 'And we will see each other tomorrow.' She and Robert watched as Larissa left the cafe. Lynda handed Robert the envelope. 'Here,' she said. 'I don't know what we're going to do with this.'

Robert put the envelope into his inside pocket. 'We'll find something clean to do with it.' He reached across the table and took her hands. 'And we'll look after that girl, no matter what.' He paused. 'The awful thing is, I just keep wondering what's next.'

'Don't,' she shook her head. 'I really don't want to wonder.'

He stroked the back of her hand. 'Are we okay? I mean, despite . . .' he spread his hands in a gesture of resignation. 'All of it. Can't even find the words.'

She looked at him. 'We *are* okay: and we *will* be okay. We'll go home, clear up the wreckage, as Katie calls it, keep Ciarán on a very short leash, and start again.' She stopped. 'We're going to need some help with Ciarán. And I suspect it's going to be a long and rocky road. He was no angel before Jon – and I don't think that either of us took that seriously enough.' She looked at Robert. 'Katie says we spoiled him.'

Robert nodded. 'Maybe we did. But that's sure going to change.' His voice was grim. 'You do know that it may not be over? I mean, Danny may try again. And again. We might have to pay the price of eternal vigilance.'

'I know that. He *will* try again – through Jon, or by himself, or some other way. The point is, he didn't win, this time. And he won't win the next time, either. What doesn't kill you makes you stronger.'

Robert pushed back his chair. He held his hand out to Lynda. 'I bless Charlie every day,' he said.

Lynda looked at him, puzzled. 'Who?'

'The Dramsoc whirlwind? The one who introduced us?'

Lynda smiled at the memory. 'Ah, yes, the night you cheated, running for the number ten bus.'

'The night I won, fair and square,' he said, indignant.

'I think we both won, that night,' said Lynda. 'It just took some of us longer than others to figure that out.'

Robert smiled. He took her arm. 'Madam, your carriage awaits.'

She walked with him across the car park. The sun was setting into a deep glow over the Wicklow mountains.

'Would you look at the pair of us?' Robert stopped so suddenly that Lynda ran into him.

'What?' She was curious to see the smile that began to flicker at the corners of his mouth.

'As the kids would say: "What are you *like*?"' He waved his arm in the air, taking in the sky, the hills, the scene before them. 'Walkin' off into the sunset, at our age?'

Lynda smiled. 'Don't knock it till you've tried it.'

Robert took her hand and squeezed it.

'Let's go home the long way,' she said, suddenly. 'So that we don't pass Emma's roundabout. Just for tonight.'

Robert started the engine. 'Home it is,' he said. 'The long way.'

And they pulled out into the traffic.

Jon is waiting for him.

It has taken Danny an hour longer than expected to make his way through the tangle of Dublin traffic. But Jon is there and this pleases him. He is sitting in a corner of the bar, his back to the door. His baseball cap is back to front, the peak shadowing the slender lines of his neck. Danny walks over and flips the cap off his son's head. Then he stands there in shock. It takes him a minute or so to understand.

'Like it?' Jon turns around and grins at his father.

Danny stares at him. His hair is now dark and cropped close to his skull. Even his eyebrows are dark. Danny is caught off-balance. Jon's build is different, of course, he is slender where Robert was always broad-shouldered and sturdy, but for a moment there, Danny caught an uncanny glimpse of Robert as a child. Something in the way Jon had cocked his head to one side reminded him too much of Pansy.

Jon's smile fades. His green eyes are suddenly anxious. 'It was part of the plan, Danny. It had to be done. You know, the whole "Golden Boy" thing?'

Danny starts to relax. ''Course,' he agrees. 'It was just a bit of a shocker. For a minute there, you looked a bit like your Uncle Robert. Anyway, how's it goin'?'

'Yeah, good,' replies Jon. 'Got away no problem. How about you? You find Larissa?'

'Oh, yeah,' says Danny, smiling now. 'Let's have a pint and I'll tell you all about it.' He orders two pints at the bar and they carry their glasses upstairs. It's a wet, chilly night, even for March. Despite the patio heaters, there's nobody in the Smoking Area apart from the two of them.

'Bloody waste of money,' the barman downstairs had grumbled. 'I told him that. A gazebo would have done the job just as well. There's fuck-all customers these days, anyway.'

Danny made some sympathetic noises. He's still cautious, even this far from Dublin. Long arm of the law, and all that. Now, he and Jon walk to the far end of the Smoking Area, well out of earshot of any random passers-by. Danny looks down at the swollen waters of the River Suir. The inner arch of the bridge is illuminated and it's reflected greenly in the hurrying currents beneath: all that water rushing against itself.

'Cheers,' Danny says, ironically. 'Your very good health.'
He pulls the packet of cigarettes out of his jacket pocket. Jon
takes one and flips his lighter, leaning over to Danny. They
smoke in silence for a minute or so. 'Right,' says Danny. 'You
go first.'

'It was easy,' Jon shrugs. 'Even apart from the Larissa thing,
I'd say that "Golden Boy" might have a bit of a problem with
coke. And ecstasy.' He shakes his head. 'He's such a wuss. I
even had to show him where to buy it.' He laughs. 'An' he's
one very confused bloke. By the time I left him, he didn't know
his arse from his elbow.'

Danny smiles. Shades of Pansy. Chip off the old block, and
all that. Nevertheless, he, Danny, should probably show some
paternal concern of his own: Jon would expect that. 'You're not
in any trouble that way, yourself, are you?' He allows just the
right amount of anxiety to shade his question.

Jon shakes his head. 'Nah. The odd joint, the odd tab.
Nothin' much.' He shrugs. 'Never had the cash. Besides, it's
weak. Not my scene.'

Danny nods. He feels oddly moved.

Jon glances over at his father again. He sounds almost shy
when he speaks. 'You were really brilliant, helping me set all
that up. I mean, the bit about the blood tests, the anaemia and
all that – that really sowed the seed. Yummy Mummy was right
off-balance that night. Got the worry wart goin'.' He pauses.
'Even feel a bit sorry for her. He was the apple of her eye, an'
all that.'

Danny doesn't want to talk about it any more. It wearies
him, bores him, now that it's all over. He's finished what they
started over twenty-five years ago. That's enough. But he can
see that the boy is yearning for a bit of praise. 'You weren't so
bad yourself,' he says. He makes sure his tone reeks of approval.
He watches his son's shoulders straighten, his smile broaden.

'Looking after the sensor lights the way you did – now that was a masterstroke. Now you see it, now you don't.' And he grins at his son, delighted with him, with them both, with their cleverness.

Jon glows. Danny can see him savour the moment. Then, out of the blue: 'Will they arrest him?' His question wavers a little.

Danny looks at him, sharply. 'Doesn't matter. They might, they might not. I made it worth Larissa's while, but who knows? She might not follow through.' Larissa. She of the blonde hair and the blue eyes – and the absolutely terrified expression.

'No, please,' she'd said, when Danny had caught up with her in Superquinn. He'd waited until her shift was over, choosing his moment. 'I tell your wife already,' she'd pleaded. 'No police! I want not the police.'

That had surprised him, right enough. Lynda must have got there before him. She always was a sharp one – way sharper than Pansy. She'd tumbled to him three years back, as well.

'Now, listen to me,' he'd said, taking Larissa by the arm. He'd spoken to her in soothing tones, kept the eye contact going. 'You don't need to do anything you don't want to. I have a little proposal for you, that's all. You are quite free to say "yes" or "no". It's your choice.' He'd watched her face relax. 'Come and have a drink with me. I don't want us standing out in the street while we discuss this. Someone might think I'm way too old and ugly for such a beautiful girl.' And he'd smiled. One of his most winning ones.

She'd looked even more nervous. But he stood in front of her, making it clear he wasn't going to go away. 'Okay,' she said. 'One drink.'

He'd bought her a Smirnoff Ice; pint of the black stuff for himself. As soon as they were sitting at a quiet table in the corner, he'd pulled an envelope from his inside pocket and placed it on the upholstered seat between them. 'There's five hundred euro in here. It's yours.' And he took a good slug of his pint.

She'd looked at him. The blue eyes were terrified; she twisted the ring on her thumb round and round. He wished she'd stop. 'What I must do?' she asked. She was wary, now.

'Make a statement to the Guards,' he said. 'The police.' He watched as alarm washed her features. 'No—' she began, but he stopped her.

'Listen carefully,' he said. 'You give a statement, a false address, and you go home. Nothing else. I'll tell you what to write. And afterwards, you just disappear. Or get a friend to do it. I don't care.' He reached for his pint again, unconcerned.

'But they will find me.'

He shook his head. He stood up, putting the envelope back into his pocket. 'I don't have time for this. In this country, there is nothing the police can do.' He waited, let that sink in. 'If you don't follow it up, there is *nothing* they can do to you.' He watched, could see her weakening. One last roll of the dice. 'You make your statement, just the once.' He tapped his pocket. 'I'll tell you the words, you take them down. Nothing else. Do you understand?'

She'd nodded, biting her lower lip.

'Then, you go home. And that's it. Five hundred euro for a few lines and your signature. Trust me. They won't come looking for you.' He'd said enough.

'Why?' she'd asked, suddenly.

'Why what?' he'd said, kicking to touch.

'Why you want so much to punish your son? I do not understand.'

He'd sighed. 'My son has been a very bad boy,' he said. 'He's done this to other girls. He will do it again. As a father, I

277

must stop him.' He'd allowed his eyes to fill with tears, then. 'Don't you understand? Ciarán must be punished. "Golden Boy" or no "Golden Boy". Do you want other girls to suffer, too?'

She'd shaken her head at that. 'Okay. I do what you ask.'

Slowly, almost reluctantly, he'd pulled the envelope out of his pocket. 'You're sure? You do understand that it's my duty?'

'I understand.'

But Danny was thinking that she understood nothing other than an envelope with five hundred euro. He handed her the notepaper and the pen he'd brought with him. Her writing was laborious, like a child's. He kept the statement simple, stark in its retelling of the facts.

'I go now,' she'd said. 'I study this and I go now. I finish this.'

He'd nodded. 'Yes. The sooner the better.'

And she'd left the pub, the door closing softly behind her.

'We've given them enough to worry about, though, haven't we?' Jon is smiling at his father. 'Even if Larissa doesn't do the business. And I have a few other things up my sleeve. For later, when things calm down a bit. Wouldn't do to have them think it's all over. We'll let them know we're still watching.'

For the first time in his life, Danny likes the word 'we'. It's like being back in the fold again, his own fold. With his own son. 'You did well,' he says. 'Couldn't have done it without you.'

Jon glances over at him. 'They had it coming,' he says. 'Cheating you out of everything like that.'

Danny lights another cigarette, and one for Jon. He passes it over to him. 'Well,' he says easily, 'we don't need to dwell on that now. We can put it behind us.' He waits for what he feels is an appropriate amount of time. 'So,' he says, 'you don't regret coming looking for me, do you?'

Jon's face is animated, his eyes shine. Not for the first time, Danny thinks what a good-looking lad he is. A real ladykiller, if ever he's seen one. Another nice bit of symmetry, that.

'No, of course not. It's been great.' Jon drags deeply on his cigarette. 'Like I told you, I never really expected to find you.'

Danny nods, pleased. 'Well, I'm really glad you did. We'll have to keep our distance for a while now, just in case. You'd better stay out of Dublin; lie low for a while. And don't go near Tina again, either.' Seeing Jon's anxious expression, he smiles. 'Don't worry. It won't be for long. It's just that Tom Phelan might begin nosing around, put two and two together. We need a bit of distance.' He grinds his cigarette into the ashtray. 'But we'll keep in touch, of course.'

'How long before I can come and live with you?' asks Jon, finishing his pint.

'You want another?' says Danny. 'Bird never flew on one wing.'

'Yeah,' says Jon. 'I'll go for it.'

'Here . . .' Danny hands him a twenty euro note. He watches his son's long, assured stride; sees his own younger self in the boy's easy grace. He really did come out of the wide blue yonder, Danny thinks. First, a letter from some agency, asking whether he'd agree to contact with his son. That had been a bit of a shocker, all right. It hadn't taken him long to put two and two together, given the boy's age. At first, he'd thought: no chance. No way. Not me. But then, he'd got to thinking. And the boy had been useful, no doubt about it. Clever, too.

He'd found Tina, as well. And through her, Amy. Jon's keeping his options open now, about Amy. He might or he might not, he says. At least he knows where she is, who she is.

And he'd been angry at her, of course. Angry at his mother's abandonment of him. It had been easy for Danny to be sympathetic, easy to fuel that anger, bit by bit. The apparently accidental meeting with Phelan in his local pub was a brilliant bit of detective work: the boy was a natural. That meeting was something Danny would be proud of himself.

Jon returns now with the two pints. He hands Danny the change. But he waves it away. 'Keep it.'

'Thanks, Danny.' His smile is electric.

They'd decided, between them, that Dad was not appropriate. Neither was Father. 'Danny' seemed to be an admirable compromise. A symbol of their relationship as two adults; equals. Two Dannies. They've stuck with 'Jon' for the boy, though. Less complicated that way.

'We'd better take ourselves off after this one,' says Danny, looking at his watch. 'I've a very early start in the morning.'

Jon nods. 'What time will you leave for the ferry?'

'About half-three,' Danny says. 'That gives me five hours of a kip. Should be grand.'

'I'll head off soon, then,' Jon says. 'Oh, here – I almost forgot.' He reaches into the inside pocket of his parka and hands his father a package. 'Your letters. You asked me to get them back for you.'

'Good man,' says Danny softly. He is surprised, gratified at his son's thoroughness. Getting the evidence back was always a long shot. 'I'm proud of you, d'you know that?'

Jon smiles. 'You didn't think I'd do it, did you?' He shakes his head. 'You come from a family of very sound sleepers.' He looks pleased with himself. 'Amazin', the things you find in the dead of night.'

The both laugh.

Danny can see his son's reluctance to go. They have bonded well, the two of them. Isn't that the term? Bonded. Like woodworkers' glue. 'I'll call you from the port,' Danny says. He makes his voice gentle. 'And we'll see each other very soon.'

Jon hesitates. 'And then can we talk about me coming to London?'

Danny nods. 'Of course. I've lots of room in my flat. We'll work it all out over the next couple of months. Maybe even head off somewhere exotic for Christmas. Would you fancy that?'

Jon grins. 'As long as my work here is done,' he says. 'Can't leave any loose ends.'

Danny drains his pint. 'You be careful, now. No point getting caught at this stage. And change hostels, if you stay overnight in Dublin, okay?'

'Yeah. Will do.' He grins. 'Left a bit of a bill in the last place, anyway.'

Danny looks at him. 'Not enough to catch up with you, I hope?'

Jon shrugs. 'Nah. People aren't very bright, are they? I mean, they keep letting you away with stuff.'

Danny doesn't reply.

'Even the university,' Jon goes on. 'No one ever checked.'

'Don't push it,' Danny warns. 'If you get cocky, they'll nail your arse.' He stands up. 'Now, you go on back to the B and B. I'll wait ten more minutes. Okay?'

Jon zips up his parka. 'Talk tomorrow then.' He seems about to approach Danny, then changes his mind.

'Yeah, talk tomorrow. And well done. Sterling work.' He says this last with a London accent and Jon laughs. Then the boy heads downstairs. Danny watches from the window as his son crosses the Suir, making his way over the illuminated bridge. He turns to the right and Danny can see him look back over his shoulder at the pub. Dungarvan was an inspired choice, Danny thinks. Its off-season quiet is perfect.

Twenty minutes later, he, too, leaves. He crosses the same bridge, but turns left instead of right. As he does so, he tosses his mobile phone into the river. Then he makes his way towards the hire car. As he walks, he reviews his work of the past few months.

Robbie. Lynda. Amy. Tom. And Ciarán, of course.

Pity about Jon. But it can't be helped.

A man can't be tied down. A man needs freedom. Great gulping breaths of it. Danny presses the key fob and the lights blink, obediently. He starts the engine and heads towards Rosslare. Rosslare to Fishguard.

Fishguard to God knows where.

Epilogue

Tom leaves the pub, nursing his hand. He stumbles on the kerb and passers-by look at him and then look away again. They avert their gaze quickly, as though he is something unsavoury. He knows he must appear drunk, or stoned. Angrily, he wipes away the stray tears that keep on coming and coming.

He can't go home. He *won't* go home, not until this murderous rage has had a chance to settle. He has to get a grip, consider his options. If he has any left.

He wanders around the city, thinking about where his life has brought him. A sham, all of it. A fuckin' sham. A job that didn't want him. A wife that doesn't want him. And all of those stupid dreams about a fishing boat on Lough Conn. Who was he kiddin'. He has no one to go fishin' *with*, even if he could afford a boat. Wide Boy has screwed him nicely. Screwed all of them, as it turns out. Robert. Lynda. Him.

Amy.

And Amy has a *son*. Tom doesn't doubt it, not for a moment. All Wide Boy has done is confirm suspicions he's already had himself, suspicions he wouldn't even have known how to voice, because he didn't know what they were. Then it hits him. If she's had a baby, then the problem, the fault between them, is *his*. Jesus. He starts to cry in earnest, sitting on the kerb outside McDonald's. He sits there, not even trying to wipe his eyes. At midnight, a Guard approaches and tells him to go home.

'I don't have one,' he says. But he stands up anyway, and shuffles off.

By the time he reaches the house, his knees are killing him. He knows they are, because they won't move properly. But he can't feel them, can't feel anything any more.

Amy opens the door to him. 'What's happened?' she cries. Her hair is tied up again, he notices, in that Amy Winehouse kind of way. It doesn't matter any more. She isn't real, *nothing* is real between them and never has been. *That's* where his life has brought him.

He pushes past her and makes his way into the living room. It seems to have changed since this morning. There's nothing here that is familiar. It looks suddenly bare and grim, like your woman's garden after he'd wrecked it. He feels sorry for that now. And the paintings. It seems such a waste.

'Tom, what's wrong?' Amy's voice is catching on something. It might be a sob, but he doesn't care any more. The kid gloves haven't worked. Staying schtum hasn't worked. All the love in the world hasn't worked. He's lost her, anyway. She belongs to Wide Boy.

'I've been worried sick. I called your mobile and then the restaurant, maybe a dozen times. What is it?' She stands in front of him, pulling at something on the sleeve of her cardigan.

Tom doesn't look at her. He sinks into the sofa and says nothing.

She comes around to stand in front of him. 'Tom?' she says. Her tone is frightened now. She has never seen him like this. Her face has an odd look to it.

'Why didn't you tell me,' he says. It is not a question.

'Tell you what,' she answers, but there is a tremor to her voice. A dead giveaway, in his experience.

He fixes his gaze on a point above the fireplace. The focus gives him a sort of control. 'That you have a son.'

She crumples. Her knees give way and she stumbles into the armchair just across from him. He notices that the crumbs have been cleaned from the carpet. The fireplace is swept, the brass polished. He almost laughs. Ironic. All done, all cared for when it no longer matters. Funny the things that catch your eye as your life falls away from you.

Don't insult me now, he pleads silently. *Don't deny it. Just tell me the truth for once.*

'I couldn't.' That's all she says. Amy looks down at her hands.

It's the truth, perhaps. Tom is stunned by the simplicity of it. Somehow, her admission makes his rage leach away and he is left with nothing but peace. This is what he has felt between them for all these years. This has been the obstruction. This, and the other child: the one he hasn't been able to give her. Now, at least, it has been named and naming it has stolen some of its power.

'Danny Graham,' he says. 'I understand he's the father.'

She looks at her husband, her eyes wide and horrified. 'How do you know? Who told you that?' she begins to rise from the chair.

'Sit down,' he says, more sharply than he has intended. Then, 'Sit down,' more gently this time. 'I've met him. Worked for him. Although I didn't know who he was – really who he was – until tonight.' He sits forward on the sofa, his shoulders hunched, hands clasped in front of him. The knuckles show shiny white under the skin. They remind him of the punch he landed on that animal's face. There is at least some satisfaction in that.

'What sort of work?' asks Amy. Her hands have begun to tremble. 'What did you do for him?'

'You don't need to know,' he says, 'it's nothing you need to know. Just some half-assed surveillance. Except that the real purpose of it was to destroy everyone he's ever known.'

Amy laughs. The sound is bitter. 'That's Danny all right. How did he find you to help him do it?'

He shrugs. 'It seemed to be a random meeting in the pub. But knowing him as I do now, I don't think there was anything at all random about it. He targeted me. Targeted *you*. He can't have been working alone.'

'Where is he now?' Amy looks around her. The terror in her eyes says that she expects him to burst through the door any minute.

'Gone, I'd say. Out of the country. Things might start to get a bit hot for him if he stays. That's all I'm going to tell you. It's best you don't know any more than you already do.'

He allows the silence to grow between them. It sits there, like a dog on a fireside rug.

'At first,' she says, as though answering the question he hasn't repeated, 'I was ashamed. They were different days, back then. My parents would have disowned me.' She pauses. 'They didn't have a lot of charity in them. A lot of religion, but not a lot of charity. I left Danny when I knew I was pregnant.' She shakes her head at the memory. 'After our last few months together, I knew that I couldn't bring up a child with him, not with *him*.' Her look is pleading. But he isn't able to respond to her, not yet. When he doesn't, she continues, her voice flat. 'I gave the baby up for adoption. Tina helped me.'

He looks up. 'And your parents?'

'They never knew. Tina and I manufactured a story between us. I pretended I'd got this great job in London. We had all sorts of celebrations. Instead, I went back to Tina and Jack's house in Waterford and hid. Jack was great. He and Tina wanted to adopt my little boy, but I wouldn't let them.'

'Why not?' he wants to know.

She shrugs. 'Too much of a reminder. If I couldn't be a mother, I didn't want to be just an aunt. And pretend for the rest of my life. I thought a clean break would be better for all of us. In the end, they agreed.'

'Why did you marry me?'

She looks surprised. 'You were good to me; kind and generous. You came along at just the right time. I thought you'd help me recover, that we'd have our own family and I could forget.' She winced. 'I'm sorry. Sorry about everything. I was selfish. All I was doing was trying to survive.'

'Did you love him?'

She smiles, looks at him directly. 'What does a nineteen-year-old girl know about love? I was blown away by him, infatuated. He swept me off my feet. It didn't last, though.'

'Why not?' He feels this compulsion to know the things that cause the most pain.

'He was a bully,' she says, simply. 'Oh, not physically. But he had me wrapped around his little finger.' She laughs, shortly. 'A counsellor told me he was a master manipulator. She was right. I'd have done anything for him. But he never wanted a relationship. I knew that once he got fed up with me, he'd be ready to move on.'

'Did he know about your son?'

She shakes her head, emphatically. 'Absolutely not. I left the day I had the pregnancy test and I never saw him again.' She stands up and searches the shelf behind her for cigarettes. She smokes only rarely, now. Her and Tina used to be like trains, he remembers, the pair of them. Puffin' away like there was no tomorrow. She lights up and continues speaking, this time without looking at him. 'To be honest, I kind of fell apart after the birth. I had a spell in hospital, with post-natal depression. Tina looked after everything for me, the adoption, everything. I never even wanted to hold my son. Some mother I'd have made.'

Her face is like steel.

'Danny told me once that he would make everyone pay who had ever hurt him. He was talking about his family at the time. That even if he had to wait thirty years, forty years, he'd pay them all back for what they did to him. And the truth is, they did nothing to him. He did it all to himself.' She tips her ash into the ashtray. 'I guess he included me in that, too.'

Tom sits quietly. 'I'm tired,' he says.

She nods. 'I never meant to hurt you, Tom . . .' She stops, sighs. 'I hate that line. It's what Danny used to say, over and over, before he went out and did exactly the same thing all over again. It sounds like an excuse. But I mean it, I really do.' She stubs her cigarette out. 'I'm glad it's out in the open. Relieved. It's really strange, but the longer it went on, the harder the secret was to keep.' She looks at him. 'I wanted to tell you, Tom, but the way . . . the way things turned out between us, I couldn't. I just didn't know how to.' She stands up. 'I'll go, tomorrow. Maybe in a few months, we can meet up and sort out what we're going to do. When we've had time to think.'

He nods. 'Where will you go?'

She smiles. 'Where I always go. To my sister.' She stands, rubs her hands on her jeans, an old, old gesture. 'I'll sleep in the spare room tonight.' She makes her way towards the door.

It's for the best, he thinks. Too much water under the bridge. Suddenly, he has an image of a garden, a woman, a tortoise set in stone. Himself with a crowbar, taking things apart. The bleakness of it takes his breath away. 'Wait,' he says.

Amy turns. 'Yes?'

He can hardly believe what he's saying. But he means it.

Oh yes, he means it. And he means it despite – or perhaps because of – Wide Boy. 'I don't want you to leave. If you leave, he wins. And all of this' – he gestures around him – 'has been for nothing, has meant nothing, ever.'

She looks at him. Her voice is incredulous: 'You want me to *stay?*'

He pauses. 'Let's just say that I don't want you to go. It's a bit different. What I really want is that he doesn't win. I don't want him to win. And I don't want to live on my own, that's the truth of it. I'm fifty-five years of age, Amy. I want a bit of peace.'

He watches as her eyes begin to fill. 'Maybe we're no great catch, either of us. But I still love you, Amy. And somewhere, I think you might like me enough to keep going. I'm tired of seeing things destroyed.'

She walks back towards him. Her eyes search his face. She's weeping now. 'Tom, I do love you,' she says, sobs catching at the words and then letting them go. 'I love you and I want to stay. I do.' She pushes his greying hair back from his forehead. 'Do you really think we can do it?'

He puts his arms around her and holds onto her. Holds on for dear life. 'I don't know.' Then, 'Yes,' he says. 'Yes.'

She buries her face in his neck. 'Thank you,' she whispers. 'You are a *good* man.'

Outside their window, there are shouts all along the street. Car engines rev into life. Partygoers call out to each other. There is laughter, cat-calling. All the sounds of the inner city. The watcher listens.

Tom listens.

He's home. Amy's all he's ever wanted.

He's home.

ACKNOWLEDGEMENTS

Thanks, as ever, to Shirley Stewart of the Shirley Stewart Literary Agency, for more than I can say.

To my wonderful editor, Trisha Jackson, and all the team at Macmillan: Eli Dryden, Ellen Wood, Kati Nicholl, Clare Stacey at Head Design, and Imogen Taylor.

Thanks to the winning combination – in all senses – of Davy Admanson and Cormac Kinsella, and to Michelle Taylor and Katie James.

And thanks, too, to Roddy Doyle, for so many things over the years, including the patient reading of manuscripts.